AIRING IN A CLOSED CARRIAGE

AIRING IN A CLOSED CARRIAGE

Joseph Shearing

with an introduction by

MARTIN EDWARDS

BRITISH LIBRARY

This edition first published in 2026 by
The British Library
96 Euston Road
London NW1 2DB
bl.uk

1 3 5 7 9 10 8 6 4 2

Airing in a Closed Carriage was first published in 1943
by Hutchinson & Co. Ltd., London.

Represented in the EU by Authorised Rep Compliance Ltd., Ground Floor,
71 Lower Baggot Street, Dublin, D02 P593, Ireland. arccompliance.com

Cataloguing in Publication Data
A catalogue record for this publication is available from the British Library

ISBN 978 0 7123 6910 7
e-ISBN 978 0 7123 6280 1

Cover Illustration © Metropolitan Museum of Art,
New York, USA / Bridgeman Images
Text design and typesetting by Tetragon, London
Printed in England by CPI Group (UK) Ltd, Croydon, CR0 4YY

MIX
Paper | Supporting responsible forestry
FSC® C013604
FSC www.fsc.org

CONTENTS

INTRODUCTION

Airing in a Closed Carriage is a crime novel written by one of Britain's most interesting, prolific and versatile women authors from the first half of the twentieth century.

Yes, "Joseph Shearing" was a woman. She was, and still is, better known as Marjorie Bowen, but even that was not her real name. Over the years, she has in some respects remained as mysterious as the fiction she produced, although in recent times—thanks, in no small measure, to the efforts of the British Library Publishing team—there has been wider discussion about the quality of her fiction and the woman behind the books. In this introduction, for convenience, I'll refer to her by the Bowen pseudonym.

This is a novel about the extraordinary life of May Beale, an American with a French mother, Madame Dumont. The opening pages may seem like a slow burn as we are introduced to May and her circle, but Bowen is careful to put in place the crucial elements of a compelling story about a group of well-realized characters.

We first meet May as a teenager in France. She is impetuous and naïve, described as a "a bit of featherhead" by her maid, Rose Bernier, but she is pleasant and attractive. While conversing with friends, she wonders idly about mayflies, with which she shares a name, and is told by a French girl that: "Mayflies do not sting, indeed they do nothing—nothing whatever but glitter in the air for a little while—but they are destroyed just the same." This image lies at the heart of the story.

Keen to enhance her natural beauty, May takes an interest in cosmetics which proves to be highly significant. After pleading to her mother for some of the face-wash that she uses for her complexion, her mother reluctantly tells her to ask Rose about the recipe, thinking her too young still to worry about such things. May discovers from Rose that one of its ingredients is "Fowler's liqueur", going on to find that Fowler's liqueur can also be obtained cheaply in flypapers, on which it is smeared. May meets two handsome Englishmen, the brothers John and Richard Tyler, who have come to meet her mother on business. Both men are more than twice May's age, but John in particular takes a shine to her.

Bowen describes the Tylers bluntly as men who "were honest men in everything that concerned their business... in everything except their business they were intensely dishonest, without knowing it." We also learn that John Tyler is a hypochondriac, addicted to a "prescription" that a French chemist warns is highly dangerous, because it is "nothing but pure arsenic in powder". As night falls at the end of the first chapter, taking his "stimulant" has emboldened John to decide to try to secure May as his wife. For her part, May is dreaming about the chance to use the cosmetic: "How charming to be light and diaphanous as a lily in the dark."

By the time the second chapter opens, things have moved on. May is living with John in Manchester, at a house called Stone Pynes. She is twenty-five, having married him at seventeen. Although she now has children, she is deeply discontented, and wondering if she would have made a better match with Richard Tyler. Lacking a head for figures, she has run up debts; John is unfeeling and unfaithful, while the servants dislike her. Madame Dumont advises her to "get rid of the man". However, May is Catholic, and divorce is therefore not an option, although "it might be possible to get an annulment at the Vatican."

The scene is set for a domestic tragedy that unfolds with a bleak and remorseless inevitability, although the death which is central to the story is a long time a-coming. The elaborate build-up is unusual in a crime novel, but it's interesting to note that—in two otherwise *very* different books—Cyril Hare adopted a comparable method in *Tragedy at Law*, published two years before *Airing in a Closed Carriage*, and so did Agatha Christie in *Towards Zero*, published the year after Bowen's book.

As Bowen says in her Foreword, the story is "founded on a much debated trial for murder that took place in England in 1889." She says she has used "the theme, the central characters and incidents, and some parts of the legal speeches taken from those uttered by lawyers and judge during the hearing of this case. For the rest, and in particular for the psychology that is at once the core of the story and the solution of the mystery in which this judicial drama has always been obscured, the author alone is responsible… This interpretation of the inside of the story is, however… one that seemed the only possible explanation of these events to this author… This is the first effort… to try to arrive at the truth not by a study of actions only, but by the study of the characters and events that produce these actions."

Bowen also makes the bold claim that "no liberties have been taken with the known details of the story… nothing that was proven in the case has been evaded or distorted. It is probably precisely those portions of the novel that are indisputably true that will appear to the reader most wildly improbable."

At the centre of the case which provided her with such rich raw material was a woman who had died in 1941, just two years before this novel was published. Florence Elizabeth Chandler, a young American who married a Liverpool cotton broker called James Maybrick, was the real-life May Beale. Stone Pynes is the fictional counterpart of Battlecrease House in Aigburth, on the outskirts of Liverpool, where the Maybricks lived in increasingly unhappy circumstances. After James Maybrick's death on 11 May 1889, apparently as a result of arsenic poisoning, Florence became the prime suspect. She was arrested and ultimately tried for murder in St. George's Hall, Liverpool. What happened at the trial and thereafter underlines the fact that truth can, as Bowen suggests, be stranger than any fiction.

The Maybrick case became a *cause célèbre*, and its sensational aspects have kept it in the public eye. Several interesting books have been written about the case, by Nigel Morland, Trevor L. Christie, Bernard Ryan and Kate Colquhoun, among others.

Florence Maybrick herself was responsible for *Mrs. Maybrick's Own Story*, which is fascinating, not least to anyone interested in penology, even if it leaves several important issues unbroached. The legendary Raymond Chandler was among those who have been intrigued by the case, which he jokily retitled "Why Doesn't an Arsenic Eater Know When He's Eating Arsenic?", and he wrote extensively about it. Chandler even put together a detailed analysis of factors pointing in favour of Florence's guilt, and innocence, respectively. Suffice to say that his interpretation of the evidence was very different from Marjorie Bowen's.

In 1993, the publication of James Maybrick's alleged diary, which amounted to a confession that he was Jack the Ripper, made headline news around the world. Since then, debate has continued to rage as to whether or not the diary is a hoax. The film director Bruce Robinson came up with a controversial variation on the Ripper theme in 2015, arguing in *They All Love Jack*, a book brimming with conspiracy theory, that James' brother Michael Maybrick was the Ripper and, for good measure, the person who killed James as well. In a thoughtful review for the *Guardian*, P. D. Smith said that Robinson's ingenious theory "strains the limits of credibility", whilst admiring the scale of his research as well as "his chutzpah".

The Maybrick case has long fascinated me, as it has done for numerous crime writers. Novels inspired by the case include Anthony Berkeley's second book, *The Wychford Poisoning Case* (1926); in his dedication to E. M. Delafield, he says that "the book... has grown out of those long criminological discussions of ours. You will recognize in it many of your own ideas, which I have unblushingly annexed, but

I hope you will also recognize the attempt I have made to substitute for the materialism of the usual crime-puzzle of fiction those psychological values which are… the basis of the universal interest in the far more absorbing criminological dramas of real life". However, although Berkeley shared Bowen's interest in true crime and criminal psychology, his style of writing and approach to the crime fiction genre was very different from hers, and his book bears no resemblance to this one.

More than twenty-five years ago, I had the good fortune to be shown around Battlecrease House by the owner, which was a memorable experience. The house takes its name from the cricket ground across the road, and I've always been intrigued by the fact that the American Florence, as well as her husband, was a member of the cricket club. I've spent many years reading different accounts of the extraordinary events at Battlecrease House, and discussing the case with friends and true crime experts. In my capacity as a solicitor in Liverpool, I was even contacted about the "Ripper diary" before it became public knowledge, although I must add that I was not tempted to become involved. All I can say is that, when I finally read the diary, I concluded that if it is a hoax (and I don't have the expertise to pronounce either way), it is nevertheless a quite brilliantly imagined hoax, one which any crime novelist might be glad to dream up.

Airing in a Closed Carriage was one of seventeen books published between 1932 and 1950 by Marjorie Bowen under the name Joseph Shearing. The Shearing *oeuvre* included a collection of short stories, a book about Charlotte Corday (who assassinated Jean-Paul Marat in 1793) and a "biography in the form of a novelette" about Madame Lafarge, who was convicted of murdering her husband with arsenic in 1840.

Remarkably, the Shearing books represent only a fraction of Marjorie Bowen's total output, which extended to about one hundred and fifty titles. Such was her productivity that she wrote under numerous pennames, including George R. Preedy, Robert Paye, John Winch and Margaret Campbell, or Mrs. Vere Campbell. Her real name was Margaret Gabrielle Vere Long (née Campbell; 1885–1952) and I included two of her short mysteries (one as by Bowen, one as by Shearing) in my first anthology of Christmas mysteries for the British Library series of Crime Classics, *Silent Nights*. She is, however, most closely associated with tales of the weird and supernatural. Several of her short stories have appeared in the British Library's Tales of the Weird series, as does her "full-bodied tale of mythical weirdness in nineteenth-century Germany", *The Haunted Vintage* (1921), which benefits from an admirably insightful introduction by Michael Dirda.

Like Marie Belloc Lowndes and Fryn Tennyson Jesse (to name two women authors whose fiction has featured in the Crime Classics series) before her, Bowen was deeply interested in the psychology of crime and in famous cases of the past. She admired the work of William Roughead, the Scottish lawyer and criminologist who did much to popularize what we now term "true crime", and even dedicated her Joseph Shearing novel *The Spectral Bride*, aka *The Fetch* (1942) to him. In 1939, she wrote to him saying that "Joseph Shearing survives on your encouragement", while in another letter she said that "your books to me are like cream to a cat".

It seems quite likely that she discussed her views on the Maybrick case with Roughead, and few (including Raymond Chandler) would disagree that the verdict reached at the trial amounted to a miscarriage of justice, whatever view one takes of the crucial matter: the means by which James Maybrick met his death. Bowen's writing style is notable for an authorial omniscience that is today unfashionable. While she portrays the Tyler brothers negatively from the outset, May is presented in a generally favourable light, arguably more favourable than the evidence about some of Florence Maybrick's documented actions would justify. This perhaps generous characterization is seen, for instance, in the portrayal of May's involvement with Jerome Thorne when compared to Florence's association with Thorne's real-life counterpart, Alfred Brierley.

What is beyond doubt is that Bowen's writing was so vivid that film-makers were frequently attracted to her work. Highly regarded films based on Joseph Shearing novels included *So Evil My Love* and *Blanche Fury*, each released in 1948. In 1947, *Airing in a Closed Carriage* was adapted for the big screen as *The Mark of Cain*. Interestingly, the script was co-written by Francis Crowdy and a woman very well-known to fans of the British Library Crime Classics, Christianna Brand. They made many changes to the story, transforming it from a study in character to a conventional mystery with a race-against-time element towards the end, no doubt to inject pace. May, renamed Sarah Bonheur, is English, and is played by Sally Gray, who had starred the previous year in the film version of Brand's *Green for Danger*. The Howard brothers (as the Tylers were renamed for some reason) were played by Eric Portman (Richard) and Patrick Holt (John), while the cast also included such capable actors as Dermot Walsh, Vida Hope, Andrew Cruickshank, James Hayter, Miles Malleson and William Mervyn. *The Mark of Cain* begins well, but becomes increasingly thrillerish in the later scenes and at the box office, it was a flop. *Airing in a Closed Carriage*, on the other hand, remains a crime novel of enduring interest. Although it faded into obscurity in the years after its publication, so that copies have long been very hard to come by, Bowen's compelling character work and treatment of the historical material makes this rare book well deserving of a fresh airing for the twenty-first-century readership.

MARTIN EDWARDS
www.martinedwardsbooks.com

A NOTE FROM THE PUBLISHER

The original novels and short stories reprinted in the British Library Crime Classics series were written and published in a period ranging, for the most part, from the 1890s to the 1960s. There are many elements of these stories which continue to entertain modern readers; however, in some cases there are also uses of language, instances of stereotyping and some attitudes expressed by narrators or characters which may not be endorsed by the publishing standards of today. We acknowledge therefore that some elements in the works selected for reprinting may continue to make uncomfortable reading for some of our audience. With this series British Library Publishing aims to offer a new readership a chance to read some of the rare books of the British Library's collections in an affordable paperback format, to enjoy their merits and to look back into the world of the twentieth century as portrayed by its writers. It is not possible to separate these stories from the history of their writing and therefore the following novel is presented as it was originally published with minor edits only made for consistency of style and sense. We welcome feedback from our readers, which can be sent to the following address:

British Library Publishing
The British Library
96 Euston Road
London, NW1 2DB
United Kingdom

AIRING IN A CLOSED CARRIAGE

"If then, all the worldlings prize,
   Be contracted to a rose
Sweetly there, indeed, it lies,
   But it biteth at the close."

GEORGE HERBERT.

"There are some strange things knocking about this house."

Remark of the alleged victim, quoted at a trial for murder (1889).

FOREWORD

This novel is founded on a much debated trial for murder that took place in England in 1889. The author has used the theme, the central characters and incidents, and some parts of the legal speeches taken from those uttered by lawyers and judge during the hearing of this case. For the rest, and in particular for the psychology that is at once the core of the story and the solution of the mystery in which this judicial drama has always been obscured, the author is alone responsible. For that reason he has altered all the names, both of people and places, while keeping to the atmosphere and historic detail of the period.

This interpretation of the inside of the story is, however, by no means the invention of a writer of fiction, it is one that seemed the only possible explanation of these events to this author, after he had read the many hundreds of thousand words that have been expended on this *cause célèbre*, without finding any suggestion by anyone that threw any light on this remarkable tale, nor, indeed, any attempt to do so. This is the first effort to remove this mystery from the arguments of lawyers and doctors and the enthusiastic debates of champions on the victim of a hideous miscarriage of justice, and to deal with it in the manner of a novelist, that is, to try to arrive at the truth not by study of actions only, but by the study of the characters and events that produce these actions. Despite the immense amount of ink spilled over this subject, there are many gaps and tangles in the original story as published that have never been straightened out or filled in; this task the present writer was obliged to undertake, but found nothing that shook his conviction as to the underlying truth of what seemed on the surface incredible.

On the other hand no liberties have been taken with the known details of the story; all the details of the house and household at Stone

Pynes are authentic, and nothing that was proven in the case has been evaded or distorted. It is probably precisely those portions of the novel that are indisputably true that will appear to the reader most wildly improbable.

JOSEPH SHEARING.

London

1943.

I

SCHOOLGIRL'S POSY
FLOWERS OF ELDER AND ROSE

THE GIRLS LOOKED LIKE LITTLE DOLLS IN THEIR MUSLIN dresses with stripes of gold and silver around the borders; they lay under the drooping willow trees that fell in ornamental lines of greenish silver against a sky where the palest of clouds made the faintest of white haze against a tender azure sky; some saddle-horses, fine and high bred, were held by grooms a little further away, and seated on a rich Andalusian shawl of light colours was an elder lady, whose dress was also white, but of sarsenet silk, shot in the folds with glistening radiance that resembled mother o' pearl.

She played with her tiny parasol with the long ivory handle and the deep heavy silk fringe and glanced, half with affectionate amusement and half with the anxious air of one who is in charge of something precious, at the group of girls, and now and then at the stiff, smart and expressionless cavalry officer who stood beside her and who stared, with the air of a man who is doing nothing but at the same time doing his duty, across the lake that appeared as bright and shallow as a silvered porcelain dish, to the charming, coquettish little pleasure house of Bagatelle.

The girls were not long quiet; one of them was French, another Belgian, the third English and the fourth American. They possessed more than the usual prettiness of healthy, well favoured youth; there was a grace about them, as if they had been specially cared for, adorned, and, perhaps, a little pampered. The Belgian girl had well tended and glossy red hair and large blue eyes and a complexion remarkably white, but perpetually smudged with red.

"Gnats again!" she exclaimed. "I wish I had a parasol like your mother has, May!"

She put her plump hand to her warm cheek with a sigh of impatience that was not altogether caused by the clouds of minute insects.

"We shall have parasols, like we shall have everything else when we are a little older," smiled May Beale.

She stretched out her little feet in pretty satin slippers and glanced at them with pleasure. She was quite satisfied with everything about her person, and had a certain sweet patience in her nature that prevented her from fretting, as the others fretted in the wild hardihood of youth, at this lull before, as they would have put it had they been articulate, life began, life, just ahead now, for all of them.

Louise continued to dab at her face while the French girl murmured, "They were not gnats, but mayflies."

The girl whose name had been thus uttered, laughed. "I wonder if I am a mayfly? What does it mean?"

The English girl took up the answer and in her own language, she knew French tolerably well but disdained to speak it except when it was effective to do so.

"A mayfly is a little creature of iridescent colours, it lives for a day only, therefore it is really a shame to do what you are doing, Louise—endeavour to destroy it."

"Indeed, I have destroyed several," replied Louise disdainfully. "They sting on me badly..."

"They are not mayflies," remarked the dark Parisienne. "Mayflies do not sting, indeed they do nothing—nothing whatever but glitter in the air for a little while—but they are destroyed just the same."

"You sound quite like a philosopher preaching at me," smiled May Beale. "I know you all think me extremely frivolous, but there's not the least likelihood that I shall ever be destroyed. Isn't that a charming little palace across the water? Do you know anything about it?"

She posed the idle question persistently to her three idle companions; the Parisienne would not reply; the English girl did not know, the Belgian murmured vaguely that she believed a prince had built it for a queen.... How artificial it looked, the elegant empty residence, like a model in sugar taken out of a box of flowered cardboard and put down upon a square of green velvet, mused Louise.

May would not have this simile; she was precise in her observations.

"The grass," she declared, "is mown very close, but it doesn't in the least resemble velvet."

"There's not a single daisy or weed in it, and that's like our lawns at home," conceded the English girl.

Françoise remarked she thought *gazon* expressed lawn much more exactly than the English word.

May sank down on the grass at full length, tipping her broad-brimmed Leghorn hat over her eyes and peering up through the very finely plaited straw braids at the double pattern made by the willow leaves through which the sunbeams fell, and the sunbeams themselves that interchanged their shapes as the long branches swayed. A pretty play and one that she was never tired of gazing at in this drowsy way. She sensed more than saw or heard her companions moving away and whispering to her mother. Perhaps they were teasing to have the picnic basket opened again, to see if there was more ice cream in the ice-box, or if any were left of the pineapples, the peaches and the bonbons. For herself she was satisfied, Louise's birthday had been quite an agreeable occasion, one made more so by the fact that it had been supplied entirely by May's mother, Madame Dumont. May liked nothing better than to be generous, Louise was far from her home in Ghent and not so rich as most of the girls in the convent at Passy, it had been delightful to give her this *fête*. May had not been sure that it had been a good idea to dress them all the same, but Madame Dumont had excellent taste and she had decreed it, and it had been successful, the four white frocks equalized taste and means.

Mayflies… why had they begun talking about them, with a good humoured hint at her? She knew that she was lazy and studied everything—well, not with difficulty but with amiable reluctance; but she believed that she had already learned all she needed to know. Her mother had taught her a good deal in the old white porticoed house in Virginia—the smaller house, for the larger had to go after the Civil War when the slaves were freed, but there was still a handsome property where the negroes, with their heads bound in brilliant coloured handkerchiefs, could be seen bending among the white fluff of the cotton blossoms. The home scene in Virginia had been something like Bagatelle, the wide carefully kept lawns, the design of space, light, air, flowers drooping in garlands from high bushes, and trees with boughs falling in tresses higher still until the eye seemed to be carried to the zenith of the heavens, "and the soul with it," said May Beale almost aloud, and sat upright and clasped her hands round her knees, her straw hat falling back.

She wondered why she had said that or what she knew about the soul… there was some manner of rapture or ecstasy roused in her by the perfection of the summer weather, the stillness of this retreat, the peace of the vistas on either side and the sense of having gratified friends, for Louise had blushed with delight over every detail of the festival and Françoise and Amy had been pleased too, and her mother was always kind and gentle and her stepfather always indulgent. Yes, it had been a golden day.

May recalled the old books the Ursulines fingered so carefully; many pages of plain print and suddenly a page on which there was a golden letter…. "You call them that, don't you—'red letter' or golden days. Days of the saints. I wonder which saint was on the calendar to-day. I ought to have looked, of course, before I came out this morning. Perhaps the nuns will ask me when I return." This gave her no apprehension. Everyone always smiled at May Beale and forgave her everything.

Her hat had slipped on to her shoulders and the ribbons strained across her throat. She was a small girl, "a pocket Venus", Amy's father had named her when he had come to see his daughter at Passy. "Five feet four," she had been taught to say, "by exact measurements," but she was so finely made and so exquisitely in proportion that she did not appear insignificant but of a just height until, perhaps suddenly, she would chance to move beside a man or a heavily made woman, and then she would appear a creature of Sèvres biscuit china.

She studied the group on the grass that had a little changed now. Her stepfather was making himself agreeable to the three girls in a very courteous way, thought May, who was quick to sympathize with all the most delicate feelings of others, but she was sure that he was a little weary of this childish merry-making. She glanced at her mother, a woman like herself—aristocratic, lazy, a little pampered, very easy. And what else…? May did not know anything else of her mother any more than she knew anything else about her own character than that she was lazy, pampered, very easy.

Her mother had been married twice before she had become Madame Dumont. There was always a gentleman to hold her mother's gloves and parasol in Virginia; now she was a French countess, and her husband a staid and well-connected officer in the Chevaux Légèrs who was, as the term went, "her devoted slave". She intended to live in Paris, she had told May, and only occasionally to visit the Virginian estate; there was a steward put in to see about the cotton-growing.

"You know I am no use at business," Madame Dumont had often confessed to her daughter, stroking her hand with maternal caresses. "We have lost a great deal of money, my dear, but that was not my carelessness. I had a very good steward and we have so many relations who are excellent business men. It was the war…" and her large, clear grey eyes would fill with ready tears, and May, also soft hearted, would feel sad, too.

The Beales could count ten men who had been killed fighting with the Southern forces. Madame Dumont had her memories of those ugly times of defeat of which she never spoke. Sometimes even in the warmest sunshine she would shiver and draw her scarves of tinsel-stripped gauze, or her costly Andalusian shawls, that were woven with the hues of a shell, closely like a protection round her sloping shoulders, as unbidden, some bitter recollection would disturb her life of elegant sloth.

She wore her hair in a style that was so becoming that even the fall of the Second Empire had not put it out of fashion, curls gathered on the nape of her neck, catching on the edge of the bodice that just fell below the line of the shoulders, that were hidden by folds of Indian muslin bordered, like those of her charges, with stiffened silver and gold thread; she sat indolently and smiled across at her daughter.

'She does not,' May told herself tenderly, 'look any older than we do,' and she wondered, in her lazy way, what life was going to be for her mother, for herself, for Louise, Amy and Françoise—like this, always?

Her mother beckoned to her, delicately. "Come over here, May. Why are you sitting there alone? You look sadly tousled, my child. See, you have crumpled the ribbons of your hat and your sash, and I told you that that muslin would not survive being crumpled like that." May smiled as she crossed to the group, knowing all these sweet reproofs meant nothing. "Now there is one other thing that we are going to do on Louise's *fête* day," added Madame Dumont. "Your stepfather, May, is going to the dêpot with his men and the horses. They have been very kind, taking us about, have they not?" The girls in dutiful chorus agreed. "He has his duties to-night, my children, but you and I will go in the barouche and choose one more little present.… No, you must not become excited, you really must not because, perhaps, it is something that you will not indeed like much at all."

"Oh, we shall like it," cried May, "but we really have had everything we want."

"No," said Madame Dumont firmly, "I must not hear you say that, because if you have everything you want that would mean that you were being pampered, and that I could not endure. There must be a great many things that you still want, May. There must be a great deal of finery that you long for, or else I should think that my darling is becoming a spoilt little creature."

Amy slightly lifted her lip at what she considered a speech both sententious and sentimental, but Louise smiled and thought it was charming; the Parisienne was silent, smoothing two fingers, pale as nacre, on the glossy bandeaux of her dark hair. Her hat she kept swinging from her elbow; it was so much more becoming than wearing it.

Colonel Dumont took his leave of the ladies and his wife put on the shawl which the girl picked up from the grass. Small fragments of grass clung to the fringe.

"I believe there *is* a daisy, Amy," cried May. "Do you know I haven't seen one daisy! Like lawns we had at home, Mother... and as you said they were in England, Amy."

"Yes," agreed Madame Dumont placidly, "the grass is excellently kept; it is to be regretted that it is a public park, too often one meets vulgar people here, and already there are too many promenading; it is time that we went to make our purchase."

The four of them were seated in the barouche that was produced by Madame Dumont's fancy and her purse; very light and well-sprung, built in England, painted in France, nothing of taste and luxury was lacking in the shine of the lacquer on the body, the glossiness of the velvet of the interior, the polish on the coats of the two well-matched light bay horses, or in the uncreased buff coloured liveries of the coachman and groom.

"The shops will soon be shut," whispered Louise, who was never quiet. "What can we be going to buy?"

"No, the shops will not be shut yet," said Madame Dumont. "You are always so impatient." She smiled amiably at them all and inside her mind added, 'Except May.... May who knows how to behave and be dignified. She *is* really better bred than any of them, for the English girl is cold and a little disagreeable, the Belgian a little sentimental and foolish, while the French girl, of course, who thinks herself perfection, is old for her age, more like a married woman.'

"I know one indulgence you are going to allow us, Mother," whispered May, drawing closer to the folds of the exquisite shawl on which hung the thick velvet azure blue ribbons from Madame Dumont's close-fitting hat, "and that is the face-wash from your own chemist—M. Bourget. Oh, you promised us, Mother!"

"As if you children needed face-wash, you can ask me that in another twenty years time!"

The girls were extremely interested. Amy and Françoise, who were squeezed on either side of Louise on the back seat, leant forward to listen, while the young Belgian's eagerness was undisguised.

"Oh, I am always flushing up and having patches on my face—and then there are the gnats, or mayflies, whatever you call them.... like we had to-day. Oh please, Madame Dumont, something that will make my complexion quite clear...."

"Why, it is clear enough, you foolish child... and the flush is very pretty and May has a nice complexion, too. So, of course, have Françoise and Amy. You must remember, my charmers, that I am an old woman and that if I sometimes use a face-wash... well, that is a very different affair."

The girls continued to plead and Madame Dumont to laugh, she knew that they would all have their face-washes and many other embellishments of their beauty quite soon now, she hoped that May at least, would know how to use them... that was all.

"Well, Rose will give you the recipe. One of these days you can send it to M. Bourget yourself and have it made up."

"Oh, Mother!" pouted May. "You know that the nuns would never allow that, and we never go out alone. I think it mean...."

"Never mind, you ask Rose. One of these days you will find a way; meanwhile, you know you can make a very agreeable complexion-wash yourself—a schoolgirl's lotion with a posy of elder flowers, some rose water and some chlorate of potash I think—but really I forget—and there's something else... but I forget the name of that also. Rose will tell you.... Now this is the shop where we are to make our purchase."

The girls had forgotten about this in the excitement of the talk about the face-wash and they all turned round quickly and eagerly stared at the shop that certainly was a disappointment, for it was a bookseller's establishment of a sombre aspect that Madame Dumont indicated by a wave of her hand.

The dusk was beginning to thicken the brilliant air of Paris and as the barouche drew up on the cobbles with sparks from the wheels, a cold and low-blowing wind came along each of the two streets and seemed to meet and blend and pass on again round the corner where the bookseller's handsome shop stood.

"It certainly blows chilly here!" exclaimed Madame Dumont, dismounting as the groom let down the step, and offering him, with kind indifference, her hand in the cream-coloured kid glove.

"It reminds me," shivered Françoise, "of the story they tell of the Gesu Church in Rome. They say there is always a wind there, and," she added impertinently and daringly, "because the devil made an appointment to meet a Jesuit there, and the Jesuit went inside and was so long that the devil went after him and has never come out... so the wind blows waiting for them."

"That's a naughty story," objected Madame Dumont, "and you shouldn't repeat it. I don't know what the nuns would say," she added mechanically.

"Are we going to buy books?" asked May, disappointed. Whatever was there in books? and they saw enough of them in the convent! Still, her mother always knew what she was doing. Amy and the French girl seemed indifferent and a little vexed, but there was a glow of ecstasy on Louise's plump face.

They passed into the shop. It was arranged like a room with a large table of tulip wood in the centre on which a few choice volumes were piled. Madame Dumont courteously saluted the proprietor who appeared to glide from nowhere and seemed in an instant to be standing humbly at her service.

"Those books I ordered, Monsieur," she reminded, and there was a reverence in her tone May noticed, as if she was in church.

The grey-whiskered, frock-coated bookseller bowed again, made an almost invisible signal and an assistant appeared with four books covered in pale blue velvet laid carefully on a polished tray.

There was no disguising the chill of disappointment among the girls; these volumes were Bibles. The azure binding was very pretty and there was a large fleur de lys in small seed pearl embroidered in the centre of the cover, and the end papers were of the purest water-marked satin, while there was a long blue watered silk with a silver fringe tie to match the cover; there were also a great number of those letters majuscule that May had day dreamed about when she had been lying on the lawn, to brighten the pages.

"This is for you," announced Madame Dumont with a demure grace, "dear Louise, with my love... and one for you, Amy, and one for you, Françoise, and one for you, May. And you are to keep them always and to remember the little *fête* we had in Paris. I came in this morning and inscribed your names into each, so there will be no more formalities. The cases are ready, so we will just take them with us and say no more about it... and if you feel a little dejected that it was not a new bonnet or scarf, well, perhaps some day you will think differently."

The girls murmured their gratitude. After all, a blue velvet Bible was a handsome possession, something to show, perhaps, to boast about.

"You must come to my apartment and drink a little tea, and then I will take you back to Passy," smiled Madame Dumont.

They were out in the street again and it was perceptibly darker than it had been when they entered the lordly shop, the cross-wind seemed to blow more coldly, so that the girls chattered about getting their pelisses out from the back of the barouche, but Madame Dumont said that it was but another block they had to go and that the wind was only at the cross-roads—and so it seemed, for the streets of Paris appeared warm again quite soon and in Madame Dumont's gay apartment there was no chill at all, but hothouse flowers, and, quite soon, a fire of fragrant wood.

May kept one intention in her light mind; with the new Bible, that she had unwrapped, in her hand and holding up her dress from her satin slippers, she left the little party who were talking to some ladies who had come into congratulate Louise on her *fête* day, and ran upstairs to her mother's bedroom where she found, as she had expected, Rose Bernier seated making lace on a firm pillow of blue linen hung with bobbins.

"Ah, Mademoiselle May, and now what do you want from me to-day? There is always something that you come to beg from the poor Rose."

The overfed spaniel turned and growled in his dainty basket; Madame Dumont's bedroom was over-furnished with lace, porcelain, satin and ruched velvet and the air was close with artificial perfumes. May did not admire this room, with the great gilt canopy bed, copied from that of Marie Antoinette at Versailles and the mirrors that must have reflected too often the still delicious figure and face of the charming owner. She preferred something simple, like her own room at Passy; but she was there on a deliberate errand, and did not notice her surroundings even by a glance. The girl could remember the ageing woman since she had been a small child, for Rose had been in Virginia and with her precise, scornful ways had made herself respected among the negroes. Rose too had her memories of the war and like her mistress, she was silent about them and seemed to live for the present only. She was an ugly woman with high cheekbones, harsh brows and a mouth that seemed drawn tight over too many teeth. The shadows in her face were grey and her hair was stiffly crimped and appeared of the texture of a horse's tail, but she had all the elegance of her class, her lead coloured silk dress shone in smooth folds and was trimly moulded over her neat figure.

She put her lace pillow with the hanging bobbins, quickly aside, lest the fine thread should be disarranged by the impetuous girl's embrace.

"I want the recipe for the face-wash," coaxed May. "Maybe I cannot get it made up now, or even for weeks—but Mother said I could have it!"

Rose Bernier laughed. "Did she indeed… that lotion which is made up by M. Bourget? Well, I don't see why you shouldn't have it, Mademoiselle."

Rose went to an alcove, pulled aside the ruffled curtains, pulled out drawers, opened boxes and returned with a fine piece of paper.

"I have several copies. You may take this one. Look, it is very thin… what we call onion skin… you must be careful that you do not lose it,"

"Oh, what is it? Let me see…."

"Well, I hope you can read it. Try, mademoiselle—you know your French is not very good."

May looked at the paper on which was written in purple ink in a foreign hand with long f's:

Liqueur de fowler	30
Chlorate de potasse	7.50
Eau de roses	210
Alcool rectifié	30

Usage externé

"Of course I can read it. It is what Mother told me in the barouche. That is purified alcohol at the bottom… but I don't know what the first stuff is… Fowler's liqueur… what does it mean, Rose?"

"It doesn't matter what it means, mademoiselle. It gives you a very beautiful complexion, but of course you are much too young…."

"Oh, but of course I'm not too young. Sometimes I'm not at all pleased with my face… besides there are other girls, and they really do get blotches or pimples… and the gnats and the mayflies! Have you ever heard of mayflies, Rose? They are little glittering insects that only live for twenty-four hours, but sometimes they get destroyed."

"Now why do you interrupt a talk about a face-wash to say that?" asked Rose shrewdly. "You're a bit of a featherhead, you know, Mademoiselle, eh!"

"And you understand English too well, Rose, I dare say I am a featherhead and a mayfly…."

"Oh, someone called you a mayfly, did they, and that's why you have got the word in your head? Well, Mademoiselle, if you will kindly let me know what we are talking about—face-wash or mayflies—perhaps I can answer you. I think mayflies are foolish little insects, who just buzz in the air and die."

"They only have twenty-four hours, but time is relative, you know! It may be that twenty-four hours to them is like a lifetime of, say, eighty years to us. Mustn't it be queer to be eighty years old? Perhaps when his day is done, a mayfly feels he is eighty years old! I am so glad I have got the face-wash… I shall find a chance of making it up. Mother says you can make a good imitation with attar of roses… and I have some, you know.…"

"You are very extravagant. Mademoiselle, a lady of your age should not have attar of roses.…"

"Well, I have some, and I can get the alcohol and as for elder flowers—we can stew them down. I know there's a beautiful bush in the garden, the nuns won't care for us to pluck it all because they keep it for wine, but I can get a bunch or two. It is really like lace. Amy says in England there's a flower like that, Queen Anne's lace, that grows in the meadows. You know, I should like to go to England, Rose."

"You might go to a worse place or a better," replied the maid. "Now what have you done with that recipe? I don't see it any more, Mademoiselle… you are very careless, you know."

"Oh, it is in my reticule, indeed it is perfectly safe." May stooped and kissed the rough pale brown brow of the French woman and ran from the room.

She put her hand in her reticule to be sure the paper was there; it would be a difficult thing for her to keep; she sighed, anticipating much responsibility; she had so often lost small trifles… there must be somewhere where she could put it safely.…

One of the ladies began to talk to her… she had to be civil and answer questions about her lessons with the Ursulines.

"Oh, I'm too delicate the doctor says to have much real schooling, I just go to the nuns at Passy now and then when mother's in Paris. Sometimes Mother lives in Rouen with my stepfather when he is in garrison there, and then I go to a convent in Rouen… and then sometimes we go to the *plage*, you know and on visits to Virginia.…"

"A busy life," the lady had smiled. "But what a beautiful Bible you have! That is indeed a delightful reminder of Louise's festival!"

"Yes, Madame, it is charming," agreed May who had felt sincerely ashamed by that moment of disillusion when the barouche had drawn up at the bookseller's shop.

She moved about the luxurious room. Tea was being poured into cups of porcelain, so fine that they could be seen through when held up to the light. There was *tutti frutti* being served on thin lilac coloured glass plates, and stems of ginger taken by a silver fork from a jar with hawthorn blossoms, white, staring against a glossy blue and napkins like spiders' webs for the ladies to wipe their sugary fingers upon and to flick morsels of cake from their dresses of French silk.

May was very happy; she had now another plan which was to make her mother keep her in her apartment for the night, and let Rose take the other girls to Passy while she could return in the morning. She really wished to be with her mother and she believed that her stepfather was attending a review on the Champs de Mars to-morrow; she had heard some such vague talk... and, of course, it would be perfectly delightful to be with Mother so long... besides, there might be an opportunity of slipping into M. Bourget on the excuse that one needed some scented powder....

She put the proposition frankly to her mother with appealing eyes and Madame Dumont considered her only child with warm affection. She wondered if May knew what great beauty lay in those eyes that were grey-green, and yet seemed flecked with gold and silver and were so fairly set under straight, wide and almost imperceptible golden brows, in that fine hair like a fleece, curling and waving in ringlets here and here, in the line of her face when she held it up, with the slightly tilted nose and the perfect chin and throat, that was like the line of a lily....

Madame Dumont refused the concession.

"You must return to the convent to-night, May. I have a business meeting with two Englishmen... imagine that! Of course my advocate will be here and your stepfather if he can return from the dêpot...."

"Two Englishmen!" repeated May instantly forgetting her vague intrigue. "I should like to meet them.... You know I want to go to England, Mother."

"Yes, we must go to England some day," replied Madame Dumont vaguely, caressing her daughter's rich ringlets. "It is the country we came from; of course we left it in the time of Charles the Second... one mustn't expect the same respect now we had then. It would not be in the least the same now... not like Virginia.... And as for these gentlemen, well, I really don't know if they are gentlemen. One is a cotton merchant and the other a cotton broker, from Manchester. Your father seemed to think that they were vulgar people, but then you know..." Madame Dumont hesitated, she did not wish to be difficult in a changing world, "they offer a high price for the cotton. You see how mercenary I have become, but we spend a great deal of money...."

"Two Englishmen! I should like to see them... are they at all like the Southern gentlemen?"

"Well, they are both handsome, and, I thought, rather different from other people." Madame Dumont spoke reflectively, like a woman who has been interested against her will. "I don't know much about them," she added indifferently. "Your Uncle James met one of them on the ship crossing the Atlantic... they had been buying cotton in Virginia. You know, cotton is beginning to pay very well with the new dyes and patterns.... Of course, darling, all these pretty things that you see about, and that you will have to have... cost money...."

May interrupted. "Mother, couldn't I see them just as I am going home...? I mean, going away... just pass through the vestibule as they are coming in?"

"You're a little tease. But I am sure I don't see the harm of that. You are so curious; you were like that when you were a child... you know, always trying to find out everything and then forgetting all about it the next day. Well, there are two of them—brothers. I am sure the elder is old enough to be your father...."

"Well what about the younger?" asked May. "Perhaps he is old enough to be my brother?"

Madame Dumont did not deign to answer this question. "They are waiting upon me before supper... one could hardly ask them yet to an entertainment. You may stay a quarter of an hour later, and if you meet them as you go out, you will just give them a little salutation and pass along quickly."

May had to be satisfied with this; it was simple curiosity that had been roused in her as her mother knew, May was one of those people who are both inquisitive, in a perfectly amiable way, and indolent. One quality would alternately cancel out the other. Sometimes laziness would predominate, and she would not turn her head to see who was passing the door, but another time she would give herself a great deal of trouble to discover all the details of the simplest event. To-night there was no trouble at all and she was able to see the two Englishmen as she left with her three companions in the charge of Rose Bernier, precisely to the hour that had been appointed by the Mother Superior.

The Englishmen were waiting in the vestibule that was overcrowded with small marble statues on bronze pedestals in the effeminate style of Canova, and the four girls noticed them with a vivid interest; these strangers were certainly different from any men whom they had seen before. They wore dark attire which seemed to increase their considerable height and their hair was also dark, and so were their brows that were very straight and level, while their faces had a pallor that seemed unnatural in a man; this was very marked in the elder, it was not a warm pallor, but the whiteness tinged with green seen in a privet flower; their features were, however, masculine and noble.

May Beale went ahead and, being the most audacious of the girls, paused and held out her hand to the first and elder visitor.

"You are my mother's guests, I think, Mr. Tyler?"

She knew she was committing some breach of discipline; the nuns talked so much about etiquette and May never troubled to remember any of it; the elder man replied in a suave manner that his name was John Tyler, and presented his brother, Mr. Richard Tyler, adding smoothly that it was an unlikely hour to come on business but that "with one thing and another the appointment had been difficult to fit in."

Rose Bernier tried with a little movement of her hands under her apron, to urge the girls on, but they remained to gaze at the two strangers who seemed out of place among the tall dark blue Chinese vases filled with the pampas grass and the trivial statues, sleek and meaningless.

The men smiled at the girls; it was a moment of undisguised appraisal on either side; May was conscious that John Tyler was definitely interested in her beauty, but this was nothing uncommon; many gentlemen had been thus impressed and she had thought nothing of their homage.

Rose Bernier had her way and the girls passed on to the barouche, the Frenchwoman scolding in her own language about the indecorum of Mademoiselle speaking to her mother's guests without being presented and the strangeness of "a talk on business" at such an hour of night, and wasn't it somehow shocking that there should be business to be talked of with a lady of the quality of Madame Dumont?

"Why don't these gentlemen go to see your stepfather, Mademoiselle?"

The girl did not know, and said so, laughing. She was pondering on those two tall dark figures that had crowded out the dainty little vestibule of her mother's apartment.

"They are like," she remarked thoughtfully, "Roman emperors."

Louise giggled. Françoise however said that the simile was correct and added "in frock-coats."

"If it was not for that absurd modern costume," May continued, "I do think they had faces like Roman emperors—classical, like you see on coins and in busts. Nero—Diocletian?"

Amy, who had been bored and not spoken for a long time protested, "My dear May, I hope you did not think that those badly dressed, badly mannered creatures were English gentlemen? They were people whom I am sure my dear papa would never receive—provincial merchants, tradesmen or stockbrokers...."

"Of course Mademoiselle is right," agreed Rose Bernier, "no gentleman would come talking on business to a lady at such an hour."

It was dusk, but one could smell the lilac; it was dusk, but one could hear the plashing fountains; it was dusk, but leaning from under the hood of the barouche one could see the tall poplars making a tracery of dark against the still faint sparkles of light in the sky; it was dusk and the stars were coming out and the air was of a piercing sweetness from the last hawthorns in the Ursulines' walled garden as the girls turned in at the white gates.

They all, although they were silent, had a sense of excitement. Nothing had happened and yet it seemed as if a great deal might happen.... The river was not far away.... You could not see it, or hear it, but there was a sense of it, hastening on.

"How strong all the flowers smell to-night!" sighed May, the first to alight, before the footman had lowered the step from the barouche, and earning thereby a rebuke from Rose Bernier for leaping from the carriage. "And see the lilies! They are almost luminous in the dark."

"Haven't you noticed that before?" asked Amy. "We grow them in clusters at home and they do really seem to light up the gardens like glow worms."

"Nonsense!" objected Rose Bernier. "They do not give out light. You must read your botany books more carefully... it is only that they seem to glow because they are such a pure white and that it must be very dark indeed before they are quite eclipsed."

"That," May confided to her in a quick whisper, "is what the lotion does for one's face... it makes you glow in the dark like the lilies." She turned to her half-seen companions. "Wouldn't that be wonderful, girls? Imagine black velvet and one's arms and shoulders and face pure white, and one's hair brushed up...."

"You're a silly chatterbox. Mademoiselle," said Rose Bernier, "and I hope you *won't* try to get that prescription made up.... Here comes Sister Jeanne, and now you really must be quiet."

The girls were duly delivered to the nun who received them amiably. Oh, they were in good time.... There was a gentle clinking of polished keys and the gentle moving back of the grille and the gate, and Rose Bernier got into the barouche and drove back to Paris.

A faint rain was falling. There had been a long drought and the dry earth gave forth a curious and delicious smell as the raindrops fell into the garden beds.

May Beale felt her excitement increase. She escaped her yawning companions and ran to the room that she was allowed to have to herself under the excuse that she was delicate, while the others slept two and two in cubicles. Everything in the room pleased May as much as it pleased the nuns; it was furnished in blue and white with a curtain of blue lined with white at the head of the bed, and at the bottom of the bed a low bench on which May folded her clothes piece by piece every night, laying over them a blue veil. On the table beside her bed was a plain carafe and glass, and some books of devotion that May never read—and yet it gave her a sense of protection to see them there.

Above the mantelpiece that crowned a small stove that May had never known lit because she had not been in the convent in the winter, was a large German colour print of the Virgin in a robe of azure blue, her thin boneless hands crossed upon her bosom and her doll-like face turned upwards while two tears rolled down her cheeks. May, though she had good taste, thought that something made the picture beautiful and she often lit two pure wax tapers underneath it and watched them burn to the sockets of the brass sticks.

There was a cupboard for May's clothes, and there were chairs painted in blue and white and there was May's medal hanging above her bed by a ribbon of watered blue.

There were times when May was tired of blue and white and would lie in bed planning the colours she would have when she was free… liberty was not far ahead now. Her mother had promised to take her to Rouen, to Virginia, possibly to London.… Meanwhile, it was quite pleasant here.

The nun came in, shading with her thin hand, on which the veins were beginning to show purple, the small night light that May, being delicate, was always allowed. May showed her the Bible and the nun praised it without opening it and delivered a little homily on the splendour of the binding saying, in a toneless voice, that it was not the appearance of the book, but the contents that must be valued.

May put the Bible down and began to undress. Her mind was not on the Bible, but on the face-wash.… It was a pity that her mother had not been able to keep her in Paris that night… Then suddenly she was alert. "Where did I put it?" She picked up her reticule from where she had placed it on the bench at the end of the bed.… She was extremely tidy in her habits. She had learned that, if nothing else, from the Ursulines; but there was no scrap of onion paper in the reticule.

May experienced that curious pang of loss that is always in disproportion to the value of the missed object. She felt as if some disaster had happened, and then she recalled that she would find the recipe or have it again from Rose any time. Still, it was disappointing… it might be many days before she went to Paris, and meanwhile there was the question of waiting.... Waiting... what word could be more detestable to youth?

"Never mind, why shouldn't I make some lotion myself? I can remember everything that was on that paper, and I know how to get it too... except that Fowler's mixture, and I dare say we can manage with something else."

She remembered the two gentlemen she had seen waiting in her mother's little vestibule. She felt rather uneasy, even in a way downcast and perhaps insulted because the English girl, in her hard, precise manner had said they were not gentlemen. May was not sure they would have passed as gentlemen in Virginia, or in Paris... but it was difficult to tell about people from another country... and as for merchants, well, that was absurd... all her mother's money came from merchandise. Without the cotton there would be no luxurious room for May in a luxurious convent, and no such day of festival as they had had on the shaven sward of Bagatelle.

She placed the Bible with her other religious books on the bedside table, repeated her devotions and lay down in her chill bed, first putting her hair, the changing colours of pale gold and silver that belongs only to extreme youth, into a little cap of Indian muslin.

May soon confided to her three friends her intention of making the face-wash, the recipe of which she had lost.

"We need a posy of elder flowers, and that is soon gathered from the big tree at the end of the garden... and then we need a little pure alcohol and some chlorate of potash and some attar of roses... and my stepfather gave me some on my seventeenth birthday and we can make the wash ourselves."

The girls were extremely interested; May's simile of "glowing like luminous lilies in the dusk," had taken their fancy; none of them had anyone whom they desired to please, yet the intense wish to please concerned them above everything.

They ran down the moist garden after they had finished their lessons with the full permission of Sister Philippe, who was in charge of the garden; she said they might pick two or three bunches of the elder flower.

"But this blossom doesn't live long in water," she had warned them, "it stains your fingers and it has rather a rank smell."

May had replied frankly that they wanted to make a face-wash of the elder, and the nun still had smiled indulgently. The nuns, the girls knew, were very good women; their lives were joined to those of the maidens in their charge by the faintest of links.... Very often they betrayed themselves by their eyes, their lips, their nostrils... but the girls never noticed.

There were novices in the convent and those who had been for long boarders, with some of them the nuns were intimate and often closeted, but these girls who came and went for a few weeks were outside everything, except the daily observance of the decorous duties—the masses, the prayers, the devotions, the lessons—and if they performed these with regularity, the nuns never interfered with them and so, for their part, the nuns were merely very good women to the girls. One was glad one was not a nun.

May came back from the end of the garden with her cluster of elder flower. Examining it closely, she could see that it was composed of hundreds of little flowerets and that it was not of the pure white colour of the lily, but more the hue of milk that is turning into cream; the blossom had a faint perfume, but it was true the leaves and stems were coarse and repellent.

All the girls had commonplace books or jottings in albums that had belonged to their mothers or grandparents, and in these were directions how to make various preparations... how you could strain jelly through a chicken skin... how you could stuff a swan... how you could make frumenty or syllabub... and how to go out early in the morning on May day and wash your face in the dew. These were now searched, the girls seated on a bench by the lily bed.

"All very old fashioned," sighed May, "it will not show us what we must do. I have the attar of roses..." She produced a thick glass tube on which were coarse gay characters from her pocket and said that had come from Bulgaria. There were only a few drops of essence inside when her stepfather had given it to her with a most formal salutation; he had said that a whole rose garden had been distilled to make this brilliant essence.

Amy, for all her detachment, was interested enough in the experiment and undertook to buy at the chemists in Passy the rectified alcohol and the chlorate of potash. This meant a delay. The girls were not allowed out alone and the sisters were not always ready to take them, whenever their whim dictated. No, not even these rich girls, who were so pampered and indolent. So they whiled away the afternoon as best they could, there was nothing in the scrap books to help them about the lotion, Françoise said she could make it—but what was Fowler's solution and how obtain it? They strolled into the house beset by the problem that was not of any importance to any of them.

May watched the cluster of elder flower dying in the white china vase into which she had put it. Yes, it was dying... drooping forward... all its light shrouded. "Oh, it's like poor despised beauty who has decked herself for an admiration that has not been forthcoming."

They went into the music room and May's small fingers ran over the piano as she played Weber's "Mermaids' Chorus".... She repeated it again and again, the melody soothed the girls, they sat with their arms clasped round their knees, thinking of nothing, hardly dreaming of anything, merely listening to the melody that seemed to envelop them, like a vapour in the air envelops an idler brooding in an empty field.

After tea, for the Ursulines gave English "five o'clock" in the modern style, Amy was allowed to go on her errands. The nuns had no objection to her visiting the chemist's; indeed that nun, Sister Clare, who had charge of them that afternoon, had very little objection to anything. She was in ill health and coughed continuously, and her blue eyes, that were circled with another hue of azure, had a sarcastic as well as a keen expression; she accompanied Amy without comment.

At the chemist's, Amy bought a new hair brush, trying the bristle with a professional air, while her lips were pursed and her look doubtful. When she had made a decision as to the brush, she bought the rectified alcohol and the chlorate of potash, that looked like salt, in a little paper packet, and then carelessly asked the young assistant, who was very civil indeed to this charming and wealthy customer and who knew that his firm had good trade with the Ursulines, if he knew what was "Fowler's liqueur?"

"Mademoiselle, that is a medicine and it cannot be sold without a doctor's prescription."

Amy was disappointed, and stood uncertainly, the nun took little interest.... She asked mechanically, "What do you want it for, Mademoiselle Amy?"

"Oh, you know," whispered the girl in a low confidential tone, "it is to make that face-wash to please May... not that any of us care for it... I've got no freckles or pimples... but she is anxious to make something that her mother's maid gave her a recipe for... and now she has lost that and wants to try to make it herself."

"Well, you must pass the time somehow," conceded Sister Clare, and she asked the young man, lifting her tired blue eyes, how it was this ingredient could not be bought?

It was a matter of the law, he answered, a formality. "But exactly the same stuff, Mademoiselle, may be bought on flypapers. It is Fowler's *liqueur* that is smeared over them."

"Flypapers!" exclaimed May in active disgust. "Horrible things! I am so glad we do not have them in the convent!"

"The convent is clean, and therefore we have no flies."

"Oh, but they are nauseating.... I have seen them in Paris with the wretched mayflies struggling over them... oh! I think they are terrible! I have often put the whole paper in a bowl of water to end their misery...."

"Mademoiselle's kindness of heart is to be commended, but I am not talking of flies, but of flypapers. If Mademoiselle would purchase some of these, which are only one franc each, and soak them for several hours she would find the liquid that comes off them was quite the same as Fowler's solution."

"Well, then," said the nun, pressing her hand to her side, "buy them, my dear, and let's be gone."

She glanced, with what seemed a calm distaste round the chemist shop, where the bunches of dry herbs in various shades of brown and green, hung from the ceiling, and where large clusters of poppy heads, symbol of Morpheus, showed with their dry brown skull-like bulbs and their sharp crowns in the shadows at the back of the shop. The shelves were lined with vases of Delft marked with the names of various drugs such as senna, ipecacuanha, quinine.

Amy liked the smell of the white castille soap, and perfume of the *eau-de-Cologne* and jasmine water was very pleasing; but she was quick to see that the nun was tired and that it was time to have done with this trivial and selfish business.

"I will have some flypapers then, please," she said quickly. "Please roll them all up together with the brush and put them down to my papa's account."

May Beale was disappointed when she saw the ugly drab flypapers; she, too, had shuddering memories of them in Paris shops, they had spoilt many a visit to the capital.

"But you must not think of that." Amy was cool. "You must put them in a basin with enough water to cover them, and the solution you find in the morning is what you must mingle with the other things."

How to prepare these was a task rather beyond the girls' skill, but one of the nuns was sympathetic. She took the drooping bunch of elder flowers from them and said that she herself was preparing a simple that evening—lime tea, which was so appreciated by the invalid inhabitants of the convent—and that she would not mind steeping the blossoms and she added, with that stillness that was too cool for contempt, "Rich girls like you must always be doing something nonsensical."

In the morning they had their ingredients; a bottle of liquid from the elder blossom, a pint or so of liquid from the flypapers (the papers themselves were instantly and fastidiously thrown away) and the little packet of chlorate of potash; the receptacle, an earthenware ewer, was soon ready; then May produced a flask of an artificial green colour with a white spiral line, as if a finger dipped in milk had been traced round it, that Madame Dumont had bought at Murano and given to her daughter; it had gold marks on it....

"I think they say something like 'Love me' or 'Kiss me'. It's in Italian," said May.

The solution in the ewer being shaken and stirred, it was poured into this flask and the stopper, which was of a fantastical crown-like shape, firmly set in place.

The nun who came to see what they were doing, for the girls were never allowed to stay alone for more than a few minutes in the gay rooms where they were permitted to amuse themselves, remarked that "whatever it was the young ladies were making, they must let the mixture stand for at least twenty-four hours."

The sharp impatience of youth was angered by this, but the well-trained Ursuline gave them a fresh occupation.

"There are some flowers to be set in the garden... you will like to do that. The gardener," she added with that calm tinge of irony that the nuns used towards these wealthy and transient guests, "has done all the work. What you will need to do is to place the plants in the beds."

The girls liked this task; the warm brown earth, soft and crumbling from the recent rain, the clean fresh plants in their small bright scarlet pots... the work was easily accomplished, and the effect was good; they left the solution in the green and white striped flask and ran downstairs.

May only paused by the chapel, not that her mood was serious, but her curiosity was aroused. She prayed there so many times a day and, thoughtless as her nature was, she sometimes wondered what religion and the chapel meant if one only could think of them in a detached way, without the nuns being there or the confessor walking about, or, as she had been taught to believe, "the eye of God" spying on one... there was no escaping that, but her buoyant spirits believed there might be a chance that at some odd moment He was looking another way.

The chapel always stood open; it was dark, and the shadows had a wine and gold colour. Everything in the building was painted, or gilded, or adorned with brocade and tapestry and vases of flowers. There were side altars with railings, and faldstools of red velvet. All the pupils who came to the convent had been obliged to work something for the chapel; even May had accomplished a chair cushion on which clusters of golden grapes, carefully couched in scarlet thread, had been laboriously sewn.

She forgot the pleasant task in the garden and crept into the sanctified place. Sunlight filtered through painted glass, but it was very little, and the air was sickly with stale incense. On the altar was a very dark picture; it seemed to be of some tragedy... of murder or torture, but the bitumen that the painter had used had eaten away the brighter colours save here and there where a ghostly white limb or the flash of a stormy sky was revealed.

May dropped her obeisance to the altar and then turned mechanically to her accustomed place and looked round, and tried, with her curious mind, to get some meaning into it all. She had grown up in this atmosphere... there had been a chapel in Virginia... there was a chapel at Rouen and there were the big churches where her mother took her on state occasions. An uneasy feeling this, that there was an invisible world of saints and angels and devils hovering around.... She pondered the question for a moment. Was her making of the face-wash a sin...? Was her deliberate lingering to see the two Englishmen a sin...? The fact that she had led three other girls, her best friends, into misdemeanours—was this a sin, too? Perhaps she ought to confess, but at the same time she knew that she would not.

She was quite unaware that she was herself the most beautiful thing in the chapel, full of tawdry dolls, meaningless draperies and windows of stained and painted glass. May Beale might have come from God's hand, if He was to be credited with the creation of all loveliness. There was no flaw in her, nor in the spirit that looked from those grey-green eyes... if spirits may be supposed to gaze from a human being's eyes.

She knelt down and put her hands together and in all simplicity prayed.

"Dear God, if I am wrong in making the face-wash—perhaps it was because I was wrong that I lost Rose Bernier's recipe—if I was wrong in staying behind to see the two English gentlemen, please punish me and not my friends for it."

The prayer gave her a sense of release. Surely God was placated now.... He could not want anything more.... It was a relief to be in the chapel when it was empty. She did not like it when it was crowded with pale-faced nuns. She did not like it when the organ played those thin melodies that seemed to belong to another world.

She rose and tiptoed out of the heavy enclosed atmosphere, but she did not go into the garden where her companions were gravely taking the tender plants out of the small pots while the gardener watched their amateur efforts, and placing them in the holes he had made. She returned to her room and sat there with her hands clasped under her chin, while she gazed at the green Venetian flask with the white spiral line.

Mr. Tyler and his brother sat in the warm sunshine at the iron table outside one of the fashionable *cafés* in Paris. There certainly was, they both agreed silently, something about Paris "that set your spirits up." It might have been the brilliancy of the air, that was like a powdered gold after smoky Manchester or even foggy London; there were airy drifting vapours, yes—but these merely served to set off the light… they floated high overhead, they did not settle down, close you in, stifle you, take you by the throat and begrime all your garments.… There was electricity about, too, in Paris… if you stroked a cat or brushed your own hair you could see the sparks fly.…

So they sat comfortably at their round table and enjoyed the passing life of the *boulevard*. They were, in their narrow way, shrewd men. They knew the value of everything that has a price, they put a price to a good many things that have no market; they often bargained for what could neither be bought nor sold and, in their own gross way, they were satisfied with existence. They had, in their own phrase, "done very well for themselves." Their origins were those of most of their class—not basely obscure, as their business rivals were quick to hint—but mean. Their father had been a small attorney in a town in the Midlands, who had scraped and pinched and cheated his clients when it was safe to do so, who had sent his boys to the grammar school in the day and himself taught them worldly wisdom in the evening, and wearied his wife to death before he was able to build the ornate marble tomb he afterwards shared with her, and invested his money very carefully in cotton when there had been all that excitement over the anti-slavery bill… a slip… a landslide… and then a boom, and now a steady settled prosperity.

The two boys had learned their lessons excellently; they had paid little heed to what the masters in grammar school had taught them, but they had rubbed shoulders there with other boys, mostly of their own type, and thus studied the world in little, and they had listened to their father's advice and respected him for his shifts and subterfuges, and early they had gone to Manchester into the office of a cotton broker, and early they had started business on their own account; one, Richard, as a broker, and John as a merchant.

Their speculations had been successful. They had bought cheaply and though their firm was in a small way, their goods had always been high class and had commanded a fair price, they had taken trouble, too; John had been to Virginia several times and made his bargains on the spot while other men had stayed at home and smoked their segars and enjoyed themselves at the Wirral Races and perhaps at the Cambridge Rooms; they had been cautious, the money set aside for their vices was always carefully spent.

"It's a fine day," remarked John.

"A fine day," returned Richard.

They were out of place and knew it; their hands more than once went to their pockets where the thickness of their bank rolls gave them confidence.

They belonged to a new class, to a new world, they considered the old classes, the old world with mingled contempt and envy. Their tastes were gross, and what they wanted to satisfy them they could have bought; yet they had all the tradesman's longing "to be like his betters", and it was not the mincing cocottes who strutted about the pavements that they gazed at, but the ladies with their clouds of chiffon, with their tilted parasols who passed to and fro in barouche or carriage behind prancing horses. Anything out of reach attracted them… not that they were going to break their hearts about what was unattainable… oh dear, no… but there was a gnawing envy, a carking disappointment hidden behind their complacency. They were extremely handsome men of their type, which was not what a foreigner would have supposed to be English;—they were dark, with smooth, thick hair and features, as May Beale had remarked, of classic regularity that would indeed have shown well on a coin. Their eyes were grey, their brows straight and heavy, there was nothing repellant in their faces save their impassive heaviness and their pale complexions; particularly noticeable in John; Richard now and then would flush, but John had an even pallor that never changed.

He settled his satin stock, drank off the *apéritif* the waiter had just placed by his elbow, and remarked, "A good deal last night, don't you think?"

"The woman is a fool, of course," replied the younger brother. "But her steward seemed to know what he was about."

"I saw the estate the last time I was in Virginia, you know, the cotton crop is worth more than that steward seems to think. The Beale cotton plantations are pretty good and with these new dyes our trade can buy the lot—if we could be first in the market with some novelty, we ought to do pretty well."

"Well enough for you to marry and settle down, eh, John? It's time, isn't it?"

"What makes you think of that now?" asked John.

"Well, you're forty-eight…."

"And you're forty-six! Why don't *you* marry and settle down? Born bachelors, that's what we are."

With their clear grey eyes, the hue of agates, they watched the phaeton roll past with large wheels like metallic spiders' webs in which were two upright ladies in floating laces and gauze; Richard was quick to mark his brother's glance at these beauties, a glance much more avid even than his own rude and jealous stare.

"You'll never do it, John, you'll never marry into a family like that... and if you did, what would it be? They'd pick you to the bone in a month, and what would be left of you?"

"My dear fellow," John used imitation worldly expressions picked up on his visits to London, "do you think I have any ambitions that way? I want my pleasures, I don't want to be tied up to a wife.... That little creature we saw last night, now, a schoolgirl...."

"Which one? There were four of them all dressed the same, and with blue velvet Bibles if you please!"

"Oh yes, they had had some festival, I suppose. They are Roman Catholics, you know. But the one who had the audacity to speak to me... I should think she's a bright little piece. I never saw such eyes... quite green..."

"I thought you had *your* eye on the mother."

"No use," said John, his clear eyes roving, his voice expressionless.

"Why not? She seemed to be gay and yielding."

"She's married."

"I never heard you concern yourself about that before."

"It isn't England," replied John stiffly. "These Frenchies don't know our ways. The husband might call one out... I don't want a bullet through my liver...."

"Oh well, if it's like that...."

"Well, it is like that, and I was thinking more of the daughter than the mother."

"She's a schoolgirl—sixteen, I should think...."

"Perhaps more," mused John. "You can't tell when they have their hair falling down and that childish look.... Not so simple as she seems perhaps.... I wonder what she was thinking of when she stared up at us?" There was silence for a while, and then he added, "I've no doubt she despised us. There's a title, you know—Madame la Comtesse Dumont...." He gave a coarse French accent and a sneer to the word. "That would be a good laugh in Manchester, wouldn't it?"

Richard was silent. He was of slightly finer material than his brother—more subtle, more patient, not so quick to betray himself. He ordered another *apéritif*, they were moderate drinkers, and naively relished the unfamiliar liqueur as they sat at the table watching the passers-by. One had to look at something... the Third Republic was nine years old, but the fashions set by the Empress Eugènie had not yet vanished; the voluble ladies who went by in their carriages, or occasionally on foot with an escort of haughty, chattering gentlemen, had still the outline that had graced Compiègne, the skirts were full, not crinolines as the Empress, now in exile in England, had worn, but full and gathered up behind in great bows and ruches, and the waist Still tight and the bodice cut low in front and the hair falling in curls under a tilted hat.

It was still the Paris where Offenbach's brilliant tunes were played like champagne flung on to the air; still the Paris where *gendarmes* walked about in couples with their cocked laced hats, and where omnibuses, though no longer a novelty, were quite something to stare at as they rattled over the cobbles.

Everywhere they glanced, the Englishmen could note with scorn the National Emblem, the gathered fasces with the motto *"Liberté, egalité et fraternité"* and above, the red cap of the galley slave or perhaps the crowing cock; it was a busy city, it was quite true what they said about it in England—a city of pleasure, more so as it was unabashed; it was ready, like a pander, to supply everybody's vices; it did not even make any comments on anyone's bad taste. A tradesman and his family could be supplied with quite innocent amusements while a broken down dandy could be supplied with amusements not so innocent while those with a great deal of money to spend on vice could find a little more value for it than they could in even the rankest purlieus of London.

"It's the air," said John with a sigh. "It's the air."

"The air is very brilliant. You going to take the cotton from the Dumonts?"

"Certainly. I shall probably go again to Virginia and look at it for myself. It's a bargain. The woman, as I told you, thinks she has a very shrewd man of business, but he's not so sharp, and as for her husband, he knows nothing at all... a wooden soldier. These foreigners...!"

"Americans don't seem like foreigners to me, nor to you I know. The woman was pleasant enough. I still think you had your eye on her."

"I've got my eye on a good many of them."

Richard, with that touch of spite he often showed asked, "What about Dora and her family?"

"You leave Dora and her family to me. What I've begun I'll finish."

"I hope you will. It's not the sort of thing, you know, people *like*. If you're going to get on in Manchester you'd better get a wife and a carriage and pair, and pension Dora off and forget about her."

"The first is easy enough, but I don't know about the last. Did you ever hear of a woman being pensioned off?"

"Well, there's that other affair in America. What about her?"

"Sheila? Oh, she's all right... she'd never ask for anything... she'd never talk either. She's a fine woman. Why this discussion of matrimony, Richard? As I say, you might get married yourself and give us this air of respectability you think we need."

"I'm not the elder brother... it doesn't matter so much what I do. This is a queer place—look at the flowers those young women are carrying... so many flowers you can't see the girls. Do you know the names of those blue things?"

"Not I. Did you notice the dresses those girls wore last night... as if they were out of a picture about a hundred years old?"

John did not know what he meant by "a hundred years old". He was ignorant of everything save his own business and the easy animal life that he had always led and with a good deal of satisfaction. One hundred years ago... merely a romantic expression.... What had the Tylers been a hundred years ago...? Peasants... great-grandfather and grandfather had been successful, shrewd, prudent Midlanders with an eye to where money was to be made and where it was to be invested... the father had been an attorney on the surface only, he was mainly a dabbler in stocks and shares—not secretly, but as a very paying side line. John and Richard had been brought up at first with puritanical austerity and afterwards ostentatiously, for their mother had been a weak-minded woman to whom the inflow of money had meant display. Both the men, as they sat there in the flush and flourish of their middle age, could recall, and did recall as a kind of protection against the alien luxury they saw about them, those early days when, after their mother's death so soon after the early success, they had moved to the large house outside Manchester where they had never seemed to fit in very well.... There had been a vinery and their father had had a saddle-horse and a groom whose manner had not been (even the boys had noticed) correct; but they had inherited their mother's desire for what was showy—her longing, too, for what was unobtainable.

John could remember going into the kitchen garden, which was the most pleasing part of the ugly neo-Gothic house and stiffly laid out grounds. The bricks of the wall there had been burnt the colour of a summer afternoon, rose and gold, and on them were growing peaches each in a small bag of net. The loutish boy had noticed the rich fruit served on dishes of painted porcelain for dessert and never wished to eat it; but seeing it so guarded by the net bags, he had asked the gardener, who was turning over the soft soil with a small rake, why peaches were so protected, "and not the plums and the cherries, Saunders, eh?"

"It's because they're so precious, Master John," the man had answered with that sullenness that Mr. Tyler's servants showed beneath the cringing manner they used to a dull upstart master.

"Precious, eh?"

John had snatched the peaches down one at a time, and torn off the net bags and stuck his teeth into them one after another.

Saunders had said nothing. He knew better than to interfere between the old master and the young master; it might mean merely a talk in the library and a few texts from the Bible; it might mean a thrashing, but Mr. John was able to give as good as he got and the gardener was indifferent both towards the boy and the fruit.

The peaches were not ripe, the flesh clung to the stone; John flung them down one after the other in disgust; he had, though he did not put it in that way, grasped at something that was rare and choice, had his way with it and flung it aside.

Now he recalled, too, the day when he had seen a strange bird floundering in the strawberry bed and asked his father, who was taking what he called a "survey of the estate", what the outlandish creature was.

"It's a peacock, your mother liked to keep them because the gentry do."

The oddity at once became valuable to John. He had waited till his father was out of sight to tiptoe his way as best he could among the creeping plants and get hold of the brilliant bird that was half entangled in the nets; it was stronger than he had thought, struggled and soon was away; but he had had time to admire the magnificence of its bloomy breast—something beyond colour and beyond brilliance—and the incredible design of the sweeping tail that was something that John could never hope to describe even in his thoughts where it was always hung, a plume of exasperating, inexplicable beauty.

John had not seen the peacock again. He did not know what had become of these glittering creatures beyond that Mr. Tyler had said that their shrill cries were disturbing at night, and John had escaped punishment for the theft of the peaches; Mr. Tyler, perhaps, had other things to think of. He was making a great deal of money and building another stove house, and he spent more and more time in the clubs, bars and exchanges of Manchester, and less and less time in the big mansion where he had installed his motherless boys; neither John nor Richard had seen much of their mother and never missed her; they merely knew she had died when they were very young, and had ceased to be interested.

There was a short interlude of female relatives coming and going in bombazine and large handkerchiefs with black borders, and the smell of *eau-de-Cologne* and dead lilies; and then there was a housekeeper who was very correct and who had been with gentlefolk, and the boys went to school; not to Rugby, but to an excellent grammar school, better than that their father had attended.

Sitting there at their iron table, looking on the Paris *boulevard*, they wished it had been Rugby; they wished it had been Harrow or Eton. They remembered an expression they had heard from their father—"below the salt". It was not a pleasant sensation remembering that.... They recalled last night; the lady had been kind... yes, that was the worst of it—she had been too kind. They were likely to make a good deal of money out of her, and they could not say that she had been condescending; but there had been that touch of aloofness in her demeanour, and in that of the stiff cavalry officer who came in so late and who bowed absurdly from the waist, and could not speak English, which set them in their place. They knew the reason why they had never married; those women who would have had them willingly for their looks and their money, the Tylers despised; and those they would have taken, even without love or liking or fortune because of their aristocratic connections, they could not even meet.

These defeats were never admitted; the brothers, if not subtle, were reserved. Each kept his inner life closed from the other, yet they knew one another very well... perhaps because they were so much the same.

The Paris atmosphere was over them like an enchantment... the big heavy Englishmen could not resist brooding over folly.

"It's the air, so different from Manchester," said John again and the stupid remark exactly expressed what he felt.

The air did sparkle and glitter and make you feel well, yet as if you wished you were not nearly fifty.... To marry and have an establishment... he brooded over that. He had been invited sometimes to dinners at the houses of merchants in Manchester and Liverpool, and he remembered now, with a certain envy, those heavy rooms, and the long damask tablecloth with the épergne in the centre loaded with hothouse flowers and trailing greenery, and the cutlery and the glass and the little vase with a gardenia or rose at everybody's plate; and then the guests—the glazed shirt-fronts of the men—a cold white, and the bare backs and bosoms of the women, a flushed and warm white, setting off necklets of turquoise or garnet.

"I should like to have such a dinner party... to have my wife at the head of a loaded table wearing, not any of that cheap stuff, but diamonds..." He imagined May Beale not in her muslins, but in satin—oh, of some rich colour or other... perhaps the colour of the peacock's breast... that would make people stare, because a dark hue would be so odd on a young girl... and on her bosom, diamonds.

He bit his nether lip; it would be a long time yet before he would be able to buy diamonds for anyone... it would be a long time before he would get as much as an introduction to May Beale....

"I think I shall go to Virginia," he announced abruptly. "I'll have another look at the Beale estate... that Frenchie don't know how to make the most of it... the steward may be a rogue... I daresay we could strike a good bargain—take the entire crops over, for several years—make a bit, eh?"

Richard agreed. They were honest men in everything that concerned their business, but "a good bargain" was considered as part of this honesty; in everything except their business they were intensely dishonest, without knowing it, neither honesty nor honour had ever come under their consideration; neither was in their traditions, their training, their nature.

They rose without speaking, but as if by mutual consent, and parted with a careless gesture; the light had changed to a richer and deeper blue, the sky had deepened to that dark violet that precedes the twilight on a clear day.

Richard sauntered off to one of the variety theatres that so blandly catered for the tastes of tourists like himself; he paused to look with approval at the crudely painted boards round the entrance on which were depicted men in top hats and white shirt-fronts, and women in black dresses with cascades of lace petticoats, dancing the can-can, a dance still fashionably daring for the simpler type of foreigner.

John did not seek any such diversion; he had his pockets full of money and coarse pleasures appealed to him… but not to-night. He had other matters on his mind. He was tormented by a sluggish ambition that was thwarted by his own character—his ignorance of anything but his own narrow world… his inability to value or judge what did not belong to that world… his complete misapprehension of what was important and what was trivial. He hated those people who had any knowledge that he was vaguely conscious he lacked and he would swagger and boast endlessly as to his own advantages, admitting no one to be his superior; but there always was the hidden desire to be something that he was not, to obtain something that he could not have. There was something however that he could have and that he intended to obtain.

He returned to the hotel that had been planned exactly for his type of tourist and walked moodily to the room next to Richard's, for which he was paying a very high price. He glanced round with satisfaction, though it was a depressing room. There were red plush curtains and ecru lace curtains at the tall dusty window, there was a round table with a green chenille cloth in the centre of the room, and the large iron bed had a chenille coverlet and a heavy bolster with fringed ends. On the wall over the fireplace was a print *The Death of Montcalm*, which puzzled John because he was sure he had seen the same print in England labelled *The Death of Wolfe*—but the subject was patriotic, John gave the French that, the English had won that battle, as always, and he could allow, as the French admitted, that they had been beaten, after putting up a fair fight; and the same picture could easily serve to illustrate the death of the two generals.

John's luggage had been taken away save for one valise upon the trunk stand, but the room held something that was entirely his own and that he daily assured himself was safe. He searched for it now, unlocking the cupboard carefully, methodically and peering into the dark and musty interior where overcoats, band boxes and hat boxes hung and stood in close array. What he wanted was a medicine chest that he at once put his hand on; it was made of snake and tulip wood and well polished. He placed it on the plush cloth and unlocked it with a small key that he took from the heavy gold chain that held his watch across his waistcoat. The medicine chest was well plenished with boxes and bottles filled with various drugs, all carefully labelled in his own handwriting. At the bottom were drawers, and when John Tyler pulled these open he looked upon packages which were held together by thin bands of purple ribbon. These, too, were labelled and some of them had such childish remarks as "For cats", "For rats" written on them. One of the bottles was empty. He took it up, held it to the light and put it back again. He examined all the other medicines with deliberation, as a man who considers something he understands a good deal about. There was also a pile of small sheets of paper, some of them almost as fine as the onion skin on which was the face-wash recipe that Rose Bernier had given May Beale.

John selected one of these, then, taking out his large silk handkerchief, dusted the interior and then the exterior of the box, locked it, hid it again and locked the cupboard door.

The big man, with a sauntering gait, then went out into the streets of Paris. There was a good deal that he did not know, even in his own line of gross and vicious living; he was now hampered by ignorance of the French language and of what he termed "the right places to go to"; but these ought to be found simply enough. He refused to allow himself to be afraid of Paris, to confess that he had never been to France before because the very name overawed him. He turned into a large chemist's shop, one much more elaborate than that neat establishment where Amy had succeeded in obtaining the chlorate of potash and the rectified alcohol for the face-wash that was to be so charmingly perfumed with elder blossom and attar of roses. John Tyler, pushed his hat aggressively over his forehead, and with his hands in his pockets, sauntered into the shop; it was full of what to him were formidable and yet silly novelties in the way of toilet articles, elegantly arrayed in gay cases and crystal bottles.

He put the paper on the counter and disdaining the few words of French that he knew, asked bluntly in English that "it might be made up."

The alert assistant spoke English without any ado, glanced at the prescription and shook his head. John Tyler's anger, that had been mounting very slowly but surely since he had seen May Beale the night before, flared. He used some coarse expressions under his breath and in his own tongue, then, rapping his finger on the counter, said, "Why can't you? I have had that prescription made up in every country of Europe."

"I dare say there are shops in Paris that would do this for Monsieur, here it is impossible."

"But it's a doctor's prescription. I need it for my health."

"Monsieur takes this for his health?"

"What the devil do you suppose I take it for? It's simple enough, isn't it?"

"No, we could not give it to you, Monsieur, on this signature—Monsieur sees the prescription is signed by an American doctor... in Virginia...."

"Yes, it is Virginia all right. I'm a Manchester cotton merchant. I often go to Virginia, I dare say I've got an English prescription... I know a good deal about medicine myself. This is harmless. You are bound to give it to me."

The Frenchman returned this rudeness by reminding him that he was not in his own country. "I do not know the laws of the English pharmaceutists, Monsieur, but in this establishment we do not make up this prescription unless we know the doctor—"

"You are speaking to me as if I were a shady customer... I shall speak to the British Consul about this—"

"Monsieur must do as he pleases." The chemist handed the paper across the glass counter crowded with showy trifles.

Then a bleak and desolate feeling, almost one of panic came over the big man standing arrogantly there. He saw before him a prospect that was almost unendurable.

He turned, as if to leave, turned again and his demeanour was utterly different.

"Can you tell me," he asked with a slight stammer in his speech, "where I could get this made up? Maybe there are other shops... I think you said..."

"Oh, maybe there are," smiled the chemist. "Monsieur may find them at Montparnasse or Montmartre."

"Shady places, I suppose you mean," challenged John Tyler. "I have no dealings with them. This is honest medicine..."

The chemist's smile became emphatic; he remarked that "the prescription" was dangerous.

"Well, what if it is? I take it because…"

John Tyler was making an effort both over his arrogance and his fear and trying to speak casually. None of this was easy for him; he had never learned either the subtleties or the graces of life, not even in the form of caricatures.

"Come, now, make this up," he insisted.

"It is impossible, Monsieur."

"Oh well, I'll get it made up somewhere… I will find an English chemist." But John Tyler lingered.

"Monsieur seems very anxious to obtain this medicine. That in itself is a bad sign," remarked the young man behind the counter.

"What the devil do you mean?"

"Exactly what I say, Monsieur. If you please, I shall call the proprietor…."

"If you please, I shall call the police…"

The Englishman laughed shortly, taking the first refuge of the uneducated in a dilemma by making a raucous joke of a defeat.

"Why, what do you suppose I want it for?—to improve my complexion, of course. The ladies like my clear skin I can assure you," and he stared at his reflection in the mirror in front of which was an elegant pyramid of soap boxes and bottles of perfume.

"Monsieur indeed looks very pale," agreed the chemist, standing his ground indolently.

The Englishman took no heed of him, but with the piece of paper in his hand considered what the mirror showed him. The gas had just been lit, but the reflections of artificial light were interlaced and crossed here and there with shadows in the depths of the large looking-glass.

It was true that he admired his smooth, white complexion, set off by the dark brown side whiskers; he was gratified that his hair was still plentiful and curled over his brow in a becoming wave; he was getting stout, but not noticeably so… he would diet a little and keep his weight down, it was the sedentary life he was leading of course. He must take more exercise…. What was the good of a saddle-horse if one didn't ride about on it, and what was the good of riding if you never had anyone to ride with? He wished that the Chorleys had been able to come with him to Paris. They were jolly people who did not give themselves airs… on the make, too, like he was himself.

"Monsieur has had the attention he requires?" said another voice, and turning heavily he saw the proprietor, a thin man with a sparse beard, looking at him with suspicion.

With the stubborn courage of his race, John Tyler again presented the prescription.

"I was telling this young fool of an assistant of yours that I wanted this made up…."

The elder chemist peered at the fine scrap of paper then at the customer and asked, "Monsieur takes this for his health?"

"Yes, I know something about medicine myself. I've knocked about, you know—particularly in America. I'm a cotton merchant…. Of course we thought everything was ruined with the emancipation of the slaves, those damned blacks, but they are working for so little that it amounts to the same thing. One makes a good deal of money but one has to keep in good trim, in rigorous health," he was talking very fast. "I suffer, you know, from this and that and I have my own medicine chest and make up my own doses…. But I require this ingredient… a pick-me-up."

"We cannot give you, Monsieur, what you term your prescription, which is nothing but pure arsenic in powder."

Richard Tyler was soon wearied with the music hall. He sauntered about the streets in the same manner as his brother had sauntered, peering at this pretty face and that pretty face, and having a drink here and there, and feeling lonely and depressed after the high spirits of the afternoon and wishing he was back in Manchester. Paris was no good unless the sun shone and the orchestras played and you could sit at an iron table and watch the crowd go past. In the evening, when you did not know where to go… well, it was lonely. He returned to the hotel bedroom to find John there, sitting gloomily by the chenille covered table. He asked his elder brother where he had been?

John flared out at him and said that his head ached and he had tried to get a prescription made up… that he had been to several chemists and they would not listen to him. What a country!… the sooner he was home the better.

"There must be something we can do to pass the time… what about a Turkish bath?"

John, in the ordinary way, would have liked the suggestion… these baths meant preserving his figure and keeping his weight down, and suited that streak of indolence in a nature that liked to make money by buying and selling across the counter or the desk and not by either the work of the mind or the hands, but to-night he was restless and thwarted.

"We'll go and see that fortune teller," he said very unexpectedly to Richard. "Madame Bondi. She's got that place in the Palais Royal…. Well, why shouldn't we? She's supposed to be the grand-daughter of the old woman whom Napoleon used to consult, and if he had his wise women, I don't see why we shouldn't. We're Napoleons in our way, aren't we, Richard?"

Richard thought this was as good a diversion as another. He was completely credulous and absolutely willing to believe anything that was to his own advantage.

The porter was roused, a *fiacre* called and in quite a short time the brothers were in the Palais Royal where the gas lamps cast circles of livid light on to the pavements, heavily flecked by the shadows of the trees that disappeared into the upper darkness.

Neither John nor Richard knew the possibilities of the Palais Royal that seemed on the surface such a decorous square of select apartment houses and hotels with chambers above, *cafés*, barbers' shops, cutlers, florists and such other tradespeople as gracefully served the smaller luxuries of life, for nothing coarse or ugly was to be bought in this trim enclosure. The cutler sold only the daintiest of knives, suitable for a lady to cut a rose from the stem... the posies in the florists were all set in frills of silver paper with lace borders, and streamers of multi coloured tissue ribbons; the milliners showed only the choicest models of velvet toques and pill box hats encircled with ostrich feathers.

John had a suspicion that if one knew one's way about (and he cursed himself that he did not) one might penetrate behind this smart façade and find a great deal that would be extremely diverting—but he did not know the password. Two of the houses at least were gaming hells, and Richard and John had visited them, but they had proved dull. There was nothing, John had complained "going on", only a crowd of quiet people seated round a table covered with baize, over which the light shone bleakly from the shaded gas, and the two strangers had been admitted, with neither hostility nor welcome. They had been ill at ease and ready for a fight, but there had been no attempt to cheat them... they had won a little and lost a little and came away feeling there was "nothing in it," and that the Wirral Races were far more exciting, yet, John felt, surely somewhere in the Palais Royal....

Madame Bondi made no secret of her profession. She told fortunes without any ado, and her abode was a small room above a lace maker's shop where the most exquisite productions of Valenciennes, d'Alcenon, of Venice and of Honiton were displayed on cushions of sapphire blue velvet.

"Perhaps the old girl's dead… perhaps we're too late," and Richard, on this excuse, hesitated; he still retained much of his provincial Puritanism, and believed, furtively, in sin and the Devil.

John was bolder and pushed the swing street door and went up the narrow stairs. There was a disappointing smell of floor polish; it seemed to the Englishmen as if the whole of Paris smelt of floor polish.… They reached to another door on which Madame Bondi's name, with insistent modesty, was inscribed in large letters. The sickly perfume of incense, by no means so agreeable as that of the floor polish, floated from behind this door, and the brothers grinned at one another sheepishly, like schoolboys venturing on a visit to the expensive sweet shop that was out of bounds.

They pulled the bell and heard it tinkle, and it was Madame Bondi herself who opened to them. She was neither imposing nor alarming. Her face was well floured, her lips, almost indistinguishable in outline, had been smeared with red. She wore a wig of the colour that wigs always seem to be—the tawny hue of a lion's mane. There were several handsome rings of antique design on her fat white fingers that uncomfortably reminded Richard, who had a little imagination, of large maggots; her shawl was Andalusian, as was the fan, which she carried always as if it were a weapon.

Her outfit was as simple as her person. The curtains had been well drawn so that there was no glimpse of the outer world… one might have been in a cabin in a ship at sea, or in a little apartment on a desert island for all there was of Paris here. Nor had she the central table that had seemed to the brothers an inevitable feature of Parisian furnishing. The room was loaded with every kind of ornament which to the two Englishmen formed a dazzling, variegated patterned background, and there was a little table of bamboo on which burned two joss sticks stuck in a small vase, the perfume of which they had smelt as they had come up the stairs.

She asked them to sit down, speaking English easily, and they took gingerly two chairs which they felt too frail to bear their weight. They did not know how to begin, but the Frenchwoman was used to every kind of awkwardness and glided into an easy conversation that soon brought the visitors to their desires—they wanted their fortunes told.

"For a bit of fun," explained John. "We are in Paris for a holiday and we do not know many people."

Madame did not betray that this simplicity was almost suffocating. It was to her like suddenly being placed in a field full of buttercups and daisies with nothing else in sight... to boast of it, too, and to emphasize it! She could hardly keep her small, blood suffused eyes from travelling to their pockets. How much had they got... and would it be safe to rob them? She thought not. They were large and powerful and would put up a fight, they also, probably, though vulgarians, were well enough known in their own detestable country... and there would be trouble with the police and trouble with the police was what Madame Bondi had always so far very successfully avoided.

John was the first to try his luck. He placed a large white hand, on which he would have liked but did not dare to place a gold signet ring, on the bamboo table; and Madame, who did not need to study the lines thereon to judge the character of the man facing her, made an attempt at gazing at it with little exclamations of wonder and amaze about "the Mount of Venus" and "the Life Line," with several incomprehensible words that she always found extremely effective. She had, underneath all her quackery, an uncertain gift—sometimes obscured for weeks and months together, sometimes flashing into life. She did not herself know what it was save that it gave her a kind of intuition, a feeling, about the person before her; and as she sat there staring at this large, white hand laid on the bamboo table, a firm, capable hand very carefully kept... a hand daily rubbed with perfume to show it had never done any manual work, that had never done any work of any kind, that had never held in a fine horse, or caressed a noble woman, or held a pen firmly to write an eloquent or passionate letter, but still a large, white, well trimmed hand—she made her judgment, "The hand of the man in the place of his master."

She knew those heavy self-made, vulgar Englishmen… they were to her utterly abhorrent; their worst fault was their closeness with their money… they wanted everything without paying for it…. She gave a little sigh and settled back in her chair.

"Well?" said John Tyler impatiently.

He supposed she was going to charge at least ten francs and he wanted something in exchange.

"I cannot tell you," murmured Madame Bondi.

She was collecting her wits. What was there to say to a creature like this… a tradesman… one who would live and grow even stouter than he was, and beget his own kind and fatten the churchyard? She wanted to spit on the floor… but she gazed into the man's face, observed the black hair up-curling from the brow and the eyes of agate brown, and the strained expression, and she felt that she had made a little mistake somewhere.

"It's not all quite so simple as it looks," she remarked. She remembered her profession and pretended to study the hand again. "Of course there is a good deal here as you are a deep one, I can see…."

John enjoyed that… anything not to be commonplace, just the same as the other fellows….

"A deep one," she repeated, and seemed a little uneasy, and her yellow teeth bit her lips; those smeared and indistinguishable lips that were a smear of paint in the floured face.

Richard was getting impatient. He found the perfume of the joss sticks suffocating, but Madame Bondi's uneasiness was genuine. She was suddenly overpowered by the presence of these two men whom at first she had despised as so raw and foolish. They were so large, with their black hair and black whiskers and black coats, overpowering.... They seemed to her to resemble the waxworks she had seen in the underground museum. What were those that she recalled... two murderers, two stranglers with large, white, wax hands stretched out to their victim's neck.

"I couldn't tell you," she panted quickly, "your future. I shouldn't like to."

"You wouldn't like to?" John was flattered. "What's going to happen to me? Aren't I going to be successful and make a great deal of money?"

When he was as simple as that she was on sure ground. She assured him that he would be successful and would make a good deal of money and have a big house and a number of servants, and horses, and carriages... "and perhaps be Lord Mayor of wherever it is you come from."

John laughed. He did not quite believe this, but it was in the line of his ambitions and therefore acceptable.

"And what about the ladies?" he asked. "Can you see a wife anywhere?"

Madame was quick to take her cue. Oh yes, she could see a wife... very beautiful... dispensing hospitality... a little thing... fair. I don't know what colour her hair is.... Oh yes, Madame is *petite* and her hair is very fair... what you call the colour of honey...."

"I suppose so." John grinned to himself. "And very young?"

"A good deal younger than Monsieur," said Madame demurely.

Richard thought of May Beale and that John was getting too near the mark, so he rose clumsily and claimed his turn.

John relinquished the seat; the nameless longing that had teased him all the evening was assuaged by this new turn.... Well, she was a wise woman and she was supposed to be descended from Lenormand who had told the cards for Napoleon when he had been a ragged young subaltern in the days of the Terror... and told them correctly too... predicted his triumphs and his imperial destiny. And John traced his fingers carefully down his own profile that so much resembled that of the man who had become almost fabulously great.

Madame had much the same talk for Richard. He would be successful… he too would make money.… What else did these Englishmen want? You could always please them with that… money ahead. She knew from their accents that they did not come from London. "And you will not marry," she added. She thought she had better make a change in the formula, and not promise another dainty beauty to the second brother.

"It is quite likely," said Richard shortly. "I'm difficult to please. Well, I think that's the end of the show, John. How much, Madame?"

"I do not know that it's the end," said John abruptly. He put his finger and thumb into his breast pocket and brought out the paper that earlier in the evening he had shown in vain to various chemists. "I wonder if you could help me here? I take this stuff for my health… my health's not very good, you know."

"But Monsieur seems so robust… so tall, so fine…"

"Ah yes, ah yes, I know, but there's always something or other laying me up—a little cough, or ache or pain—and I had malaria badly and, being a stranger here, I am not able to get this medicine that keeps it off—no joke, malaria. Could you help me?"

He put the thin paper down in front of her on the bamboo table.

Madame Bondi flicked it aside after glancing at it casually. Then, without raising her eyes or her voice she said, "The fee will be a thousand francs."

Richard laughed coarsely. "I've heard something of what they are in the Palais Royal! Come along, John, give her ten francs—that's all the stuff is worth.…"

John had stepped up to the old woman's chair and taken up his paper.

"How much?" he asked. "For a thousand francs—how much?"

"Quite sufficient for Monsieur's needs while he is in Paris."

"Are you sure it will be the right medicine—pure...? I don't want too much of that indigo or soot in it."

"Monsieur may be assured that what he gets will be of the purest quality."

Madame Bondi rose and spoke in a caressing tone to a white cat on the sofa that had hitherto been indistinguishable among the cushions and draperies of the room, but that now uncurled itself as the one beautiful object in the hideous apartment and as it yawned, showing delicate pointed teeth, she pulled aside a curtain and disappeared.

Richard spoke brusquely in a low tone, standing close to his elder brother.

"What are you doing, having dealings with a woman like that? She is probably a criminal! What do you think is going to be the end of it?"

John, with the savagery of a man who does not take much trouble to control a vile temper, ordered his younger brother downstairs; and the younger smiling, went—not from cowardice, for he had that fighting blood that is one form of courage, but because it was greatly to his advantage not to vex his elder—and, after all, if John liked to make a fool of himself it was nothing to do with him.

Madame came back with a packet in her fat hand. John snatched it, opened it and peered at the contents—a white powder, very faintly tinged with blue.

Madame apologized, hunching her shoulders, screwing up her rouged lips. "The police, you know...."

"The same in England," he muttered, adding, "but it is all nonsense, there's nothing in it.... If I was at home my doctor would give me more than this."

"*Mon dieu!*" muttered Madame Bondi, for once losing her impassivity, "but there's enough here..."

"... to poison a regiment! That's what we say," laughed John, showing the even teeth that he so carefully preserved.

He took out of his pocket an empty tobacco wallet made of leather and lined with oiled silk, and put the powder in it and snapped it together; and then, from an inner division he brought out a thousand-franc-note and placed it on the little bamboo table in front of Madame Bondi.

"I suppose," he suggested, being unable to resist the temptation to bargain, "that covers the fortune telling fees also?"

But Madame Bondi was too old at her trade to be "cheated" as she termed it, so easily.

"Monsieur knows what the power is worth to him—more than a thousand francs—and there are not many places where he would be able to obtain it—and if he had not chanced to come—"

The Englishman cut her short; she was fast falling into a whine; he wanted to get away.

"Well, how much? Say five francs...."

The old woman stood out for fifty francs for the two "fortunes", adding with a leer, "Remember the beautiful young wife with the fair hair that is going to sit at the head of Monsieur's table when he is rich—when he is Lord Mayor...."

"I don't want to be Lord Mayor," sneered John, though the idea, new to him, had a strong fascination. "Tell me more about the girl—what coloured dress is she wearing?"

Madame Bondi was as floundered as the peacock which John had once seen in the strawberry nets. What colour would this brute admire? She had no idea... it was clear he possessed nothing in the way of taste.

"Rose?" she murmured.

"Rose...?" protested John. "She's got that in her cheeks and honey and gold in her hair.... Oh, I should want something rich—like peacock feathers...."

"Peacock feathers," repeated the old woman, "but they are unlucky—very unlucky. You must never have peacock feathers in a room or at a marriage."

"Oh! superstition!... But why did you say that?" he asked reflectively.

The impression of his boyhood had not worn off; there was beauty, sheer beauty, that for a moment he had clutched in his hand before it screamed and struggled and flew away... burnished... heart shaped... green and gold glimmering together... purple and blue and violet.

"Well, have her dressed in peacock feathers if you wish, but it'll be another fifty francs," insisted Madame Bondi.

"I suppose you'll leave me my fare home?" He put the money on the table and left her rudely.

Richard was waiting for him, walking up and down under the light shed by the tall gas standard that was dappled with the to and fro shadows of the moving poplar leaves.

"You ought to be careful with that stuff, John. And a thousand francs..." he ventured this much of reproof.

But John was on him again savagely, like a big bulldog turning on one of slightly lesser weight.

"I've done pretty well for you, Dick, and you know it. You know you've got to keep your mouth shut. Who told you anything about my affairs...? That was a stroke of luck... it keeps me going, I tell you. I get palpitations, the doctor said I ought to have it. It will ward off an attack of malaria.... I know how to handle it and I keep it locked up."

"For pity's sake, don't let it come near me!"

"What do you think it is—poison? It is strychnine—strychnine, I tell you... a tonic."

"And they wouldn't let you have strychnine in the shops?"

"No! some rule of the French police. These foreigners... after all; I shall be glad when we're back in Manchester."

"Well, I don't think too much strychnine is good."

"It doesn't matter what you think, my dear Dick," said John, suddenly agreeable, elated at the prospect of the undisputed possession, of the means of providing himself with ease and comfort for many days to come.

"And a thousand francs!" grumbled Richard. "Why, that's forty pounds. When I asked you to lend me a fiver...."

"You shall have your fiver if you stop complaining. Let's go home now. I'm sick of these streets..."

"I should like to investigate the Palais Royal," objected Richard, looking with mingled curiosity and contempt round the quiet square.

But John discouraged these yearnings and Richard knew, though he did not say so, that neither of them was the type who would easily find out more than was on the surface. Even the interview with Madame Bondi had been crude. Richard was quite sure that John had said too much. A blackmailer's price... it could not have been strychnine. Forty pounds.... Richard thought of the money in the terms of the counting-house. He saw it entered up in the ledgers. He saw it buying cotton. He saw it invested and changed into fifty pounds, sixty, seventy or eighty pounds—and John had clapped it down without thinking as it were, just for a packet of powder. Richard had made an accurate guess about the nature of that purchase.

John wanted watching. He seemed inclined to make a fool of himself over that girl. Of course she was quite beyond his reach, or Richard would have made a fool of himself, too—or rather, not so much of a fool, he would have come forward and clapped down whatever they wanted for her in the way of settlements and taken her back to Manchester as his wife. Why not? Who were they anyway, the Dumonts?

The brothers went home and the clouds blew up suddenly over the sky, and the pavements darkened with the quick downfall of the rain. They entered their hotel and went to their several bedrooms, both taciturn again, with impassive faces.

*

John took the powder out of his pouch, looked at it carefully, placed a portion of it (weighed out in a minute pair of scales that he took from his medicine chest) in his mouth and chewed it with great satisfaction. The rest he locked away in the chest.

Now that he had had his stimulant he felt another man; stronger, bolder, more inspired. He certainly would try to see if he could not have May Beale as his wife. It might take a little while to bring that marriage off, but he could not see what was in the way of ultimate success; girls of that age were easily impressed, in his opinion, and after all, he had had some experience, and the mother, for all her little disdainful airs, was a fool; while the stiff wooden soldier had no control over another man's child, and there was the common advantage to be gained out of the cotton crops. Well, he was sure that Paris apartment took a great deal of money to run.... They'd be glad of a man like himself in the family to bring them in some cash for all those opera tickets, green coloured barouches and all the rest of it... and cavalry officer's pay wasn't much and he did not suppose in these days an aristocrat had much left after three revolutions.... No, there wouldn't be many pickings on M. Dumont's estates, so went the big, heavy, formidable man's musing.

He did not light the gas, but had taken his dose by the glow from the little night light that had been placed in the grate, and he sat there staring in front of him into the half darkness, flecked with pale trembling light, his hands clenched unconsciously on the table with the chenille cloth.

At the same moment May Beale was sitting up in bed in her convent with her hands clasped round the knees of her lawn nightgown, dreaming of the green bottle with the white lines in which was the delicious lotion with which to-morrow she and her three friends would bathe their faces, arms and hands.... How charming to be light and diaphanous as a lily in the dark.

II

LADY'S POSY
FLOWERS OF LACE AND TINSEL

'I WONDER IF I SHOULD HAVE BEEN HAPPIER IF I HAD MARRIED Richard?' This came so sharply into May Tyler's mind that it seemed to be written across the book of accounts at which she was staring. She did not trouble to regard her self question as a problem. It was like everything in her life—aimless, a chance reflection that came and went like the gnats that buzzed in from the garden; there was a little cloud of them that she watched idly, crossing the room and disappearing into the shadows.

She stared at the accounts again; a disagreeable array of figures. She never could make a satisfactory business of finance. It was endless—so much was needed for the household, the servants, the nursery, for her husband's office and for herself—that was the only interesting use of money for May. She had money of her own and she felt, though she was too sweet tempered to cherish a sense of injustice, that she was quite entitled to spend a good deal on furbelows. But these accounts of the housekeeping that had to be ready at the end of the month, that she must take into her husband's room and put before him, that he would check with alarming rapidity, running his pencil from top to bottom of the column and writing down some figures, then challenging her on the details.... Her arithmetic was not good and she "did not know where the money went," that was all she could ever say in self defence.

The servants were continually being changed at Stone Pynes; they all of them seemed to May Tyler as careless and thriftless as the negroes whom she remembered in her childhood, and a great deal less amiable.

Sometimes she had a suffocating sense of a huge silent conspiracy against her among these foreigners she employed. What did they talk about downstairs in that casement that was so carefully shut off by the heavy baize doors from the upper part of the house so that no noise or smell penetrated? They were human beings after all and the inquisitive side of May's nature could not forget that, though ladies were not supposed to concern themselves about their servants. She knew that she was what was known as "a bad manager", the domestics did much as they pleased, were wasteful and extravagant and talked spitefully about her and the master behind their backs. She was so easy going that this did not trouble her save that she had to come into contact with them, make some show of managing them and there had to be meals on the table and very often dinner parties.

Nurse had been with her twelve months; she must get rid of her; Lizzie Burt was not to May's liking at all. She was young, but ill looking, with small eyes. Of course she knew her work, had had the best recommendations and came from a gentlewoman's house; but the children did not seem fond of her. "They don't seem very fond of me either," mused May. "I wish I could take them away, I wish we could go to Virginia—I and the babies."

She sat in a lolling attitude, staring out of the window. The geraniums were arranged in stiff squares either side the gravelled drive, like platoons of soldiers in their scarlet uniforms. They had not the effect of flowers, but of ornaments made in paper or tin, arranged symmetrically, bright red and bright green—not to be touched, or smelt, or a leaf taken off and crushed in the hand; but to be left correct and hard, until the gardener took them away. May disliked them. She remembered the Virginian garden, the colonnade of the old colonial house and the shaven lawn; and she remembered the gardens in Paris, too, with, this time of year, the tresses of lilac, laburnum and mock orange, and the poplar trees which grew so tall they seemed at night when quenched in darkness to reach the heavens. Here there were no trees whatsoever, but bushes of laurel that had a sickly yellow pattern over the thick leaves like a disease.

May Tyler tapped her teeth with her pencil. The accounts would have to wait until to-morrow. It was always the same, though she knew that she ran into trouble by putting everything off to the last moment. What did it matter? She would get a lecture from her husband whatever she did; he would tell her of her extravagance and her wastefulness, and she would have to hear of his complaints of the servants. She was astonished when she reflected what a keen eye he had for the weak spots. Sometimes in irony she would set the whole day aside to arrange everything in the house to please him… all that he had ever complained about, she would try to remember and set right. She would dress herself to his taste, she would have the children hushed and in bed as he wished, she would have the meal that he preferred on the table; she would have his evening paper folded and in his napkin—oh! everything! all the things, to May such stupid things, that he had teased her about, ordered her to remember. And then the man would come in, and taking no notice of any of her endeavours, go straight to some fault, as he called it, and speak of that.

Once she had said, "Isn't anything ever right? Don't you ever say a word of encouragement?"

And he had replied, a-straddle on his own hearth, with his hands clasped behind him underneath the long skirts of his frock-coat, "I expect everything to go well in my own home under my wife's supervision. When I say nothing, you may understand that I am pleased; when I am displeased I shall complain."

May tried to put the recollection of her husband out of her mind. Indolence was over her like a muffling cloak. Would not there soon be some excuse to go to London, or possibly to Paris, or to return to Virginia with her mother?

Madame Dumont was staying at Stone Pynes; that did not make life any easier. The two women were never allowed to be alone together for long; and Rose Bernier was definitely an object of suspicion to the English servants, towards whom she adopted a very condescending attitude. There was something to the English maids intensely exasperating about the ugly Frenchwoman who always ironed and goffered her mistress's lawns and laces; but May preferred Rose Bernier to her servants like she preferred her mother to her husband. She was happy when she could escape into her mother's room which Madame Dumont, with total disregard of the wishes of her son-in-law, had transformed into the kind of apartment to which she was used. Her husband had been sent on garrison duty to Africa, and though she was far too wise a woman to stay long with her only daughter, she had not been able to resist this English visit.

May wondered if her mother or Rose could help with the accounts, but she was too good natured to torment them. Besides, she was quite sure that her mother would be no better at this task than she was herself, and Rose would have—well, something sharp to say about John.... Perhaps a good many people would have something sharp to say about John if May had told her tale. But May kept quiet and, in the language of her generation, "preserved appearances".

She wondered about Richard, in a detached fashion. Richard had never married. Sometimes she saw him looking at her in a manner that made her think that she might have married him instead of John. She was not at all sure of his feelings towards her; she did not know if it came to open dispute with John, if Richard would take her part or not. Richard came and went a good deal; on business, of course, though there was an office for that. He was frequently there for luncheon or dinner, or accompanying them to the Wirral Races and other amusements. May wondered about him in a cool fashion, it seemed to her strange that one of her warm temperament should be so cool, surely she had not been supposed to be without feelings? She seemed encased in ice. That was a stupid simile; she dismissed it as soon as she had made it. What was she encased in—disdain, pride, self-respect?

She closed the unfinished account books, rose sighing and glanced round with distaste on the overcrowded room that bore evidence of John Tyler's prosperity and total lack of taste. Useless objects in marble and bronze, in velvet and satin filled the apartment. Everywhere were screens and tables, porticoes with fringes, and sets of painted china in racks stood out to be admired; and vases, jugs, platters, silver, brass and copper that had no use at all... that kept the parlourmaid busy every morning, taking them down on trays to the pantry, and cleaning them with pink powder and brushes, grumbling all the time that there should be a pantry boy to do that work and nothing else. What a deal of grumbling there was at Stone Pynes... it was about May like a miasma. She could not endure to think of it, and with her quick step left the oppressive room and went upstairs to her mother's chamber.

Madame Dumont was sitting, with an air of nonchalance, by the window waving to and fro a fan of ivory though the air was, if anything, chilly, and gazing down on to the suburban street below. Rose Bernier was at her eternal task with "chiffons"; yards of Chantilly lace were under her lean, brown fingers.

May silently took a stool at her mother's feet. She was surprised when Madame Dumont asked sadly, "I think you should put an end to it. Have you come to talk to me about it?"

"Mother, I didn't know that I had shown so much uneasiness and I have never said a word...."

"Well, you don't suppose that you need to say a word, as you call it... and as for your uneasiness, I think you have disguised it pretty well, but I have had some experience, my dear, and I know that you are unhappy. I really cannot understand," she added, "why you married him."

"And I cannot understand why you allowed me to..." and then both the women laughed, being incorrigibly lighthearted.

"He seemed to me something tremendous," smiled May, wistfully trying to explain herself. "You know, like a Roman Emperor.... And I was only a schoolgirl, and I did admire him and it seemed so important and in a way magnificent... and I wanted to go to England. I liked the idea of marrying an Englishman."

"You might have married an Englishman," replied Madame Dumont, "and gone to London. Instead of that, you married a vulgarian and came to Manchester and it is, my dear child, an entirely odious place."

"I have some good friends," protested May flushing painfully.

She had been married eight years and had a woman's pride in her home, in her friends, in her atmosphere. She did not like this blown upon even by her mother.

"People like the Chorleys, I suppose?" said Madame Dumont.

"Amelia and Henry.... Oh yes, they come here very often. They are quite good..."

"Don't say friends, May," interrupted Madame Dumont sadly. "Rather friends of your husband and acquaintances of yours."

May was silent, wondering how much her mother knew. She had not been prepared for this onslaught on her defences—and before Rose, too; yet Rose almost certainly knew more than her mistress about Stone Pynes; May Tyler, having no subterfuge, glanced at the maid whose lap was full of lace, and Rose peered up and nodded and grinned, "Madame Tyler—"

"Oh, you *will* call me that!" interrupted May. "You know you shouldn't and it annoys me!"

"Madame Tyler," persisted Rose, pursing up her lips until her mouth was like a bag with the string caught tight, "you should dismiss all the servants you have in the house. I think nothing of any of them."

"But Lizzie's a good nurse," May was quickly on the defensive. "I would never have allowed her to look after the children if she did not have the highest recommendations, and Dr. Harman says that she is really very clever with both John and May."

"John, indeed, for the boy's exactly like his father," said Madame Dumont, "and I don't know that May is much like you, dear. She seems rather yellow and wizened to me. Why doesn't she have more fresh air?"

May maintained her pitiful, futile pretences.

"Dr. Harman says that Lizzie knows better than I do. She's had a great deal of experience, though she is still young—not thirty, I think."

"Leave Lizzie and the doctor alone, Madame," scolded Rose Bernier. "What of those people you have in the kitchen? Now I don't say anything about Maggie Pilch, who is your good cook...."

"Oh, I'm very fond of her. Cooks are always pleasant people, are they not, Mother?" asked May, delighted to come at last upon an amiable topic.

"She's a stupid woman," insisted Rose Bernier remorselessly. "She's no control over those girls... what do you call them? Nelly and Dolly and Jane..."

"Nelly Tanner, Dolly Hoey and Jane Chase," said May nervously. "They all had the best recommendations and came from very respectable homes...."

"Not the best houses," remarked Madame Dumont coolly, "or they wouldn't be here, my dear child. You should face the truth. This is not a gentleman's establishment. You have made a *mésalliance*... admit as much—my advice to you would be, if you could, to get rid of the man."

"But our religion forbids it," May sighed quietly.

Her mother looked at her sharply. Her terse advice had proved that her sad surmises were correct.

"Why of course it does," she said, tapping her daughter on the cheek with her fan. "Divorce is not to be thought of by a Catholic, but it might be possible to get an annulment at the Vatican—you're twenty-five only, May, and still very pretty."

"Twenty-five years old and eight years married," thought May mournfully, she rested her head on her mother's knee. Had she been asked to give an account of that wooing, of that marriage, of that married life she would not have been able to do so. The man had been so strange… from another world. She had understood so little about him. She had been very flattered when he had come to her mother's apartment so often—and then she had had the migraine and left the convent, and he had been most attentive—taken her entire attention with his letters, his presents and his bold, yet veiled stare. Her stepfather had been against the match, but her mother had thought the girl should "please herself". That was Madame Dumont's great weakness—she would always allow people to "please themselves"; and May had only to lift her grey-green eyes and plead to be allowed to marry John Tyler for Madame Dumont to agree at once that it was a most suitable match. After all, so it seemed to be, on the surface. The man had plenty of money and was making more and likely to make more still in the future; and his settlements were handsome enough and there was to be a large establishment in Manchester which the American ladies had never seen but which they were told by the Tyler brothers was the second city in the Empire; in the brilliant sunshine of Paris everything had seemed so different.

Madame Dumont remembered those days, and with an air of lazy regret remarked, "Perhaps I was careless.… But you cannot live in this terrible place."

"But you've been here before, Mother, and you've never said it was so terrible—and believe me, there are a great number of amenities… I'm not a prisoner, not spied upon, you know… and as for what Rose says about the maids, I can get rid of them.… They never stay long anyhow and I don't think I'm a good manager."

"Your husband should give you a housekeeper. How are his affairs? Does he ever tell you?"

"Oh no, Mother, of course not. Why, that would be too confusing. He gives me something for the housekeeping, and I fear I am sadly in debt."

"How much in debt?" asked Madame Dumont, who was used to that state of affairs, but knew how to strike a nice balance between what one could afford to owe and what one could not afford to owe.

May was confused again. She really did not know. So many people did not send in their bills and others she was afraid she had lost, and some her husband had taken and said he would pay.

"With a scolding too, I suppose," suggested Madame Dumont, and then she asked, with a thin edge to her voice, "I suppose he's kind to you—I mean always, and respectful?"

"Yes," replied May, too quickly, and looked away.

Over her bent, proud head, mistress and maid exchanged a narrow glance.

"I must get away from Stone Pynes," said Madame Dumont. "I shall not wait for your stepfather's return from Africa. I shall go to Paris and I shall ask your husband's permission to take you with me."

"But the children, Mother... I couldn't leave the children?"

"Why shouldn't the children come too, and we could find another maid, as Rose doesn't like this woman Burt, and get an Alsatian *bonne* in Paris."

"Oh, it would be delightful!" cried May, clasping her hands and looking up radiant and sparkling. "And then I could really have them to myself and we might play together in the garden— You know, I never feel that there is a garden here.... Just those geraniums with those laurels.... Oh! to get away, that would be splendid—and those *bonnes* are so kind and would let me have fun with the children."

"Don't you ever have any fun with yours, May?"

"Well, John doesn't like me to spoil them, and Lizzie Burt is really very capable...."

"I shall go up and see them now."

"Very well, Mother."

May Tyler rose, a lovely woman; her dress was unsuitable for that hour of the morning—thick cream lace over pink taffeta with flounces, and soiled round the hem. She never could contend with the dirt that gathered on the thick carpets and the difficulty of persuading one of the housemaids to clean her gowns.

"You ought to have a maid," Madame Dumont had once said.

And May had replied that she did not need one—she could indeed take care of herself, which was so obviously not true that Madame Dumont had never referred to the subject again.

May knew that she spent too much on clothes and that there were too many soiled and torn frocks in her wardrobe, and that she did need a maid. She did not even know how to thread a needle, if she ripped a frill the gown had to hang on the peg until it occurred to her to send it to the dressmaker who would probably report that it was not fit to be mended and had better be given to one of the maids. Such domestic trifles were always too much for her and there were so many of them, like invisible battalions of foes pressing around her inner life.

She walked silently behind her mother who well knew the way up the stairs that were carpeted with a heavy red pile that caught and showed every speck of dust. On the landing outside the nursery was a clutter of tables, on which stood various bowls and ewers, not very clean, with pots and jars of patent food and meat juices and where were piled stained aprons, napkins and work baskets with broken lids and untidy contents.

Madame Dumont gave this disorder a contemptuous glance and walked into the nursery without knocking; resentment at this breach of etiquette was shown on Lizzie Burt's flushed face as she rose stiffly.

She was very properly in her place between the two children who were seated at their little school desks; John, the elder, cutting out letters from a small book and the girl sticking a needle, threaded with Berlin wool in and out of a piece of canvas.

Madame Dumont remarked, "The room is very hot. You should have the window opened, Lizzie—and why don't you take the children out? The sunshine is beautiful to-day. I think they look pale and sickly."

"Dr. Harman is very pleased with them, Madame," replied Lizzie with a tightening of her ugly mouth.

"There shouldn't need to be a doctor always in attendance with healthy children. I never had a doctor for May—she used to run out in the garden quite free. She had a swing and bright balls to throw about in the air."

"Oh, I take the children in the park, Madame, once a day, regularly...."

"The park?" repeated Madame Dumont. "I have found Manchester very deficient in open spaces, also too symmetrical in arrangement. Indeed, I should think that a more hideous place could hardly be conceived, and the air is usually so thick that when you have a little sun as you have to-day you should take advantage of it."

"It's a splendid city, Madame," retorted Lizzie bitterly defending her native place. "I'm sure there's nothing your ladyship could ask for here that you wouldn't find. Why, the number of medical charities and houses of recovery and dispensaries we have—and, as your ladyship has noticed, the Royal Exchange—"

"I don't think any of those things are very much good for children. What is the park that you take them to?"

"Oh, it's the Peel Park in Salford on the river, Madame."

"That's a long way off," remarked Madame Dumont sharply. "How often do they really go?"

"Oh, Mother, don't tease Lizzie so," pleaded May. "The children are very well, though they always appear peaky and yellow, Dr. Harman said they were in excellent health."

"Well, if you're satisfied…" Madame Dumont spoke with her air of sweet detachment. "But I should take those draperies down from the window. What are you doing, John?"

"Cutting my letters, grandma," mumbled the boy without raising his head.

He was well made, with his father's features and dark hair; pale and expressionless, correctly encased in a long blouse and trousers with patent leather belt and shoes that, to Madame Dumont's eyes were far too polished and far too little worn at the toes.

"And you, my dear—are you trying to make something charming with the Berlin wool?"

"It's a text," replied the girl primly. "'Love thy neighbour as thyself'—but it will take me a long time to do it; you see, grandmamma, there are a great number of stitches…."

"But Miss May will do it in time. She is a persevering child—and Master John doesn't like to leave his letters until he's finished."

"I suppose," Madame Dumont attacked suddenly, "they are not so persevering and patient because their father punishes them, are they?"

"That wouldn't be any business of mine what their father does in the way of punishment," flared Lizzie Burt insolently. "If they are naughty they are reprimanded."

"John wouldn't be unkind?" said Madame Dumont to her daughter.

"Not to the children," replied the young woman on a forced note of cheerfulness. "Of course not. Shall we go downstairs—you see that we really only disturb John and May and nurse, too, has a great deal to do."

"Yes, indeed I have Miss May's new suit to hem and her bonnet to trim," said Lizzie. She had remained standing with her hands folded while the ladies were in the room but she managed to convey a deep disrespect.

No sooner had the door of the nursery closed than Madame Dumont said, "May, did I bring you up to be such a fool that you are afraid of your own servants? Why don't you do what you like?... You talk down your own heart. You could have the children in a pleasanter room than this."

"But, Mother, you don't understand. I must please John—I'm his wife, and this is the kind of establishment he likes. Cheetham Hill is a very good suburb. The houses have only just been built.... Stone Pynes is considered a splendid mansion... indeed it is. It is much finer than the villa we first lived in and John gives me every luxury.... And oh, Mother, I cannot do anything but let things go."

"You're weak and foolish," reproved Madame Dumont, "and so am I—but only to a point, May. It seems to me—well, I suppose you meant what you said... John *is* always kind to the children. But you must get rid of that woman...."

"I don't like her," admitted May, clinging to her mother, "but she frightens me and John chose her... she came from a most genteel place, and if the children don't like her they're very obedient and good and they don't seem to want to be with me very much," she confessed at last on a breathless sigh.

"That's because this woman is turning them against you. I suppose she is more or less in your husband's employ?" Madame Dumont was about to say, but checked herself. She, too, was indolent and she, too, had her own pleasant life; and perhaps May was right in not confiding more to a woman who could not help very much. An interfering grandmother—that was the last role for which Madame Dumont was fitted. She was still a beautiful and elegant woman. It was impossible for her to do anything unbecoming. Even her affection for her daughter would not induce her to make an ungraceful gesture.

★

There were guests to dinner that evening. John Tyler had risen in the business world since his whimsical marriage; risen since that first dinner party when May, in a dress that she considered very old-looking and unsuitable, of peacock coloured satin, had sat at the head of a modest table to entertain a few cotton brokers and merchants of the meaner sort and their dowdy wives. To-night there were some quite considerable people—those who had grown opulent on the rising prosperity of Manchester… an alderman, the family doctor, George Harman, who seemed to fit his part as hand to glove, and a more eminent physician, Edmund Fitch, who had "condescended to grace the board", as he would have described his appearance at the home of John Tyler, who sometimes consulted him about diseases that Dr. Fitch considered entirely fanciful; he thought the man a hypochondriac, but Edmund Fitch's practice was largely composed of people with imaginary diseases.

May rattled off pretty nonsense as usual, at the head of the long table. She had to talk, laugh and drink champagne so as not to think; everything was glossy, expensive and in the meanest taste. There was too much food, too much wine, too much plate and too high a polish on the napery; but it was not luxurious enough for John; he was vexed because there were housemaids serving instead of footmen and because there had not been a butler to admit the guests; if May had not been so extravagant he believed he could have managed a better show; as it was there was only the saddle-horse, not even a carriage; it was no use for a man to get up in the world, and marry a woman with a comfortable dowry if he could not make more of a show. He believed almost all his guests—not quite all, because he was careful always to include some promising strugglers on the lower rungs of the ladder of commercial success in his invitations, in order to flatter his own pride—but almost all kept their own horses and barouches and rode about behind them with their womenfolk along Piccadilly and the smart crowded ways of the city, Infirmary Square, Mosley Street, Portland and Church Street... he had seen them going to the cathedral in style on a Sunday; he had seen the women waiting for the men outside the Exchange.... He felt as he had felt when he had seized the peacock netted in the strawberry bed, when he had set his teeth into the forbidden peaches... always this gnawing discontent.

Yet the housemaids were very neat and quite efficient. They were afraid of him. He saw to that, even if May was indifferent, his temper was something to be dreaded. And he knew how, when he came back from the races always in a good humour from some self-indulgence, to fling the money about. May never gave anything; she had nothing to give.

Talk was brisk and without any meaning; the diners discussed what they already knew, agreed on commonplaces and avoided anything that might have had the least interest and ate the heavy food as if hungry.

Madame Dumont as a foreigner was questioned pointedly as to her opinion of Manchester. Was it not growing in a prodigious fashion... such a number of small townships had been absorbed.... Did she realize that it was now sixteen miles in circumference?

Madame Dumont, who never read guide books, had realized nothing of the kind. She remarked that the air was always full of smoke and that the rivers, of which there seemed many, were very black. This comment brought a laugh of gratified superiority from the company. One did not call those rivers of course, though it was the kind of mistake a foreigner would make... they were but little canals or branches of the Irwell. The information was given carefully, almost in words of one syllable. And the other side of the Irwell was called Salford, "like Southwark in London," one lady informed Madame Dumont.

"Oh," replied the American. "And the river... or canals or whatever you call them... why are those so black?"

"Ah, that is from the dye factories. You see, the dye is discharged into the water and so the rivers and canals and even the Irwell itself is always black."

"Mon dieu!" sighed Madame Dumont. "This is a charming city... you have smoke in the air, you have chimney pots and factory stacks to shut you in and when you go abroad you may look on rivers that are dyed inky black."

John Tyler understood the implication of this remark though it passed as a foreigner's jest with most of the guests—clumsy enough, but still amiable.

He heartily disliked his mother-in-law. She was ranked in his mind, though he never put such things into concrete form, with the peacock, the peaches and with May.... Only Madame Dumont had escaped him, the others had not... he had eaten the peaches and trampled on the stones, and he had held the peacock and ruffled his plumage—and May was pretty well in her place by now; but Madame Dumont with her fortune and her foreign husband and her visits that always came at some unfortunate time, and her French maid, was quite beyond John Tyler even to disturb.

He asked her sharply if she had noticed the Albert Bridge and how well the two great high roads to Liverpool and Chester were kept.... Well, he dare swear that she would find the Exchange on days of the cotton market extremely interesting....

"I find these underground rivulets interesting." Madame Dumont still smiling was looking at her son-in-law across the loaded table. "Little streamlets that seldom come to the light; a stranger like myself carelessly crossing them where they are visible is puzzled to know whence they come and where they are going to. Only they are black, my dear John, extremely black and it is a pity, mark me—a pity that they should *ever* come to the light, even to the murky light of Manchester."

May rose, a signal that the ladies automatically obeyed. Madame Dumont drawing her gauzy shawl over her smooth polished shoulders said as she passed John, fumbling with the port, "Will you allow me to take May to Paris for a short visit?"

He was dumbfounded at her impertinence and arrogance; cornering him with such a question at such a moment! The devil was in the woman and he would have liked to have put his large white hands, now curdling into the coarseness of middle age, round her neck and shaken the impertinent life out of her slender frame.

"May has her home and her children to look after," he replied, the age-old hypocrisies coming smoothly enough to his lips, "and Paris is hardly the place for a young woman...."

"What a strange part of Paris you must know," remarked Madame Dumont, and with no more than that turned away and went upstairs, the women following, May agitated and laughing to cover her agitation and wondering how much her mother knew, and if it were possible that John would allow her to go to Paris. Oh, why not? It would cost him nothing and he could easily run the house without her, if it was only for a fortnight. They might stay in the convent.... No, that would never do... but they might stay somewhere where there were trees and grass and the children could become golden in the sun, learn to be fond of her and play with her and be free of Lizzie Burt and pull instead at the coloured ribbons of an Alsatian *bonne*.

She sat beside her mother who had nothing more to say about Manchester and did not respond when the ladies praised the fine new park where there was a statue of good Sir Robert Peel, and asked her if she had noticed the splendour of the Royal Exchange. "Really, dear Madame, you should go there on cotton market days as Mr. Tyler suggested—that is, Tuesdays or Fridays between one and two. There are all the spinners and mill hands and printers, and there is such an ado...."

"It is nothing for a woman, that kind of business," replied Madame Dumont. "All one cares about is the money the creatures earn.... The noise and the dirt, they make earning it... well, that is very disgusting."

May, as she had expected, was rebuked by her husband after breakfast the next morning. Madame Dumont had her *petit déjeuner* in her room and husband and wife were alone in the heavy over-furnished dining-room about which still hung the fumes of the roast and the boiled, the sauces and the soups of the dinner party of the night before. They had not met since they had parted on the stair head when the last guest had gone and May's eyes were downcast under the straight brows.

John Tyler laid down his copy of *The Times*. He found it a dull newspaper and he was not a Tory in politics, but it was a gentlemanly journal to have delivered and he noticed that as men came up in the world they took in *The Times* and read the local papers in secret only. You could observe that... there was less talk of the Reform Bill and of one's father remembering the Peterloo massacres and more about supporting the Government and the stability of the country as one became successful.

"What is this nonsense, May, about your mother taking you to Paris? I really must forbid her visits if they are going to be so unsettling.... And I hope your accounts are in better order this month. I gave them to Aitken and really he could make nothing of them. I have spoken to the bank manager and he says you draw a great deal of cash. I think it is a mistake for a woman to have her own banking account."

"It is my own money. You never put any allowance in the bank for me—you give me money for the housekeeping only.... The account is my own money...."

"Surely, my dear girl, there is no need to remind me of that twice. I am only too well aware that you have your own money and as far as my observation goes, it is spent entirely on frivolity. I am speaking of my money, that I give you for the housekeeping...."

"But what you give me is not enough and I have to spend a great deal of money of my own, and what my mother and my stepfather give...."

John Tyler cast up his hands as if in horror.

"Such confusion.... I never heard of anything so extravagant. You should put your affairs entirely in my hands... you should not expend this money on presents without accounting to me for it...."

"Well, to-day is not the day for the housekeeping books, and we were talking about the visit to Paris...."

"Which is quite out of the question. As I told your mother last night, I should be ashamed to have a wife who was so careless of her duties as to wish to leave her small children for a lengthy period...."

"But I should like to take the children with me...."

"You would like to take the children with you to Paris?"

"It would be with my own mother. We might stay with the nuns...."

"I will not have my children contaminated, that has been understood. I remain a member of the Church of England..."

"And I remain a member of the Church of Rome. Before I was married you said there would be no difficulty about that and I have not obtruded my side of the question upon you."

"Indeed, my dear May, you have obtruded it upon me so little that I very much doubt the depth and sincerity of your faith."

"You would be very angry if I had a priest about the house, or if I went to mass more often than I do. And I suppose I am forbidden to go to Paris with my own children and mother even if spending my own money...."

"You seem to have a very good opinion of yourself... it is my own this and my own that, and a constant reminder that you have a small pittance of your own. And as for this running away—I entirely forbid it."

May rose and walked up and down the room. Her gown was of white silk with blue poker dots, very much frilled, and set off her delicate, finely formed figure. John gave her a glance over his newspaper; something like the glance he had given her when he had met her in the vestibule of her mother's apartment eight years ago, then set his lips and turned away.

"You know," said May, "that I could say something."

He was silent and stirred his cup with a spoon on which unfortunately he was not able to put a crest, but which had instead a large, flamboyant initial. "I supposed," he parried slowly, "bygones were to be bygones."

"Oh, I am sure," sighed May uncertainly, "I have no wish for any more argument, but if you won't let me and Mother go to Paris, will you not let us go to London?"

"You will not take the children," said John Tyler unpleasantly, "Lizzie Burt will look after them, under Dr. Harman.... If your mother cares to ask you to leave your household to go to London for the sole purpose, as I am sure, of attending theatres, concerts and spending money at milliners and dressmakers, I am sure that I cannot restrain so independent a young woman...."

His words could hardly have been more stinging and unkind, but the consent had been given and that was sufficient for May. She moved away, for all her easy-going bewildered air, not without pride. And John Tyler looked at her, for all his formidable mastery, not without fear.

Madame Dumont and her daughter stayed at the Grand Hotel Bristol, Waddington Street, near Hyde Park Corner and the squat yellow magnificence of Sussex House. May found London if not as delightful as Paris, at least a great deal more delightful than Manchester. The air was cleaner, though it lacked the brilliant sheen of the other capital. There was a certain amount of company that her husband's city entirely lacked. Madame Dumont, a rich cosmopolitan, had friends wherever she moved, and there were intelligent worldlings willing enough to spend an hour or so in the ladies' sitting-room in the Hotel Bristol and to pass the gossip of the day with them.

May found this very diverting but it was a diversion that soon staled. She sipped at it as one might the frothed cream on a drink, and then let it go as being a tasteless, cloying sweetness and nothing more.

"You are not so easily satisfied," remarked Madame Dumont. "Are you, my child? I have given you company and taken you to concerts, to the theatre, and you have been very much admired and, most remarkable of all, your husband has let you alone...."

"He has written to me every day," interposed May quickly, "and Lizzie always sends a report about the children's health...."

"That is neither here nor there. As long as John does not disturb us with his presence.... What would you *like* to do, May?"

May knew, though it was foolish to take this question at its surface meaning, what she would *like* to do.... She would have liked to go far away with someone who loved and admired, someone who petted and pampered her.... She checked her day-dreams. What she would *like* to do, in her mother's phrase, merely meant a choice between a visit to a hairdresser's, a milliner's or a shop, where, seated on stools before a long counter polished smooth by continuous use, a servile shopman would unroll before them glittering lengths of stiff satin or sparkling lengths of coloured brocades.

"We will go to Madame Clorinde," May smiled, rousing herself. "You know, I never get clothes as splendid in Manchester.... John wouldn't approve of my spending so much money...."

"We don't need to ask for John's approval," replied Madame Dumont. "I think you have a little money of your own... the cotton has paid very well this year."

"I suppose you must thank John for that," put in the loyal wife quickly. "Yes, and Richard too—they are keen men of business—but we still keep a very dingy little office, and we only have a hired groom and one saddle-horse."

"Do those things concern you?"

"In a way," replied the young woman frankly. "You see, they would fret anyone in the world in which we live, and it vexes John not to be as fine as his neighbours, and I always feel a little small and put down because—well, we don't do things in such style..."

"The style in which the good citizens of Manchester do things, as you call it... (I am afraid you have learned some vulgar expressions. May) is not one to be imitated."

"But if I am to live among them..." protested the daughter. "Don't you understand, Mother? That is my life. I am condemned to live among them...."

"Condemned is the right word," agreed Madame Dumont. "Now I wonder," she added softly, "what can be done?"

"Nothing can be done, and he knows it, because we are Roman Catholics."

"That makes the marriage-bond sacred to us. Well, do you know what it is to your husband...?"

"Very little," admitted May in a low voice. "A convenience... a conventionality... I don't want to talk about it any more...."

"My poor darling, I can guess it all without you saying anything. I am afraid that we were both fools and that your stepfather did not give me very good advice. But then," she added, with an unwonted touch of wistfulness, "I had never met people like the Tylers before."

The salons of Madame Clorinde were overcrowded with furniture—gilt, plush, ornate sofas, chairs and screen and what were known vaguely as "knicknacks"... carved brackets on which stood small statues... mirrors round which gilt cupids crawled... alcoves before which puckered and goffered curtains were drawn; tables with marble tops and fantastic shaped legs and figurines of porcelain set off in cabinets lined with pale blue padded silk. Among all this medley it was difficult to see the gowns that Madame herself brought out and showed discreetly on a revolving dummy that was full bosomed, well-laced about the waist, trim as to the hips and head lines.

May noticed with real interest these "creations" as Madame called them.... The fashions were not really very attractive. They were, though none of the ladies present knew it extremely old—as old as Crete, a civilization that had been for many thousand years buried. The bodices were tight and cut extremely low, with no more than a strap over the shoulders. Steels and whalebones held them exactly in place over the waist, the skirts were drawn backwards into huge flounces that were sometimes accentuated with big bows. At the foot of the skirt were frills and ruches. The day dresses were on the same models, save that they were buttoned tight to the neck and had long sleeves. Over them were worn mantles shaped to the figure with exaggerated points at the shoulder, or short jackets of sealskin or other fur, hip length and rather clumsily cut. The hair, in imitation of the style recently adopted by the Princess of Wales, was brushed on to the top of the head in a multitude of curls and away from the nape of the neck where stray ringlets were usually unsuccessfully kept in place by slides and pins. On these ringlets were arranged for the younger women hats of various shapes and sizes, over adorned with ribbons, plumage, flowers and ornaments of almost every known material, even ivory and glass; and for the older women bonnets, with broad ribbons that tied under the chin.

Madame Dumont, an American by birth, a Frenchwoman by taste, did not wear a bonnet but May told her, half ruefully, that the Chorleys had said that she should be wearing one soon herself—"before you do, Mother."

"As the mother of two children and the wife of a successful Manchester merchant, I suppose," agreed Madame Dumont, "it would be most suitable—but Amelia Chorley doesn't wear a bonnet?"

"No, she's very vulgar looking, I think," replied May absently gazing at the dress on the stand which was of guipure lace mounted on shot blue-green taffeta, closely shaped to the dummy and buttoned down the back with steel buttons.

"That's a strange way to speak of one you said was your friend...."

"Oh, she's a friend in a way because she's about the house so much... and then we make up parties," explained May vaguely. "John and I, Amelia and Thomas...."

"And Richard?"

"Oh yes, Richard, too. He comes and goes...."

"Do you like the dress?" asked Madame Dumont, putting up her lorgnette.

"Yes, but I prefer that which was cut lower."

"Well, this would be for different occasions—for the afternoon. Here is a French newspaper...."

Madame Dumont picked up a sheet from the side table and Madame Clorinde was careful to assure her that it was a new issue that had come by that morning's post.

"Well, May, choose what you wish among the dresses and the gauzes and the tinsels and do not stint yourself, for what you cannot afford out of your own allowance I can certainly afford for you."

May turned aside from her mother who was soon engrossed in the journal. She was not thinking of any question of extravagance; a darker woe weighed her heart. What opportunity had she of wearing such dresses—and for whom? Would it be considered suitable for her to put on the guipure lace gown to go up to the drab little nursery, with the hideous oleographs on the wall, to see her dull children sitting over their primers with Lizzie Burt in correct attendance? Would not John frown and make some sarcastic remark if he saw her at the breakfast table in that "confection", as Madame Clorinde called it, of black chantilly lace and thin pink silk? And what would the good dames of Manchester say if she was to appear in the cathedral in one of those plush jackets of grape colour with pinched sleeves, with a tartan skirt looped back with enormous bows of green ribbon, and worn with a hat that was like a purple plate piled with green and scarlet cherries? Madame Clorinde's taste was described by many people as *outré*, and she was not patronized by those more timid females who, when they went to choose their designs and their patterns always began with "I want something quiet and ladylike..."

But May could not resist the childish pleasure she felt in these garments. She turned them over, noticed the fine sewing and "finish", the whaleboning, the braiding, the minute stitches, the linings and the interlinings; some of the dresses seemed to weigh as much as a suit of armour in the hand. These had been selected as being her size—"a little below the medium," judged Madame Clorinde carefully surveying her small client.

"I'll try them on," agreed May, glancing at her mother who in elegant pose was turning over the cheap paper stamped with the cheap ink that formed her favourite news-sheet.

It was stupid of her not to have ordered *Le Journal*, Madame Dumont thought, to be sent to the Bristol; she must remember when she went home to do so; but Madame Dumont's reflections went lazily from this point to another; it was really no use for her to remain in London, or in England, much longer... she had given May all the support she could. Obviously the poor child was married to a brute—an ugly, unappetizing brute, Madame Dumont considered, and she could not quite understand her own lapse in allowing her beloved daughter to make this marriage; but at the time it had seemed so suitable, and she was never a woman to interfere. She could not interfere now, and divorce was out of the question since they were Roman Catholics. A Papal Dispensation would cost—well, far more than the profits of ten years on the cotton fields, and it would take an acute emergency to rouse Madame Dumont out of her elegant sloth and force her to direct action. She had done what she could for poor May, both in that horrible house, Stone Pynes, and in giving her this little pleasure in London. So her thoughts drifted away again from her own affairs and those of her daughter, on to the morsels of gossip that were on the page at which she looked, many of which concerned friends and acquaintances of her own.

May stood in a cabinet lined with heavy plated bevelled glass. She was wearing the guipure lace dress. Madame Clorinde pronounced that it was "too old" for her, and May thought so too.... Twenty-five years of age, but married eight years, remember that—and with two children, and the wife of a Manchester merchant.

"I don't think it is too old..." she began. "It is heavy though, and stifling round the neck. I'll try on the other... of course it is cut too low."

It was a pleasure to feel the rustling folds round her. The colour was something like that which she had worn, by what masculine caprice she did not know, at John's desire soon after their marriage.

"It is the exact hue of a peacock's breast," smiled Madame Clorinde.

"That's unlucky, isn't it?"

"Oh, no!" Madame brushed any suggestion of such unpleasantness easily aside, as if nothing like ill luck could touch her establishment. "It is the feathers only which are considered of evil omen, and then only when they are associated with a wedding."

May put on the gown. After a good deal of lacing and hooking and pulling into place, it was discovered, as Madame enthusiastically declared, to fit her perfectly; May was surprised herself at the figure that she saw reflected in the long plate glass; not the Manchester matron, but rather the woman who might have been supposed to bloom from that girl who, in the pale muslin striped with tinsel had lain on the sunny grass and looked across the placid water at the artificial trimness of Bagatelle; the rich tinted dress showed her smooth arms, her white shoulders.

"You require no jewellery," announced Madame with her head on one side and a few pins in her mouth.

She was an insignificant person herself, but could throw any amount of zeal and ardour into embellishing the charms of other women.

"And your hair piled up like that.... The present fashion suits you very well. Madame is lucky... some ladies do better with their hair in the style that the Empress Eugènie used to wear it, but Madame, with her hair on the top of her head and brushed away from her ears that are so beautifully shaped..."

May laughed good humouredly. It might have been Rose Bernier speaking; women of distinct classes seemed to have distinct manners. Those whose profession it was to deal with chiffons always spoke in this soft and flattering way. May wondered if she had her own peculiar manner, the manner of a woman who had lived for eight years in Manchester, who for eight years had been the wife of John Tyler.

"I will take the dress," she said, in utter recklessness, knowing that it would be neither liked nor admired where she would have to wear it, though it might be, in an odd way, envied. "And now the other one—the plush jacket and skirt and the hat with the cherries...."

Even Madame Clorinde's eyebrows raised a little. The costume was considered, even in these salons, slightly extreme, and it was known that while Madame Dumont was an honoured client, Madame's daughter had made a most unfortunate marriage with a provincial gentleman and did not live in London. But Madame was too discreet to murmur, 'For the provinces—hardly'; instead she glided away and glided back with her assistants, and May was soon in the tartan skirt, with the bows of green ribbon forming a bustle behind the plush jacket of a grape colour, and the hat with the little cherries.... Standing there in the frivolous salon with the chairs of damask and white paint and scrolled ornaments, it did not look, after all, so extraordinary.

"Ladies are wearing such things this season," said Madame Clorinde, a little doubtfully. 'I do not know of course in Manchester...' she would have added, but coughed instead and when this pretended impediment to her speech was removed she added, "It's rather old and heavy for Madame, perhaps... the colours too brilliant...."

May did not think so and she knew that she was right. The ash blonde hair that was the colour of new cedar wood, and that curled naturally into the little coronet that was so fashionable and so difficult for many women to achieve, was becomingly set off by the little hat that was fastened coquettishly by a band of ribbon at the back. The jacket, with but few alterations, would fit admirably; the tartan of no known clan was, after all, sombre enough—there was nothing vivid or startling about it... If one was distinguished in one's manner, Madame Dumont had always said, it hardly mattered what one wore. There were some women on whom nothing could look vulgar. May, in her more sober moments, would have known that such lofty talk might have gone down well in Paris, but would be only matter for scorn in Manchester. As it was, she ordered the purple dress and the lace one and the walking-costume, but then said she had bought enough—but of course there must be a blouse to wear under the jacket, and she selected one of white lace that fitted her very well and went out into the outer salon where Madame Dumont was still turning over the pages of *Le Journal*.

"I have bought both frocks and the walking-costume and the hat, Mother...."

"And I suppose you will be scolded for extravagance, my dear. It is such a *gaffe* to bring one's husband into these matters."

"Oh, how can you tell what I was going to remark?"

"I know perfectly well that you are going to say 'I don't know what John will say.' You are certainly becoming provincial, May. Do you know," she went on, "what I have seen in the paper? Old Madame Bondi has been arrested at last.... She was the fortune teller, you know, in the

Palais Royal. I was nearly persuaded by a foolish friend once to go to consult her myself, but of course she was never considered respectable and I was far too wise to meddle with her…."

"I remember hearing about her, Mother, I think." The younger woman spoke without interest, and her small fingers smoothed down the gleaming silk of the tartan skirt.

"Oh yes, she was famous—she used to have her advertisements in this very paper. She was supposed to have second sight and to tell the tarot cards with which Madame Lenormand had foretold Napoleon's fortune…."

"What's she been arrested for?" asked May indifferently. "It is permitted to tell fortunes in Paris, isn't it?"

"Yes, but it seems she'd been engaged in some quite illegal trafficking in drugs—cocaine, morphia and arsenic, it says here. How very strange. I never supposed she had anything to do with such things."

May had scarcely heard of the matter of which her mother spoke. She was surprised and a little shocked on hearing the older lady mention them so casually.

"What do people buy drugs for?" she asked, and was conscious by the look that passed over Madame Clorinde's face that she had made what her mother would term "a *gaffe*".

"Oh, it is to ease pain—migraines and that kind of malady—opium, or laudanum does, you know," replied Madame Dumont vaguely, putting down the journal from which she had extracted all possible entertainment. "And then it becomes a habit and of course it is not allowed by the English or French police to be bought openly, so people go to these kind of people and buy it—the drug, whatever it is, I mean."

"That must be terrible," mused May, and her brow wrinkled. "I wonder."

"What do you wonder?" asked Madame Dumont, turning slowly towards her. "What should you be wondering on a subject like this…?"

"Nothing," replied May. She meant, 'Nothing I can tell you.'

Madame Dumont continued, "Imagine that old creature—her name of course was not Bondi, she was an Irish woman; she has had many aliases in her time… they think she was Bridget O'Neill—that's an Irish name, is it not?"

May was not in the least interested in Madame Bondi, though she was slightly sorry for the fate that had overtaken her. She did not care to think of anyone meeting misfortune.

"I do not like to think of her being in prison, even if she has been a wicked woman," she remarked. "Imagine, Mother, to be in prison! They keep them in prison in France, don't they, before the trial?"

"Oh yes, and here too I believe… but really I know nothing of the English law, but I don't suppose, my dear girl, that it will ever concern either of us,"

"I suppose not."

May studied her reflection again in the long cheval glass that stood in the middle of the overcrowded room. Invoices were being made out, orders given… she must wait while the skirt was measured… it was half an inch too long… and the bows might be drawn tighter with more luxurious effect over the slender hips…. As she stood thus in the white blouse and the dull, rich, sombre tartan skirt, the assistant on her knees beside her measuring and pinning the brilliant bows, and her mother lounging gracefully in the plush coloured chair, the gilt door was opened suddenly and another of the trim assistants said that there was a gentleman waiting in the vestibule who wished to see Madame Tyler.

Neither of the women moved. Their poise was perfect; they had inherited much from ancestors who had been taught how to behave. Both of them believed that it was John who had come to London to reclaim his "errant wife", as he no doubt would term May. The younger woman, well skilled both in the dutiful and the prudent action to take, left the next move to her mother, and Madame Dumont, with a languorous movement of her head, asked, "What's the name of the gentleman? It is strange that he should have followed us here and not wait for us at the hotel."

"Monsieur says that he went to the hotel and was sent on here and that what he had to say to Madame Tyler is important."

The girl spoke haltingly, in an accent like Rose's clipped English... a Breton, May guessed mechanically. Why did one think of stupid details at important moments? She felt sick, as if she was on board ship; a dull nausea gripped her body. She alone of the people in the room knew what John might want.

But Madame Dumont, still casual, said, "Ask Mr. Tyler to come up. It is Madame's husband—perhaps there is some news about the children...."

"The children..." repeated May in a concerned voice.

But Madame Dumont's level eyes under the level brows, so like those of her daughter's, flashed a signal that this had been but a subterfuge. There was no fear for the children.

The assistant, like an automaton went on with her task of carefully pinning together the rich folds of stiff silk.

'Oh, what does it matter,' lamented May inwardly. 'What does it matter... an inch, or half an inch, or a quarter of an inch here or there... and why did I buy the dress at all...?'

She stared at her reflection in the cheval glass. John would hate her. She was wearing the hat with the cherries and the lace blouse that was too low on the throat and bosom, and the tartan skirt....

The tall gilt and mirrored door opened and Richard Tyler entered, May could scarcely keep her equanimity, the relief was so great.

"Oh, Richard... you!"

"It is flattering that you should be so interested in our feminine activities, Mr. Tyler," smiled Madame Dumont. "I hope you have not brought bad news from Manchester?"

"I've brought some news," replied Richard. "It is for May and I wouldn't think of concerning you with it."

"To your platitude I may reply with another—that what concerns May concerns me."

"Well my news, such as it is, is for May herself."

Richard spoke with the determination of the conquering Englishman firmly established on his own hearth; he was at the moment nothing of the kind, but netted in feminine frivolities,—clothes, hats, flowers, tinsel, silver lace, golden gauze and furniture that looked as if it were made of sugar, and ornaments that appeared to be miniature wedding cakes surrounded him; but his manner was inherent, a part of his character. The little polish that he had acquired never lasted him long, nor served him at a crisis.

May turned to stare at him. She retained that essential candour that never can learn that the truth is not to be found by gazing into everyone's eyes—that essential candour that never suspects the lie or the deception.

"What news can it be, Richard, from Manchester? Tell me."

Instead of answering her, he asked bluntly, "Are you going to buy that dress and hat?"

"My dear Richard... or Mr. Tyler (I don't know which you prefer to be called) pray spare us!" put in Madame Dumont. "May will doubtless have to go through all that when she returns to Manchester. I am afraid we thought that it was John and that he had some news about the children—"

"—Or I should never have been allowed up," interrupted Richard, concluding her sentence with an abruptness that was scarcely courtesy.

"I'm afraid not. Why should you be?" Madame Dumont rose. "I suppose you have come to inspect the dresses and lingerie," she added impatiently, "that Madame has been buying?"

"May's purchases have nothing to do with me," returned Richard, and this time the shaft had gone behind his guard, for his face, that was usually nearly as pale as his brother's, flushed an unbecoming red. "I came on here because it seemed the most sensible thing to do."

"No doubt, like a good business man…" smiled Madame Dumont, picking up her long cream-coloured gloves, her reticule of small opal-hued beads, and a silver filigree flower holder in which she had placed two sulphur-coloured carnations, "no doubt, like a good business man," she repeated, "you always do the sensible thing. What would you suggest would be the sensible thing for *us* to do now—discuss our family affairs in this *décor*, or to return to the hotel for what you, I suppose, would call a conclave?"

"Madame Dumont," replied Richard Tyler doggedly opposing his firm purpose to her feminine teasings, "I want to speak to May—and alone. I don't often get a chance. It is something to do with John."

"With John?" echoed May, at once afraid and helpless.

Her mother glanced at her with pity, also with helplessness, it was all going to be extremely stupid and tiresome, and perhaps tragic; but there was really nothing that Madame Dumont, easily married for the third time, indolent, expensive and good natured, could do in the way of interference.

She nodded to Madame Clorinde and May thanked the assistants in tones that were not as rich and full as usual—she had a very musical voice and one that had far more power than might have been expected from her frail body. The women all understood one another without needing even to turn their heads; the man understood himself, and that was sufficient for him.

With determined, if clumsy courtesy, he got the women away from the dressmaker's into the hired carriage that Madame Dumont had selected for her fortnight in London. May had changed into her usual clothes—grey and dark-blue poplin. They seemed like a disguise after the brilliant hues she had worn in the dressmaker's salon. How strange, she thought, for Richard to come on them like that, and what was the news? She was resolved, as he was, that it should not be told in front of her mother. Madame Dumont had all her love and all her confidence, but May Tyler had her own peculiar reserves and sanctities which she would not reveal to anyone. She had no intimate friends. Amy was married and living in another part of England. She never corresponded with the wife of the Manchester cotton merchant. Louise was in Brussels and wrote affectionate notes now and then about her children and her dear husband. Françoise had retired to a château in Normandy and wrote only at the Christmas season, notes that had the air of being both enigmas and epigrams—and May had made no new friends since she had come to Manchester, for she did not count Amelia Chorley as anything—well, if she had told the truth to herself, that ugly truth that one so seldom tells to oneself—as anything but an enemy.

When they reached the hotel Madame Dumont gave up an already lost battle with a graceful gesture. May's affairs were impossible, the girl herself had very little spirit… was secretive too. Madame Dumont could not see what she could do to help—not even if her husband had been with her to consult, and he was away in Africa; so tedious and inconvenient… and she had a headache from the close atmosphere of the dressmaker's salon, and from the drive through the London streets, where a sharp east wind was blowing. The islands seemed to lie under the winds, the American thought, as under a curse. There was the may and the laburnum in bloom, but it was tossed to and fro by this incessant wind like the tresses of water nymphs struggling under angry waves, and the sky, that Madame Dumont desired so ardently should be an azure blue, was a grey that she likened in her own mind to vinegar and ashes. No, she had migraine and she desired the ministrations of Rose Bernier, and perhaps May could settle her own difficulties best, so she laid down her arms lightly.

"Well, Richard, I suppose you must be allowed to tell your tremendous secret to May. Don't keep her too long. It is the most trying thing in the world to visit the dressmaker's… you have about an hour before luncheon. You are lunching with us?"

"I'm afraid not—I have a business appointment. What I want to say to May won't take long. You mustn't think there is any mystery about it—it is only that it is just a family affair and I shouldn't think—"

"—Of bothering me," interrupted Madame Dumont. "I understand.… I am so grateful.…"

She was gone, ignoring Richard, blowing a kiss from her finger tips to May.

May gazed piteously at Richard. All she remembered then was that he was kinder than her husband. Perhaps that was because he was not her husband—but at least he had never shouted at her, or banged doors in her face, or told her of her faults, or been atrociously rude or coarsely discourteous. Sometimes he had been a pleasant companion when he had taken her to the races or a dance and paid her attentions that were clumsy enough, but, she felt, well meant, as if he had been a little sorry for her… it was at times like those she wondered if she would have been happier if she had married Richard.

What was he going to say to her now? That did not matter so much… at least it was a chance for her to say something to him. It was quite true that they were never alone at Stone Pynes, although she had never thought of that before. John was more often in his house than in the office, and there was always the servants… Lizzie Burt, Jane Chase, Nelly Tanner or Dolly Hoey, in and out on some excuse or other—to fetch letters, to answer bells.… What did they come in and out for…? She knew she had very little time alone with Richard. Even when he escorted her to an entertainment there would always be a third person present.

"Oh Richard!" she began. "Is it something terrible that you have come here to London to tell me?"

"I didn't come to London especially to tell you," he replied. "I had to come to London... we're doing some business.... There is a man who has got a new substitute for cotton—ramie he calls it—and there might be a big fortune in that if we can get it first. That is what I came up about."

"But it must have been something important, Richard..." May's beautiful eyes were beseeching, "for you to have snatched us from the dressmaker's...."

"Why, it was only a question of saving time. I might have kicked my heels here for another hour or so.... I know what your mother is when she gets on clothes...."

"I'm just the same," admitted May with great simplicity. "Of course, I know John won't like the clothes I've bought...."

"No, but perhaps it won't matter by the time you return to Manchester what John likes."

She stared at him not in relief, but in alarm.

"I wish you wouldn't frighten me, Richard. You ought to know that life isn't too easy for me at Stone Pynes."

"My dear girl, I daresay I know your position perfectly well. How many years is it," he added with coarse abruptness, "since John kissed you?"

She turned her back on him and walked to the windows, then she turned, also abruptly, and faced him.

"What are those white powders he takes? I believe it is strychnine."

"What makes you think so?"

"I don't know. He said something about strychnine once. He has large quantities of it made up in London and sent to him. It worries me."

"Does it? Why does it worry you what John takes? These aren't matters to concern women. John's always been clever about medicine. He's made up his own concoctions for a long time. You must remember that he is old enough to be your father."

"I think you are talking very strangely, Richard."

"Oh, it is you that are strange. You're a foreigner here, you know… we find you very odd indeed. You have heard people say that in Manchester, I suppose?"

"Odd?" said May, who had not taken the least offence at these abrupt words, but who was still staring at her brother-in-law with an almost appealing air, as if she hoped to find in him some kindness—possibly some championship or protection. "It is certain that I have very few friends, but I go about a good deal and do what the other ladies do."

"Oh, they are all different from you and you know it. It is not like you to pretend."

"It is so unlike me, Richard, that I do not pretend—but still I ought to bring you back to the point, and ask you why you came here so suddenly and unexpectedly. Odd…? I think it was odd seeing you in the dressmaker's room…."

"I daresay I did look peculiar. A plain business man who is not used to furbelows amid all your laces and ribbons."

He walked up and down, seemingly communing with himself. She felt that he was very much aware of her, that he was considering—not her personality, for she assumed, nay, she knew that he had long since dismissed May Tyler as an insignificant creature—but just how he should deal with her… there was a suggestion of the iron claw in the velvet glove about his attitude; but she still hoped for what she so greatly needed, kindness from Richard.

"I don't know why you live as you do," he continued. "John is scarcely civil, much less kind. He married you on a whim, you know, and for the money. It's been pretty useful but you don't fit into his life—you haven't made friends or entertained for him, or cut a dash, or kept his house very well; and John's an ambitious man and wants to make a figure in Manchester."

"Would there not be," asked May gently, "another side to the query? Would you not consider how young I was when I married, and how unthinking… that I am of another religion and another country from yours, and that I have never been able to feel at home in Manchester, nor to like the factories, the streets and the slums, and those heavy public buildings and those sooty parks very much…."

"Oh come! you've lived there eight years and enjoyed yourself too, I think. You like dancing, and the concerts and admiration, don't you? I wonder why you always stop in time…."

Now she did not understand him, and he as plainly saw it and gloated over the pleasure given him by his mistake.

"I suppose you don't take being a Roman Catholic very seriously?" he suggested. "You never see a priest and you don't often go to mass…."

"Oh but I do sometimes, and I get absolution. It would be impossible to explain to you—but it isn't *being* a Catholic… what can I say… it is a kind of *state*…."

"Oh, I know all that fantastical and high-flown talk. We've always been plain folk in Manchester. We stood out against the King in the Civil wars, you know, and against the King again in the '45 in the North; and some of our ancestors went to the block on Kennington Common for it…. Oh yes, there was a Manchester regiment enrolled to fight King Charles…. We're Puritans and always have been."

May felt a woman's distaste at the conversation being turned from the particular to the general. She wanted to talk about herself, but Richard continued on the theme of his native city.

"You've heard of the Peterloo massacre… that's a good many years ago, but my grandfather was there…. The field's built over now by the Free Trade Hall. We've done something in our time, you know. Who talked louder among the general discontent fifty years ago than we did? Who made louder cries for reform and got it, too? We've had a few other things as well… a charter… an archbishop's city…. We were made a city, oh not so long ago! You seem to think it is a poor place. Have you seen the parks and the statues?"

"Oh, I've seen everything," said May wearily, "the Natural History collections which are housed in the Young Men's Christian Association, and the Free Public Library and the Royal Institution and the Athenaeum," she added with a sparkle, "founded by some very moral gentleman for the advancement and diffusion of useful knowledge. There, I believe, you can consult a library of sixteen thousand volumes for an annual subscription of a penny a day."

"Now you're making fun of me," he retorted with sullen humour.

"I must make fun of you, Richard, if you won't tell me what you gave me this alarm for. If it is anything private," she added rapidly, "you had better be quick for Mother will come downstairs soon."

"So you keep your private affairs from your mother? I knew it, of course. I was not so sure that you would admit it."

"Why shouldn't I admit it?" said May simply, "since I knew you knew it."

Richard seemed in a sudden good humour. He smiled at her and his face appeared quite benevolent. He was certainly milder of aspect than John and did not so quickly betray himself by boldly staring eyes and darkly frowning brows. He had softer tastes also. She had heard him play both the pianoforte and the violin with some skill, though both the instruments, to her innate taste, went absurdly with his modern clothes. In other garments, she reflected, he might appear quite a remarkable creature, and again there drifted into her idle, troubled and yet lively mind, like a drifting leaf on a breeze, "Should I have been happier if I had married Richard?"

Aloud she said, with the air of one who cannot be at pains to conceal her misfortune, and indeed the candour of her nature was such that she had never yet been at pains to conceal anything, except what was to another's hurt or beneath her own dignity to disclose: "John and I have been apart these four years and more. I suppose everyone knows it, and the servants gossip about it. I see now that you know. But what can one do? They say most married people get like that—just friends, or only acquaintances. I agree, Richard, with what you say about my faults. I'm frivolous and lightheaded, I suppose. I was brought up to be lazy, and John has alarmed me...."

"Alarmed you?" Richard fastened on the word. "Has he ill-treated you, or threatened you?"

"I thought you knew everything," continued May with a guarded look. "John has alarmed me by his coldness, which seems to chill all the warmth in any human relationship; and his friends are like him, and his children too. You must have seen that—even May, who is named after me, she never smiles or puts her arms round my neck. She was taken away from me when she was so very young—they both were. They said she was delicate. I was kept at school for the same reason, Richard... you see I have stood rather apart from life."

"I know," agreed Richard, and, unexpectedly, quoted a line that he had heard in church, but that had no religious sound as he repeated it, "a garden enclosed is my sister, my spouse."

May supposed that this was some puritanical password. She gave it but little attention. She felt that she must force herself on to her trouble as an advancing soldier might force himself on to the spears of the enemy.

"Did you want to tell me that John has been unfaithful to me, Richard? I know it... I have found their handkerchiefs and their caps, and sometimes their letters.... He is quite careless, you know, and indifferent...."

"If you weren't a Roman Catholic and could get a witness that he had been brutal to you, you could be divorced," said Richard.

She stared at him in great surprise, her smooth brows, that were so seldom wrinkled, frowning.

"A divorce…? Why should you say that to me? I expected the suggestion to come, but from my mother…."

"I am no great admirer of John's," said Richard, slightly hunching his shoulders. "He drinks too much, plays the great gentleman absurdly—makes a fool of himself at Wirral Races, spends too much, doesn't keep his accounts too well…. And those men he's got in the office, they're old and peevish and past it. Of course it is not my business—I'm not a cotton merchant, but a broker." He changed his tone and his subject again. "You asked about that powder he takes. You say it worries you. 'Worry'—that's a woman's word, like 'nice'…."

"I don't think it can be right. He has a parcel of pills and bottles that Messrs. Joshua and Blunt send every week or so. He keeps them locked away, of course. Sometimes I hear him when he thinks he is alone, groaning; and he complains of stiffness in his legs and of feeling sick."

"He was always a fool about his health," said Richard curtly. "John's a strong and healthy man for—fifty-six, is it, May dear?"

"I suppose so."

It was like a dash of cold water in her face to be thus curtly reminded that she at eighteen years of age had married a man forty-eight years old…. There had been a fool somewhere, but where, May did not yet quite know.

"Well, it's natural he should begin to cosset himself, especially as he has not a fond wife to do it for him—or has he, May? *Has* he got a fond wife to mix his medicines and his cordials, to groan over his losses with him and to spend the guineas that he wins at the races?"

She was silent and the life went out of her face, leaving it with the stillness and texture and colour of a magnolia bloom. This was something totally unexpected. She had been broken by degrees to the little insignificant infidelities that she had never envisaged, that she had never thought about, that she had never put into words stronger than these—"John is flirting with another woman whom he thinks prettier than I am". But this meant something more. This was what Richard had come to tell her. He seemed more anxious to know how she would take his news than to impart it. He had been for a long time preparing her for what he had come to say. Two hours had passed since he had come upon her in the sombre tartan skirt and the coat of grape hue, and the hat covered with cherries in Madame Clorinde's salon.

Now he said quite casually, "There's a woman named Dora Lestrange whom he keeps at Salford. She's more his wife than you are. Oh, I don't mean he's a bigamist—but they have four children, and 'where your heart is there your treasure is.' That's an old saying, isn't it? You were only something that took his fancy. I think the great attraction was that you were a gentlewoman. Of course you know that we have not any pretensions to gentility...."

She answered, not his shocking revelation, but his last foolish jibe.

"I think John has great pretensions, and that is where all the wrong has been done."

"Well, I've made none in coming to tell you what I've told you now."

"I mustn't believe it. Women don't believe those things—they don't think about them. I suppose in any case it would be John's life and John's money... this other woman's too. I don't know their story and I mustn't judge—but above all, I mustn't believe it, Richard."

"I knew you'd say that. I know you quite well, May, and why you've remained so aloof and so apart. And John knows too, and that's why he can go away for weeks and feel quite safe about you, certain that no one can come as far as you can toss your glove...."

This expression was not in character with the man and what he had said before. She looked at him and saw that he was slightly changed as by some powerful passion long suppressed at last mounting up and revealing itself. He turned away quickly again and fingered the coarse imitation net and lace at the window.

"Will you go and see her, May? Have you enough courage for that? She's quite a sensible person, and the children are kept quite well, and friendly. She lives in a neat house at Salford. Of course, it's the wrong side of the city—Dora's the wrong side of the hedge altogether, but it doesn't say that the browsing there is not quite luscious, my dear."

May replied almost immediately, not with the haste of one who makes no reflection, but with the serenity of one who has long made up her mind on life and such problems as it is likely to present.

"Yes, I'll go with you and see her. John would dislike it, I suppose. It seems like a treachery, but if I were to tell him, he would be very violent and prevent me—and I suppose there must not be a scandal because of the business?"

"No, no scandal, May dear, whatever we do."

She did not catch the implication of his last words, spoken quickly. She was trembling, felt cold and sick as she had felt sometimes on the Atlantic crossing when she had stood too long on the deck, and the sun had seemed to go down suddenly and the long beams to be quenched in the acrid winds, and all her blood to curdle in her veins.

"I suppose it makes no difference," she whispered, as if to herself, and she turned away and gazed at her own reflection in the glass as if gathering courage from the contemplation of a stranger.

"It's *proof*," urged Richard, "that you didn't have with the other women. A bit of lace, or a letter—that don't count; but Dora… he couldn't get out of that. And it wouldn't be difficult for someone—someone…" he touched his own breast, "to put John in a temper with you before witnesses and make him *say*, or even do *something*… it would be worth it, May, even if he struck you."

She still stared at that stranger in the mirror.

"I don't know the divorce laws of this country," she murmured. "I never thought about it save recently, and my mother spoke of a visit to Paris and taking the children there and making them, perhaps, different… and I knew I couldn't go because of John."

"It's only the children, and wanting to go to Paris, and your mother," he demanded between passion and a sneer, "that made you think of divorce?"

"What else should it be?" asked May, turning. "And now, Richard, you must go. I wonder," she added simply, "why you hate him so?"

"Perhaps it is not because I hate John so, but because I am fond of someone else. I never had a sister, you know, May, and you are my sister-in-law as they call it."

"Do you want to protect me?" she asked. "I think you've done it in a very cruel manner. I don't see it clearly yet…" She was thinking her thoughts aloud more than composing a speech for him to listen to, and she was silent for she had almost said, 'no gentleman would have done it like this.' And yet perhaps he really was sorry for her, perhaps he wanted to help her get free from a life that was becoming fast intolerable. She had realized in the last few minutes how intolerable it was—the humbug, the hypocrisy, the shut-away nursery, and the shut-away kitchen and servants' hall… and the whispering of the maids who ate her food and took her money and cringed for her cast-off clothes… and the loud laughter of people like the Chorleys who mocked at her in a coarse yet friendly way, Amelia's blasé kisses and Thomas's hearty handshakes, and the long dinners that seemed endless, when dull men and dull women drank too much claret and the polished damask cloth was soon stained with gravy and wine and wet with flower vases pouring water—upset by clumsy, shaking hands.

Manchester, with the tall factory chimneys and the smoke, and everywhere one went the black rivulets, and everything one touched dirty, and the sprawl of houses in the old town on the east bank of the Irwell where the workers lived diseased and cowed, unless they were intoxicated with gin… and that north-eastern suburb which had once been what was termed "stylish", but was now out-of-date and neglected… the bleak, dreary country beyond, and factory on factory between the Oldham Road and Ancotes and that suburb as fearful to her as any outpost of hell, Moss Side, where she had once been taken by a district visitor into a wilderness of broken-down houses. Genteel residences were moving further and further away from the factories and slums it was true, and at Stone Pynes on Cheetham Hill she had little to complain of…. But it was not so far from Moss Side, it was not so far from Oldham Road and Ancotes….

She stopped her thought as by virtue of her breeding she was able to do; Stone Pynes was a long way from Salford.

She went to the carafe that stood on the round table in the window-place and poured out a glass of the London water that tasted flat on her dry lips, and when she had sipped it, turned to Richard and said with amicable courtesy; "If you will come to Stone Pynes when it is convenient, when he is at business—"

"No, when he is at the races at Wirral," interrupted Richard.

"Oh, you have it planned, then I need take no trouble. I shall be glad to go to Salford to see this lady."

May experienced no coherent emotion. She was one who had always refused, with the obstinacy known only to the idealists, to be vicariously disillusioned. What she had heard seemed to her like an interchange of shadows. She knew that it affected her real life, the way in which she would pass her future days, the manner in which she would hold herself before her fellows; but she did not see it as something clear and definite as she knew Madame Dumont and Rose Bernier, and as she knew John and Richard themselves would see it; she was playing, as it were, with the ghosts of cards, not with the cards themselves.

This was due to her natural indolence of mind and to the ignorance that had been fostered by her convent education and increased by her life as a foreigner in Manchester.

She did not concern herself with endeavouring, as a clever woman would have done, to discover Richard's motives in thus betraying his brother. She vaguely thought they might be kindness, as she was very eager to discover kindness in anyone and Richard had so often appeared to her under the guise of the kinder, more generous part of John, as if there were one man divided and Richard had all the good qualities and John all the evil. She did not concern herself either about her mother. The friendship between the two women was and always would be intact. They were at liberty, as each knew, even to deceive one another should occasion arise. Madame Dumont's last kiss and pressure of the hand had, in a way, sanctioned such deception, as if she would say, 'You have something to do that I must have no part in. Whatever it is, I shall support you and help, if need be.' Madame Dumont could not help. May knew this with the self containment of a woman eight years subjected to the private torments of an unhappy marriage.

Richard escorted her back to Manchester and his mood seemed as usual. He was a far pleasanter companion than John had ever been since the Paris days. He could make jests that, coarse as his nature might be, were not offensive to May, just little homely jokes on ordinary things—and he could look after her comfort during the depressing miseries of the long train journey from Euston to London Road Station in a way that John never thought of… he had a carriage waiting for her at the station, and John never thought of that either, but allowed her to find her own public conveyance.

"You should have a maid," said Richard as he helped her into the interior of the brougham that smelt of old leather and polish, "and John should be able to keep a barouche and pair. He does not spend his money well."

"What should I know about that?" replied May. "You have told me one way in which he spends his money, and," she added with an inconsequence that was childlike, "he says I am extravagant, too. I never get my accounts straight...."

"And John never presents any," replied Richard.

He left her at the door of Stone Pynes, after having learned from Nelly Tanner that the master was still with the Chorleys at Wirral Races.

"I'll call for you to-morrow evening," he said, "unless..." and he looked at her steadily, "you want rest?"

"No. I'd rather go at once."

This was spoken in hushed tones beneath the portico that had an air of pretentious fake, as had everything in that heavy, expensive mansion that appeared to have been built by a bricklayer without the aid of an architect, a man who had only followed rule of thumb and designs in the pattern book. There were turrets and oriel windows and pointed roofs of slate, and jutting balconies, too small to accommodate a human being and always in the ugliest possible brick and slate, so that the eye was teased, not only by the hideousness of form, but by the poverty of material.

May unconsciously always drew her shoulders together when she entered Stone Pynes, as if she was trying to shield herself from a blow. The air was always the same, stale and enclosed; despite the baize doors above the kitchen stairs, there was the reek of cooking stagnant in the atmosphere—roast meats, stale savouries, other odours not comfortably defined. Nothing in the place was quite clean and May knew it; when the flounced curtains were lifted from the floor, dust flew out; when vases were moved from one unserviceable table to another, a ring of dust showed. May's clothes, even in her large closet cupboard, showed dust when shaken. Away from Rose Bernier and the ministrations of the London hairdressers and her mother's intimate friend, Sophia Byrd, who was so clever with the hands and the complexion,

May Tyler felt that she would soon become dingy, blotted with the soots of Manchester.

She passed into the drawing-room, forgetful that she was wearing the brilliant costume that she had chosen in London. Richard had insisted, with a quiet, brotherly friendliness, that she should wear this on her journey. They had travelled first class, with red plush seats and a wicker luncheon basket, and May's costume did not seem inappropriate until they had arrived at London Road Station. Then she had felt, amid the drab and the dun of the moving figures, and the shifting soiled light, enclosed under the sooty dome, out of place, a bright bird that had strayed into a flock of crows. But now she had forgotten her costume—the skirt of sombre tartan, the jacket of grape-coloured plush, the hat with the vivid cherries—but it was recalled to her by an exclamation of delighted surprise that she heard as she closed the door of her drawing-room.

Not John's voice—even if she had not been assured that he was at Wirral, she would have known that it was not he who spoke for she was sure that this was an exclamation of pleasure at her costume.

The man who had spoken came to meet her. He wore a light coat and he was fair, a last straggling beam of light that was full of motes burnished his pale, harsh textured locks. This made him different from anyone whom she had seen lately; certainly very different from both John and Richard. She knew him and liked him. Something for his smile, something for his tact, something for the admiration—distant, respectful, that she had caught in his glance now and then. He reminded her of one of the knights described in Tennyson's enchanting verses. She read Tennyson's poems frequently when she should have been doing other things. The web of her own lazy fancy had been quickly spun round Jerome Thorne, because of his name, that was unlikely for a Manchester cotton broker, because his mother had been a Roman Catholic, and his fairness—she was not sure whether that pleased or not, but it was uncommon for the English to preserve it until maturity. As children they shone like gold, but as they passed their earliest youth, they became the colour of the factories where they worked, the counting-houses where they checked their ledgers, the smoke-laden atmosphere they breathed; but Jerome Thorne had remained bright, in his eyes, his complexion, his locks.

It was strange, if not improper, that he should call upon her alone at this hour, and she was pleased by his bold unconventionality.

"How did you know I was coming back? It was unexpected," she smiled with her ready reaction to the moment.

He replied at once, allowing her kid-gloved hand lightly to fall from his, for she had spoken to him without any more greeting than the handclasp, that he had come on a chance—that Amelia Chorley had sent him on a chance.

"She said you were capricious and might easily return from London unexpectedly."

May was nearly saying in her simplicity, 'Richard came to fetch me for something important,' but she checked this with a troubled air, and asked with equal candour, "Why have you come? Is it something important?"

"Well, it is bad news in a way, Mrs. Tyler. You see I was at the Wirral Races with your husband..."

"Yes, I know you often are...."

"Why didn't you come?" he asked obliquely. "We were all expecting you. It is a fine sight, don't you think, to see the field flash past—the glossy horses, the jockeys' gay colours.... And you like the entertainments afterwards—the dancing and the waltzes...?"

"Yes, I like it, but Liverpool is as ugly as Manchester, only at the races one seems far away from reality."

She sat down, aware of his eyes over her strange resplendent plumage. She felt it to be that—plumage, soft and shining.

"It's nothing serious, Mrs. Tyler," continued the young man, whose voice was deep and caressing, "only your husband was taken slightly ill and they put him to bed at the hotel. You know—'The King's Head,' where you usually stay at Wirral."

"Taken ill? John? I think he doses himself too frequently, Mr. Thorne. As perhaps you are aware, he sends for medicines from London."

"Yes, I know. He prides himself a deal on being an amateur physician—but you mustn't trouble yourself about that. I really think he knows what he is about. He gets his stuff from Joshua and Blunt and they are first-class people. He has been abroad a good deal, you see, and learned to doctor himself when he was in outlandish places."

"He takes a white powder frequently," said May. "I suppose you know it," she added with a disdain of subterfuge. "I have spoken to Richard about it, and as you are his close friend you'd know...."

"Yes, I've seen him take it, but he doesn't care for anyone to remark about it. It is strychnine, I think. It is a harmless tonic, you know. There's a young fellow to whom he lent a helping hand in a chemist's at Deansgate who gets it for him."

"Is it difficult to obtain then?"

"Oh, I don't know about difficult—it depends on the quantity."

"What are you trying to tell me?" asked the young woman, rising. "Has my husband taken an overdose of this medicine? It is extremely disturbing. What is his illness? Have you called in a physician?"

"Oh yes, there is the best of care given to Mr. Tyler—and the Chorleys are doing everything. They are very close friends, as you know...."

"Close friends of John's," repeated May, and she roused herself. "It was kind of you to tell me. I suppose all his friends know what he takes. He becomes very angry if I..." she paused, "if I find him taking it."

"What's it to do with you?" asked Mr. Thorne. "He is a man well over fifty, and should know his own mind."

She wondered if this was another reminder that her husband was almost, in the cant phrase, "old enough to be her father".

So John was ill, comfortably so according to Jerome Thorne, at Wirral, and would not see the conclusion of the races; and she had longer time in which to go to Salford and think over afterwards what she had seen and heard there, to make her plans. She stripped off her gloves and played with them. Jerome Thorne should go now. His message was delivered. His manner had been abrupt, yet full of an almost beseeching tenderness. Nelly Tanner came in and asked if they would like wine. Her mistress ordered sherry and biscuits, hardly caring what she replied. Jerome Thorne allowed the maid to depart and then remarked that he cared nothing for the sherry. He thought that John had been taking too much at Wirral… it was inferior sherry too… they cheated you at the races.

She looked at him, her vague, indolent and inquisitive thoughts trying to reconcile his appearance with his words and what she knew of his life and occupation. Yes, he had the appearance of one of Arthur's knights, remote from worldly pleasures if not from worldly pain, different from the other men who seemed roughly cast in the same mould—that of the Roman emperor with the crimped dark hair and the heavy chin. This man seemed golden—face and hair—and his features were very finely shaped, with wide nostrils and that short upper lip that can express mockery and ecstasy—every shade of emotion without hardly changing their contour; but his glance, though contained and manly, was as gentle as her own; there was neither sneer nor any harshness on those well-formed features.

She wondered at him. She had heard nothing about him except that he ran, rather ineffectively, the business bequeathed him by his father and was, as John said, not allowing "the old man's money to burn a hole in his pocket"—that he frequented the races, public ballrooms and private dining-rooms, and at thirty years of age was not married.

She had heard women, when she was closeted unwillingly with them, discuss him as part of the local gossip—because he was a man remarkable in looks, comfortable, at least, in fortune (though that comfort might lessen if he continued to live so extravagantly) and yet one who had outraged conventions, in not taking himself a wife.

The maid brought in the sherry on the tray of Sheffield plate, with its scrolled edge and engraved centre, and May Tyler was conscious of an atmosphere of watchfulness, of tension, of all that goes with secretive whispering, welling up from the kitchen, from the servants' quarters, emanating from the person of Nelly Tanner, and enveloping her as she stood there in the fashionable gown over which the severely dressed housemaid had cast one flicker of a glance while she, the mistress, was drinking mechanically a glass of the wine that she knew well enough Maggie Pilch had taken from the bottle labelled "cooking".

In her vague, yet inquisitive mind, May Tyler wondered if this atmosphere was imaginary or real, and how long it had lasted. Was it the nervous results of what had happened to her in the last few hours that had seemed to cause this miasma of doubt, misapprehension and suspicion about her? Was it she whose glance and gesture were conveying alarm and despondency? Or was it true that she was surrounded by the fine nets of a conspiracy? But that was absurd... a conspiracy? Who should be concerned to conspire against her? Servants gossiped of course, and she knew she was what was termed a bad mistress—careless, speaking her mind in a way that gave offence, for though her words were always pleasant they were often misinterpreted and her easy-going dealings were much exploited by those she employed.

She had noticed that among her friends, too. From sheer indifference she would be so amiable with them that they would encroach and claim to be, not what she held them—acquaintances—but intimates, then she would draw back and they would be offended and a coldness would arise.

"What are you thinking of, Mrs. Tyler?" asked Jerome Thorne as the maid left the room.

"I am thinking that life's one consolation prize is the fact that we can keep our thoughts secret."

She poured him the sherry that he left untouched. No doubt he knew at a glance what she guessed, that it was not the wine that gentlemen drank but only what women in the kitchen flavoured their messes with.

"I'm really hardly mistress here," she said with her disturbing and disarming frankness. "You see, the servants do very much what they please. Whenever I try to interfere they talk to me of English customs and English ways—and indeed I know very little about them although I have lived eight years in Manchester."

"It is quite apparent," replied the young man, "that you are ignorant of our ways. But you mustn't learn them, this ignorance gives you a fascination which none of those whom you honour with your friendship find easy to resist."

She was used to stilted phrases, but this sounded to her particularly awkward. She smiled at him gently, as if excusing a fault. She asked about her husband's health, pressed for details. A chill... what did that really mean?

"He doctors himself rather recklessly. He carries that medicine-chest around with him, you know, and takes this and that. Well, sometimes one can make a mistake.... He told me himself that Dr. Harman had warned him—"

"Did he?" asked May, quickly raising her eyes and interested now in this point and in nothing else. "Did he tell you that—and about the white powders?"

"Oh, I don't know anything about the white powders, Mrs. Tyler. I daresay there are powders of all colours. But your husband did tell me that he had come to a disagreement with both Dr. Harman and

Dr. Fitch as to his own treatment of himself. You see, there is nothing wrong with him but this malaria, and I suppose sometimes a glass or two of inferior brandy taken on top of a chill…"

May laughed. "I wonder why John should drink inferior brandy…?"

"I don't know in the least, Mrs. Tyler."

He still had the air of a knight champion, somebody who would defend her, on whom she might, at a pinch, rely. She studied him and could find no disharmony in his features. He was of a surety different from these other Englishmen and more might be expected of him; she wished that she was going that dreary journey to Salford with him, not with Richard, though Richard, of course, was kind….

"Your mother was a Roman Catholic, Mr. Thorne, I believe?"

"Yes, you've noticed my name? It is in the calendar of saints and uncommon among the Protestants. I daresay it sounds fantastical for a cotton broker."

He considered her very steadily and she was endeavouring to interpret that gaze. She made a gesture with her right hand, an unconscious movement as if she swept aside all the incumbrances of ugly, unwieldy furniture, stiff and dust-laden draperies, dun pictures and misshapen ornaments and stood alone with the young man in some open place, perhaps a wind-blown hill with the clouds sinking below the horizon from the smooth grass before the little toy palace of Bagatelle outside Paris.

"I wonder if I was in a difficulty if you would help me?" she asked, and even the integrity of her own simplicity was startled by the effect on him.

The colour came into his face, blotching it unbecomingly and he turned his eyes away as if he did not wish her to see the expression in them.

"I hardly know how to answer you, Mrs. Tyler."

"Do you call me Mrs. Tyler because you emphasize that in this country a married woman does not ask help of anyone save her husband? I know that of course. In Virginia it is different—a gentleman is always at the service of a lady."

He seemed half flattered, half vexed at her reply. The words that she had used had already become staled in England though they might retain the elegance of their former value in America. She was certainly what she claimed so unconsciously to be—a gentlewoman. As for himself, he was the son of a small tradesman who had been fortunate and who had spent a great deal of time in what he termed "polishing his manners" until he was able to meet anyone in Manchester on equal terms, but he acquitted her of sarcasm and came a little nearer. She was on the sofa, her bright dress blurred into the incongruous hues of the cushions behind her graceful outline.

"There is no one who knows you who would not be glad to be of service to you, Mrs. Tyler. You have kept yourself very much aloof since you have been here. We all feel..." he took a careful refuge in the plural, "that you have troubles. John—a friend of mine of course and the best of fellows—is... well, not easy... not an easy husband," he went on clumsily, "for a woman so much younger than himself."

"John's health troubles me," she replied steadily. "I think there is nothing the matter with him, but he goes frequently to doctors and then there is, what you mention yourself—this white powder that he takes—sometimes at night, sometimes by itself and sometimes after food; and always after he has taken it he seems well for a while, more cheerful, and then he has attacks of sickness and numbness in his legs, and pains. I have spoken to Richard about it, but Richard makes nothing of it; but now you come and tell me that he is ill at Wirral. I wonder," she added impulsively, "if I should go to him?"

"Certainly not, my dear Mrs. Tyler. The Chorleys have already got a hired nurse in for him. That was why I was sent to you—to reassure you and to tell you not to concern yourself about his absence."

"It is very good of you, Mr. Thorne. I appreciate it... indeed I do."

She rose on a well-bred instinct that the interview was at an end and that it was time to release him, time, too, to let those women clustering in the kitchen, the other woman watchful in the nursery, be aware that this unusual and unconventional visitor had departed.

"I am much obliged," she continued in her soft voice, with its slight accent that her residence in England had not lost. "I shall write to my husband to-night."

To May's observation which, though lazy, was always quick, Mr. Thorne appeared to be like one poised on the edge of a precipice, ready to take a leap, yet doubtful and then at last restraining himself. His casual man-of-the-world manner copied from the men he had seen in the Argyle Rooms and the parade at the Alhambra in London, slipped on to him again like a slightly ill-fitting glove over a nervous hand.

"You are looking extremely charming, Mrs. Tyler. Let me compliment you on your costume. I see the taste of Madame Dumont there. It reminds me of the gown you wore when I saw you first.... Do you remember that dinner party?"

"Yes, it is something the same colour, the colour of a peacock or a plum or a grape. That was an old dress 'made over' as we say. I had had it since I was first married, but fashions change... the stuff, however, was so excellent—the stiffest Lyons silk—that I did not care to discard it."

"I hope you have it still, Mrs. Tyler, and that I may see you in it again."

She pulled the bell; she did not notice how quickly Nelly Tanner appeared, for her musings were already far away.

The young man had gone, bowing. There was no sunlight now to shine upon his smooth gold head, but even in the dusk he appeared to her as a figure of brightness.

"Shall I light the gas, Madam?" asked Nelly Tanner, coming back quickly with her firm emphatic tread and a crackling of her starched apron.

"Yes, I suppose so. Everything as usual, Nelly.... Why not? The master isn't coming home.... Mr. Thorne came to tell me so. He is taken ill at Wirral..."

"Oh, indeed, Madam. I am very sorry, and I am sure Dolly and Jane and Mrs. Pilch will be—"

"I am sure you all will be... but it is only a chill and my husband has his friends, Mr. and Mrs. Chorley with him, and they have put a nurse in and there is a good doctor there—so there's no need at all for us to worry."

The woman had pulled the long chain that hung from the chandelier in the centre of the room and four heart-shaped jets of gas—blue merging into orange and white—sprang up inside the opal-coloured globes, faintly engraved with a design of ferns. The lights, at once wan and garish, picked out all the dismal details of the overcrowded room, showing Nelly's upturned face, bloodless and wrinkled above the stiff starched apron, the hair thin and pulled back under the crimped muslin cap, her lips of a faint lavender colour and her expression closed and malignant.

'I won't keep Nelly,' thought Mrs. Tyler, 'although she does her work quite well. I don't think she's fond of me. I won't keep any of them except Mrs. Pilch, and she's kind.'

The parlourmaid spoke more familiarly to her mistress than she had ever done before.

"I beg your pardon. Madam, but may I say how very smart I think your London costume is? We have all been admiring it."

"You can hardly have seen it," replied May Tyler sweetly. "I know it is rather extravagant for Manchester, but my mother liked it and wished me to have it.... You may go now, there will be nothing to do until dinnertime."

The woman gave her a look that was not wholly respectful and May, without taking offence, wondered why. She was almost sure that they disliked her and were banded against her, yet there was nothing to be said against her, nothing except that she shared their faults, was a little wasteful, extravagant, indolent and shirked her duties. She was shirking duties now. She ought to go upstairs and see John and May, but she could not face Lizzie Burt. She would only be told that the children were in bed… and they never seemed to want to see her, or to ask where she had been or what she had done or to do the things that she had imagined children would do—stroke her dress, or her cheek, or put their heads in the hollow of her shoulder.… No, not Lizzie Burt to-night… and not those children who were so much more John's than they were hers.…

It was lucky, she supposed, that John was detained at the Wirral Races… of course his illness was largely imaginary.… She knew that on occasion he drank too much and allowed himself the dangerous luxury of a bad temper. He had the Chorleys with him, his friends but not hers, and into her brooding mind flashed a recollection of a day when she had come home and found Amelia Chorley in the hall talking very familiarly with Nelly Tanner. She knew that ladies did not talk with other ladies' servants yet she had hardly been surprised because she had even without mental comment known from the first that Amelia was ill-bred… but now she remembered the incident.…

Did they gossip about her, John's friends and her servants… and if they did gossip, what could they say? She had lived, as Mr. Thorne had remarked, a very aloof life, taking part only in a disinterested fashion in the activities of Manchester… always amiable, always smiling, but unattainable in the way of friendship.… She added now to herself, candidly, "Unattainable in the way of love.…" Four years separated from her husband and living a life that was neither that of wife, widow or spinster.… She had heard, though they had hardly impressed her, remarks that other women had made on such matrimonial conditions. It would no doubt have been possible for her to have found someone who would have given her all her husband did not… but such a design had not entered into her conception of life. It was possible for her to wither in the shade, not possible for her to thrust herself into the sunshine.

She went upstairs slowly. The carpets were thick under her feet… she could almost feel the dust and grime from the factory oozing from the thick pile… she could almost hear the thin voices of the servants complaining they "never knew such a house for dirt", and "where did all the soot come from?" as with open pans and soiled brooms they stirred the dust from one stair to another, from one curtain to another, beating it out of chairs and carpets until the whole of Stone Pynes was enveloped in dancing motes.

There was nothing in her room she liked. From the moment that John had refused permission for her to furnish it according to her own taste, she had acquiesced in the odious conventionalities of the people among whom she had married. She had ceased to regret her Virginian bedroom with the white walls and the muslin curtains that looked out on a stretch of lawn so like the lawn at Bagatelle, with the large broad-leafed maple and sycamore trees that, no matter how still the day, seemed always to be moving in an invisible wind and that towards the autumn changed to colours of the most brilliant gold, orange and scarlet; so did the trails of creeper across the classic portico with leaves that hung clear-cut as ruby coloured stones across the white front of her childhood's home.

But at least the bedroom was her own. John never entered it now to criticize or to sneer. He slept when he was at home (and she hardly knew when he was at home or not) in an adjoining closet which was entered by an alcove leading into her room. This alcove was draped and fitted with a bed, beyond which was a door the key of which was now never turned.

May sat down among all the furbelows and hangings. There was always something at Stone Pynes that required mending, cleaning, washing or renovating. On the floor was a quantity of the boxes she had brought with her from London—smooth, gleaming, white cardboard boxes prettily tied with coloured tapes. She found a pair of scissors lying by the heart-shaped blue-satin sawdust-stuffed pin cushion on the toilet table, and snipped these tapes and took out some of the now useless treasure she had brought from London, as a mermaid exiled from the sea and imprisoned in an inland town might turn over her corals, pearls, seaweeds and under-water flowers. Here were the roses of tinsel and braid, the fringed sashes and the long gloves of thin skin, with enamel buttons—some from wrist to elbow, that her mother had given her as bountiful, uncounted presents. Here were the hats of feathers and veils that had seemed so charming and appropriate to the scene when worn in a brougham driving round Hyde Park, but would soon be draggled and a cause for merriment if worn along Portland Street or George Street or Market Square.... Here was the guipure lace gown, and the other in purple colour that she had bought and was not likely to wear... and slippers to match, that she had never thought of, but that her mother had ordered as a matter of course... slippers from Paris, high in the instep, narrow in the toe, with paste buckles and high heels....

May put her forlorn trousseau into the wardrobe; she noticed on the upper shelf among the untidy medley of hats, muffs and gloves, the Bible in the azure blue velvet that her mother had bought on Louise's feast day in Paris when they had waited in the barouche at the windy street corner; for a moment she was tempted to take the holy book down and open it... it never had been opened... but it was beyond her reach, it would mean the effort of getting a chair.... She was ashamed, too, to touch something that had been so long untouched.... The blue velvet Bible remained with its clasps fastened.

She put the boxes, as was her fashion, half with the lids on, half with the lids off, with the papers tumbled and the trifles within disordered, into the large mahogany wardrobe that occupied half of the wall opposite the window, and that was in such ludicrous taste compared to the flimsy imitation French bed with lace valances and curtains. The dresses she hung up by the tapes inside the neck, noting the name "May Tyler" that Madame Clorinde had placed on a neat label within each. Yes she was *May Tyler*. She felt as empty as the dresses so labelled.... To-morrow she would have to go to Salford and see a woman named Dora who had four children, and who was really her husband's true wife....

She went down to dinner in a quiet dress such as she usually wore when there were no guests, and Dolly Hoey waited upon her. There was no respite from the steady flow of ill-cooked dishes, the thick greasy soup, the mess of cheese and cauliflower, the joint slightly burned and wholly unappetizing; the trifle that was sickly, odorous of the cheap sherry that had been offered to Jerome Thorne... and no savoury to-night because "the master wasn't at home" as Dolly remarked.... Then a few nuts and a few sweets handed in filigree dishes traced with a design in the worst of taste.

"Seeing the chocolates reminds me, ma'am," said Dolly, "Mr. Thorne left a parcel for you and it quite went out of my head to the present moment."

"Pray bring it up, Dolly."

May left the dining-room with the air heavy with the strong odours of cooking.

"Pray bring it to the drawing-room where I shall sit a little while."

She considered the girl coolly as before she had considered Nelly Tanner when she had lit the gas. The second parlourmaid was still young, but not comely. Her face had the same bleached look as had Nelly's. Her lips had a little more colour and pouted, but her air was sly, silly and lazy. All the servants, with all the movement they made and every word they said, seemed to insinuate that they were ill-paid and overworked and that this was not a gentleman's house, such as they had been accustomed to… that there ought to be a butler, and a boy for the silver, and there ought to be a brougham and a coachman and his wife who would help cook and do the housekeeping, perhaps living in one of the small ostentatious lodges with Gothic turrets and small dark rooms that stood at each of the entrances to Stone Pynes. These lodges were empty save for a few oddments of lumber; and a perpetual irritation to John Tyler, and a perpetual reproach to May. It seemed somehow her fault that the establishment was not on a more magnificent scale. If only she had been a little more careful.… If only she had known how to manage.… Eight years of lamentations and rebukes on these lines could not but ring in her head at a nervous moment.…

Dolly brought up the box and placed it gingerly on the table.

"Mr. Thorne brought it for you with his compliments. He said the master had sent it. I'm sorry, Madam, I forgot to bring it up to you before."

"Thank you, Dolly. It is no matter, I shall go to bed quite soon, then you may turn down the gas and all of you go to bed yourselves… and pray ask Cook to lock up the door of the silver-closet for your master is not home to-night and I am very tired.…"

When the maid had gone she allowed her thoughts to spring into action. Every nerve in her body was at a tension… a present… and from John.… Was it a bribe? Had he any idea of what Richard had gone to London to tell her? Did he think that any of her actions could be controlled by presents? Quite probably he understood her very little, and she was honest enough to admit that she did not understand him very well herself. There had always been a deep estrangement between them—but now this present, when he was lying thirty miles away, ill. Had he had some inkling from some spy of Richard's purpose? And what exactly was Richard's purpose?

*

May Tyler took the parcel upstairs. It was fastened almost as elegantly as those she had brought from London—much longer than wide, and addressed in a hand that was not that of her husband. But being ill he would get somebody to write it for him.... 'I suppose it is Thomas Chorley's...'

The scissors were out again in her small fingers that had always been so idle and yet which looked so capable in their exquisite proportion and delicate flexibility. The string was cut.... Again there was tissue paper rustling on the tawdry bed, on the thick dusty carpet.... Within was a large box of chocolates of the most expensive make, tied with a saffron-coloured ribbon... the sheen of the paper covering the box broken by a precise representation of a bouquet of yellow roses. Under the ribbons that matched these decorations was a visiting-card... not that of her husband... the name was Jerome Thorne.... He had written nothing on it and thereby had been the more expressive.

May, in her usual fashion, opened the box and looked at the chocolates lying in neat rows, carefully decorated—some with sparkling fragments of ginger on top, some with silver rondels, some with violet leaves and some with rose leaves.... She saw that the sweetmeats were the most costly possible kind, and sighed a little.

Was this, as she had supposed, a knight errant, and if so, in what way might he be used? In none, she thought almost instantly... and yet, if a woman beset as she was, wanted help, would it not be safer to ask this young man than to rely on Richard? Her brother, and yet bound to her by no tie of blood, and acting from a motive that she might suppose kind, but she could not be sure was not perhaps malicious.

She put the box, half open, in the wardrobe with the clothes she had brought from London. It was an enormous wardrobe that John liked to think had been used by his father, mother and by his grandparents before them, but which in reality he had bought second-hand at an auction sale, and that had been the property of a decayed family who had lived in a large house, now demolished, miles beyond the smoke of Manchester. It was so large that a little woman like May could have almost lived in it, and two or three average people could have hidden there for days. She did not like its forlorn, dark and ghostly look and the dresses hung there in a gloomy fashion like so many empty sacks or scarecrows suspended by the necks, for Nelly who unwillingly acted as maid to her mistress, would carelessly hang up her hats on the same hooks as the gowns and stick the shoes beneath so they seemed like so many inanimate figures.

Well, the key was turned on all of them—the chocolate box, the flowers of tinsel and braid, the long gloves with the enamelled fasteners and all the finery which she would find it difficult to wear.

May moved about the room softly. She had pulled the chain that jerked off the gas with a gurgling hiss, and lit the candle with an innate desire for the more beautiful light. The shadows seemed not to represent darkness, but rather the forms of protective phantoms. With her hands under her chin and her elbows on her knee, she sat in the gilt and plush chair at the foot of the bed, thinking—or what she called thinking.... Illusive pictures crossed her mind... a childhood that had been over so soon, almost like a whiff of perfume... her girlhood that she had almost missed altogether, there were only those visits to Paris, those visits to Rouen... interludes—so brief—in the convent at Passy... and then these eight years at Manchester... and she was getting old, a married woman, and some of her acquaintances told her she could no longer wear low dresses but should begin to put on caps.... And was that all there was in life? Nothing else at all...?

To-morrow there would be Salford and Dora.

III

INVALID'S POSY

FLOWERS OF ARSENIC

MAY TYLER, WITHOUT CONFUSION OF THOUGHT OR AGITAtion of movement, prepared to meet her brother-in-law at the place he had appointed, where it was easiest for them to cross the Irwell to Salford.

It was early afternoon, the air still and colourless, Richard had requested May to wear her "town finery", as he termed it, and she had gratified his wish, with that well-bred indifference that takes little notice of small personal matters. She did not any longer consider her appearance, nor that the dress was anything out of the way for Manchester, nor that it mattered a great deal if it should offend those neighbours who had already become extremely remote. It might be possible to escape them yet, not to have to care what their judgment was....

She recalled the image of Jerome Thorne with some satisfaction, as they passed by the Town Hall in Albert Square that had been only recently completed. A fine peal of bells was ringing in the clock tower; and May Tyler pictured the large organ and the columns of polished granite and gleaming marble, to her innumerable, that filled the tower. She had, when she had first come to the city, been indulged with a view of the bells as one of the sights of the place. She remembered each bore lines from Lord Tennyson's *In Memoriam*—lines written a long while ago now, but that she was constantly reading, as she read all the Poet Laureate's works, though she seldom spoke of them; and the thought of the bells and the legends they bore lifted her spirit from contemplation of the black streams that, bridged, tunnelled and built-over every few yards, came and went beneath her feet.

Jerome Thorne resembled one of the characters drawn by Tennyson, she was sure... the young man in *Aylmer's Field*, or perhaps one of the knights in the *Idylls of the King* with his golden look and his remote air; a man to whom women looked for help.

Richard guided her elbow; everything was dingy, and the echo of the bells was fading on the tainted air. May repeated one of the legends to herself:

> O life as futile, then, as frail!
> O for thy voice to soothe and bless!
> What hope of answer, or redress?
> Behind the veil, behind the veil.

She did not know what these words meant, but they seemed to hold out the expectation, the promise of something better than these dark and filthy streets.

"You're listening to the bells," whispered Richard Tyler; she considered it quick of him to have noticed in what direction her absorption lay.

His voice came muffled out of the collar of his upturned coat, the air was damp and foul, though May did not notice this and her companion had wound a scarf round his chin almost to his lower lip.

"You've seen, I think, all the sights of Manchester," and he began to tell her, as he had often told her before, of the amount of money that had been spent on the city, of the amount of money that had been made there, and how they had copies of some of the finest buildings of the ancient and modern worlds in solid stone adorned by massive carving. He informed her with pride that he could remember the opening of the new jail in Salford which took the place of that built according to the designs of John Howard, the prison reformer, who lay dead under arid grasses so far away from Manchester in a light as brilliant as this was dingy.

"There's City Jail too in Hyde Road," he remarked, "with accommodation for nearly a thousand people. You should visit it one day. I assure you, my dear girl, you will find there some amazing studies of human nature. I will take you if you wish—it is at the rear of the assize court."

'Curious conversation,' thought May, 'for a curious errand,' and the words of the poet, whose works were so often in her hands came into her withdrawn mind.

> The niggard throats of Manchester may bawl.
> What England was, shall her true sons forget?
> We are not cotton spinners all,
> But some love England and her honour yet.

Were there such people, *forgetful of honour*, honour as May dimly, and yet with unalterable firmness understood it? Ever since she had come to Manchester—to her Manchester was England since she had seen no other place—she had felt that everyone was acting from self-interest, from greed, from the lust of making money, of spending it ostentatiously, of flinging it away at the races and visits to London, where, she had heard in furtive whispers, much was spent in places like the Argyle Rooms on the cheapest of pleasures… flinging it away too on women who lived secretly with their children in Salford.

They had crossed the Irwell and the shadows darkened and changed about them, cutting the masonry and roadways into different shapes so that there was a confusion of what seemed natural in the day-time into what was odd and even fantastic.

"The dark seems to have come very early," said May.

Her brother-in-law replied that they had been walking much longer than she seemed to have realized and that the clouds had blown up suddenly from the Canal and were obscuring the last afterglow.

He then fell into his commonplace, almost vulgar talk, asking her if she had ever seen the Zoological Gardens, the Botanical Gardens or the Pomona Palace on a Bank Holiday.

"It is a sight to behold the industrious poor indulging themselves!"

This was all so remote to her that she did not answer, when Richard spoke like John he scarcely existed for her.

They were out in the Peel Park and the river that, black from the dye works ran like ink through the filthy city, was here a little clearer, though it still had a dun and urban air.

Richard Tyler remarked upon the half-seen statue of Queen Victoria. He said that he could remember his father talking of the great lady's visit to Manchester some thirty years before when she had been welcomed by a spectacular display—no less than eighty thousand Sunday School scholars gathered in the Peel Park had sung the National Anthem in her honour.

May glanced up at the statue muffled in shade that did not seem to her a representation of any possible human being. Other effigies, upright, dark, gloomy, were placed at intervals along the public ways of the park standing forlorn and haughty on their square plinths of granite.

"The Prince Consort, Richard Cobden and Robert Peel," announced Richard, directing a thick finger in a dogskin glove in the direction of each worthy.

May supposed he must be mocking and told him so, indifferently.

"You were desperately anxious for me to come on this errand. You journeyed to London on purpose to persuade me and since I have acquiesced and come with you, you have talked like a guide book...."

Richard's gross laugh came muffled but, as it seemed, gratified from behind his scarf.

"I am trying to get justice done to you, my dear May. You must please yourself as to what action you take, but I should recommend divorce."

"Would you? And why...? I am a Roman Catholic, you know."

"You have told me that before. For a woman of wit, you have been rather dull for the last few days. I don't think your religion hampers you very much, though I must say you have behaved yourself very well since you came to Manchester."

"Behaved myself," whispered May, speaking softly, moving so quickly through the shadows of the park that he had to lengthen his pace to keep step with her. "I don't understand what you mean—how is it possible not to behave oneself?"

"That's what I like in you. You couldn't be vulgar if you chose. You are so different to everybody here—you are so well-bred that you don't understand what good breeding is."

"I understand when people are vulgar, understand that one must endure the consequences of a mistake. I understand that I am very idle and useless and a poor wife to John.... My mother would be very pleased if I left him. I don't pretend I have an overwhelming love for the children. I sorrow over them very much, but what can I do...? They are taken from me and put in the charge of Lizzie Burt. They don't even look at me now.... I am never allowed to see them alone. I believe John thinks I have a bad influence over them."

"A bad influence...?" The man seemed ironical, amused. "I told you, you have behaved yourself in a way that no one would believe possible."

It was no affectation on her part to refuse to understand his meaning. To her he spoke in puzzles scarcely worth unravelling. She could only have answered as she had answered before, that she did not know any way of behaving beyond the way she had behaved. She knew nothing of what was in this man's mind, and in her husband's mind; nothing of the meaning of the purple-green dress she had worn when she had first sat at the head of John Tyler's showy table, nothing of those early incidents of the peacock and the peach. She had, as a woman of sense and spirit confronted with a crisis in her affairs, to endeavour to make up her mind how she should behave now. John's roaming fancy was an old story and one that had ceased much to interest her; but this woman with her family, and Richard as an ally and the chance of freedom, of being able to take the children with her (was it not correct that in a divorce case they gave the children to what was termed the "innocent" party?)—this was a prospect not lightly to be forgone. It came—even the slight glimmering hope of it—as a ray of light penetrating the underground cell of a prisoner suddenly admitted by a careless or indifferent hand pulling aside the shutter or lifting aside the cover from before a grille.

Richard's motives... well, they must be, as he had said, a sense of justice and desire for her peace of mind and comfort of body. She did not think him capable of malice or of wishing to do his brother harm. They seemed to agree very well together, both in business and pleasure; but though she forced herself to consider Richard in the best possible light, and as her likely liberator, the image of the man who should rescue her persistently took on the knightly outline of Jerome Thorne.

Richard rang the bell at a modest, drab house, situated inconveniently at the corner of a street. May was instantly reminded of the shop where her mother had bought the Bible bound in blue velvet on the day of Louise's festival, a shop at a corner, with a slight wind blowing low along the ground then as now, but there, unwholesome as July in Paris was, fresh with the perfume from tresses of laburnum and hawthorn.

A maid, indifferently clean as May noted, admitted them into the narrow passage of the house that was lined with brown wallpaper heavily glazed and the colour of tobacco. The stairs were narrow and mean, covered with a brown linoleum on which was printed a key pattern in rubbed white. The banisters were cheaply designed and cheaply painted pitch pine; the inevitable smell of English cities, that of badly cooked food, hung about the passage and stairway but all was, according to the standards of the place, clean. There was a rack and a stand and pegs for coats in the hall. On one of these hung a dark masculine garment; May drew away from what might be John's coat. Although she knew he was ill in the hotel at Wirral, she felt a sudden nausea lest she might walk in upon him upstairs.

Richard, with a fineness she had not credited him with, understood her agitation—the first she had shown since he had given her this news.

"We're safe from any intrusion," he remarked. "Dora is alone."

"What does she name herself?" asked May, mounting the cramped distasteful stairs. "I cannot name her Dora, you know, unless we like one another...."

"She calls herself," replied Richard in a very low, almost choked voice, "Mrs. Lestrange; I told you, I think. They always do, you know," he added, "give themselves a fancy handle. I daresay when she next moves—or any minute, if it suited her—she'd call herself Lady Lestrange. She's too well-known in this neighbourhood...."

"Who do people think she is?" asked May, pausing on the first landing. "Has she no relatives, nor friends... and don't the neighbours ask about her husband?"

Richard's heavy figure paused immobile for a moment by her side.

"Dora belongs to a world where this sort of deceit is nicely contrived, and one that you, my dear girl, know nothing about yet."

He rapped with his knuckles on the door in front of him, the maid, who seemed to serve for the entire house, had disappeared into the basement. A thin voice shouted nervously, "Come in."

Richard turned the handle and May, without a falter, entered the room, looking among that tasteless furniture and meaningless ornamentation like an aristocrat sleek and beautiful, neat and orderly from quite another society than that to which this room belonged.

The woman who named herself Dora Lestrange had risen from a small sofa of black horsehair on which were piled several gaudy cushions of ruffled and pleated silk and velvet, all arranged without symmetry or colour.

The two women said "How do you do" and in a second had appraised one another. Dora Lestrange was a woman of thirty-five or so, not wearing, as May in her ignorance had expected, some flaming garments only possible to open shame, nor displaying in her person any brazen effrontery, any flamboyant defiance of the good opinion of the world, but rather a meek creature with a harmless face; her features were regular and her hair, though without gloss or curl, was becomingly banded on a well-shaped head. She wore a merino gown, well-made and fitting, of an unbecoming green colour and swung nervously at her throat a long tassel from the centre of which depended among the scarlet threads of floss silk a long amber bead.

Looking at May with flickering glance, she saw before her a woman who to her was as brilliant as the fashion-plates that she often idly gazed at in the London or Parisian magazines.... May, with her modish gown, her grape-coloured jacket, her sombre-hued tartan skirt, her cedar-coloured hair brushed into curls on which rested the hat with the velvet cherries.... May with her clear eyes and complexion, and her bloom of luxurious youth and well-being that gave her almost the unnatural brilliancy of a wax model in a modiste's or a hairdresser's window....

"I don't know why I have been brought to see you, Mrs. Lestrange. Richard will tell us both."

"You may sit down," replied the other woman, "if you please, both of you. I have been expecting this."

"I was ignorant of it," replied May, seating herself out of courtesy though she would have preferred to remain standing, "until Richard came to London to tell me."

Dora Lestrange asked, "Does John know anything about it?"

Odd, thought May, to hear her husband's name thus familiar on a stranger's lip and yet she knew how often it must have been thus used by many women during her married life, women she had never known.

Richard put in, "No, John doesn't know. He's sick at Wirral, after the races...."

"It is that white stuff he takes," said Dora uneasily. "He brings it here and takes it before—a good while before his tea, and before those foods in tins he brings. He doses and cossets himself too much—"

"The white powders!" exclaimed May quickly. "You've noticed it too, then? I have been speaking to Richard about it, I'm sure it's dangerous."

"He says," replied Dora, "he takes it because it keeps off the malaria. I don't think it does him any good. I don't know where he gets it—"

"The fact that he does get it," put in Richard brusquely, "shows that it's not harmful. I've told you on several occasions that John knows how to doctor himself. You ladies are always the same—you keep your mind on the trivial matters that are not of any importance."

"Why were you expecting I should come, Mrs. Lestrange?" asked May Tyler. "Of course you have known all about me for a long time, and I have known nothing about you until a few days ago.... And then what did I know...? Of your existence only."

Dora replied with a stumbling haste.

"I don't know anything about you, except that you live in a grand house and live a smart life and have got all you want as I suppose—money of your own and John's as well—"

"Come, come," put in Richard. "You've had your share of that, Dora. He keeps you very comfortably here, for a woman of your sort, and intends to give the children a good education. He might easily resent that, you know, and feel it a strain on his resources. John's not a wealthy man, my dear girl."

May glanced at him. This was the same term as he had used with her. His way with women seemed to her indescribably vulgar.

"He doesn't make the money he used to—that's why I've been working so hard at this ramie grass product. There's a great deal of competition to be faced nowadays," he continued.

Dora interrupted. "Have you both come to tell me my allowance is to be cut down?"

"No, we haven't. I just wanted May—Mrs. Tyler, to meet you, to make quite sure you were here. You see, she might decide to divorce John...."

An expression that May could quite well read, of a long hidden secret hope kindled and joy at the wild chance of possible marriage with her lover, crossed Dora's gentle face.

"But he couldn't divorce her just because of me, could he?"

"I'm afraid not," said Richard brusquely, "but there is very little else needed. He has to be cruel you know—a blow, for instance, in front of witnesses..."

May was silent. She rose and remained erect, looking away from both of them.

Dora spoke hurriedly, as if in shame.

"Oh, you mustn't think like that, Mr. Tyler, if you please. John wouldn't do such a thing—I know he wouldn't—and I'm sure he respects his wife."

May turned at that. "Why shouldn't he respect you, Mrs. Lestrange? You must have known him longer than I have—perhaps you loved him—and I couldn't say as much for myself. I don't know how it happened, my marriage. I was eighteen only and had my head full of fancies. Why didn't he marry you?" she asked with a directness that took away all offence from the question and gave it instead an air of sympathy.

"I was nothing," replied Dora with a painful flush. "I am nothing now. I met him in the flower shop where he used to come and buy posies for his ladies, and he took a whim to me and there was no one to look after him, and I thought he was—"

"Like a Roman Emperor, I suppose?" interrupted May.

"Well, I suppose that was it, something in a play. There was no one to look after me either.... I've had nothing to complain of," added Dora quickly. "Of course I know that he's not true—to either of us," she added. "He spends his money on sluts and trash. He doesn't listen to good advice.... Still, I've got the children. They're like him, and fond of him, and they're to have a chance in the world if there's no scandal. He says he knows how to put them to good schools and have them properly looked after. Two of them are away already—the boy's being taught in Liverpool. He's friends there and knows how to put up a story. The other two, the girls, are here with me. You wouldn't like to see them, of course?"

"No," said May. "I don't care to see my own. They are quite taken from me. No, I shouldn't care to see your children who, as I suppose, are very happy with you... and it's not my duty to do so. Tell me," she turned and smiled at Dora Lestrange, "does he—does John ever speak of me to you?"

"Oh, he wouldn't have the bad taste I am sure," replied Dora uneasily. "He only says of you that you're proud, and a foreigner and put yourself up above all his friends and set—Mr. Richard will say as much too—beyond that, why I'm sure..." She was obviously hesitating whether she should say "Mrs. Tyler" or even "Madam" but reserved her independence by continuing, "I am sure everyone respects you. It couldn't have been so easy to have been married to John for over eight years and never to make a false step."

This was an unknown language to May Tyler, as had been her brother-in-law's talk of good breeding. What false step was she then, even admitting that she was an alien and slighted wife, supposed to make?

"I see you don't take my meaning," added Dora humbly. "You're just the kind of woman I supposed you would be. I saw you once when I came over to Manchester to shop… you were on foot like I was—coming out of the chemist's with some poppy heads in your hand. You didn't see me at all I think, or anyone else…."

"One tries to forget what one sees in Manchester," replied May, "but I should have noticed you had my glance been turned in your direction… you're different from the others…. Do you think," she said, in the same kind, level tone, "that if I divorced him he would marry you?"

Richard was silent. Neither of the women were disengaged enough from their own thoughts to notice his cynical, sideway glance at Dora.

"I think he might," replied John's mistress with an eager boldness, touching for May to behold. "Don't you think he might? He promised to marry me once, and in his way he has been faithful to me… always coming here and looking after me and the children and telling me his troubles that I don't understand, about his business and the accounts—"

"The extravagant way I run his home and my foreign mother and my extravagant maid—and the money I spend on clothes and how I never keep the servants, and how I am never cordial enough to his friends…. Does he complain to you of these things?" asked May Tyler.

"I wouldn't say," replied the other uneasily. "You know what a grumbling man is… they just complain at anything…"

"But you'd marry him if I were to set him free—if he were to set me free…? I do not know how the terms go in this country, one would have to see a lawyer—"

"That could easily be arranged," put in Richard quietly.

"I think he might," answered Dora with childish hope. She pulled at the amber bead on the tassel of pink silk… a tawdry ornament… (May was sure John had given it to her) valueless too—and yet it must cost something to keep up even this meagre establishment and feed, educate and clothe four children.

"You ought to have married him," she said, with the air of one announcing a long considered decision. "You would have pleased his friends much better than I have. You would have kept his house better—and I daresay your children would never have been shut up in a nursery at the top of the house with a servant over them, so that they never even glance at you when you go to see them...."

"No," said Dora warmly. "I have looked after my children myself. I have only a little servant girl to help me. They're quite strong and healthy, all of them, and fond of me. He never interferes with them.... He's fond of them too...."

"I don't want to see them!" protested May, "even though you have them in the next room. Pray oblige me in this. And now..." she moved towards the door, "I don't see that there is anything more to say. Richard desired me to be assured of your existence. I couldn't have done anything without that. I must now act for myself."

"What will you do?" demanded the other woman, moving closer to her visitor.

She was animated, not only by her new wild hope, but by the eager curiosity as to human affairs and the love of melodrama that animates so many weak natures who live dull and lonely lives.

"I don't know what I'll do. I've been in the shallows for years now, and shall have to think and get advice. It seems to me, if John could marry you after all, and I could go away with my mother and live abroad, or in Virginia again, it would be the happiest thing for all of us...."

She said good-bye courteously, but did not hold out her hand, nor did Dora Lestrange offer hers, but turned aside to set straight a white vase painted with roses.

They came down the stairs again, the man and the woman, silently; she walking ahead, as there was not room for two of them on a tread. The gas on the small landing had been lit and the acrid flame shone through the dirty glass of the globe. They were out in the street again, and here everything had been changed with the lighting of the lamps at long intervals in the darkness that was now almost complete. The humid atmosphere caused these gas jets to throw out a luminous ring, a heavy rainbow round their glowing centre. The wind was colder, but May did not shiver.

Richard took her arm to guide her through the strange streets, across the rough places. His mood seemed exalted. He was pleased indeed with the interview... both women had behaved so well. He had always admired Dora's correct demeanour in her incorrect position, and he felt a definite pleasure in the now sure knowledge that May Tyler was, as he had always guessed, a woman who, under no circumstances whatever, would, in his own phraseology, "make a scene". She was indeed a treasure and a delight. A man could feel secure with her; there was a great deal, after all, in good breeding—as much as there was in money-making. Where she had obtained this extraordinary possession he did not know, but he knew that he valued it very highly as John had once valued all that was represented by the trapped peacock and the netted peaches. His better qualities admired her as did his baser, there was courage here and gallantry that appealed to the Englishman's standards of reserve and fortitude.

He took her arm familiarly as they turned across Salford Park again.

"If you don't care to divorce him," he whispered, bending down so that his face was close to her ear, "remember you can get a separation and a settlement and be free."

John Tyler received a business visitor in his offices in Exchange Street. The building was handsome according to the taste of Manchester; so heavy that it appeared ready to sink into the ground by its own weight, and the interior of the Tyler offices, according to the same standard, had been handsome also. They had been somewhat neglected of late. The dust had been but patchily removed from window-sills and bookshelves. The leather of the large comfortable chairs lacked polish, save that given by the occupants. The monstrous iron fireplace was unblackleaded and there were a number of miscellaneous articles about that showed untidiness and lack of taste. Two men's overcoats on a peg, three men's scarves over a chair... on the massive desk a number of incongruous objects, together with all the impedimenta for writing—glass ink-pots, standishes and pen cases, all now stained with ink and soiled....

Among this confusion of trifles was a photograph of a woman wearing a hat with a feather pinned unbecomingly, almost upright... a large, clumsily cut silver bracelet with an oriental design... boxes of cigars... boxes of lucifer matches, and several piles of paper loosely pinned together....

John Tyler appeared the orthodox business man in his frock-coat, his glossy tie, his highly starched linen, with his pallid face, regular features and the smooth dark hair so precisely brushed back, in which as yet no grey showed. He was not much heavier than he had been when he had first met May Beale in Paris, the corpulency of late middle age was softened, if not disguised, by his ponderous clothing, and his stately air. By his gross, plump, white hand, that rested amid the dusty confusion of the ornate desk, stood a jug in two shades of brown earthenware, heavily and coarsely embossed with a design of vines and grapes.

His visitor, on whom none of this interior, nor the occupant made much impression, was a much younger man, earnestly engaged on his task—one Joseph Tarrant, of better birth, better manners, more attractive appearance than John Tyler, now wholeheartedly engaged in soliciting the favours of the cotton merchant.

Mr. Tarrant had an open case before him in which were several labelled packets, and he was explaining with diligent patience how he had before at several interviews made clear to Mr. Richard Tyler the nature of the secret he desired to sell—a process by which rheagrass, sometimes called ramie, could be used as a cheap substitute for cotton.

As he proceeded with his well-informed account of this money-making discovery, going thoroughly into all technical details, Mr. Tyler listened in silence, occasionally stubbing the end of a pencil, the cover of which was plain cedar the hue of May's hair, into a pad of blotting paper. Joseph Tarrant, alert and anxious for the business deal, was secretly worried and impatient at the other man's pompous silence.

'I have explained it all to his brother,' he thought. 'Why must I go over it again? Surely the fellow should know by now whether or not he wants the stuff.'

But Mr. Tyler seemed in no way disposed to make up his mind. He put in a few casual objections to the scheme that Mr. Tarrant quickly disposed of, reminding the cotton merchant of the many brilliant discoveries that had made the fortunes of those who had put them on the market, and instancing in particular the discovery of aniline dyes by William Perkins and the sensation that the discovery of the colour mauve had made both in the fashionable and the business world.

"You've not got anything like that there," replied Mr. Tyler, still keeping his regular and rounded profile towards his visitor. "Richard, my brother, made me tolerably well acquainted with your proposal, but it will require a good deal of capital—and that's not so easy to come by these days. . . ."

Mr. Tarrant was braced to meet the opposition of the commonplace, the timid and the dull-witted; he smiled in a way that he tried not to make too indulgent, and then waited, in an effective pause, for Mr. Tyler's decision.

That personage took out his watch, considered it, pursed up his lips and muttered something about another appointment, but Mr. Tarrant was firm. He said that there were other people interested in the project of ramie grass and that it would not be to the benefit of either of them to waste more time in a discussion where Mr. Tyler seemed to take so doubtful a part.

"What have *you* been doing all your life?" asked the merchant with a sudden attempt at easiness. "New to Manchester, aren't you?"

"Yes, I come from London. I have been studying commercial chemistry. When I came into my fortune (I have some estates in Scotland) I went into partnership with a man who was making paraffin wax for candles. We didn't do very much… it was successful… our candles had a peculiar gloss, but the process was too expensive."

"What did you use to give this gloss?" asked Mr. Tyler, still looking away. "Richard said something about it to me, but I declare I've forgotten."

"Arsenic," replied Mr. Tarrant.

"Arsenic.… Now how did you get that?"

"Oh, it's easy enough to get if you are a wholesale manufacturer. You see, as chemists we could buy anything we wanted in that way.… Our arsenic was obtained from iron ore… we made it ourselves."

"That must have been an interesting process." The face that had appeared so like a profile on a Roman coin turned and looked out of blank dark eyes at the younger man.

The chemist, with professional enthusiasm, was not reluctant to explain briefly how he had very cheaply manufactured arsenic out of the iron ore. At first it had come in small particles like stained glass, but afterwards changed to white, stained with a pinkish yellow. "Then we heated it in an earthen vessel filled with cold water that reduced it to powder, and afterwards to vapour, which we condensed at the bottom of a cold glass vessel. When we scraped it off it was pure crystals, it looked like ivory dust but slightly more yellow."

"You didn't have to mix it with charcoal?" asked Mr. Tyler, "like they say you do when you buy it retail from a chemist's?"

"No, when we used it for the candles we put charcoal in it, but that was because it improved the polish it gave to the wax. I used arsenic also in my next employment, making isinglass and gelatine from bones.

There we mixed soot with the arsenic, but again, because of the process it was too expensive." Mr. Tarrant was explicit and brief, keeping his eyes meanwhile on the long packets in his case. It contained the results of his experiments, samples of ramie grass and descriptions of what the cotton made from it would be like.

"You've done some different kinds of work in your time," remarked Mr. Tyler. "Arsenic twice, that's odd."

"I never took much notice of it one way or another. A chemist doesn't, you know. I went from glue taken from bones to fish manure, but I found the smell unendurable, and since then my partner and I have taken up this ramie grass discovery. Now, sir, here I am at your disposal. Can I persuade you to put this on the market as a substitute for cotton?"

Mr. Tyler still sat immovable.

"I suppose," he remarked, "I must not pry into trade secrets and ask exactly how you obtain this substitute for cotton? Why, the very expression sounds like a miracle, doesn't it—substitute for cotton after all these years!"

"Well, there's substitutes for everything I suppose," said the young man. He undid one of the packets in his case and took out a length of material, the colour of lilac sprigged with flowers of the same hue but darker. "We made this ourselves. We thought it worth while to go to the expense of the plant."

The large white hand came out and fingered the stuff. "It looks good, stout and as glossy as those candles you were talking about."

"That's the arsenic," explained Mr. Tarrant indifferently. "I prepared all those myself from my laboratories. I took over the chemicals from my first partner. We have a good store."

"A good store," repeated Mr. Tyler. "Well, I would like you to tell me just how much you use. It's not a question of trying to steal your patent—I suppose you've got the thing patented by now—but if I took this scheme up I might be able to buy the stuff cheaper in Manchester.

Besides, I've got to cost the thing—add up, you know, how much it will mean to market it."

Mr. Tarrant obligingly had all the figures ready and produced them; but Mr. Tyler seemed to take but little notice of this piece of paper so precisely laid on his desk. He turned instead to the brown jug, looked into it, produced a dusty spoon from beneath a pile of accounts and stirred the contents of the jug.

"My luncheon," he remarked. "I have not been at all well since an odd attack I had at the Wirral Races. I live on these slops. My wife prepares this every morning for me."

He took several spoonfuls of some thick, yellowish liquid that appeared to Joseph Tarrant so utterly distasteful that he instinctively glanced away. It would have been impossible for him to say why he found so abhorrent this picture of the heavy business man in his correct attire feeding himself out of the jug of two dingy shades of brown with, as he himself termed them—slops.

"I think I might take it up," said Mr. Tyler, when he had slowly wiped his mouth with a large silk handkerchief. "Why not? I don't disguise that I'm not making the money I used to. I have a very extravagant wife and an expensive establishment to keep up."

'Put it in the plural,' thought Mr. Tarrant with cold impatience. Aloud he remarked, "I do not feel that I can tell you anything more, Mr. Tyler. I think the subject is exhausted."

"By no means exhausted," said the merchant with a sudden gleam of energy. "Come, I'll make a bargain with you."

Mr. Tarrant stiffened slightly. He did not like this part of his work. Indeed he did not consider it part of his work, which was, properly, in the laboratory or supervising experiments in the workshops... but as he had a pleasing address and a contagious enthusiasm, his partner had persuaded him to the task of trying to convince a cotton merchant and a cotton broker of the excellency of this discovery.

"It's a business matter," he said with some dryness.

"But suppose," replied Mr. Tyler, taking more spoonfuls of the liquid that looked and smelt like biscuit crushed in milk, "I like to make it a bargain? I'm always one for a gamble. That suits me...."

Mr. Tarrant thought that it did not suit him. He had been working hard all his life without ever playing a game of hazard or chance. All his money was in this, the third commercial enterprise in which he had been engaged. He had heard some stories of John Tyler. His morals were no concern of those who had business with him; but if he were a reckless gambler, was the scheme safe with him?

Mr. Tarrant's bright eyes glanced round the office. There were signs of stability there. His furnishings must have cost something... there were two clerks in the outer office and he had watched while he had been waiting for his interview, a number of people going to and fro. The day before—it had been a Tuesday—he had seen Mr. Tyler and his brother under the vast roof of the Exchange, closely engaged in conference with spinners, printers and bleachers. The two, who had stood under that vast dome, had seemed energetic, shrewd business men and Mr. Tarrant had noted that they had been greeted with respect and consideration by a number of rivals and colleagues. It was therefore, being too prudent, as stupid a fault in Mr. Tarrant's well-balanced mind, as being too extravagant, to wonder if the precious secret was being entrusted to a wastrel or a spendthrift. Mr. Tyler had repeated, however, the word "bargain" and added that he did not care for "any hard and fast rules".

Mr. Tarrant waited. He had in all honesty laid his cards upon the table. He had also, in all honesty, stated his case and his genuine opinion of the merits of the ware he was trying to market. There was nothing more for him to do. He sat erect on the hard heavy chair, his case, his top hat and cane on the floor beside him. The dull-faced clerks had not offered to relieve him of any of these burdens and he would under any circumstances have wished to carry his specimens into the inner office. The atmosphere of the place and the personality of the cotton merchant were alike distasteful to the young man and he wished that the interview was over.

'An odious class,' he mused. 'No training, no thought of anything but making money from other people's exertions. What does he know, what could he do… uneducated, without any knowledge of anything worth knowing… vulgar and gross, and yet with that air of'—a usual simile that was applied to John Tyler slipped easily into Joseph Tarrant's mind—'a Roman Emperor on one of those antique busts. Yet I suppose in the labour market he wouldn't be worth twenty shillings a week. I wouldn't employ him as the least of my workmen, nor allow him to set a foot in my laboratories.… No idea of spending money either… the races and drink and a little gambling…'

Still he waited; a shade of scorn trembling on his lip. It was always thus—skill and industry, knowledge and enthusiasm had to wait—hat in hand or lying on the ground beside a worshipper in the temple of Mammon—and wait Mr. Tarrant did until this tall and heavy man chose to speak.

When Mr. Tyler did open his thick lips, his words were indeed different from anything Mr. Tarrant, who thought he was prepared for any possibilities, expected.

"How much arsenic have you got?"

Mr. Tarrant was silent while Mr. Tyler continued in a monotonous tone, as if he were reading aloud from a book that did not interest him.

"There's some difficulty in getting it here. Of course the chemists will supply it, but not in any great quantities."

"I've no licence to sell drugs."

"I don't suggest selling," replied Mr. Tyler with a duller monotony. "I said, didn't I, a bargain? How much have you got with you now?"

"I brought some with me as a sample of the ingredients needed. I want to sell the project for making the cotton, not to manufacture it. I've used all I need of the stuff in getting this sample made... I suppose I've 150 grains." He brought out three packets in stout white paper from his valise and laid them on the corner of the desk. "One of these is the white, or the ivory-dust I told you of—the others are the black arsenic, as we term them; one mixed with soot, the other with charcoal."

"You're willing to part with it?" asked John Tyler, looking straight over his visitor's head at the large square of dirty window pane against which a few flies buzzed.

"I told you, I use it only for experiments. I've had some by me since we were making the paraffin wax for the candles."

"It gives," remarked Mr. Tyler, "not only a polish to wax but a becoming pallor to the countenance. Ladies use it, I believe, as a face-wash."

Mr. Tarrant was not interested. He looked at the three packets of arsenic and asked, "What's the bargain?"

"That you give me the arsenic and that I market your ramie grass for you. The terms you can draw up afterwards. I shan't quarrel with them."

Mr. Tarrant cast down his glance. Besides themselves there was a third entity in the dun coloured and dingy office, that was not by any means agreeable to the young man, now there was no longer anything commonplace in these drab surroundings.

Mr. Tyler continued in his even tone, stirring the contents of the earthenware jug beside him.

"I took it first for malaria in Virginia, a little of it wards off an attack. Besides, I find that whenever I'm depressed it enlivens me at once. You've read De Quincey, I suppose?"

"Yes," replied Mr. Tarrant, "and often wondered if he could have taken as much as 900 drops of laudanum in a day."

Mr. Tyler replied with heavy dryness. "One man's meat is another man's poison—and certainly this poison is like the rarest liqueur to me. I cannot explain to you the effect it has. Indeed, it's impossible for me to live without it; of course I don't tell everybody and I wouldn't have told you, except that Richard mentioned you used arsenic."

"You wouldn't have seen me otherwise, I suppose? So that was the attraction, was it?"

"I didn't say so." Mr. Tyler was grinning ludicrously. "Come, what do *you* say? You won't get that stuff marketed very easily, you know. Though I'm not rich, as I say, and I'm saddled, as I told you, with a wife who throws the money away, still I'm sound enough, and you'll find you've done a good day's business. I'll do my best for you, you can be sure of that." He added, "Is that all the arsenic you've got?"

"It's enough to poison everybody in this street," replied Mr. Tarrant shortly.

"Well, it will do for a while. The doctors won't give it me. They're fools, you know, they never understand what's good for a man; all I can get out of them is a trifle now and then in my medicine that only tantalizes me."

"You take a good deal of medicine I suppose, Mr. Tyler, and yet you appear a strong and healthy man."

"I've always looked after myself," said the merchant with some pride. "I have my own medicine chest and make up my own prescriptions when I can get the ingredients. Did you ever hear of the peasants in Styria who take arsenic and thrive on it and live to an excellent old age?"

Mr. Tarrant shook his head while the other chuckled.

"I have no difficulty," he added, "in getting it in Virginia. There was an old sea captain there who always had a good supply and a lady whom I knew pretty well, Miss Kitty Minton, used to get it for me."

Mr. Tarrant rose. "Very well, you may have the arsenic. It's your responsibility, not mine. You appear to know a great deal more about it than I do. Be careful of the packet of white crystals, it can be so easily substituted for something harmless."

"I shall take care of all of it," replied Mr. Tyler rising also, with that faint, slightly tremulous smile on his full lips which appeared to bear no relation to anything amusing, that was not ironic or bitter but merely a slight quiver of the muscles. "I'll take precautions of course." He picked up the pencil in the cedar case. "Which is your packet of the white stuff?"

"This," replied Mr. Tarrant, consulting some minute figures in the corner of that packet nearest to him.

Mr. Tyler wrote on it "For cats" and then laughed in the same meaningless way as he had smiled.

Mr. Tarrant thought this extremely childish, also possibly, dangerous behaviour. He did not know whether or not he was doing an illegal thing in letting this man have so much poison, but if the fellow took the responsibility and had been living on the stuff for years, and he did not sell the drug but merely gave it—well, he supposed it was all in the way of business.

The merchant slipped the three packages into the pocket of his frock-coat and then wrote out in a laborious and careful hand, an acceptance in his own name of the responsibility of marketing the ramie grass product on terms that were to be hereafter discussed between himself and Mr. Tarrant, representing the firm of Tarrant & Glaister.

"You industrious fellows who work so hard with your glue factories and your candle factories and manure works, deserve a little reward." The large white hand came down heavily on Joseph Tarrant's straight shoulders. "Here's your letter—that's my acceptance. Your partner will be pleased. Would you care to come home with me to Stone Pynes? There will be something to eat and something to drink, though I'm on a diet and May—that's my wife—is one of those gad-abouts who always likes new dishes and lets the cook spoil 'em."

"I'm much obliged," said Mr. Tarrant, putting the letter carefully in his pocket book, "but I've a train to catch. I promised to return to London to-day and make my report."

"You must come to Manchester again, when your partner has decided what he wants. I shan't quarrel about terms, I've told you that. I can make the cotton substitute and Richard can sell it."

"You seem to care very little, Mr. Tyler, about costing and profits, though you mentioned just now your doubts as to the price of the raw materials."

"Did I? I was thinking of something else. I've no doubt we will make our profits all right." He turned to the soiled window where flies and gnats buzzed, and flapped the white handkerchief with which he had wiped his lips at the swarm of buzzing insects. "Mayflies," he murmured, "some of 'em. Don't live a day, but while they do I think they can sting...."

Mr. Tarrant remembered that part of this word, Mayfly, in itself of such ambiguous meaning, was the name of the merchant's wife and he took a sidelong glance at the ostentatious woman with the tilted hat who smiled so complacently from the gleaming surface of the cabinet photograph.

"Taken by the new electric light," observed Mr. Tyler of this portrait as he moved towards the door to open it for his visitor. "Good, eh, don't you think...? Lively... a pick-me-up in itself."

Mr. Tarrant had no reply, bowed, hat cane and case in his right hand.

In the outer room, Mr. Tyler's two employees, Peter Aitken and Timothy Young, glanced up quickly, and quickly glanced down again. Seated on high stools they were curved over their desks with an air of such absorption in their ledgers that they appeared to blend with the nondescript colour of the room. Joseph Tarrant noted that both were of unwholesome appearance with complexions like suet and wearing steel rimmed spectacles. He bowed himself out, not wholly with satisfaction.

'Enough to poison the whole street.... Well, I suppose that fellow's used to looking after the stuff and after himself and I don't think that if he was to take an overdose there are many who would mourn him.... So that was it all the time.... We poor humans get some surprises one from another.... That was it....' Joseph Tarrant repeated to himself as he steadied himself and his top hat against a squall of fine rain that fell through the dirty smoke of Manchester. 'Not the money, not the new invention, not anything at all... the arsenic.... I wonder how he's been getting it so far... since the Poisons' Act it's been very difficult.... He didn't want opium or hashish or laudanum.... Arsenic.... What did he mean about his Styrian peasants...?'

Mr. Tarrant picked his way neatly towards the station, passing the mighty Exchange that seemed the temple of all the money-makers in England, massive and gloomy public buildings, pressing lightly in and out of the crowd the same colour as the smoke through which they moved, and arrived with some time to wait at the London Road railway station.

He could easily have taken a later train; he could easily have stayed the night if the other man had offered him hospitality, but he had no desire to dine with John Tyler, to drink his wine, to listen to his conversation, nor even to meet his wife, the extravagant gad-about who had been likened to the mayfly dashed out of existence by Mr. Tyler's large, heavy silk handkerchief stained by the thick farinaceous food from the brown jug.

When his train came in, he stepped briskly into a first-class carriage and extended himself with a sigh of one released from an unpleasant duty on the plush-coloured seat.

'I wonder,' he mused idly, 'what she's like, married to a man like that.' Then he tapped the pocket where he had the merchant's acceptance of the ramie project and thought no more either of John Tyler or May his wife.

As soon as John Tyler was alone in the office, he opened the packet of white arsenic on which he had written "For cats" and after finding with some difficulty a small spoon among the confusion on his desk, he ate a liberal portion of the crystals, cleaned the spoon by passing a lighted match over it, then sat back. For a while he indulged himself by considering the promised delight; then, exactly half an hour after he had taken the powder, dipped the larger spoon into the brown jug, and slowly fed himself with the patent mixture. How alarmed, and perhaps disgusted, that neat Londoner had seemed underneath his careful manners, at the suggestion that anyone should eat arsenic! "As if it wasn't the finest tonic in the world," said John Tyler, speaking aloud, but in a muttering kind of way. "Why, it makes a man of me and anyone but a fool would know it and try it too."

He regretted Virginia where there had been no such difficulties and where Katie Minton, with whom he had lived privately before his marriage, had enabled him to obtain a constant supply. Then it had been easier a few years ago when old Johnstone had slipped a packet in those parcels that he sent off regularly from Joshua and Blunt, containing the various medicines with which John Tyler doctored himself. Now the old fool had become cautious.... What was the need of caution... nobody ever touched the packets but himself... nobody suspected anything.... May had her guesses, but she was on the wrong track. She thought he took strychnine. Richard was half in the dark at least or pretended to be; no one knew... one white powder looked much the same as another....

As the heavy man sat still in the heavy office chair he closed his eyes and felt a new vigour flowing through his veins. The cramps, pains and stiffnesses with which he had been afflicted since the chill he had caught at Wirral Race Course, vanished. He smiled, and his easy state of body passed into easy dreams. His financial affairs that had been bothering him, no longer seemed formidable. The ramie grass, apart from the great advantage he had obtained in the gift of arsenic, might well prove a paying investment. Glossy it would be... arsenic gave a gloss to paraffin candles, to this cotton substitute, to his own smooth sleek hair.... He opened his eyes suddenly in order to gaze with satisfaction at a plain square mirror hanging on the opposite wall where he might see a reflection of his own face. People had often remarked on his clear and white complexion, without remotely guessing the cause. He was proud of that and fingered his firm bluish chin with fat white fingers reflectively. He showed little signs of his age, he was sure of that; he had always been stout and heavy, but he had inches to carry off his bulk. Many women apart from the submissive and infatuated Dora, thought him handsome; a handsome man with regular features.... That is how he would be described.... As the drug spread its glow further over his body that had been feeling aching and flabby, he reflected, as a man will in moments of drowsy ease, on the past. He had been a successful man, that is according to his own standards. He had made a good deal of money... he had spent and wasted a good deal of money.... He had Stone Pynes, a house not as fine as it might be, in a suburb not as select as it might be, but still a place very different from anything in which his forebears had ever lived. A residence smeared within and without with the false gentility of Manchester. He could go to the races and put on his money, if not with the best, at least with the second best of them—with people like the Chorleys, good humoured, jolly people with whom one could speak one's mind and needn't mince one's words.... He had achieved servants and a saddle-horse, a garden and a gardener.... He was asked to visit houses better run, better furnished, that cost a good deal more to keep up than his own... at once a compliment and an irritation. In any way of looking at it, a sign of success. He had May... he had left her to the last of his meditations deliberately.... May was not to be classed with anything else in his life. To deal with her, his slow mind had to go back to the only vivid images that his childhood had left him... the peaches that he had robbed from the scornful gardener, the peacock floundering in the strawberry nets.... He had wanted May in just the same way as he had wanted the guarded fruit and the exotic bird... and he had had her too, and kept her in Manchester, set in his house to play the wife, the hostess and the mother....

To play was the right word, though John Tyler had found it unconsciously. It was almost unconsciously also that he was aware that May was playing, and always had been playing a part. She was as alien to him and his surroundings as if she had been a Spaniard or a Congo negress. In common with most English people he forgot that the common language does not make the common heritage, and though May spoke (though with many subtle differences) as he spoke, she came from the other side of the world; her breeding, her background were as widely different from his as were her Virginian accent from his thick, provincial tongue.

There had been early differences. He had discovered her to be what the Chorleys termed "a woman of spirit". There were some things she would not do; others to which she would not submit. She had a simple, yet skilful manner of withdrawing from his life and his interests, without marked coldness or giving any just cause for offence. He could accuse her of extravagance, of carelessness in the housekeeping, of running his home on different and therefore inferior lines from those of his acquaintances—but this was the worst charge that he could bring against her, and this was somewhat invalidated by the fact that she had her own income and a considerable fortune awaiting her at her mother's death. She could—and this was exasperating to a man of his station and disposition—command money.

He was relieved when he had first realized that she was indifferent to this power she possessed. Money to her was merely to buy pleasures with, including being very generous. She knew nothing of her own business, which somewhat balanced his irritation at not being allowed to take it into his own hands. She put her money, together with the allowance that he made her, into her bank account and spent both indifferently. He wondered what her debts were now and if the firm could afford to meet them.... He had a number of creditors' notes of his own, and his losses at the races had been heavy enough to aggravate his illness. 'If I'd had this stuff then,' he thought reflectively, looking at the white packet labelled "For cats", 'I need not have had that bout of sickness.'

There was no fault to be found with May and she did not trouble him very much, though she had the most maddening defect that a selfish, vicious husband can find in a wife—she never showed emotion. She never questioned him on any subject whatsoever. She appeared incapable of what he termed "making scenes". He was quite sure that she did not know about the establishment in Salford, but there was a great deal that she must know about, for he had become too indifferent to conceal his vices from her, and never by a look had she shown that she cared; never either had she revealed that she fretted at the life she was leading. The utter loneliness of her life sometimes penetrated even his gross self-satisfaction. He would sometimes glance at her with secret surprise at her courage, glance at her sitting idle, for May was always idle, she neither sewed, nor read, nor played with pet animals; enclosed in the midst of so much company, she was utterly by herself, imprisoned among so much assertive noise, she was always silent. Yet he had to concede her the art of graciousness. She neither sulked, nor lamented.... She kept the perfect breeding that he had admired in Paris without knowing why, in the way she took her misfortunes.

It was only rarely that John Tyler thought of his marriage as a misfortune for his wife. He was too dense, too self-centred to concern himself with her possible sufferings. After all, why should she suffer? She had what most women would have been delighted to secure—a fine home, servants, two children and himself—a handsome, upstanding man with a successful business—as a husband. Even if the word husband, like everything else that May possessed, was a mockery.

Still, he was not either remorseful or concerned about May. He had, without feeling any regard or tenderness for her, a jealous sense of possession. He still believed that Richard would have married her if he could, in Paris, though he was incapable of supposing that Richard either still nursed this passion, or fancy whichever it had been, or that he bore any resentment against his brother for securing the rare and delicate gentlewoman. The Puritan very often is not conscious of the passions that may lie, not only beneath the hard surface of his own hypocrisies, but behind the hypocrisies of others. John, who had never shown any reason in his own conduct why anyone should respect or trust him, apart from some conventional business honesty, still did respect and trust Richard without knowing why or even questioning the matter.

He trusted May too... and here was a considerable satisfaction. May was unobtainable. He was sure of that. He had watched her closely when she had first come to Manchester, afraid that he might have to bend or break a French coquette, a flirt. That she had been instantly admired by many of his friends and acquaintances as keenly as he had at first admired her himself, he was well aware. He was also well aware of the opportunity for intrigue offered by a society outwardly strict, inwardly corrupt and lax; a society of materialistic people who never inquired deeply into anything, but who kept the conventions openly and indulged their desires secretly with complete unconcern, and without any probings into the nice questions of ethics or honour.

John Tyler was quite satisfied with this attitude to life. He looked no further than the home that served as a mask for his real activities...

the office, where he could make the money to keep that home going, to throw about at the races and such places of entertainment as he patronized, and to keep Dora in Salford....

Dora and her four children represented to him the lynch pin of his existence. He knew that he ought to have married her; not for the reasons that his vicar would have given him, but because she would have made him happy. Living with Dora in Salford, quarrelling with her, watching her submissive and steady devotion, her ceaseless toil on his behalf, pleasant and jolly with her when he chose, discussing his affairs with her in a language familiar to them both—that went as far as John Tyler could go in the way of an ideal existence. He would have been easier without the frock-coats, the striped trousers, the stiffly starched linen that cut his neck and wrists, the top hat, the large untidy house with the wasteful servants, and the clutter of objects, to him not only useless but entirely incomprehensible; but ambition and a stubborn desire to do as well as the other fellow, had made him leave Dora, as it had made him leave Catherine Minton and forced him, almost against his own volition, to marry May Beale, buy the Pynes, dress like a gentleman, sit in his office often doing nothing, go round to his club and talk with other men like himself of the petty affairs of Manchester and of nothing else. It was not really the life he would have liked, scarcely the life he had planned for. It represented at once a compromise and a falling between two stools. He had Dora in Salford and he had May in Manchester. Both in their different ways were a good deal to his taste... but Stone Pynes was not as splendid as he would have liked it, he had no chance of being mayor or of distinguishing himself as a local celebrity, nor of making so large a fortune that he could shine ostentatiously before his envious fellows, and the life with Dora was furtive, maimed, often marred by disagreeableness; for Dora did not behave like May. She was capable of tears, of reproaches, and though she was a good manager where May was careless, yet his straitness in dealing out her meagre allowance often caused her, as he termed it, "to pester him about money and bills". Then there were the children... of May's children he took very little notice. He believed that at their age they were best in the charge of a nurse or governess. Soon there would be someone in the house to teach them, and soon a school—a good school—for the boy, and perhaps later on a Frenchwoman or Paris for the girl. He didn't know.... It depended on what his position would be.

This was no ideal towards which he strove. He made no effort to save or plan for his children's future. He merely day-dreamed of what he would like them to be.

May seemed to make no plan or scheme either. He thought her passive attitude towards her children rather shocking. A Christian woman should surely have more maternal feeling. She had asked him several times if she might have the charge of them, if he would send away Lizzie Burt. It was only a short time ago that she had made the suggestion that she should take them with her mother to Paris, but these to him were but fitful whims that he despised as fugitive rebellions. She should be always solicitous; other women were. He had seen them walking out with their children and the nursemaid, driving round the shops with the children and the governess, taking the children with the nurse or the governess to the dentist.... He had heard of them sitting up all night nursing their children and heard the husbands, gratified, exclaim, "My wife's such a wonderful mother."

It was true that neither the boy nor the girl had ever been ill, but John wondered, with some dull impatience, if they had ever been well. They seemed lifeless.... The reports of their behaviour were always excellent, but he could not find either little John or little May attractive. He never concerned himself about their possible secret thoughts, their possible secret games, their possible secret condemnation of himself. Once he had found the boy looking at him blankly and had felt a tiny prickle of uneasiness that was gone almost immediately. Once he had heard the girl laugh as he came into the room, and again there had been a tingling of his flesh, he thought—or was it what people called the mind or the soul? But this had soon been forgotten. When they were older he would take more notice of them. The boy, of course, would be a smart, good-looking, knowing chap like he was himself. He would go into the business and earn enough money to fling about like a gentleman. He would belong to better clubs than his father belonged to; he would have possibly some aristocrats among his acquaintances. He would make a marriage with… who knew? Perhaps the daughter of a noble house. And the girl would be beautiful and charming… with all May's grace and fascination, but with more worldly wisdom and more adaptability. She would not remain aloof, enclosed, smiling and untouched.… No, she would mingle with the world and get the best out of it.

How these two attractive creatures were to be produced from the small wizened children who lived in the perpetual twilight of the ugly nurseries, except when they were taken for short routine walks, John Tyler never concerned himself to think. He was not dealing with a problem or planning action; he was dreaming a dream.

Well, things might have been worse. He rose and smiled. Three packets of arsenic… enough to poison the street, or a regiment, as the saying went.… That would last him awhile.… He had been getting it at a chemist's shop in Pendleton where one of the assistants was under an obligation to him with regard to a racing debt; but this source of supply had failed. The young man had been removed and the owner of the shop had shown little inclination to submit to Mr. Tyler's insinuating overtures. That, with the discretion of old Johnstone, had made matters very difficult for Mr. Tyler lately.

He continually went to the doctors—the family man, Harman, who had attended him ever since he came to Manchester and Edmund Fitch, a man of higher standing who often attended the better houses. They had always insisted that his aches, pains and cramps were "nerves only" and that he was a healthy man and that he could cure himself.... Why not? as they both put it 'leave off fussing so much over your health.'... But he knew better. He knew that if either of them had given him the arsenic that he craved, he would have been cured, as he had been cured now with the arsenic he had obtained from Joseph Tarrant, which he had drunk half an hour before he had taken the slops in the brown jug....

The weather was close; a smoke screen hung thick over the city. So much he could see from the soiled windows of his office; but his spirits were not lowered by this gloom. He was summing up, with some complacency, his position and his possessions. He saw nothing much to concern himself in his situation. There was the question of May's debts, and of his own too, but they could be met no doubt.... Richard would come to his help if need be. Richard, as a single man and one who knew how to manage his affairs, was very well to do, and though it was difficult to induce him to invest money in his brother's business, yet he would, on good security, now and then advance a loan.

May's debts...? Well, they gave him a hold over her, anyhow, and she was so ignorant in these matters that he could salve his conscience by adding his extravagance to hers and putting the entire blame on her. What he had lost at Liverpool could be added to the losses on the housekeeping books, and the sums that she spent in an errant fashion on entertainment or in buying the children now and then costly toys or clothes. He always made her suffer for these indiscretions, but he was secretly rather glad of them. They meant that his own imprudence could be covered up, and that he could play the self-righteous, hard-working man with a careless and heedless wife.

He passed into the outer office where the two grey and faded men, Aitken and Young, bent over their ledgers. He knew that their assumed industry would cease as soon as he left the office and they would fall to chattering over their own affairs, which were very much the same as his affairs... the gossip of Manchester and such opportunities for self-indulgence of various kinds as Manchester afforded....

Mr. Tyler paused in the street, thinking of paying Richard a visit. Richard lived in comfortable rooms near the Exchange where they had both lived before John's marriage and the purchase of his grandiose mansion; but he decided he would not do so. He was not even sure that the loan was necessary.

Then he thought that he would visit Dora—but it was too far to Salford. He felt a grievance that he could not yet keep a carriage; besides being a sign of prosperity it was so extremely convenient.

Usually when he left his office, he made a call on Dr. Harman and teased him with his symptoms—stiffness in the legs, cramp in the arms, a feeling of dizziness and so on, all of which the physician dismissed as mere querulous fancies. But to-night he had taken his panacea and had no desire, for once, to brood on his own health. He'd go home then, and perhaps talk to May.... He had not yet sufficiently reproved her for the money she must have spent in London; those dresses, grotesque too for a Christian lady and the ways of a Manchester merchant of his standing.... Yet he thought of them with a certain gratification also. She was a very beautiful woman; it was pleasant to see so many regard her with envy and to know that she was quite aloof and unobtainable. Curious that she should have bought a gown almost exactly like that in which he had dressed her when he had first brought her to Manchester, in memory of the peacock....

He turned then, walking with unwonted briskness towards Stone Pynes, and met the very man who had been recently in his thoughts—Dr. Harman, who was as intimate with the Tylers and their domestic lives as anyone in Manchester. The two men, muffled against the fog and the chill air of the spring evening that seemed to congeal about them, stood muffled and greeted one another. John Tyler nervously put his thick silk scarf tighter round his throat. Dr. Harman regarded him quizzically.

"You'd better come along and have a talk with me," he said. "I've just come from Stone Pynes. Your wife wants a divorce..."

Dr. Harman lived soberly with a sober niece in Pitt Street and there he conducted John Tyler, guiding him now and then by a touch on the arm until he had reached the sombre sitting-room beyond the surgery where the dark red flecked paper was relieved only by the ornate gilt frames of pictured landscapes, so sombre that little could be discerned of their subjects beyond stormy skies and foregrounds where lonely figures, bent before the winds amid the cracks and blisters of bitumen. Two black urns of what Dr. Harman termed "classic shape", stood on top of a bookcase of gleaming mahogany with polished glass that protected volumes of medical works and a few of the more decorous classics.

George Harman was what was known as a comfortable man with a comfortable practice. He was family physician to many of the less ostentatious cotton merchants and brokers, and had always had the reputation of being genial, tactful and kind, though the truth was that he was indifferent to everybody and everything except his physical comforts, the work that paid for them and his pastime, a laborious translation of Dante that proceeded at the rate of a few lines a day.

All the implements for this work (and he treated it as if it was a sculptured statue of weight and size) were locked away in a cabinet by the window and only brought out when the physician could forget his patients, Manchester, and the prim conversation of the niece who so efficiently ran his establishment. Even now, although he saw his inescapable duty before him, he gave a jealous and an affectionate glance towards the hidden treasure.

John Tyler was seated by the round table on which was placed a chenille cloth, and was wiping his face with his large thick silk handkerchief. During the walk to the doctor's house he had had time to grasp something of the meaning of George Harman's words, but no time to consider them. To think out the situation was altogether beyond his capacity; Dr. Harman knew that well enough. John Tyler would act only from impulse, from cunning.

"May wants a divorce?" he said with the tedious reiteration that the stupid use in order to gain time. "Wants a divorce, does she?"

"I had been expecting it," said the physician, rubbing his dry hands together, and then adjusting his spectacles.

He settled himself down in the worn leather chair with a half sigh because by the calendar it was warm weather and fires unnecessary. The empty hearth with the fire screen on which was a parrot garnished with white beads, depressed him; so did the prospect of being the go-between in the affairs of May and John Tyler—but he was the family physician and this was expected of him, he was a Christian and must do his duty in bringing husband and wife together. He was a man of business and must not lose a chance of ingratiating himself with well-to-do people. The Tyler household afforded him a steady income. John was frequently consulting him about nothing at all; the doctor had told him as much, but on the patient's refusal to agree had accepted the other's folly and made him pay for it. The children were puling and ailing also, if never ill, they swallowed large quantities of medicine... and then there were the servants to whom he did not disdain to give his services since Mrs. Tyler always paid for them extravagantly. Except at the birth of her children he had never had occasion to treat May Tyler for anything. She seemed an almost exasperatingly healthy woman although he had heard she had been too delicate to go to school when a child, the whim of a fond mother, he supposed.

"Well," he said with a judicial air. "I, of course, have long been a friend of yours. I knew your father—"

John made an impatient movement of protest; even in his distress he did not care to be reminded from what stock he had come.

The physician continued steadily. "I have watched you become a very successful business man. I have been sorry you've not been so successful in your home..."

"I don't know what you mean," replied the cotton merchant with heavy indignation. "My wife has everything—comfort, even luxury. She's waited on hand and foot, doesn't bother with the children in the least.... I've always seen there were several servants and an excellent nurse...."

"Perhaps that was a mistake," suggested Dr. Harman. "Perhaps you should have allowed her to have more to do with the children. Remember I suggested it once or twice.... I know you are not a man to whom sentiment appeals, but you must allow that to give a woman—a young and pretty woman, a very fascinating woman—the charge of her children is also giving her something to keep her occupied...."

"I don't understand you," replied John, filled with gloomy fury he found impossible to express. "Indeed I don't understand you, Dr. Harman. My wife has had everything she wanted, always has had—and as for this question of the children... Why, a woman of her class, she couldn't look after them as if she was the wife of a factory hand. I tell you," he repeated, "she's had everything she wanted."

"She's means of her own with which to help to obtain it, hasn't she?" asked the physician. "The case is not difficult for me to understand. She's had about the last sort of upbringing to fit her for this kind of life. She's a foreigner here. I'm almost certain—although she's always so amiable and so courteous—that she dislikes Manchester and all of us in it—"

"Including myself?" asked John Tyler harshly, and the doctor answered:

"Including yourself. I told you that she sent for me and suggested that I put it to you that you were divorced...."

"Why did she send for you?" John's voice was suspicious. His face, usually of unhealthy pallor, was patched with red.

"She had no other friend, I suppose."

"Well, there's a priest, isn't there?"

"She gave up going to the priest; I think she sees one sometimes when she visits Madame Dumont in London, but I understood that you, as a correct Anglican, never cared for your wife's faith, so she more or less gave it up."

"Not much of a faith!" exclaimed John coarsely. "Well, she sent for you as the old family doctor and said she wanted to divorce me. Anything more harebrained I never heard of. She's in a tantrum, I suppose, or something. She's frightened perhaps of what I'm going to say about her debts. She's been putting off even showing me the household accounts... she's a most extravagant and wasteful woman... she cannot run the house or servants as I would like.... No wonder I had to get someone of experience for the children.... Divorce? Why, she's talking nonsense. She's no cause..."

"Perhaps not—and I'm sure that you haven't...."

Mr. Tyler stared. This aspect of the case had never occurred to him. In a moment he had laughed with triumph.

"Oh, May! She's above all that kind of thing—there's no one dare look at her twice."

"Then," remarked the physician, "she must be extremely lonely. Have you ever thought of that? Pride and courtesy... perhaps a little disdain for all of us... perhaps the mere warm, undefined hopes of youth keep her alive; but you are no longer husband and wife in anything but conventionalities, and she's young and born to gaiety and kindness. You have taken her away from a world where she was cherished—"

"Pampered and spoiled," put in John Tyler.

"You ought to have known that before you married her. You are a man almost old enough to be her father... she was a girl of eighteen....

Madame Dumont, an extremely attractive lady, is also extremely unworldly... her stepfather had no influence over her and was continually away because of his military duties... Now, Mr. Tyler, I put it to you, a man who had had the experiences you had had when you married this girl, and who should have been able to judge the chances of content for both of you... a man I say who should have had judgment, prudence and discretion—"

"Well?" John Tyler interrupted the ponderous sentences which seemed to be delivered with the weight of a judgment. "A man like myself...?"

"Fifty-six," put in the physician, "and she twenty-six. She asks for a divorce, completely ingenuously, because she is unaware of the laws of this country.... How should she know them? She's seen nothing but Manchester, heard nothing but the talk of your friends...."

"She's seen her mother often enough," replied John Tyler, again drawing the thick handkerchief over his face.

"Not so very often. Madame Dumont was not made very welcome in your house, your wife's visits to London have been rare and Madame Dumont, as I judge it, is not the woman to interfere, nor is your wife the woman to complain. I believe that she will know very little of her daughter's story but of course she will guess her unhappiness and the cause of it—"

"You seem to have got the whole story pat," put in Mr. Tyler fiercely. "You seem to know more about my affairs than I do myself."

The doctor, who had been expecting exactly this attitude, and almost these words, replied coolly, "A family physician sees a great deal of what is going on in the houses that he visits. Your wife has never taken me into her confidence—not even now. She has only asked me, being the only possible person to whom she could turn, about a divorce...."

"What is the reason?" asked Mr. Tyler, with a deepening of his fury and suspicion.

"There may be no reason about it," replied Dr. Harman, "It may be a matter of sentiment." He looked regretfully at the locked door behind which seemed to murmur the melodious silver tongue of the long dead Tuscan.

"Sentiment.... Now there I'll swear you are wrong. May isn't entangled in as much as a flirtation... she's not that sort of woman...."

"I am as aware of that as you are. I said a matter of sentiment. She wants to get away from you, from Manchester. She feels (and this she put to me) that she has paid enough for a mistake she made when she was in years a girl and in mind a child. Convent bred, mind you, Mr. Tyler. Well-bred... but quite innocent of the world.... She's remained like that—aloof from all these people. I know. Not a lover among the men," said the doctor, "and not a friend among the women. It speaks for a good deal of fortitude on her part...."

"Of watchfulness on mine, perhaps," replied John Tyler, but he knew that what the doctor said of May was correct.

"Then it's all fiddle-faddle," he added impatiently. "I wish she hadn't troubled you with it, doctor. Of course she cannot get a divorce. She's idle... why doesn't she do what the other women do?... There's plenty of work to be done—visiting the poor and all that sort of thing. She doesn't go about in society either, like she might. I tried to get her to go to the carnival balls they give in the Pomona Palace, but she won't. Refuses flatly..."

"Not so flatly, I think," said Dr. Harman, who was beginning to find the interview even more tiresome than he had feared it might be, but speaking with conventional, casual interest. "Still I'm bound to tell you, having undertaken the thankless office of go-between, that she really is determined on a separation."

"The loving mother would leave her children, I suppose?" sneered May Tyler's husband.

"I think she would. I believe she feels that they are scarcely hers, that they are taken from her and given to strangers and maybe turned against her. I have always felt that everyone in your household is hostile to your wife. Servants allowed too free a hand will often despise the mistress. Servants," he added with a definite sharpness in his tone, "who were asked by the master to act as spies on their mistress.... Well, you ought to understand what the victim will feel like...."

"Suppose I don't know what you mean? Now and then I may have asked one of them if she were in, and what she had been doing that afternoon—or who called.... But what's in that?"

"Nothing, I suppose, except the bribe that is slipped from one palm to another."

John Tyler swore, though he was usually very careful in his language as in his behaviour.

"You know too much," he protested. "Not that I admit what you say is true."

"Your *wife* knows a little too much. She knows about Mrs. Lestrange...."

John stared again and again employed the habits of dull repetition so detestable to the precise doctor.

"May knows of Mrs. Lestrange?"

"Yes, she's visited her. I think she feels quite sympathetic towards her. She believes you ought to have married her—for both your sakes, Mrs. Tyler said. Dora would have made you a much better wife than she ever could, so she says, and I agree with her. You and Mrs. Lestrange are very suited to one another—the same ways, the same class..."

John Tyler winced at that, but couldn't deny the words of the man who had known him since he was a child; though he had never admitted it even to himself, he and Dora Lestrange, the shop girl, were of the same class.

"Well, it's very generous of May," he said with vulgar sarcasm. "Very good and kind I'm sure. I don't intend to marry Dora Lestrange, and wouldn't even if I were free of May. Whether she knows or not, it won't make any difference—I'll see to that. It's not cause for a divorce in this country."

"No," the physician agreed coolly. "Mrs. Tyler did not know that, she said someone else had told her so but she couldn't be sure. She has no lawyer here. Perhaps you'd hardly understand how forlorn her position is. Her mother has left England, her school-day friends are scattered, all her childhood friends and relatives are the other side of the Atlantic—"

"Excuse me, Doctor, but you're a physician, not a clergyman. I didn't come here for a lecture on morals."

"I didn't ask you here to give you one. Your wife appealed to me and I'm trying to help her and you. You'd better endeavour for a reconciliation. It won't altogether improve your business if it's known publicly that you have another establishment in Salford."

John Tyler looked sly. "There's a great many do know it," he remarked with a chuckle.

"Publicly, I said," emphasized the doctor.

John Tyler considered that. The old man was right. Divorce—why, it wasn't to be heard of... he'd never known any case of a divorced man continuing to be successful. The only commandment that he believed in was one he wouldn't have found in the Bible—*Thou shalt not be found out*. It was quite true that he couldn't afford a divorce, and his mind darted to the legal cost and maintenance for May, and the fact that she had money and might through her mother get more. No doubt, if it were necessary, considerable resources might be found in Virginia for the young woman who had been May Beale, and who had distant relatives placed in positions far beyond those to which John Tyler had ever dared to dream of attaining.

He looked uneasy now, instead of angry; bewildered and baffled.

"I don't see why there need be a reconciliation; why can't we go on as we are doing? She's got a house and her children and social life—"

"As you have remarked, Mr. Tyler, she takes little interest in the house, she dislikes the social life of Manchester, and the children were taken away from her almost at birth...."

"How did she find out?"

John charged with clumsy directness at another aspect of the hateful situation.

"That she would not tell me, of course. I'm only surprised she didn't find out sooner. If she had gone about more and listened to gossip like most women do, she probably would have heard it."

"I didn't think she cared about that sort of thing. She's long known she's not been the only one."

The cotton merchant spoke with a certain satisfaction and drew his hand down his profile as if underlining the fact that he was a very personable man.

"I couldn't tell you how she arrived at her decisions," the doctor assured him. "I suppose there comes a moment when no one can be kept on the bearing-rein any longer. She's a woman of spirit and breeding. She is stripped of everything. She may have been decided by her discovery of your second establishment to take this resolve, she may have had it in her mind for a long while.... All I know is what she told me...."

"Roman Catholics cannot divorce," declared Mr. Tyler, rising.

"That's what she wanted my advice about. It seems she is not sure. She knows that the Church—her Church—is against divorce, but the poor lady was quite unaware that Catholics as well as Protestants can obtain relief from the English law."

"Relief!" replied John Tyler. "I like that! May's lived like a lady—a rich idle lady, ever since I married her..."

"It rests in your hands, Mr. Tyler. I'm sorry for your wife. I can see it from her point of view which you can't. I should suggest either a reconciliation and that you try to come together, that you give her more liberty, a greater share in the management of the children, that you allow her to choose the servants—"

"Did she complain of that?" demanded the angry husband.

"She did not even mention it, nor the question of the children. She kept entirely to the business matter, as she termed it, of the divorce. But I have seen these things for myself on my visits to Stone Pynes."

"It seems to me that you doctors see a good deal too much," but John Tyler curbed his rage. He realized that it would not do to make an active enemy of this man in whom May had confided her intentions, to whom she had gone for advice and who knew about the Salford household. "I shouldn't think of a divorce! I consider it a womanish bit of nonsense," he said, trying to show far more fortitude than he felt. "And I wouldn't of course divorce her. I know, with all her faults, she's a good woman...."

The doctor smiled acidly, nodded his head and did not speak.

"I should have to assault her before two witnesses," grinned John. "Knock her about before she could get her divorce...."

"Being a gentleman," said the doctor quietly, "you would, of course, never do that."

"I've been tempted to sometimes. She with her head in the air, smiling through me when I've told her about something that's gone wrong, and given her the blame for her faults...."

"What are her faults?" asked George Harman with another glance at the cabinet that contained his books, papers and the three volumes of Dante's poems bound in vellum with sepia titles.

"I've told you..." But the cotton merchant was not loath for another chance to repeat them. "Money slips through her fingers... she does nothing... takes no interest in anything, though she's always civil...."

She buys this and that without any thought… she runs up debts… she gives away anything that anyone admires.…"

"Well, you can translate that," the word came easily off the doctor's tongue, as he gazed at his cabinet. "She's never been taught to keep an account of the cost of things, or how to run an establishment like yours. She's warmhearted and likes to see everyone happy.… I believe she gives a good deal away in charity. She even sent—no, it was not she who told me, I learned it from somebody else—something to the prisons." The doctor's use of the word showed his attitude towards those who had offended the law; it was not noticed by John Tyler who instantly began to complain of his wife's spendthrift habits.

The physician interrupted to ask what were Mrs. Tyler's other faults but John could not think of any. Although her whole existence, her entire bearing and attitude to life were offences to him, they were not offences that he could define.

"I'd like to know who told her." He fell back on that aspect of his grievance.

"I shouldn't concern myself about that. There's a hundred ways in which she might have found out. She might have known for a long time. That French maid of her mother's is very skilful and very fond of your wife. I daresay when she was in Manchester she may not have been altogether occupied with laces and ribbons. She speaks English, you remember, perfectly."

"I'll find out from Dolly if anybody has been to see her.…"

"I don't suppose Mrs. Lestrange would tell…"

John Tyler was baffled sufficiently to ask the physician if he would give him some advice, trying to conceal his awkward sarcasm as he spoke.

"If you will act reasonably I will help you. I'll come to Stone Pynes and talk matters over with you and your wife. I think she's concerned about these debts. If you could help meet them it might make matters easier for both of you."

"I've got my own duties to think over and she's got her own allowance. It is intolerable that a woman should spend not only her own money but her husband's as well... and what's to show for it...? We don't even keep a carriage...."

"Bad management undoubtedly," George Harman agreed smoothly. "I suppose your business is so excellently managed that you find your wife's blunders inexcusable?"

"The business does well enough. I'm putting a new invention on the market... there may be a fortune in it... then I shall move from Stone Pynes. Cheetham isn't as fashionable as it used to be."

"My dear sir," the doctor rose to show that the interview was at an end. "Pray remember that nothing in Manchester is fashionable for a woman of your wife's type."

"Oh I know I've married a great lady and all the rest of the nonsense; but I *have* married her. It takes two to make a divorce like it takes two to make a marriage, and I don't intend it. I won't have the expense or the scandal. I'll ask Richard's advice; he's the only man I know, besides yourself, I suppose," put in the cotton merchant ungraciously, "who will be able to help. He's known May as long as I have. At one time when I was courting her I thought that he'd have had her himself, but she preferred me. Richard and I have always been good friends. He's often advised me not to give her her head too much, and to keep an eye on her."

"I don't know whether Mr. Richard Tyler will be able to give you any disinterested advice or not," answered the doctor gravely. "If you will make the appointment, I will wait on you at Stone Pynes. I advise you, as your doctor and your well-wisher," Dr. Harman avoided the word friend, "to deal as kindly and courteously as you can with your wife when you speak to her of my mission."

May Tyler waited, without trepidation, the result of Dr. Harman's interview with her husband. She had considerable faith in masculine freemasonry and trusted that the proposal of divorce that, had she put it forward, would have only provoked John's cruelty and scorn, might be quite reasonably received when advanced by the family physician of whom John had always seemed slightly in awe.

She could not see what objection her husband could have to the request to release her from what Dr. Harman had often told her was "an unnatural state of affairs".

It was incredible that he still valued her as anything but a figurehead, and to May's ingenuous, aristocratic mind, incredible that he should not accept her refusal to play this farce any longer; she realized that there would be scandal, and that the second marriage that she hoped for, that with Dora Lestrange, would be difficult, but, with the optimism of the unworldly and the romantic, she did not consider it impossible; men knew how to adjust these matters and she was far, even after eight years of residence in Manchester, from understanding the puritanical hypocrisy by which she was surrounded, and she believed that John would find her discovery of Dora so overwhelming, that he would come to terms. 'I want only to get away,' she told herself, but one of her mother's sighing, laughing phrases was in her head—*"le besoin d'etre aimée"*; after all, what did one do, when one was so lonely, so beset, so alien to all one's surroundings?

She looked wistfully into the large mirror that rose from floor to ceiling, that reflected her delicate figure leaning on the gilt chair, in the manner of a full-length portrait; without the least vanity she was conscious of graces, elegances, charms utterly wasted.

Why had John married her? She was hardly aware how old was this bitter question that genuinely puzzled her; she had seen her mother's smooth domestic life, and the apparent felicity of her mother's friends, equable ladies whose husbands valued and flattered them; she had always supposed that men only married women whom they knew they could always treat with respect and kindness, at least. She had been prepared to accept her destiny cheerfully, to endure the smoky city, the vulgar people, the commercial atmosphere, the tawdry amusements, if John had continued to love her, if he had allowed her to have the children; she thought of them now, and in her heart whispered—'Oh, children, children, come away with me, into the open air, away from the drab nursery, the copy books, and Lizzie Burt!' But she had ceased to woo them; once, all her fascinations had been spread to gain their interest, she had offered them all she had in tenderness and gaiety in return for a smile, but they had been taken from her too early, kept from her too long, trained too long by ignorant servants, overlooked too long by a harsh father; they were both cowed, the boy furtive, the girl sly; they knew that to encourage their mother's fondness meant trouble from their father and from the nurse of the moment. May knew this also; she had long since accepted defeat; perhaps John knew better than she did, and she, indolent, frivolous, "a bad manager", was not suitable as a companion for her own children, perhaps her wishes, her longings for games and laughter in the open air, for fewer lessons and more fun, for a life for her babies such as she had had herself, were wrong.

But if there was a divorce, could she not, even now, have the children for half the year?

Dr. Harman had said something about that when she had quietly asked him to be her advocate with her husband, "an arrangement, amicable, if possible—a legal separation."

He had not told her all she wished to know about the English divorce laws, patting her hand in "a fatherly fashion", as he termed it; he had said that "ladies couldn't understand such affairs", and when May asked, "Can one be divorced without understanding how?" he had sighed—"Well, after a divorce one is hardly a lady any more and you must understand that, too."

May was not troubled by this; she knew she would always be herself whatever happened, and that there were no ladies, in her sense of the word, in Dr. Harman's practice, or the city of Manchester.

"Only to get away," she had pleaded, "to go abroad, with my mother, with the children."

The kindly adviser had pointed out the expense as well as the scandal of divorce, and she had reminded him of her own income, of the capital on which she could draw, of her numerous wealthy friends and relatives in Virginia, "I wish I could return there—scandal? No one knows me here, no one would care, besides, John has behaved wrongly, not I...."

She shook the memory of the interview from her; Dr. Harman was a good man, who would do his best, though he made mistakes, as when he had asked her, "Is there no one your side? You have many admirers, anyone can see that—perhaps you want to marry again?"

"There is no one," she had smiled at so gross an error. And when, puzzled, he asked her how she passed her life, that was not that of wife, widow or spinster, she had answered, still smiling—"By learning to endure."

She rose and went to the wardrobe, too large for her use since John's clothes had been taken from it four years ago; there were mingled scents of *pot-pourri*, cedar powder and lavender water, the dresses being limp, like so many caricatures of herself, the smart London gowns among the provincial garments, the suit she had worn on the Salford visit, the purple evening gown, cut so low, the rich lace dress.

On the floor of the wardrobe were shoes, several hat cases and the chocolate box that Jerome Thorne had given her; on the upper shelf were hats, bonnets, boas, shawls and the blue velvet Bible bought in Paris nearly nine years ago.

May had often meant to take it down and open the pages at random, in search of some inspiring text, but the shelf was too high for her to reach, one of the maids had to fetch down the other things when she needed them, and May, unconsciously preferred to leave her mother's gift apart, not to have it handled by a servant; it was a translation of the Vulgate into the French language, with a calendar of saints laid within the covers, and the florid inscription from her mother—May knew how that would be regarded by John and his household, although separated from her husband she had no privacy, he came continuously into her room and turned over her possessions, and she sensed that all the servants, save the stout asthmatic cook, were his spies. Why? She pondered on this, as she took four chocolates from the long, glossy box. Since he had no interest in her, why should he be so possessive, so greedy of her least look?

He had condemned her to a mental and spiritual starvation, she was not to be loved, caressed, admired, respected, neither was she to be free; her position was that of an idle slave.

She ate the chocolates daintily, one ginger-flavoured, one vanilla-flavoured, one with a silver ball on the top, one with a crushed violet; she had indulged very sparingly in Jerome Thorne's sweetmeats, but the box was nearly empty; she had met him at several dinner parties since he had come to her with the news of her husband's illness, and liked him more and more; they had been of the same company often enough before, but it was since his journey from Wirral only that she had carefully noted him; she was sure he had a noble disposition, like the men of whom Lord Tennyson wrote; it was really surprising that he should be a Manchester cotton broker and live in the same street with Richard.

She pondered on Richard, she did not doubt the sincerity of his motives in taking her to Salford; he wished to see justice done to Dora and her children, he wished to give her, May, a chance of freedom; he was more honest, kinder than John; if she had to marry one of the brothers—well, Richard would have been a more reasonable master.

She pulled aside the curtains of red rep that screened the alcove that led to her husband's room, she was supposed to see that everything was ready for his return from the office—the hot water in the brass can, the clean towels, the evening clothes laid out, the slippers and dressing-gown ready if he did not choose to appear at dinner, matches for the gas, glasses and a carafe of fresh water.

Everything was in order in the ugly room with the narrow bed, the marble-topped washstand, the marble-topped pedestal table, the stiff backed chairs, the red Axminster carpet, the Nottingham lace curtains depending from a polished massive pole behind dusty draperies, clumsily fringed and tasselled, of a shade of crimson that jarred with the hue of the carpet.

A mahogany press held John's clothes, an oak stand his boots and shoes, a wooden horse his towels, a glass fronted case his books on racing, the cotton trade and the home treatment of disease. His medicine case stood on the floor near the bed; May always saw it with disgust, almost with dismay, she was uneasy at the amount of drugs he took; not only was she incapable of wishing anyone harm, she knew that if he were ill, became an object of compassion, she would not be able to leave him, she would be trapped. Her mother had taught her to be fearful of drugs, there had never been any in her mother's chambers, aromatic vinegars, hartshorn, sal volatile, *eau de Cologne* had been kept in an elegant casket that was never locked, and no one had ever been ill with more than a slight headache or lassitude in thunder weather. But John was continually taking medicines and continually going to the doctor though Dr. Harman had assured May again and again that "there is nothing the matter with him, he is much too fussy".

Now she observed a parcel of a familiar appearance on the bedside table. Medicines from the London chemists, Messrs. Joshua and Blunt, she knew, that arrived regularly; these packages contained, she believed, the white powder John consumed, taking it from an onyx box and using a special spoon; she had described it, in her anxiety, to her mother, who had said it was probably strychnine, a tonic of no great harm, but Madame Dumont had gently deplored John's constant dosing of himself and condemned his faddy ways.

May had spoken to Richard, to Dr. Harman and neither had taken much notice, they seemed to think she was "fussy" and that John could "look after himself"; their little catch phrases that might cover nothing or so much, hung in her mind; she had noticed how they fenced themselves about with conventional words like a ring of bayonets, as she fenced herself about with pride and breeding like a halo of frost.

There was no one to dinner this evening. John might have seen Dr. Harman and take the opportunity of speaking to her, though she had asked the physician to be present at any interview with her husband on the problem of divorce; John could be cruel with his looks, his voice; he had once advanced on her with clenched fists, exercising a painful control, because he had thought that some casual remark of hers had reflected on his assumed sham gentility; besides they had been avoiding one another for so long, it would be very disagreeable to be alone with the heavy saturnine man without the protection of the servants coming and going during their occasional meals together. She considered what the procedure of divorce was, what it cost, how long it took, in some of the American states it was simple enough, she knew, and carried no stigma; sighing gently with tedium she slowly ate the last of the four chocolates and pulled the bell that would bring Nelly Tanner with the hot water.

Two extra covers had to be laid on the long mahogany table at Stone Pynes. John brought Dr. Harman and his brother Richard to dinner. May guessed this meant a conference when the long meal was over and played the civil hostess without effort; her husband did not as usual grumble about the badly cooked food nor her careless housekeeping,

Richard seemed in a good humour, and the elderly physician was correctly non-committal before the housemaid who eyed the four of them, as she handed the dishes, as if she saw through all their pretences. Meals at Stone Pynes were always too long and served with too much silver, too much porcelain, too much linen, too many knick-knacks; John Tyler liked an epergne loaded with wax fruit in the winter, real fruit in the summer, an armoury of knives, spoons and forks at every plate, as many rests for carvers, as many mats, glasses, stands and vases as the table would hold. He liked large quantities of hot meat, following soups in huge tureens, *entrées* in silver dishes, fish lying full length on long platters, sweets rich and spiced, wines of all kinds, mostly decanted in flagons with enamel labels hanging on them; yet he ate very sparingly and with the air of a man too careful of his health, and drank moderately with a plebeian indifference to the quality or the mixing of his sherry, claret, hock and brandy.

May found the dinner more than usually dull; she had long since given up the effort to please her husband or to cope with English housekeeping; the shopkeepers sent what they would, and Mrs. Pilch cooked as she pleased. May touched even less than her husband of the abundant, coarse food that was put on the overburdened table; she had ceased to regret American and continental customs of eating, but now she thought, "Perhaps if I can get away, I shall never have to sit through these meals again—so much cutlery—so many plates painted with fishes, painted with flowers, painted with fruit, so many finger-bowls, mats, dishes of sweets—and all ugly."

She civilly maintained a conversation with Dr. Harman in whom she felt a friend, perhaps a protector. The physician related some of the exploits of his maternal ancestors, one of whom had held Manchester successfully for Parliament against Lord Strange and, oddly enough, another who had served under Colonel Townly when the Manchester Regiment was enrolled in the service of Prince Charles Stewart.

"Have you seen, Mrs. Tyler, the house in Market Street Lane where the Pretender lodged?"

"Richard is the one for that history book stuff," said John; he seemed uneasy, and drank more than was his custom, complaining about the quality of the brandy, and that the wine merchants had "cheated" him—and he "would have satisfaction".

George Harman continued his safe discourse; his grandfather had told him of the days when all the cotton came from Cyprus and Smyrna, when the merchants were in the factories by six o'clock, and shared their breakfast bowls of porridge and milk into which all flipped their spoons among the looms, with their workers.

"Very different from this, eh?" John glanced over the edge of his glass at the opulent table.

"Very different. It was a simple life—they dined, sparingly, at midday, and every day the ladies were visiting by two o'clock and at the collegiate church by four o'clock."

"They worked that we may play—times have advanced a bit since then," remarked Richard complacently. He glanced, as if at a signal at his brother. "Shall we have coffee in the library, John?"

"In the library? Oh, by all means! What do you say to that, May?" asked John avoiding his wife's gaze.

"Of course. I'll tell Nelly..."

"I wish you would say Tanner, May, it sounds so common to give the servants their Christian names."

"I am sorry that I forgot, John, we have that custom in Virginia."

"Oh, Virginia! And those blacks—no better than slaves, even now—"

Richard said, directly checking this bravado, "We have something serious to discuss and should keep our tempers cool."

"I agree," added the physician readily, "and as your medical adviser, Mr. Tyler, might I say—? No more spirits."

May rose, and led the way to the library; there was no port to-night and the men followed her directly; Nelly Tanner and Dolly Hoey going towards the baize lined doors that shut off the kitchen, with loads of crockery and plate it would take hours to wash, gave their mistress sly and hostile glances.

This was a dreary room even for Stone Pynes, John Tyler had ordered a library in the same way as his father had ordered a peacock and a garden with peach trees, he thought it a sign of prosperity which it was, and of gentility, which it was not; the cold tastelessness of the upholsterer had not been disturbed, glass fronted bookcases lined the walls and contained the complete editions of all the works of all the better known of those writers termed "classics", together with handsome volumes on theology by well known divines of Low Church views; none of these books had ever been opened.

The opal-coloured globe covering the gas jets hanging from a brass cord in the centre of the ceiling showed a carpet and wallpaper of a dismal sage green, chenille curtains of a darker shade of this hue, stiff-backed horsehair chairs and a large desk furnished with all a writer's paraphernalia from pens to reference books and a bust of Plato.

As this desk was very seldom used it was very neat, and did not appear to belong to the same person as John Tyler's desk in his office; he had taken pleasure in ordering and overseeing the furnishing of this room but he did not know what to do with it beyond occasionally interviewing his wife about her accounts, his children about their misdemeanours, and his doctors about his ailments.

'My library,' and 'I'll see you in the library' had, however, he thought, a dignified sound, and for to-night's conference it was peculiarly suitable.

May did not think so though she smiled so gallantly from her hard seat that Dr. Harman remarked kindly, "Hardly a lady's room—perhaps you would prefer another, Mrs. Tyler?"

Richard put in smoothly, "May furnished none of the rooms in Stone Pynes, not even her own."

"She had no wish to," retorted John. He sat by the tidy desk, staring downwards. "May has always had everything she wanted."

His wife's smile did not fade at this monstrous statement. Her large clear eyes, brilliant under the level brows gazed candidly at the three men; she faced the situation as she had faced a fence when riding with M. Dumont.

"Dr. Harman told you I wished for a divorce, John? You have told Richard, I suppose, since he is here."

"Richard is my best friend, he'll give us both good advice," returned her husband sullenly.

May turned her frank look on Richard, as if she accused him of treachery, but, with her ingenuous habit of idealizing everyone, at once acquitted him of any but wise and generous intentions.

"I hardly need advice," she replied gently. "I want a divorce, John."

"Just because you found out about Dora! Who told you?"

"I shall never say," smiled May, and he knew she never would, though he continued his bitter complaints about the gossips and the scandalmongers. "But it is not altogether because of Dora, John; I want very much to go away, to have another kind of life. Our marriage is over."

"A fine way for a woman to talk! What do you lack? I never stinted you because of Dora—that's *my* affair, after all."

"A necessary result of Christian marriage," remarked Dr. Harman, who read books on science condemned by the clergy. "Well, I am here to effect a reconciliation, if I can—"

"There has been no quarrel," said May. "Sometimes my husband is angry with me about the accounts, that is all—"

"I don't want to become bankrupt."

"May's debts are not so large, surely," Richard spoke from the window-place where he had taken his stand; he had an air of being master of the situation, almost of enjoying himself.

"What *are* your debts, Mrs. Tyler?"

May turned to the doctor.

"I am stupid at arithmetic—I think, about a thousand pounds, but I shall have some money of my own due again next quarter."

"You hear!" cried John. "A thousand pounds!"

"But it is more than a year," said May quietly, "since you gave me any money for the housekeeping. I have had to run bills, and you go to race meetings and are providing for another family."

"That is sound sense," remarked Dr. Harman.

"I call it damnable impertinence!" John's voice was almost a shout, his face was at once flushed and haggard.

"This will get us nowhere. What are your objections to a divorce, John? The scandal and the money?" asked Richard.

As his brother groaned, the physician added, "Pray consider that your wife's existence is very hollow—you dine under the same roof, and that is all your marriage, you have taken your children, your household from Mrs. Tyler, you keep another woman and four children, you give your wife no comfort, no solace, she is financially independent, a foreigner here—without relatives or friends."

"You should be in the pulpit, Dr. Harman!"

The old man smiled at this trite childish outburst, and replied, "Look at your wife, Mr. Tyler, and consider if she is fitted for the life to which you have condemned her."

The brothers did look at the young woman in her fashionable London purple dress, cut so cleverly to her charming figure, low over the white shoulder and bosom, with her lovely face, and pitiful smile, brave, yet beseeching, her delicate head with the coronal of pale curls....

"She is twenty-six and you are fifty-six," added Dr. Harman bluntly. "Set her free, or treat her as she deserves. Come, what have you to say for yourself?"

"Don't lose your temper," added Richard swiftly. "Explain yourself, John, your side of the story now, things rather go against you, you know."

John put his hand to his thick neck and stared uneasily round; he felt baited and also the necessity for "putting up a fight" as he termed it. With an effort ugly to see, he muttered obstinately:

"A divorce would ruin me—and the business—which is looking up… I'm putting a cotton substitute on the market; there ought to be a fortune in it.… Dora—that's an old arrangement… I hardly ever see her.… I can't let them all starve.… I work hard in the office. May is a bad manager, lazy, no good with the children—it costs me a deal to keep pace with her extravagance—her mother comes here, interfering and putting her against me. We don't agree—I made a mistake. If it wasn't for the servants I should be ruined. May doesn't make friends, doesn't help me socially. Everything came to an end four years ago—I wasn't well, my health isn't good—and she's so infernally fastidious."

Dr. Harman soon overthrew this angry apologia.

"Your wife isn't concerned with the effect of a divorce on your business. She asks no alimony, the scandal would be of your creating, not hers—you've been married eight years and Dora Lestrange's youngest children are aged six and four. You are a healthy man who thinks too much of his fancied ailments and you would be well enough if you'd leave off dosing yourself. If you, who were a man of forty odd admit a mistake in your marriage—you should have compassion on the error of a convent-bred girl of eighteen. Madame Dumont holds so deliberately away from your affairs that her daughter has not even told her what she has told me. As for this charge of careless extravagance perhaps you, from the first, chilled and disheartened this untrained and *fastidious* lady."

"Bravo! Another sermon!" John Tyler rose. "I think, Dr. Harman, you come here more as an advocate than a judge...."

Richard crossed swiftly over to his brother and took his arm.

"There isn't much to be said for you, John. Dr. Harman and I are doing our best to keep you out of the divorce courts—infidelity is proved."

"But not assault before two witnesses—I've never touched her...."

"Pray don't talk so brutally, Mr. Tyler. I've come to effect a reconciliation, so far I have seen no consideration for your wife in your talk and that makes it difficult for me."

Dr. Harman spoke with asperity; he was forgoing an evening with the Florentine's *Inferno*; covertly, and without envy considering May, he thought of Francesca da Rimini—odd that this seductive young creature married to a dull brute like the elder Tyler had no lover; he was sure that she had not, he was well-versed in human nature, besides if there had been anything of that kind, he must have known of it, for he heard all the gossip of his circle.

"There is no thought in your mind of a second marriage, Mrs. Tyler?"

"No," she replied at ease, but John Tyler broke out:

"Is this a Christian country, sir? A wife is asked in front of her husband if she wants another!"

"You took two wives," said May, "and you go to church oftener than I do...."

"It's different with a man. In Heaven's name what are we talking about? Will you be satisfied if I pay your debts and give up Dora?"

"No," May answered. "The debts tease me—but I contracted them for you...."

"What about the London finery?" he struck in, heavy as a blow.

"My mother paid for that. I can pay the other debts too, shortly." She turned to Dr. Harman. "I asked you, sir, to persuade my husband to a divorce. Reconciliation? I repeat, we have never quarrelled. I have no spite against Mrs. Lestrange. John should marry her."

At this statement, so simply and innocently made, the men could not avoid glances of mutual sympathy.

"You don't understand," the doctor put in kindly, "how impossible that would be."

"There seems to be so much I don't understand—I am a foreigner here. My mother is abroad. I have no one to advise me—could you not tell me the divorce laws of this country? Am I entitled to be free of this—marriage?"

Her pause was more forcible than any adjective and even John looked sullenly ashamed as he took the weakling's last refuge.

"I don't feel well," he muttered, rising, "ever since that damned chill at Wirral, I've been low—and now this—divorce is out of the question. It would ruin me. I'm too upset to talk any more. I've offered May all I can—"

He turned, rubbing one leg, and half limping towards the door. "It's these infernal pains in my legs, doctor—stiffness, too, sometimes I can hardly walk."

"Stop dosing yourself," returned Dr. Harman going with him to the door. "You've left this heels in air, haven't you?"

"Oh, Richard knows my mind, he'll speak for me, I'm sick of the whole damned nonsense."

John Tyler left the room, drawn, as by a lode star, by the packages that Mr. Tarrant had given him, and that lay securely under a pile of clean handkerchiefs in a locked drawer.

Dr. Harman caressed his chin.

"By no means satisfactory." He glanced at Richard. "What sir, can you do?"

"Give May some good advice, if she'll allow me. There is no need for families to break up like this—for lack of a friend.... May knows she can rely on me—I've her interests at heart; John is in the wrong, of course, but his offer was generous enough—I know he's fond of May.... Dora and her children might be sent to Canada with a little capital."

This smooth evasion of a tiresome affair was exactly what George Harman wished to hear; he thought Richard Tyler a useful, honest, conventional man who would "patch things up"; he, the hard worked family doctor, had done what he could, he was sorry for the little Virginian, who was much too "ladylike" for this sort of thing—and for the divorce courts, but he could not see how he could help her any more.

"Well, good evening to you, Mrs. Tyler, I hope you'll take a sensible view of your difficulties, you've the children to think of, you know. Sorry I wasn't much use, you've a real friend in your brother-in-law."

For all this breezy exit, Dr. Harman did not look at May who allowed him to go without protest, and with orthodox gratitude for his good offices.

To quiet his not very lively conscience, the physician said to Richard who accompanied him to the door:

"Poor soul, so pretty, too, see your brother treats her well. I was obliged to do as she asked me to do—but divorce! Pah! She doesn't know what she is talking about—imagine her in the witness-box! A woman can't do better than her own home."

Richard Tyler found John's wife sitting in the large chair where he had left her, her hands clasped in her lap, the light from the opal globe making her and the dull purple gown appear insubstantial against the dismal background of the tasteless room.

"You spoke more like John's advocate than mine," she said softly. "Dr. Harman was no help to me—I have no home, the children are not like mine...."

"My dear girl, I know it, the man is a meddlesome dotard...."

"Oh, not that! He is trying to keep me here, in my place—a woman's place." May spoke with a vehemence unusual to her, "Is a woman's place tied to a decayed marriage until the stench kills her, is not that unladylike? *Is* it a woman's duty to play these dull, empty farces?"

"Yours isn't—that's what I meant—the doctor is a fool." Richard took the chair near her and spoke in a carefully detached manner. "You're a very pretty woman—John is fifty-six—as you say, he has taken the children away. I had to speak as I did, but don't believe a word of it—I want to get you a divorce."

"You play double."

"No, I don't. But you see how unmanageable John is, and it was foolish of you to go to that old doctor, you heard *his* mind."

"Yes, I did, and John's too. What am I to do? I feel as if the whole weight of this house, the whole weight of Manchester was pressing me down...."

"You must get away. You'd have a case if he'd only just flick you with a napkin in front of two of the servants."

"Please, Richard, that is very horrible—it sounds as if you wished me to *arrange* something disgusting—and the servants are *his*—except Mrs. Pilch. Oh, I never could..."

"Perhaps I might..."

"What do you mean?" She stared at him piteously. "Indeed I cannot be degraded."

"No, I don't think so." Richard looked aside and his full lips twitched. "I meant I might help you—it is all difficult—a lawyer's business...."

"I know of none."

"I do—in London, though. A sound firm. Could you get to London?"

"I suppose so—but it would mean deceit, I have tried to do this openly."

"You see the result. Remember that John is a sick man—"

"Then I must stay with him."

Richard's dense dark eyes turned on her a stare of searching annoyance.

"I mean merely nerves—from all that stuff he takes."

"The white powder?"

"All kinds of powders—he is always fancying himself into an illness. Of course, really, he is as strong as I am, though years older."

"I cannot go to London if he is ill."

"May, if I am to help you, you must be sensible. If John were ill he'd have nurses—if he wanted coddling, he'd go to Dora. Now do listen to me, this divorce would be to his advantage as well as yours...."

"Would it?" she asked wistfully. "He doesn't seem happy. Would he marry Dora?"

Richard smiled. "Perhaps—anyhow, it doesn't do a man any good to have a fretting wife—it's a false position for both of you."

"Then why doesn't he set me free? You see, Richard, I know nothing about it—divorce."

"I couldn't explain now—it's complicated. There are many points I'm not clear about myself. Messrs. Gay and Dawson will soon explain! Dawson is very able, I know him well. No do listen to me, May. I'm about your only friend."

"I know, I'm listening and I'm grateful."

"You remember the Binghams? Retired brokers who live at Blackheath? You've a standing invitation to go there."

"I did not like them."

"Never mind. Write to Mrs. Bingham and say you'd be pleased if she'd put you up—tell John where you are going—to think things over, eh? Leave here two days earlier than the date you're due at Blackheath—and put up at this hotel...." He took a card from his pocket and laid it on the desk. "And I'll meet you there and take you to the lawyers."

"Will you?" She sighed, eased by the burden of decision being taken off her shoulders; she read on the pasteboard: *Hotel Mentone, Villiers*

Street, Strand. "But Mother and I always stay at the Grand Hotel Bristol in Waddington Street. . . ."

"You're known there," explained Richard patiently.

"I'd rather not do anything underhand."

"Then," cried the heavy man suddenly rising, "if you call this underhand, you must live and die in Stone Pynes, for I'm powerless to help you!"

"Please forgive me. I *cannot* remain here."

"Remember the address," he picked up the card. "I can't trust you with this, ingenuous as you are. Hotel Mentone, Villiers Street, Strand—a hansom will get you there from the station in a few minutes. I'll bring all the money you want."

"Thank you, Richard." He was touched, amused, excited at her quiet acceptance of his bounty. "And you will arrange with these lawyers?"

"Everything. Then you must go to the Binghams and stay a week. I suppose there will be no question of a priest interfering?"

"Oh no—I feel a renegade. I have said nothing."

"Your Church is against divorce?"

"We do not allow it—but I am not married in the view of my Church, since John would have the Protestant ceremony only."

He considered her keenly, his glance flickering over her delicate person, too richly dressed for his brother's house, much as John's glance had once flicked over the netted peacock, the guarded peaches.

"Not a word of this to anyone, mind you."

"Whom should I tell?"

"You've no friends in Manchester?"

"None."

"You're a queer girl." He suddenly bit his forefinger and said abruptly. "Don't have so much to do with Jerome Thorne."

He was gratified by her astonishment and wished he had not spoken.

"Why not? I like him better than anyone here—but I seldom see him. What do you mean, Richard?"

"Nothing. The fellow thinks himself a lady-killer, he seems to go where you go and to come here, pretty often.... Keep him in his place. Now remember, Hotel Mentone, Villiers Street, Strand, and let me know the date when you go...."

Richard took his leave cheerfully and May went slowly upstairs, lifting her long gown from her bronze shoes; she was intensely grateful to her brother-in-law, but how he misjudged Jerome Thorne, by imagining him capable of a vulgar flirtation; she was sure he, too, as firmly, and more delicately than Richard, would champion a helpless creature; she liked to ponder on his fair face that had a golden look, on his slim, upright figure, on his serious and courteous manner. May felt suddenly fatigued when she reached her room, and drew the curtains across the alcove closely to shut out the sound of her sleeping husband's heavy breathing.

Mr. Tyler considered his affairs with a gloomy eye. He had been in every way dispirited and angered by May's most sudden and most unexpected move. Her discovery of the existence of Dora was something that he had never reckoned on. He was still puzzled as to how she came by that information. He turned over sombrely the people he knew who might have betrayed him. His mind, slow and malicious, even turned towards the Chorleys with suspicion, but he never thought of Richard.

In a way that he would have found impossible to explain he was angry with May for behaving, as he considered it, below her own standards. In his opinion it was "unladylike" of one whom he had always thought of as so aloof and well-bred to talk about divorce, to talk about it so coolly too. It was really a shocking subject and one not fit for a lady to discuss. May had been indeed a little lowered in his estimation by that interview in which Dr. Harman had so vainly tried to act as mediator.

It had been humiliating to his masculine vanity to have to discuss this subject before his wife and even before two such friends as his brother and his physician. It was May's fault; whatever she had found out, she should have been quiet about it and done her duty as his wife. He felt he had a legitimate grievance here. Why, he knew any number of fellows whose wives overlooked their peccadillos in exchange for a good home and a handsome allowance; and May *had* a good home, however she might affect to despise it and a handsome allowance even if she did overrun it and supplement it with her own money.

It was a pretty problem, and one that he saw no way out of. He certainly did not intend to give up Dora; loyalty, decency and selfishness kept him bound there. He was interested in her children who were far more to him than May's dull and sickly pair. Besides, Dora supplied so much of what he needed—rough-and-ready companionship, unquestioning devotion, affection that had much of adoration in it; in Dora's eyes he was a very considerable person, a notable, almost a great man.

While in May's eyes he was not even a gentleman, not even an admirable human being and there lay her unforgivable offence. She had never said as much, any more than she had ever said or conveyed by a sneer or a glance her feeling of disdain for Stone Pynes and the servants whom he had set over her; but he knew what her judgment of him and his had always been, and now she'd have to be placated—distracted from this nonsense about a divorce.

Of course, she had no case. He'd take care there was nothing like an assault; but if she once began to complain to her mother or her stepfather, or to her friends in America, he might be put in a very ugly position. His affairs were not in such a state that he could afford to leave Manchester and start life afresh; and he was past the age for fresh adventures and had neither the desire, nor, he considered, the health to go away with Dora and live humbly in a paid position, nor indeed the courage.

May wanted to go to London to see the Binghams. It had been a long standing invitation and she had said frankly that she wished to accept it now, at this crisis, because she desired to think over his proposals—that still remained the same. He would pay her debts and give up Dora. The last she had waved aside as an injustice to the woman in Salford, but the first she was definitely concerned about and John, slow witted even when angry, thought it quite likely that she might want to withdraw to Blackheath to ponder the position, and had agreed to allow her to go.

He did not suppose that she would make a confidante of Mrs. Bingham, whom she knew slightly only, and he was well assured that she had no friends in London with whom she could consult. Therefore, suspicious as he was, he was half looking forward to this pause in the struggle. He would be glad to have the house to himself. There was an appearance to be kept up before the servants. There was George Harman, and Richard, continually at his elbow with their "sound advice". The Chorleys, too, continually hung about and railed him on his sour groans. They were very much his allies, but he was becoming fretted by their constant criticism of May—not that he objected to hearing his wife's faults dwelt on, but he found it galling to have it forced on his notice that he could do nothing to correct them. Amelia's "Why don't you make her do this, John?" and "You really should see that she doesn't do that," and Thomas's advice as to how the house should be run and how May should be obliged to see it was run were becoming very vexatious to John Tyler.

He did not wish perpetually to hear, "You're a prosperous man… you're making a good deal of money.… If May knew how to manage you ought to be able to keep a carriage and at least one man servant.… You've got a saddle-horse but not even a groom and it isn't good enough, my boy. You ought to talk to May. Those London clothes of hers really are ridiculous.... I don't like to repeat to you the comments I hear."

John knew quite well what Thomas Chorley and his wife heard. May had no friend in Manchester. That must be her fault as she had lived there for eight years. She went her visiting rounds and had her reception days and behaved herself with smiling courtesy to everyone, but they all sensed, as he did himself, that she was alien—different; aloof and inwardly apart.

It was just as well then that she should go to London; he allowed her a week, though she had asked for ten days to think over the situation. He had even permitted her to discuss it in its broad outline with the Binghams who were sober, discreet and orthodox people who would be certain to advise any woman, even if her supposed wrongs were greater than any May could point to, against anything so scandalous as she proposed.

When he had ponderously emphasized to his wife how shameful and disgraceful divorce was, she had asked him, why it was the law, if it could be used only by those who would be blighted for life by it? And he had replied with some furious evasion....

Well, let her go, and let the key be turned on her untidy room until she returned; and he would put through the time in his own way (leaving Dora alone, to his secret annoyance, for with her would have been comfort and consolation) discussing his case gloomily with Richard.

He relied, he had realized, a good deal on Richard... his second-self in a way, but a man of more stability of character, of a shrewder judgment, of more self-control. Not that John allowed his brother these virtues. He merely said that Richard, not being married, had nothing like the responsibilities that he, John, shouldered, and that Richard's business as a cotton broker would not have been worth much if he had not had John's help as a cotton merchant.

This support, however, was not forthcoming. Richard had to go to Birmingham to consult, he told his brother, a chemist who had undertaken, at a very moderate charge, to put in hand the initial processes of the ramie grass cotton substitute that Joseph Tarrant had brought to the notice of John Tyler.

"It's a matter of business, you see, John, and your own affairs are at a standstill. Better leave May alone. I think she's a light-minded woman. It will all pass over, if you're careful. She cannot come to any harm with the Binghams... they won't as much let her out of their sight."

John had retorted, "There's no fear of anything of that kind with May. She won't go gadding about." He grinned, even in his misery, with a certain cruel satisfaction. "I doubt if she knows the name of as much as a single playhouse in London. She's got no one to take her out either."

He gloated over the unapproachableness of his wife and Richard cordially agreed with him that May was in that respect immaculate.

"You must give her her due, John. She's kept your name high in Manchester and she's had opportunities enough. After all, for these last four years she's hardly been a married woman."

John did not care for this bluntness but he continued to glory in May's reputation for respectability, it pleased him that many men had eyed her from afar, but that none had dared to approach her and that she moreover (and this was a further gratification) had not even been aware of being desired. He remarked, however, with a grudging and reluctant venom:

"Young Thorne seems to follow her about. I notice he's put next her at a good many dinners. I saw them together in the street when she was shopping—he's got a nasty reputation."

"May doesn't know that," replied Richard coolly. "She reads a deal of trashy poetry, you know. She thinks he's a kind of knight of old.... I know, by what she's said of him.... That kind of silliness is a good safeguard for a woman. You ought to be glad, John, that May is foolish in just the right sort of way."

"She didn't seem foolish when she was talking about divorce the other night."

"She's got intelligence but no worldly wisdom."

"She's had no experience of anything," said John in a voice that if it had not been so level might have been sarcastic, "but of Manchester and us."

John thought of sending Nelly Tanner in the capacity of personal maid to his wife at Blackheath but Richard had advised him against this crude method of espionage. "It will only make her feel, however ingenuous she may be, that she's being spied on, and you know quite well there will be nothing to report as she will be in the Binghams' house all the time. Tanner hasn't a very correct manner or a pleasant temper, she'll only make trouble and let us down before the Binghams."

So John, deferring to Richard's advice, allowed May to go alone to Blackheath.

May arrived in London with the feeling of being a guilty fugitive. She had never been in the capital before without her mother or Rose Bernier being on the platform to meet her, she had always gone to stay at the familiar hotel in Waddington Street where the porter, the chambermaids and the waitresses all knew her so well. Now she was alone on the dirty platform underneath the high dirty glass roof, and on an errand that seemed to her distasteful, if not wrong.

She was to pretend to John that she had gone straight to Blackheath. She was to post a letter with the Binghams' address, informing him that she had arrived safely; and Richard had even told her to explain that the postmark would be "London" because she was going at once to her bank to interview the manager about a draft from America.

"John," Richard had advised her, "will be quite satisfied and even pleased about that." But the letter that lay in her handbag was not to be posted until to-morrow.

To-night she was to go to the Hotel Mentone in Villiers Street off the Strand; Richard had promised to come round that evening to tell her what appointment he had made with the able and courteous Mr. Dawson. He had soothed her apprehensions by saying that both the lawyers were elderly and kindly men who would give her excellent advice and complete information as to how she stood, while Richard's friend would be in every way invaluable. But for the moment she was at a loss.

In the soot-laden atmosphere much like that to which she was accustomed in Manchester, staring at the rows of hansoms and four-wheelers, at the porters hastening past with their trucks, at the groups of people meeting and hurrying away all half-hidden in murk and colourless gloom towards the barriers, she felt forlorn and lost, when a voice that was always agreeable to her addressed her and caused her to turn with eager pleasure.

"Can I see to your luggage for you, Mrs. Tyler? Can I help you? Perhaps there is someone meeting you whom you have missed?"

It was Jerome Thorne who spoke and she looked at him a moment before she could adjust him to these surroundings; he smiled at her childlike bewilderment. "I've run up to London for a day or two, like you have yourself, Mrs. Tyler, and taken the same train. I didn't notice you at the other end."

"No, nor I you," she replied, and he turned aside to hide the grin that would have revealed, surely, even to this piece of innocence, 'It would have been strange if you had, seeing the trouble I took to conceal myself.'

Then he was all respectful attention, the easy part he had set himself. Her luggage was one small trunk and the few cases she had had with her in the carriage. Without thinking that possibly she was being indiscreet, she told him that she was staying in London for the night and then going on to the Binghams at Blackheath.

He knew them… yes, very well… they were friends of his, too, he would like to be able to come over to Blackheath and see her, but his business was "pressing" and he feared he would not be able to get so far. What was the name of her hotel? May was so little used to intrigue that she nearly gave him this as a matter of course, but recollected herself in time and replied with a flush of shame, "Oh a little place that Richard told me of… not the Bristol…."

She was, perhaps for the first time in her life, confused and incoherent as she glanced at Jerome Thorne's slim and upright figure moving with authority among the porters, she wondered wretchedly if she had disobeyed Richard's instructions? No one was to know that she was going to the Mentone… but Richard had not foreseen this contingency, that she should meet an acquaintance…. Yet what was more likely…? Business people went to and from London and Manchester every day, and she had chosen a popular train. She had made a blunder; obviously she should have told the young man that she was proceeding to Blackheath and somehow have shaken him off, even at the cost of a false direction to the cabman… now there was nothing to do but to rely on the chivalry she was sure he possessed.

When he returned with her luggage on a truck, and hailed the foremost of the hansoms waiting on the rank, she began nervously, ingenuously, "I have some private business to transact with a lawyer and my bank…. I should be so much obliged if you would not mention that I am not going straight to the Binghams…."

Mr. Thorne, who was by no means unskilled in the bypaths of amateur subterfuge, could scarcely restrain a deepening of his impassive smile at this naive confession. He had what he thought the correct reply ready.

"Why, Mrs. Tyler, it is no affair of mine where you are going, and I hope you wouldn't think me the kind of fellow to gossip over a lady's affairs...."

But though he considered this a very chivalrous statement there was something about it that May could not either define or like.

He saw her into the hansom and there was nothing in his manner to which she could object, yet she was sorry that he insisted on knowing the name of the hotel that he might give the directions to the cabman, she had no resources even against his vulgar skill and reluctantly said, "The Hotel Mentone."

"I'm staying there myself—that's curious," he smiled coolly. "May I share your hansom? I always think the Mentone is a delightful place to put up at, I commend your taste, Mrs. Tyler," and he was beside her, his light dust-coat touching her grape-coloured jacket, for she had come to London in the bizarre outfit she had bought from Madame Clorinde.

"Richard," answered May, "found the place for me. How odd that you should be going there."

"Why, not so odd," he replied easily, "it's well known to Manchester people, that's why Richard recommended it to you. I suppose he'll be calling to see you?"

"Yes, on a matter of business."

"As John's deputy no doubt, John being too busy to leave Manchester?"

This was her own excuse put ready-made before her, but she did not use it, and sat silent.

The narrow cab forced her into an intimacy with this young man that she did not like. She had admired Jerome Thorne because of his name, his appearance, his mother's religion. She had believed that he was someone to whom one could appeal in distress—a wraith as it were of one of Lord Tennyson's spotless heroes. But sitting so close to him in the hansom cab, watching the bright flanks of the horse before her, hearing the jingle of the harness, with the perfume of the cigar and *eau-de-Cologne* from the young man's person, she was not at ease. Why, she did not know, save that it ill-suited her nature to be party to any kind of subterfuge. She almost wished now that she had brought Nelly Tanner with her; she almost wished that she had not taken Richard's advice to consult these London lawyers and was really going straight to the haven of the Binghams' dull conventional house at Blackheath, for there was no spirit of adventure in May Tyler—but the appearance of the Hotel Mentone was reassuring. It was a homely place in a narrow street that sloped directly down to the Embankment and the river, and it had every air of decorum and respectability; not that May had remotely supposed it would have anything else, or that she needed, even knew of anything else than decorum and respectability, yet she was subtly comforted by the cheerful neatness of the chambermaid, the solid furnishings of the bedroom so like the room she had left at Manchester, and the long dining-table already set with damask cloth, folded napkins, slim bottles of wine and of sauces for the evening meal; after all, she knew, even if she would not admit as much, even to herself, that there was some sort of world no decent woman was aware of, that John visited, that was, perhaps, familiar to Dora Lestrange.

As a matter of course Jerome Thorne shared her dinner with her. His manner was calculated, he believed, to put her entirely at her ease. He did not, however, please her as much as she had supposed he would should she speak to him alone and for a considerable space of time. The chance remarks she had heard from him when in company, what he had said when he had come to tell her of her husband's illness at Wirral, were more to her taste than the flattering chit-chat that he uttered now; yet she still liked him; candidly studying his face she found in it nothing but frankness and goodwill and she cut through his superficial compliments which did not affect her much one way or another, for though she had received none since her marriage, she had been used to them before, by asking him straightly: "I think you would be a friend to anyone in trouble, would you not, Mr. Thorne?"

He was a little discomfited at what he considered these odd tactics.

"I should always be at the service of a lady," he remarked, using a jargon that she did not understand.

"I mean—if anyone was really in great distress, alone and forlorn—I think you, without any consideration for yourself, would try to assist them—that is what I mean. I had that impression of you. I have not had it from anybody else whom I have met in Manchester, except from Richard."

"I am very flattered, Mrs. Tyler, to have had this effect on you—very flattered indeed."

He was a little bewildered at her complete ignorance of what all his acquaintances must know about him; his debts, his difficulties, his haunting of the race-courses and the clubs, the precarious position he occupied in the business world, his carefully cultivated reputation as "a lady-killer"... she certainly was very different from any other woman he had ever met, and he flattered himself and boasted to others, of his great variety of amorous experiences.

He eyed her curiously, not knowing quite how to proceed; but she was waiting for an answer; her clear grey eyes, under the sweeping brows, were turned on him with a glance at once proud and wistful. His reply was more honest than he had meant it to be.

"I certainly would do all I could to help you, if that's what you meant, Mrs, Tyler."

"Yes, that is what I meant. I'd rather you spoke frankly than paid me compliments. I cannot tell you my affairs now, but they may be public quite soon—and there is really nothing in them for anybody to be ashamed about. Richard is helping me, but Richard is a very busy man. He has," she continued, with a simplicity that further astounded Jerome Thorne, "a difficult business on hand just now. He is putting a cotton substitute on the market and has to go to Birmingham. My mother and stepfather are abroad, and all my relatives are in Virginia; Dr. Harman has been very kind to me. I wondered, if I were in need of it, you, too, would be kind?"

"Kind? That's a word capable of many meanings, Mrs, Tyler. I'm prepared to be a good deal more than kind."

"You must not think that you can say that you admire me. I do not mean a flirtation or a coquetry—I think you above that. Naturally one could ask any young man to help one in that sort of way.... I mean that you would do it out of chivalry?"

The word sounded completely "out of date" to Jerome Thorne who had not read the works of Lord Tennyson and who had only heard of chivalry in drawing-room ballads. He understood vaguely, however, what she meant and he began to suspect her sincerity. He could not believe in such single-mindedness, never having met it before—and what was she doing secretly at the Hotel Mentone... and what sort of game was Richard playing?

He had, however, enough subtlety to be cautious. He assured her in a low tone that she could rely on him, and when she protested, sincerely enough, fatigue, he allowed her to leave the dining-room and go to her own chamber without suggesting what he had intended to suggest—a visit to one of those places so well known to him, the Argyle Rooms, the parade at the Alhambra or Lemoines where there was music and dancing nearly all night, and every opportunity for illicit "love-making", as Mr. Thorne termed his dull intrigues.

May Tyler spent an ill night. She felt (for the first time in her life) friendless—despite the open championship of Richard and, she believed, the secret championship of Jerome Thorne—and a fugitive, almost a wrongdoer. Her surroundings were different from any she had known before; they depressed her already fluctuating spirits. Several times she rose, turned on the gas and put about her own personal possessions on wash-hand-stand and dressing-table, without effacing the alien appearance of the room that seemed to have an odour of strangers, where dirt concealed beneath neatness half-suffocated.

She was late in the dining-room, having at the last overslept and not heard the chambermaid's knock. There was a letter on her plate from Richard with a Birmingham postmark. He expected to be in town immediately after this communication and would call at the Hotel Mentone to take her to the lawyers, he wrote in kind, cheerful, brotherly terms and May's spirits rose a little.

Jerome Thorne was loitering over his breakfast at a table in the window-place and came over easily and joined her; it would have been natural to her to give him her confidence and show him Richard's letter, but she was a little baffled by her situation and so said nothing of her business in town nor of Richard's forthcoming visit.

The young man made elegant small talk, fencing with her as he supposed, quite unaware of the extent of her simplicity; he asked her how long she was likely to stay at the Mentone, and she answered "Several days", at random, her thoughts far away; he asked her if she had liked the chocolates he had given her and she replied at once, glad to be able to be both truthful and courteous, that she had enjoyed them very much and that there were still a few left in the box in her cupboard at Stone Pynes. Mr. Thorne then at once proposed that he should buy her a further supply of these dainties, and asked her if she would accompany him to the shop in Regent Street where he purchased them. "I had the box prepared especially for you."

May thanked him and declined the invitation. "I have some shopping of my own."

She was eager and amiable now she was on safe ground.

"I shall see you perhaps at luncheon time, unless you remain in the city," she added, remembering her husband's custom that she supposed was that of most business men, of staying in his office for the midday meal.

But Jerome Thorne did not seem so strenuously occupied. He said at once that he would meet her at luncheon at the Mentone and that he would order a better repast than that hotel usually provided; then not content to let her go on such vague terms, he pressed her, with some adroitness, as to any possible visitors she might have, and May admitted that her brother-in-law might call to see her and take her to the Binghams at Blackheath. She was too inexperienced in any kind of intrigue to realize how foolish and even incredible her story must seem, or even to realize that she had given no reasonable excuse for being at the Mentone at all.

Mr. Thorne accepted her statement with a casual air and merely asked that she should not mention his presence in the hotel to Richard.

"Why?" asked May directly.

"I have a reason of my own," he replied coolly. "Will you oblige me, Mrs. Tyler?"

"I do not think," replied May sincerely, "I should have thought of speaking of you being here to Richard. I suppose, as you said, there are many people from Manchester here, is it not so?"

"Yes, it is. I have a particular reason… something to do with the race-course… something a lady would not understand… for your brother-in-law not knowing I'm in town. Oh, it's something you would find very foolish I'm sure, but pray oblige me."

May promised, and the young man left her with a lingering glance, that seemed to hold respect, protection and help. May regretted his company. She felt more at home with him than with Richard. She would rather have been going with Mr. Thorne to the lawyers than with her brother-in-law whom she certainly trusted but who was personally not so attractive to her as the younger man, who kept for her, not quite untarnished, but still kept, his air of chivalry.

Richard had, in a lesser degree, the obtuseness, the coarseness, the heavy dullness that made John so distasteful to his wife, whereas Jerome Thorne had no taint of the middle-class trader, but seemed to her, more definitely every time she saw him, to be of the same quality as the Virginians and Frenchmen whom she had known in her childhood and early life.

She waited in the public sitting-room for Richard to arrive; turned over an old newspaper and retired into her thoughts, regardless of the comings and goings of a slow-faced waiter of such insignificance that she hardly noted him as a human being, who asked her if she would like coffee… if she was waiting for anyone… if she would ring the bell should she require any service.

May did not know that it was strange for a lady in costly and flamboyant clothes, that were in the very best of modish taste, to be waiting alone in the coffee-room of the Mentone, nor that the waiter was a keen observer of the only types of humanity that he ever saw, those who used a disreputable hotel on disreputable business.

On the stroke of twelve, that boomed and rattled from a tall grandfather clock, Richard appeared; he had an air of suppressed excitement and told May rapidly, standing before her with his hat and gloves in his hands: "It had been difficult to get away from Birmingham without causing suspicion." There had been, he emphasized, many people to mislead.

"I do not like that at all," protested May. "I think the whole thing might have been done openly. It is hard for one of my temperament to be a woman," she added irrelevantly.

"Oh you," he answered brusquely, "would spoil everything. Now I've got an appointment for the lawyers this afternoon. Dawson will be there—with plenty of time to give us—we'll put the whole case before him and you shall hear what he has to say as to your chances of getting a divorce. I want you, too, to tell them all your financial affairs, so we can straighten up the matter of your debts. I'll go with you to your bankers afterwards. Part of your trouble, my dear girl, is getting into a mess with money matters. It gives John a constant cause of complaint. You will have luncheon with me here, I suppose? I shall be staying at the Mentone myself. I always do when I come to London.... Did you give your own name?"

"Yes."

"Did you forget that I advised something quite ambiguous like Mrs. Smith?"

"I'm afraid I did. When they asked my name I could think of none but my own."

"Well it doesn't matter, Tyler isn't such an uncommon name."

"I don't want to stay here any longer. It's too near the river and the street's so narrow. I'll go out I think, for a walk about the city."

"There's nowhere you can walk round here, it's all business premises and shops, and there's nowhere a woman can get a meal when she's by herself. You'd better let me take you somewhere."

But May did not want for the moment any more of Richard's company. She desired very much to be alone. She had forgotten, in her personal preoccupations, Jerome Thorne's presence in the hotel and therefore was not apprehensive of the two men meeting after the younger one's request that his presence should be kept secret; she was only desirous to get away from the place, from Richard, to prepare herself in some kind of solitude, at least mental and spiritual solitude, for the coming interview with the lawyers.

"I shall go to Shoolbred's," she said. "There's a restaurant there where ladies can dine alone. I have often been there with my mother. I have some purchases to make for Stone Pynes, and I think I shall try to buy a gift for Mrs. Bingham. They had some very pretty china roses when I was last there. I think she would like one of them; they were made in Dresden and are of the finest possible manufacture."

Richard smiled, she was amazingly ingenuous; this quality of hers was like a zestful flavour on his lips; he escorted her to the Strand, found a hansom, put her in it and gave the address of Messrs. Shoolbred's in the Tottenham Court Road.

May walked aimlessly through the large shop where she was well known, as Madame Dumont had an account there, and the ladies would frequently visit the large showrooms to make various casual and often extravagant purchases. She was now too distracted to notice the various and pretty articles displayed, but she bought the china rose in the hardware department. It was an elegant object and yet there was something amiss with it; the delicate leaf petals of the flower were ill-rendered in the glossy porcelain, however exactly this might be tinted saffron and pink; it was useless too; merely, as the attendant suggested, to stand on the table—a lady's table—as ornament; it reminded May of the rose printed on the shining surface of the chocolate-box.

May had luncheon in the ill-lit restaurant at the top of the building, reached by so many flights of stairs decorously dark and gloomy, a long room with a row of small narrow windows opening on to the huddled chimney pots that were partially hidden by the crude yellows and reds of the stained-glass panes. Solitary ladies, but none as young and conspicuous for looks and clothes as she was, one or two elderly men, nursemaids with children, occupied the square tables with the white damask cloths, and May felt secure in an atmosphere that so nearly resembled that of Manchester.

She ate her meal thoughtfully, ordering with care and eating with indifference. She had no desire to go back on her adventure, and she had enough courage with which to go forward, though it was definitely unpleasant, worse than she had supposed it would be; and yet nothing had happened to revolt or jar, it had even been an agreeable surprise to meet Jerome Thorne, to accept his sympathy that was at once so eager and so restrained. He did not know her trouble, and yet she felt that had he done so he could have helped her more efficiently than did Richard; yet Richard was kindness itself. She had no cause to complain of him, and after this little relaxation she must put herself in his hands and that of the lawyers.

Would it be possible to get this divorce? How was it Richard did not know and had not informed her already? Men had a baffling way of behaving. She rejected Richard and John's talk of an assault before two witnesses; this was something brutal from which she must avert her eyes. Then there was the question of "custody of the children" which had come so glibly from Richard's lips. She must find out about it... possibly the English law might give her a legal claim to them, and her face flushed at the hope. Perhaps they would be really her children, and perhaps she could after all take them away to Paris, to Virginia, out of the smoke and fog, away from the possessive excellency of Lizzie Burt, away from everything and everyone in Stone Pynes.

With this prospect still in her mind she rose impulsively, and taking her money carefully (she was ill-used to taking a meal away from her own home so it seemed odd to have to pay for it) out of her bag, went to the little cashier's desk that stood inside the large folding doors. A tap on her shoulder and a loud voice exclaiming her name caused her to turn round quickly. It took a great deal to disturb her well-bred equanimity, but now she stood at a loss. It was Mrs. Bingham who confronted her, and with a stare of astonishment that seemed touched with reproach and menace.

"My dear May, where have you been? What an extraordinary chance meeting you here! We should have expected you it seems yesterday... what has the mistake been? I have your letter and you distinctly said next Tuesday...."

"Yes, I did say that date," replied May taking up her change mechanically. "What made you think that wasn't right, Mrs. Bingham?"

"Why the message—the telegram… it must have come almost immediately after you left Manchester. John is ill… quite seriously ill.… Dr. Harman thinks you should return at once. Now what on earth was I to do when you had not arrived and I was not expecting you till next Tuesday? Is there any trouble?… Do you want to speak to me privately…? Shall we go into the ladies' waiting-room…?"

"I suppose so," whispered May looking round at the long dimly lit room where in a frigid and rigid silence and attitude conventional people were eating their conventional meals. "We cannot talk here, of course."

"Where are you staying, my dear child?" Mrs. Bingham's shocked curiosity was not to be easily satisfied, but May paid but little heed to her constant questionings as she walked beside her towards the green glass door on which in transparent glass was written the words "Ladies' Waiting-Room".

So John was ill… that was all that mattered.… It meant an end of everything, at least for the time being; no interviews with the lawyer, no further consultations with Richard, no possible assistance from Jerome Thorne.… She would have to return to Manchester at once.

"When will be the next train?" she asked.

"My dear child," replied Mrs. Bingham sitting down heavily on a large, darkly upholstered chair. "Don't run away with all sorts of crazy ideas. You must come to us for to-night of course." She looked at May shrewdly, with mingled firmness and reproach. "It was really very foolish of you to get matters so confused. If you didn't wish to come and stay—"

May interrupted. "I had a little business to do in London, Mrs. Bingham. My husband doesn't care for me to stay in hotels by myself but I thought I had the right to do as I wished."

"You had no right to deceive him," put in Mrs. Bingham sternly. "It's an absurd deception. May, to seem to be staying with us when you were not. The telegram was addressed care of me at my Blackheath address; I've been half out of my mind… I didn't know what to do or where to find you…."

"I'm sorry, I understand I put you in a very embarrassing position. I do apologize—but it is a thing one never could have thought of, John seemed in good health when I left him."

In her mind she was thinking of the white powders and John's angry distress at their last interview. Had he, in an attempt to console himself for what no doubt he considered her harsh treatment, taken too much of his own medicine? She said nothing of this, believing it to be John's secret, but remarked, "He was taken ill at Wirral Races, Mrs. Bingham, but he seemed much better. John is quite a healthy man and fusses too much over his fancied ailments. I don't suppose this is anything for us to disturb ourselves about. Who sent the telegram?"

"It was not sent by your husband," replied Mrs. Bingham with an ominous look, "but by the doctor himself, which doesn't appear as if your husband's disease was so very imaginary this time. Anyhow, I'm very thankful for this chance meeting. How odd that I should meet you here…."

"Not so odd," said May with a slight smile, "since we both deal at Shoolbred's. There are few other places where a lady can have luncheon in London. My business appointment was not till this afternoon and I could think of nowhere else to go."

"Well, this is the day I always come up to give the week's orders, and I, too, find the restaurant most convenient, but it is certainly most extraordinary that we should chance to meet. You're taking it all very coolly, my dear child."

"I'm so sure that there is nothing serious the matter with John, it is most vexatious and I am most sorry that you should have been put about."

"You should have told me where you were, where you were staying—at the Bristol as usual, I suppose?" questioned Mrs. Bingham.

May did not reply. Her composure, which was not in the least arrogant or insolent, but rather sad and aloof irritated the older woman who had a sharp eye for any lapse from orthodox behaviour.

"Well," she continued in a ruffled tone, "I'll come round to the Bristol with you and help you to collect your things, and you must come with me to Blackheath. You've missed the only possible train for Manchester for to-day. We will see you off in the morning. I dare say that I or Charlie could do your business for you if you'd confide in us. It isn't anything serious I hope?"

"Yes, it's quite serious, at least to me… it involves other people… it's something to do with my income from Virginia," she added with less than her usual candour.

"Well then," retorted the other lady, "John should know about it. I don't believe in wives having secrets from their husbands… it really is a pure deception on your part, May, and I don't like it at all. I shan't mention it, of course, because I don't want to create bad feeling, especially when John is so ill."

"I don't think he is so ill, Mrs. Bingham. The doctor would have said so. What did the telegram actually state?"

Mrs. Bingham at once brought a flimsy form from her bag. On it was written in a scrawled pencil: *Your husband seriously indisposed. Advise your immediate return. George Harman.*

"I'll return to-night, no matter how inconvenient the trains."

But Mrs. Bingham was obstinate. "If I am to say that you have been staying with us, you *must* stay with us," she insisted. "I cannot begin telling lies at my time of life just because you're rather flighty. Oh, I know, my dear girl, that you were brought up with other ideas and I dare say between America, Paris and a convent you do not look at things the way we do, and of course it's very odd for you to have business affairs your husband doesn't know about.... But it's not my affair, I'm sure."

"I suppose it is, Mrs. Bingham," said May rising, "as I have involved you in it. I shall send a telegram at once, and I think it would help keep the peace—shall we call it that?—at Stone Pynes if you don't say that I had come up to London on some matter of my own. Therefore, to make that kindness of yours on which I count, go with your conscience, I shall come to Blackheath to-night."

Mrs. Bingham could hardly find any objection to this nor any excuse for further probing into what she felt was a considerable mystery. She was not, however, an ill-natured woman nor one overprone to gossip, and she had never heard a single word, even among the most vulgar people in Manchester, against the correct behaviour and discretion of May Tyler who was apt to do what might appear perhaps odd and independent actions, but who never had overstepped the barriers of the most ladylike conduct. Mrs. Bingham was really convinced that this escapade was nothing more than some piece of wilfulness due to foreign upbringing and as such prepared to pass it over, she had no desire to be a tell-tale, and secretly preferred May to her husband, but she was a little disappointed in that young woman's tranquillity; after that first start and flush May had seemed unmoved, secure and dignified; as if she were neither contrite nor repentant; Mrs. Bingham took it for granted that she would go with her to Waddington Street to fetch her luggage, and walked beside her to the street door.

May gave neither yes nor no, but when they reached the street smiled "good-bye" with an air of grateful civility, and jumped into a hansom, that she had beckoned the porter to bring up from the nearby rank, so quickly, that the elderly woman had no chance of following her, nor of hearing what she said to the cabman.

"I shall be at Blackheath as soon as possible," and lifting the flap with a pale gloved hand, gave a rapid direction.

'That was not courteously done,' regretted May, 'but I have Richard, who has been so kind, to consider, and probably Mrs. Bingham wouldn't approve of my staying at the Mentone which seems indeed to be more suitable for gentlemen than for ladies. There were certainly some women staying there but I found them ill-bred.'

May's disappointment lay about her heavy as a cloak of lead. She left a note with the sharp-eyed waiter for Mr. Richard Tyler in which she said: *John is taken ill and I am returning to Manchester to-morrow. To-night I shall be with the Binghams at Blackheath.* She had no excuse to write to Jerome Thorne, but she was sorry not to see him again.

The hotel was very dark and quiet, the rooms shrouded, the skies were grey, the wind icy from the river, there was no sign of spring save in the tight posies in the baskets of the flower women who sat by the dirty, sombre station at the top of Villiers Street.

May paid her bill, fee'd the chambermaid and the porter and went away in a four wheeler to the Temple Station for Blackheath; the distance was short, but she could not carry her trunk.

The blear-eyed waiter who was such a good observer and so sharp a judge of such samples of humanity as came his sombre and sordid way, handed with secret relish May Tyler's note to her brother-in-law. When that gentleman, flushed and stimulated by a good meal, appeared precisely at three o'clock at the Hotel Mentone, the waiter watched that high colour fade, those bright animated eyes harden and look aside, those well-cut lips that middle age was beginning to blur at the edges harden and stiffen, and the whole man become taut, as if ready to receive a blow. The waiter enjoyed these signs of discomfiture and the effort that was made to conceal them. They were by no means unfamiliar to him. He, like all the members of the staff of the Hotel Mentone, was well used to getting private zest out of the delivery of these little notes to the woman or the man who had been left behind, to the woman or the man whose appointment had not been kept, to the losing party, in brief, of some underground intrigue.

Richard Tyler flung down a florin and put the note in his waistcoat pocket.

"I shall be leaving this afternoon. I'll take the four-thirty, there'll be just time to catch it."

The waiter murmured agreement and Richard Tyler sat down in the dull coffee-room that was polluted by enclosed air and the smell of the week's cooking, to confront the severest disappointment of his life. John had turned the tables on him nicely by this damnable illness which was certainly his own fault, brought on either through overdosing himself or chagrin at the divorce project; but own fault or not, that was no consolation for Richard Tyler.

She had returned, and as long as his brother was ill, she would not leave Stone Pynes and all his carefully thought out scheme had fallen to the ground. There was however one thing he could do. He could provoke his brother to deliver what would be an insult from which May would never recover or forgive—the last legality required for a divorce, an assault, a blow before witnesses. He fee'd, not thinking what he was doing, the waiter again for bringing down his valise, and his cab rattled up the cobbles two minutes before Jerome Thorne in his light dust-coat returned to the Hotel Mentone, also to be informed with secret zest by the drab-faced waiter, that Madam had gone and left no note.

John Tyler was abundantly glad of the opportunity to recall his wife from the London visit of which he had never thoroughly approved. It was true that he was ill. He had been to see Dora at Salford and come home in a bitter May night of drizzle and rain, and taken what he termed "a chill" that terminated by cramp in his legs, a feeling of nausea and impotent rage for Dora had been helpless and even tearful before this catastrophe in their fortunes. He had remained in bed in his dreary room and asked Nelly Tanner to send for Dr. Harman. It had been easy to persuade the physician to send the telegram that was to bring May back to Stone Pynes. It was a wife's duty to be by the side of her husband when he was unwell, and this time George Harman had not talked so much about imaginary illness but given the invalid some medicines that further increased his discomfort and persuaded him that he was seriously ill.

When May arrived he had a sour welcome ready. She found him, as she had expected, by no means prostrate; in a brown girdled dressing-gown seated in the library in which sombre apartment, despite the time of year, a fire had been lit. His eyes, glazed by sickness, flickered over her purple jacket and the rich subdued tartan of her skirt.

His greeting was, "You know I don't like the way you dress. What did you need to put that finery on for if you were just going to see the Binghams?"

"Mrs. Bingham admired the dress," said May quietly. "I am aware you don't like it and I would have taken it off before I saw you, but I was anxious to know about your health."

John Tyler resorted to his usual tactics of which she took little heed; he grumbled that she cared little for his peace of mind or ease of body, that he might die for all she cared, that she had no right to have left him on any excuse whatsoever; as for "thinking things over", couldn't she do that at Stone Pynes?

"I don't suppose I can do it anywhere, I have to act from day to day on instinct. I suppose you'd say my instinct brings me back to you.... We cannot talk about anything until you're better."

"I shall never be better," he replied peevishly. "I've been a sick man for many years now although you don't seem to realize the fact. You're the most thoughtless and incompetent of wives...."

"Then why not be rid of me?" put in May quietly.

He turned on her at that. "You've got somebody else in view I suppose? I've heard some stories since you've been away.... Amelia Chorley's a good friend of mine... she had something to say about you...."

May was astonished, knowing her behaviour to be without fault.

"Amelia Chorley is a vulgar woman. Why should she gossip about me to you... and when my back is turned...?" She wouldn't say any more nor listen to his angry reply because it had always been her endeavour to avoid recriminations of any kind. Quarrelling—especially domestic quarrelling between husband and wife—were to her so abhorrent that it was impossible for her to submit to it.

"If you're not well, John, I'll get a nurse from Miss Rose's Home. You remember Nurse Goff whom we had for John when he was ill, she might come and look after you..."

"You ought to look after me yourself."

"Why, so I would, only, as you say, I know nothing.... Then there's Mrs. Crimpton, she might come in... she's not trained but she's excellent at nursing...."

"Laying out corpses you mean," jeered John bitterly. "Why do you want to put all these hags about me?"

She could not answer all these inconsistencies; at one minute she was incompetent and impossible and another minute he expected her to do everything herself; it was a hateful task that lay before her if John was to be really ill, but it was one she could not possibly, according to her own standards, avoid.

"Has Richard returned?" he asked sullenly. "Have you seen or heard anything about him?"

"You would hear before I should," she answered evasively.

"He's been in Birmingham. Some business to do with that ramie grass—I wish he'd come along, I've no one sensible to talk to."

May did not reply though she might have said—'This is your native city, you have all your friends and acquaintances,' but she neither smiled nor sighed, but considered him pleasantly. He asked her questions about the Binghams and she was able to answer truthfully, then he broke off peevishly and told her there was to be a series of entertainments at the Pomona Gardens in aid of the Royal Infirmary Charity and, if any money was left over after that estimable institution had been satisfied, for the Ladies Committee of the Women's Prison.

"They're spoiling these people... imagine raising public money to help those criminals!" snarled John Tyler.

"I'm sorry for them, one should have the courage to go to such places and see how these unfortunates are treated."

She mused over that lost world full of human beings, women like herself, accused, sentenced for she knew not what crimes, sunk into an abyss for she knew not what reason....

"I'm glad they collect money for them. What is it spent on?"

"Heaven knows," replied John bitterly. "Pampering them, I suppose. It's squandered on schemes like giving them baths and a library, materials to work with to undersell the shops.... I don't know what the country is coming to. It seems to me you've got to be a criminal before you get any consideration."

He continued in the same strain of gloomy complaint of which May took little notice; she was used to this tone which exactly reflected his mind but she was surprised that he desired her to go to these entertainments; was it an offer of reconciliation? There was to be a gala performance of a play, the name of which he had forgotten; there was to be an afternoon concert and a carnival ball....

"You'll like that," he sneered. "You enjoy dressing up... look at what you're wearing now... hadn't Mrs. Bingham something to say about that?"

"She admired it, I told you, it's quite fashionable and modish."

John raised his hand and let it fall in a silent gesture of despair and irritation. He had not mentioned the divorce; neither had she; yet she felt it to be in the minds of both.

"Well," he announced, again showing that inconsistency so hard for her to endure, used as she was to it, "the house has been all to pieces since you've been away. I hope you'll go down and see Maggie Pilch and order some decent meals."

May resisted the temptation to reply, "I thought I was such an inefficient housekeeper," and answered, "It will be no use this evening, I'll go to-morrow morning and do what I can. Now I am going up to see the children."

"They haven't missed you," he replied brutally.

"Do you know that?" she challenged at the door. "Have *you* been to see them?"

"No, they're safe and happy enough with Lizzie Burt. Dr. Harman is coming this evening, he'll tell you what is the matter with me…"

May went up the narrow dark stairs to the nursery. She found what she had expected to find; Lizzie Burt, with a censorious look was cutting out coloured pictures from a tattered volume of stories and pasting them into a scrap-book, a proceeding of which neither of the children seemed to take much notice. John was sitting digging the stump of a broken pen-knife into his desk and only giving an occasional sideways glance at the lambs and rabbits, the horses and cows which Lizzie Burt, with stiff sweeps of the hand, was pasting into the book; little May, with feminine subtlety, affected an interest she did not feel, but her idle hands were pulling aimlessly at the lace on her apron.

"Here's your mother," said Lizzie Burt rising. "Good evening ma'am. The children will be glad to see you back again."

"I've only been away three days altogether," smiled May. "The children haven't missed me?" she questioned.

"No, I wouldn't say they missed you." Nurse was slightly venomous. "They're more used to me than they are to you, madam, if you will permit me to say so, and the master quite approves of all I do."

May felt as usual that she had been dismissed from her own nursery and her own children; neither boy nor girl took any notice of her beyond the mechanical rising to their feet and the "Good evening, mamma, I hope you are quite well."

May Tyler returned to her room and sat down in what would have been in another woman, the blackness of misery; but she had the aloof and resigned spirit that kept her outwardly composed and inwardly resolved to face with courage whatever was ahead, John as an invalid... all her projects for the divorce defeated... whatever Richard might argue, she could not leave her husband while he was ill. Perhaps it had been her gesture towards freedom that had overthrown his health, perhaps it had been those white powders against which she had protested, but against which she could protest no more for she was only snubbed by John, by Dr. Harman, by Richard and even by Amelia Chorley to whom she had once ventured to remark on the amount of medicine that John took....

She went to the large wardrobe, opened it and saw the large cardboard box covered with the glazed paper on which was painted the saffron rose. Jerome Thorne's gift, and he had offered to buy her another such present, and to take her to the shop where such dainties were laid out in sumptuous display... that would have been a pleasant expedition... May looked, as through a peephole, at a life of ease, of gallantry, of wit and leisure that she might have enjoyed had she not been married to John Tyler, a life in which neither she nor her mother could see any harm whatsoever, a life that expected and gave happiness as a matter of course.

Well, it was not for her, she did not even open the box though there were a few chocolates remaining; she glanced up at the blue

Bible on the upper shelf as she took off the flat hat trimmed with the cherries, and slung it up dexterously beside the Holy Book. She ought to open that of course—her mother's gift, and associated with the delicious day, so warm and slothful, in Paris, when she and the friends now scattered, had lain on the grass in the *bois* near Bagatelle. Now she had grown up, woman's work to do... a sick man to wait on... She put her hand to her smooth brow, a little baffled by the difficulties. To whom was she to turn for advice? She knew nothing of illness. To-morrow she would order patent foods and invalid concoctions... Perhaps Dr. Harman would confide in her and tell her what John's illness was; he certainly had appeared different; his cheeks were sunken and he was puffy under the eyes, his hands shook and she noticed that when he got to his feet his limbs trembled; and yet he had spoken of going to the Pomona for a series of entertainments.... She was not shrewd enough to realize that he wished to be seen in public with his wife in order to dispel those rumours that had somehow got about, that he and May were on the verge of a separation or a divorce, and that the second establishment at Salford had been discovered by May Tyler.

Idleness, confusion and frustration confronted her like three spectres. It was almost horrible to see Nelly Tanner coming in, without waiting for the signal, with the brass can of water and the clean towel; she was expected then to take up her old routine at once... to dress for dinner, to go down to the large dining-room, to sit through all the courses of heavy and detestable food....

With a warm, human desire to be friendly with all in her time of distress she said to the stiff-faced woman, "Have you got on all right while I have been away, Nelly? There's been no trouble or difficulty?"

The housemaid had her back towards her mistress, under the excuse of arranging the can precisely in the basin on the marble-topped wash-hand-stand. "I'm sure I don't know, madam. It don't seem to make much difference… it's the master and Mrs. Pilch that run the house as far as I can see, with Lizzie Burt for the children…"

"I can always trust Mrs. Pilch," said May sweetly, "and I hope you too, Nelly. I had to go to town to see a friend and on business, but as you say, I have so little to do with things at Stone Pynes that I don't suppose there was much difference."

The woman looked at her sharply out of her acid eyes, silenced at this candour with which she did not know how to deal; threw back her head and left the room.

John did not come to his bedroom that night. May waited up for him, expecting to be called to attend him in some fit of coughing, sickness, cramp or moaning complaint, but he must have slept, and slept heavily, down in the library. It was dawn before she slept herself and then her dreams were ugly and chaotic.

Mrs. Pilch eyed her mistress with compassion, reserve and a touch of defiance.

"It's not my place to be speaking to you, madam," she repeated for the third time, "but I'd rather forget my place and take the consequences," she added primly, "than see what I do see going on, and you made the victim of it."

"I wish," smiled May gently, "you would not talk about your place, Mrs. Pilch. You know I was brought up in another country and we don't have these ideas. I have always tried to be friendly with anyone who has been working in this house."

"Yes, I know you have," replied the cook stoutly. "And whose fault has it been if it's not been a success?" she added sombrely. "There's things going on that you ought to know of, and that I don't like at all—and if it wasn't for you I shouldn't stay."

May had always liked Mrs. Pilch and had exchanged many a lively conversation, and many a good-humoured agreeable jest when they were making the list for the month's household accounts, or going through the stores in the provision closet, the china in the china closet, or the silver in the cupboard lined with green baize; but this was the first time that Mrs. Pilch had spoken candidly, and it was, though with respect, in a tone of intimacy that she addressed her mistress.

"But what can be happening that I need know about?" asked May. "I suppose Nelly, Jane and Dolly are always complaining that I'm extravagant and don't arrange their outings properly, and ask too many people to dinner and work them too hard?" May smiled pleasantly. "Well, you mustn't take any notice of that, Mrs. Pilch. I give them extra treats and am very free and easy with them on other occasions..."

"That's the trouble," asserted Mrs. Pilch firmly. "You're *too* free and easy, madam. Tanner, Chase and Hoey want keeping in and," again she resorted to the catch phrase, "taught to know their places."

May was silenced; she had not been home long since her short and abortive visit to London. John was better in health, Richard had subsided into the position of friendly elder brother, and life at Stone Pynes had closed on her like a trap, commonplace routine held her firmly in John's house in her position of John's wife. Now there was Mrs. Pilch who had asked to see her on some trifling matter connected with the non-delivery of cheese biscuits coming straightly to this point when she was offering sympathy and friendship to her mistress—for what?

May was standing; she had an instinctive dislike of sitting in the presence of servants who were obliged to remain on their feet. She looked at the woman's impassive face with the brushed-back grey hair, the round cap, the bulky body that was given a rigid outline by the large plain white apron.

"You've always been very kind to me," repeated Mrs. Pilch and again with a sigh as if at her own limited vocabulary, she repeated, "I don't like what's going on."

"Can you tell me what it is?" asked May candidly. "I suppose you know, as much as I do of my concerns."

"I know a good deal more, ma'am, if that can be said without offence. There's talk here I'd never join in. Nurse—that Lizzie Burt, she's no true friend to you."

"She looks after the children very well. You see, my husband chose her and the maids—"

"And the gardener," said Mrs. Pilch, "and me for that matter… but I don't hold with what's going on…"

"I don't think you may say that, Mrs. Pilch, unless you tell me what it is, and even then it sounds like—"

"I know what it sounds like," interrupted the cook. "It sounds like spying and tale-bearing and making mischief; but it isn't, it's trying to put a stop to all that sort of thing."

"There's nothing to make mischief about, Mrs. Pilch. Indeed, you mustn't concern yourself… nothing could be more dull than my life, there's no cause whatsoever for gossip so it seems to me; but if you think there is," she added, with a swift turn of her head so that her large grey eyes gazed steadily at Mrs. Pilch, "why, you must tell me."

"There's this, madam," replied the cook suddenly. "They think you're flighty… idle… that's what they think, I say—wasteful and extravagant, that you don't look after the master like you should do, that you're too much of a foreign lady for Manchester and altogether too grand and too fond of pleasure… It's your mother being foreign, madam—more foreign than you are, if you know what I mean… but we don't count Americans as being as outlandish as the French. And then that Rose Bernier, she's got her airs and graces I'll allow, but what I say is that the maids and the men that Mr. Tyler chooses aren't used to the houses of the gentry like I am, and," she added, in a manner that was incapable of giving offence, though the expression was strange, "I could never find anything odd or what shouldn't be about you, madam.

I think you behave like a lady, and *they've* never seen a lady before and so it seems funny, and *they* start making up tales and carrying tales—"

"Mr. Tyler," said May, instinctively defending her own standards, "wouldn't listen to tales brought by the maids."

"Wouldn't he! He might pay them to bring them, and if you'd like to give me notice for saying that ma'am, well you must."

"I shan't give you notice," replied May, "and I thank you for what you've told me because I'm sure you mean it out of kindness and affection, but as I do nothing wrong, I cannot concern myself with what they say about me, can I?"

"It would be wise to, ma'am," replied Mrs. Pilch earnestly. Her hard eyes moistened. She felt a genuine affection and compassion for this beautiful young woman whom she had long respected and liked, and whom she saw, in her role of shrewd spectator, as a creature being trapped. "I know more than I can say," she added gloomily.

"They think, I suppose," May tried to smile, "that I'm indiscreet. I sometimes see a gentleman alone."

"Yes, ma'am, Mr. Thorne's seen you alone once or twice."

"Always..." May realized she was about to justify herself to a servant and checked herself. "Are there any other complaints against me?" she asked with an increasing lightness.

"Only that you are going out so much to parties and not seeming to care whether you go or not, and never doing anything but read poetry, and having such handsome clothes, and going off to London with your mother and then going off to London alone. That's an unheard of thing, you know." Mrs. Pilch smiled in a manner that made the social difference between the two forgotten. It was an older woman with much knowledge of the world speaking to a younger who had very little, not, at least, of the wrong side of the world that is like the dark side of the moon, unknown to many who see nothing but the glitter and the shining disc with its silver air of purity and candour.

"I soon came back from London," said May; she remembered with a start she could scarcely control that on that occasion she had behaved as the servants said she was behaving—she had deceived her husband, she had tried to deceive Mrs. Bingham, she had laid a plan and played a trick, she had been trying to get a divorce that would very likely ruin her husband's business and his social reputation, as she had since been told by Dr. Harman, as Richard had admitted; in the light of the cook's speech, it was disagreeable to recall her last interview with Dr. Harman.

She had not told him of her attempt to avail herself of Richard's championship and consult the London lawyers, but she had gone to the doctor with a renewed plea for his help in obtaining release from her present life and he had assured her with some impatience that there would be no sympathy with a woman who tried to obtain a divorce from her husband when he was ill and on May's timid mention of the white powder had impatiently dismissed this, saying no medicine caused Mr. Tyler's ill health but that he had probably caught a chill at the Wirral Races, the effects of which he had never completely shaken off… there might be gastric complications… May's duty was plainly at Stone Pynes. "It was unfortunate," he had added sternly, "that you were in London when your husband was taken ill. I was thinking of you as much as of him when I telegraphed you to return."

"I am really confused, Mrs. Pilch," said May frankly. "I'm in a difficult position and I don't know what to do."

"That's plainly to be seen, madam," replied the other brusquely. "I'd help you if I could but I'm not able—only just to give you this warning… you'll get rid of Tanner, Hoey, Chase and the nurse as soon as you can? I daresay I might find you some nice girls or decent young women who would be glad enough to come here; if Mr. Tyler would keep to his bed for a day or two it would give us a chance. He wouldn't interfere so much with the housekeeping… Why don't you get a nurse in from Miss Rose at the Institute to look after him?—or Mrs. Crimpton? that would keep you free to go your own way."

May Tyler trusted and liked Mrs. Pilch so well that she took no offence at this advice, but she shook her head, remarking, "Indeed it is hopeless, Mrs. Pilch, for me to endeavour to get out of..." she was going to say "the trap" but altered the word which had been in the other woman's mind to "Stone Pynes. And now I think we should talk about the cheese biscuits that didn't come from Sorrel's."

"Indeed, ma'am, we certainly should, and I have said my say and hope you will take notice of it, for a kinder mistress I've never met and don't want to." With that, Cook listened to the directions about the undelivered cheese biscuits, the Normandy pippins, the arrowroot and invalid food for Mr. Tyler.

Richard Tyler possessed what he would have termed "brilliant business ability". This combination of qualities included a hard selfishness that no ulterior considerations could affect and that capacity for opportunist intrigue that goes with a low opinion of humanity and the instincts of a trader.

The London visit that he had planned with much trouble had failed through no mistake of his, but through John's illness with which Richard felt no sympathy; but something might be made out of it yet as regards furthering his design to assist May in escaping from her marriage, and in establishing her in unprotected freedom and easy financial circumstances in some of the less reputable suburbs of London, such as he had vague but useful knowledge of, May a social outcast, May with her own money, May a cheap and easy victim for a sympathetic relative.

An increasing dislike of his brother spurred him to exasperation. John represented all the success Richard would have liked to have had, more money, and marriage to a fair and brilliant woman of better birth than himself. John had his own establishment and John had been both socially and commercially more sought after... In short John had led in every way a life that from Richard's point of view compared very favourably with his own. He despised his elder brother for not doing better with his good fortune, and contempt as well as jealousy sharpened his animosity towards one who had walked with him, step by step, as a rival, and outstripped him, not by merit.

He had always felt an irritated scorn of these continual illnesses with which John plagued all who came in contact with him, as he felt a scorn for the careless way John conducted his lucrative business, the slipshod manner in which he ran his expensively rented office, the manner in which he threw his money about at the races. Richard argued to himself that if he had only had John's luck he would have made much better use of it, but he affected, and that without difficulty, a complete sympathy with his brother for they were so much alike that they fell into automatic agreement when they were together since they saw all from the same level, and the focus of their lives was identical; self-interest, greed and the grosser sensual passions combined into a hard core of dogged brutal complacency in the minds of both these men.

Now Richard insinuated to John that May was extremely shallow and tiresome, more than he had supposed her to be, and that her visit to the Binghams should not have been tolerated even under the excuse that she had "gone to think matters over".

"You see," added Richard, gazing at the dust that covered his brother's untidy desk, "it took a bad turn in your illness to bring her back. Supposing she'd stayed in London...."

"She was with the Binghams," grumbled John uneasily, "and she returned at once, and you forget she's got the upper hand of me—she knows about Dora...."

"So many people know about Dora that I shouldn't let that concern me. Why permit it to get on your nerves, John? She cannot get her divorce."

"She could make it very unpleasant for me," replied the other with the hint of a smile. "In the business world, and the clubs, and at the Exchange...."

Richard turned his face away to hide a sneer. Didn't John realize that he was not accepted, even in Manchester, as a man who could belong to any but the third-rate clubs, one who only occasionally found his way to the well-spread tables of his betters, and then merely because of some business deal? He did not remark on this exposed weakness, but continued to emphasize May's revolt and to hint that it would be wise to insist on her using more matronly manners, on dressing more plainly, on going to fewer places of entertainment....

"She's made up her mind to go to all those gaieties at the Pomona, John. You should take her yourself as you offered. To keep up appearances. Or you should refuse to let her go."

John now refused to escort his wife to entertainments that he found impossible "when drowsy with pain"; he pretended he had neither the health nor the money; the truth was he no longer had the courage to be seen in public with May; although this might have done him good socially, it was more than his temper and nerves would stand. Besides, he was not going to ask for her company and risk a refusal, as she might, in one of her high-and-mighty fits.

"Well," slipped in Richard smoothly, "I'd better take her myself."

"Why need she go?" grumbled John, drumming in irritation with his thick fingers on the medley on his desk.

"Why indeed? You should have trained her so she was content to stay at home and look after the children, but I suppose if she's made up her mind to go and has bought the tickets it's better for me to go than to go by herself, or with..." he stopped deliberately.

"Or with whom?" asked John, and it was he now who sneered. "She's got no friends... the Chorleys would take her, but I should have to pay for their tickets, and she's not fond of them and very likely she would refuse, if she knew they had to take her,"—and there was a faint note of admiration in John's voice as if he respected and liked his wife for despising the Chorleys.

"She might go with young Thorne," continued Richard in an expressionless voice. "He seems to follow her about a bit—he's even been *here* to see her—when she was alone—and I think it's a bit indiscreet. You know what servants are...."

"Yes, and I know what May is; there's nothing in it on her side."

"There might be on his...."

"Yes." John's smirk was gratified. "I daresay. He'd lose his head for her if he was given the least encouragement. He's not been the first—you've seen that for yourself—you've seen how May handles them."

"I know." Richard was as gratified, as certain as was his brother. He liked this confirmation of his own convictions as to his sister-in-law's aloofness, but he pressed his point. "It's a question of manner—she's very free and easy...."

The complacent husband repeated this. "Free and easy—flighty, extravagant, brought up on the continent and in Virginia and yet educated in a convent.... It doesn't seem to go together, not according to what we were taught."

"It does go together and *makes* her," said Richard.

He thought to himself, 'something elusive in this breeding as they call it, and neither of us will ever understand it'; aloud he tried to increase the impression he was endeavouring to make on his brother.... May wanted "looking after"... she was idle... she shouldn't be allowed to run up to London again, even if she did say she was going to see the Binghams. He went as far as that; but John, complacent in his trust of the wife whom he disliked almost to hatred, smiled arrogantly and Richard had to leave the subject; his finesse was not equal to any further attempt at cajoling one so like himself.

He turned the subject on to John's health. John looked pale and puffy, "the colour of lard," Richard remarked, and wanted to know what was the opinion of the second physician, a man of higher standing than George Harman—Edmund Fitch, who had been consulted recently by John. This matter of his health was one on which the elder Tyler was always able to talk at great length and as he leant back in his fine leather chair and went with great detail into his symptoms and his remedies, the follies and ignorances of the doctors, and his own skill in self-dosing, Richard's mind had travelled far away, to the Pomona Rooms on a night of carnival.

Richard had led an empty life, the world in which he had always moved was exceedingly small, like his parents and his brother, he was never, for a moment, more than a peasant at a fair, with more money than was good for him to spend. Besides the plebeian coarseness that was his heritage he had to the full the national defect that had spread like a slow cancer over England for three-quarters of a century, the raw aimless ambition of the ignorant business man of the industrial age, who could make money without working for it, who believed that power lay in money and nowhere else, who copied the external differences of their betters, without knowing what the internal differences were. With new wealth in new hands had come a new hypocrisy, a new smugness, there was the clergy-ridden peasant's fear of vice and the rich man's ability to buy it combined, and there was the smugness of the puritan who had come to good terms with his conscience, who had turned all his suppressed abilities to cunning, deceit and intrigue and termed the result trade. The Tylers had all of this new morality, their wealth was founded on the black slave trade, a proportion had gone to found the massive temples to good causes that further darkened their city already dark from the smoke of the industry of white slaves.

Richard did not know how empty his life was because his days were so full of petty detail that blotted his perspective; he had no wish to leave the place where he had made his money and where he was so much at home; even that exciting visit to Paris he had no desire to repeat; it had been expensive and tantalizing, and what good had John done himself by his repeated visits to Virginia? Richard was content with Manchester, but not quite with his life that was, even for the Midlands, definitely second rate. And he did not know even how to begin to climb; he was steady in his business and continually piled up money, then lost it, in sullen desperation, in some shady club gambling, or paying the expenses of a companion whom he felt to be as costly as luxurious, a woman who laughed at all his shrewd tricks, and often, for all his precautions, left him stripped of more than he could afford to lose. And all the while there was May, whetting his appetite with her unconscious innocence; he would not have had her different; her gay, aloof unapproachability was a fascination for him, more potent even than her bodily graces, so tempting to a sensualist irked by the inevitably sordid nature of his indulgence. He despised John for his handling of May, he had envied and hated John ever since, by some unlikely chance, he had secured the foolish girl, under the nose of her foolish guardians, but he held, unquestioned, his puritan code. May, as his brother's wife, was out of his reach, but May divorced, very much the other side of the hedge, May innocent, silly and friendless, yet with a comfortable income, might not by any means be so.

Yet he respected her; she too had always upheld the code, not the meanest gossip in Manchester had been able to blow upon her, though he had used Thorne's obvious professional snares to annoy John with, he knew that May did not even see them. But he had no compassion for her, and should she be brought within the legitimate range of his desires, he would find her lawful prey. He did not think this likely—her behaviour on the London visit had shown how guileless and above reproach she was—but divorced, living perhaps in Maida Vale—his own fear put even a divorced sister-in-law out of range, and her mother might take her out of his way; yet there might be underhand chances; his deep hidden instincts dared to suggest this, his deep outer crust of traditional morality refused to listen, his conscious mind only schemed mechanically to set May free of John, to humiliate the man, and to release the woman from the close confines of middle-class respectability.

Mrs. Bingham wrote to her imprudent young friend, as she thought of May, an anxious letter asking for news of "dear John's health", and repeating her invitation for another visit to Blackheath under happier circumstances, and this time she added on what she conscientiously meant to be a note of kindly warning, concealed in playfulness, "I shall meet you at the station to see that you come directly to us. Those little escapades, however harmless, dear May, don't do a married woman any good."

May read the letter without interest. The Binghams could not arouse any emotion whatsoever in her mind. She felt that it was not likely that they would touch her life, nor did she attach so much importance to her stay at the Hotel Mentone that she was under any effort to conceal it; of course, it would be unwise to mention it to anyone; Richard kept telling her that; but deliberate attempts at subterfuge she did not trouble to make and the letter with the tell-tale last sentences was left where she had opened it, with a pile of other letters, invoices and bills on her desk in the drawing-room, a frivolous piece of satin-wood and ormolu that she had brought from Paris, of which she had long since lost the key, and that was always overcrowded with papers, empty scent bottles, twisted chiffon handkerchiefs, white kid gloves, dancing programmes to which minute pencils were attached by silk cords, and any pretty trifles that May collected as she passed through her sad, empty, but outwardly gay and elegant existence.

*

The spy, whose monotonous and so far fruitless task it had been to watch her correspondence, almost omitted to do so that evening. It had become dull and tedious—looking over those scattered bills left so freely about, so openly discussed, those little notes of refusal or acceptance of an invitation, those appointments with dressmakers or hairdressers that littered May Tyler's desk. But the spy was diligent and carefully with a reluctant sigh at the thanklessness of her occupation, she came down as usual, felt-slippered and cautious, with a small hooded candle in her hand, when everyone else was in bed, and cautiously turned over as usual, the day's correspondence that Mrs. Tyler threw down on the charming little bureau.

Lizzie Burt was yawning as she glanced at the familiar bills and accounts that was the sole satisfaction she had had hitherto for this work. She was able to indulge in a vicious sneer. "If she don't pay those soon she'll be in real trouble... and think of all that money on clothes, or hats or having hair curled." But to-night there was more. There was a letter with a London postmark... Blackheath... something about that mysterious visit... for Lizzie Burt was quite sure it had been mysterious. She did not know Mrs. Bingham's hand or the difference between a male or female script.... She pulled the letter out, set down the hooded light and read the large writing eagerly. At first it seemed nothing but one of those useless little scrawls that hitherto had comprised May Tyler's whole correspondence, but as she reached the end she thought she had discovered a prize. With an instinct to conceal her treasure at once she, without fully grasping the sense of the letter, put it into the pocket of her prim frock and went cautiously upstairs, her felt slippers making no sound on the thick dusty carpet.

John Tyler returned from Salford in a sombre and evil mood. He was sure that walking through the wet, chilly June evening he had renewed the chill that he had caught at the Wirral Races. His limbs felt heavy, his head hot, and alternate shudders of heat and cold encumbered his heavy body. He dreaded an attack of malaria, the recurrent disease that he believed he had never been free of since his youth. He remembered, with relief and even with zest, that secret help upstairs—the three packets of arsenic that he had received from Joseph Tarrant. He kept them at the bottom of his pigskin hat-box, and now, after going slowly and painfully upstairs, for his legs were aching and numb, he took out one of the packets and gave himself a dose of the stimulant. The effect on him was as usual instantaneous. He smiled with a certain satisfaction in the midst of his temper and discomfort as he considered how he was increasing this dose without any ill effects; he was becoming as clever as De Quincy himself.

He nodded at his reflection in the mirror with almost insolent complacency. He had conquered something powerful that other men were afraid of; he could take arsenic and be the better and not the worse for it. How the doctors—old Harman and Fitch who thought so much of themselves—would feel the laugh turned against them did they know that while they were refusing him more than a minute dose of his favourite drug, he had such large quantities of it under his control. When he had satisfied his own vanity by gazing at the pale, slightly swollen face beneath the thick black hair that the mirror and the candlelight showed him, he went upstairs to where Lizzie Burt sat with a demure, secretive air over her work—tunics for Master John and aprons for Miss May lying in piles beside her neat basket.

She rose as the master entered and stood silently waiting for him to speak. She had decided to keep Mrs. Bingham's letter for a suitable occasion, by which she meant one that would yield a good return both in pecuniary profit and in the satisfaction of her instincts for the melodramatic.

She disliked her mistress for purely abstract reasons, since May Tyler had never in any way affronted her, nor even disputed her dominion over the children; Lizzie Burt considered her as an enemy because she was, in the nurse's estimation, rich and free and pampered, as well as beautiful and idle—like a buzzing mayfly to be brought down and crushed, as a vexation in a busy life. She made, too, a paying business out of reporting her mistress's actions to her master, though all she had had to say so far had been very flimsy, for she feared to lie.

He was not without some shamefacedness, that passed, he thought, for delicacy and tact, in his questioning of May's nurse about May's behaviour and their conversations on this subject had always been whispered and evasive; but to-night John did not feet inclined to exercise restraint; the London visit rankled, Richard's attack, lightly dismissed at the time, stung in his memory, the problem of the divorce was still unsettled. May had, he knew, spoken again to the doctor on this subject, and though the cautious physician had succeeded in quieting her, still her possible future action hung like a menace over John Tyler's future life.

He bade the nurse sit down, asked her about the children's health; she respectfully questioned him about his own, her fingers flying over the long seam of the blue tunic the while.

"I should be well enough if my domestic affairs were better," he grumbled. "Everything seems to go wrong in this house. You're the only person of sense to whom I can talk."

She knew that he had said this to everyone whom he employed, but it was none the less quite gratifying to hear; what was even more gratifying was the knowledge of Mrs. Bingham's letter that if he had had quick ears he might have heard crackling beneath her bodice and her apron as she bent over her work, holding it between the circle of light cast by the pale-coloured glow of the lamp; there were no gas jets in the attics.

John Tyler inspected the room with a resentful glance—the nursery was shabby—nothing in his house ought to be shabby. He remembered the costly dresses May had bought in London. He peered sideways at Lizzie Burt's discreet face.

"I suppose your mistress doesn't come to you with any complaints?"

"Never, sir," replied the nurse primly; "she doesn't take enough interest in me or even the children to bother her head about making complaints."

"She's not satisfied, though."

"She's a difficult lady to please then," remarked the nurse, glancing up. "I'm sure a more comfortable home and a more devoted gentleman no lady could want."

He would have liked to have stopped these insincere compliments, but he had not the subtlety necessary to come, without offence or danger, straight to the heart of the matter. Lizzie Burt, like all the servants, acted tacitly as his spy, but it *was* tacitly, and he often had an angry impression that he paid too much for very little. What indeed was he paying for? Peace of mind, probably. He liked to be quite sure that May was, as he termed it, "behaving herself". Nothing would have surprised and shocked him more than any evidence to the contrary; but though he was thus morally assured of his wife's aloof and immaculate discretion and reserve, still his native jealousy, his sense of his own infirmity, caused him to spend money—that he would have liked to have had for his debts or his gambling—on having her perpetually watched.

Lizzie Bert had always proved herself the most able and unflagging of these fee'd spies. He trusted her absolutely. He was sure that May could not do anything without Lizzie Burt knowing of it, and while he was wondering how he could come directly to the point and ask Lizzie if she knew anything as regards Richard's insinuations as to May's flightiness and in particular her careless behaviour with Jerome Thorne, Lizzie Burt was pondering the price she might get for the letter from Mrs. Bingham that surely was of tremendous importance because well-bred ladies, respectable women and faithful wives did not, Lizzie

Burt was quite sure, go and stay in hotels in London when they were supposed to be on a visit to friends. Certainly Mrs. Bingham seemed to treat it lightly, but then that must be either because she, too, was an easy going lady or because she was afraid and ashamed for May Tyler.

"You look as if you'd got a fever, sir, to me," said Lizzie at length. "You're quite flushed since you came in, and the room's cool enough.... I kept the windows shut all the evening because of the wind and the rain."

"I got wet coming home."

He looked gloomily at a worn screen composed of scraps from old picture books and Christmas numbers. The pattern had been worn off the brown and mustard coloured linoleum, the walls required re-papering, the paint was cracked.

"I shall be glad when John goes to school," he said, half to himself. "May can move downstairs to a better room."

Lizzie noted this thoughtless comment. Her rule, then, was to come to an end in not so long a time.

"Master John won't be old enough for school yet awhile," she remarked, "will he, sir? I was wondering if you would get a governess whom I could work under." She saw that he was calculating the advantages of a governess against the cost and she checked one of his hopes by remarking, "A governess wouldn't do a nurse's work, sir. You'd have to keep a nurse until Master John goes to school, and Miss May is old enough to keep a maid—and the nurse generally gets the maid's part if she's been with the family a long time, and faithful—at least in all the gentry's houses, doesn't she, sir? Though you'd know better than I."

"I never concern myself much about such things," he replied heavily. "I must go and see Harman again to-morrow; I don't know what's the matter with me—one day up and another day down—it's all this worry, I suppose.... How are the children? I haven't seen them for days."

"Oh, they're very well, sir. I take them in the park almost every afternoon and they employ themselves very well. I just set them easy lessons out of the copy book and then correct them in the evening. They're very good children, I'm sure, sir, and I cannot help saying, if you'll overlook it, that I'm sorry their mother doesn't take more interest in them."

"She's always thrown her children on others," complained John. "You'd indeed wonder how she *did* spend her time—what does she do all day when I'm at the office?"

"Why, sir, how should I know? I'm up here with the children and doing my duty; I never see the mistress except when she just puts her head round the door now and then and goes away at once. She's visiting and pleasuring, I suppose… she's quite the most smartly dressed lady in Manchester; and she spends a good deal of time with Cook—Cook's a great favourite of hers…."

"She's a bad cook; I think that's partly what's the matter with me—indigestion and bad cooking; and that stuff she gives me to take to the office, it's no good at all… sometimes it makes me feel sick…."

"I could make it for you up here if it's one of those patent foods just heated in the pan…."

"I don't know what my wife buys for me, it's all kinds of stuff—first this and then that—messes, I call them…."

"Oh, they're very good really, sir. I bring the children up on some of the things you have," replied Lizzie Burt with an air of efficiency. "It depends of course on how they're made… if the mistress doesn't know how to make them…"

"Mrs. Pilch makes them, not your mistress. I get some in a jug to take to the office every day for lunch, and reheat it on the paraffin stove… it's so often lumpy, and sticks to the jug and cup…." He continued, as people will who are preoccupied with their own health, in complaining of the doctors, the cook, his wife, how they all were wrong in what they said of his case, and the food and attention—or lack of attention—that they gave, or did not give him.

Sitting there in the ugly, shabby little room, his grievances crowded round him thick as flies round carrion. How detestable the world was, even with a favourite secret drug to keep one going… the effects of the powerful dose he had taken were beginning to wear off, leaving the usual depression. He was on a fidget to be at the pigskin hat-box again… his mind seemed to him to work with difficulty, to be somehow blurred.… How was it all going to end? How get rid of May, or keep May…?. Why, he was a young man yet… without going into precise details as to his age or expectation of life, he put himself down roughly for another ten or twenty years of enjoyment—but not with May round his neck; and yet, not as a man whom May had divorced. He must ask Richard again; he must go up to London and see his lawyers.…

He rose and was turning heavily from the room, having no further use for Lizzie Burt; but she had some further use for him. Her mind darted ahead—the future might be barren of opportunity. She had in other situations hoarded some titbit of gossip until it was discounted.

"I picked a letter of the mistress's out of her waste-paper basket in the kitchen," she poured out glibly, "when I was going down to see Mrs. Pilch about the extra milk for Master John… you know he's growing very fast just now, sir, and needs a quantity of milk.…"

"A letter of your mistress's in the kitchen—" John was alert, standing by the door, but frowning and suspicious.

"Yes, it wasn't torn up—of course, there's no harm in it—but you know what the girls are.…"

"Girls…" John had a coarse laugh for that phrase.

"The maids, I should say." Lizzie's look and tone emphasized the superiority in her station to that of an ordinary servant. "Of course I didn't read the letter, but I saw it had got the London postmark on it and just thrown in like that, so I thought I'd give it to you, sir, in case there was some business in it that shouldn't be—"

"Knocking about in a waste-paper basket, I suppose," interrupted John Tyler harshly. "Well, give it to me...."

The nurse slipped her hand behind the starched bib of her apron and drew out Mrs. Bingham's letter neatly folded across; John glanced at it with mingled contempt and relief.

"That's Mrs. Bingham's writing—Mrs. Tyler is hopeless with her correspondence.... I'll speak to her about being so careless. Thank you, Lizzie."

She was gazing at him with sharp expectancy and he added clumsily: "I ought to give you something for looking after the children; I'm afraid neither I nor your mistress have been able to give you much help lately." He took two sovereigns out of his pocket and laid them, the price of the letter, on the table by the box of needles, the reels of cotton and the scissors....

Richard eyed his brother cynically. John certainly appeared sick; he had not spent, for the last weeks, more than an hour or so a week in his office. He seemed overcome by lassitude, slack in his movements, halting in his voice, his eyes heavy, his usually pallid cheeks frequently and unnaturally flushed.

Richard had laid on the desk—that was dusty and untidy, and on which stood the dark and light brown jug containing the patent food that John took for his lunch—papers relating to his business deal in Birmingham with another firm of manufacturers who were willing to undertake part of the responsibility and to provide part of the capital for putting the ramie grass cotton substitute on to the market.

John gazed at them indifferently, and listened indifferently to the younger brother's business explanations, though these were satisfactory enough. There really seemed as if there might be a considerable fortune, both for the merchant and the broker in Joseph Tarrant's invention; but even Richard was not as interested as he appeared to be.

He had talked smoothly and intelligently, but his mind had the while been revolving his own peculiar schemes. He was very much baffled as to his brother's moods or thoughts, and May's remoteness and candour had made his part with her difficult too, but he was resolved that the affair could no longer hang like a poisonous cloud in the air; it must be brought to earth, made solid and used directly to serve his own purpose. Somehow this evil must be condensed into a weapon useful to himself.

He asked, at last outspoken how May was getting on… how she was behaving… if she was being less tiresome and extravagant, and if Dr. Harman had succeeded in affecting a reconciliation.

"You know, John, I have not been to Stone Pynes for several days; I thought it wiser to keep away and leave you to settle things among yourselves. Harman is an experienced man, he ought to be have been able to do something…."

John laughed most unpleasantly. "I've not seen much of May myself, either… I don't know her mind…." John Tyler spoke with difficulty and after a heavy pause.

"Perhaps I shall find out something when I take her to the carnival at the Pomona," suggested Richard with an air of cheerful efficiency.

"You can take her if you like, but it won't solve my difficulty for me."

"No, I suppose not. What is your difficulty exactly, John? You want all scandal avoided, you don't want the divorce, and yet you do want to get rid of May…. How's it going to be done?"

John, with a large pale hand that was more than usually unsteady, took a letter from the breast pocket of his black waistcoat and placed it on the table beside Richard's business correspondence.

"It was only by chance I read this, I came upon it lying upon the floor, all screwed up…. I was going to throw it in the waste-paper basket and then I saw it was Mrs. Bingham's handwriting and I wasn't sure if it was addressed to me or to May, so I glanced at it, and saw this at the end...."

While John had been making these unneeded and discredited excuses, for Richard believed not one word of them, the younger brother had been reading Mrs. Bingham's indiscreet epistle.

"Oh," he remarked thoughtfully, "so May stayed at a hotel before she went on to Blackheath.... Well, there might be nothing in it... have you spoken to her about it?"

"No," replied John gloomily, "I wanted advice from you first. I do not think she was up to any mischief, but yet why the deception? Mrs. Bingham," he added almost eagerly—"*she* doesn't think much of it...."

"I believe she thinks a great deal about it," remarked Richard gravely. "She's a kind-hearted woman who doesn't want to make mischief.... It's very wrong for May to stay at a hotel, especially at some hotel Mrs. Bingham doesn't know of...."

"It was not the Bristol in Waddington Street, eh?"

The two brothers faced one another: John, sour, sullen and bewildered, Richard inwardly alert, outwardly sympathetic, across the desk on which stood the brown jug with the farinaceous food.

"I don't think so—from the way this is written—but it would be easy to find out."

John brooded over Mrs. Bingham's foolish letter and Richard's half-casual, half-mocking condolences—for thus they seemed to the angry and baffled man. He began to suspect some plot, as he termed it in his mind, being hatched against him, and he could not even dimly understand what this might be and who was working it; but his sense of grievance against May, the most helpless of the possible conspirators, the most irritating of the possible personalities ranged against him, since she was at once in his way, and necessary to him because of the respectability her presence gave his establishment, while he needed her money, and she was the person most in his power... all his musing and gathering rages sharpened by his increasing malaise that he was dosing in vain with his secret pick-me-up, fell on May twenty-four hours after he had read the stolen letter, when he entered her room and suddenly, without control or finesse, demanded, "what the damned words meant." This crude action was all his day and night's reflection over his dilemma had produced.

May stared at the letter, more concerned for the moment in wondering how her husband had come into possession of it than of what she was to say in answer to his demand that he repeated thickly and hotly.

"How did you get it?" she asked. "I left it on my desk, I thought.... I suppose you do read my letters?" she added reflectively.

This composure cost him his last scrap of control. Walking up and down the overcrowded room he raged against her, using language that she could barely understand, nor did she try to; she had her own problem: and that she now dealt with precisely, rising from the padded blue velvet seat by the wardrobe and saying: "We cannot settle anything like this.... What Mrs. Bingham says is true, but you shouldn't be reading my letters."

"You should not be lying to me," he replied, almost inarticulate with passion, so that his words came like those of a man half-strangled.

"I did not lie to you, John, save by implication. I never said I was staying anywhere, except with Mrs. Bingham, and you see that she, though she is a very prudent and discreet person, finds no great objection to my 'escapade' as she terms it.... But I want to know your reason...."

John had enough sense and cunning left to realize that only by restraining himself could he hope to discover anything from May, whose quiet manners always gave her an advantage in their disputes, so he waited, still pacing up and down.

"Put it down as a woman's folly," added May with a sad smile. "So you would call it I should say.... I had to—or I thought I had to—go to my bankers in the city.... You were going to be away or I should have stayed in Manchester. There was some business to transact—"

He bore away her excuse in a flow of wrathful language, the meaning of which she understood was that she had no right to be conducting business, that all her affairs should be in his hands....

"But you know that is not so," she put in when she could make her low voice heard. "You know, John, that I am in control of a great deal of my own money.... That was in the marriage settlement; it is useless for you to once more tell me you regret the days when a married woman's property was entirely in her husband's keeping. Won't you forget about this? I assure you I meant no harm and did none. I'll promise not do to that sort of thing again if it annoys you so much. It was my first deception of anyone, even indirectly, and I'll never deceive you again, John, if you will try to consider me a little.... We must," she endeavoured to be strong, her flush deepening and the eagerness increasing in her voice, "come to some kind of agreement. There are those debts to be paid and some of the creditors are pressing.... I'll take the terms that Dr. Harman spoke of if you will pay these people; I'll do as you wish and try to behave like a dutiful wife while here at Stone Pynes, though I doubt," she broke out wildly, "that I can do it for ever, or even much longer...."

Her husband paid no heed to her rising despair; he had plunged into this interview without thinking out anything, and he was thankful when Nelly Tanner came in with her discreet smirk and said that Mr. Richard was below in the drawing-room, as she had been told by her master to term what May called the parlour....

"I'll talk about the rest of this in front of my brother," said John rudely. "If you want it threshed out, he ought to be there. We'll come down, Tanner."

May agreed, thankful not to be shut up alone with this evil-tempered man, thankful that Richard who was at bottom, she believed, her champion, should be present. She was conscious that there was something unpleasant in this continued, if oblique and slight, deception of her husband, but then the childlike intelligence that, indolent and disdainful, lay behind her high breeding and her sweet nature, did not regard John as a rational human being and considered Richard as being in every way able and capable. 'John,' she said to herself as she followed him downstairs, 'is a sick man, mind as well as body, and must be treated so, and if anyone can manage him it must surely be his brother.' She was relieved, in a way, that he had discovered her stay at the Mentone. It was her own carelessness, of course, that she had left the letter lying about, but never so far having had anything to conceal, deceitful ways were unknown to her, and after all, where was the mischief? Even from John's point of view it could only lie in the fact that she had not told him before of one of her reasons for wishing to go to London. Now she would, if need be, tell him—"I wanted to get the legal opinion on the possibilities of a divorce which you, or even Richard—even Dr. Harman—didn't seem able to tell me."

She wondered, as they entered the overcrowded, ugly parlour where the late afternoon sun fell pallid and without warmth through the soiled glass of the large window-panes, if she should tell Richard frankly that their scheme had been discovered, but a look on his face (he seemed to flash her a glance of warning) decided her on silence. She owed him some loyalty too; he had been her adviser from the first and it was he whom she should obey, not John.

Richard looked from her faintly troubled serenity to John's ill-controlled agitation and remarked, with an air of hearty goodwill towards both, that he was "sorry if he had come upon any domestic misunderstanding."

"It's more than that," blurted out John, taking the easiest chair in the room without any courtesy towards his wife or his guest. "I found out that May didn't stay with the Binghams all the time she was in London. She put up at a hotel alone."

He made no reference to the fact that Richard knew this.

Richard glanced sideways at May and she read his query and answered it. "John discovered this because he found a letter that Mrs. Bingham wrote to me. I did not tell him, not thinking it his affair."

"You hear that!" broke in John. "She doesn't think it's my affair!"

"Well, women are beginning to have independent ideas," returned Richard casually. "What was your reason. May," he asked her, "for staying in London instead of going directly to Blackheath?"

By this question he allowed her to understand that she must not reveal his part in the episode. He also left her the onus of making up instantly some plausible excuse. This she disdained to do and answered pleasantly and composedly as she moved towards the window, instinctively wishing to be as near light, air and freedom as possible, "It was some business of my own, some financial business—there was really no need to trouble John about it, things being as they are between us—"

"I demand to know what that business was," said her husband quickly.

He was encouraged by his brother's presence, for Richard had moved behind him as if to support and strengthen him.

"You've every right to know," agreed Richard, at the same time looking at May as if to assure her that he was working entirely in her interest.

The young woman remained indifferent to both of them; she was seated in the ornate chair, with too many silk cushions of too many colours, that was placed clumsily by the coarse lace and heavy chenille curtains, the last showing on the rough pile the greyness of dust and soot.

"I'm glad," she remarked, "that the fog and smoke have lifted. Sometimes even on the sunniest day Manchester is quite dark."

"It is to do with the direction of the wind in the upper air," replied Richard, not sorry for this diversion. "I wonder if you would let me talk to John by myself for just ten minutes, May. I think I could put him in a better mood."

His glance seemed to implore her forgiveness and her trust. She was ready to concede both. She had no actual enmity towards her husband, she only wished to be free of him and of Manchester; free even of Richard also, who might be a good friend but who was to her in no way attractive.

"Ask Tanner to bring us in some coffee," said Richard, going to open the door for May, "and liqueurs, up here."

"A reconciliation feast," smiled May, faintly pleased. "Richard, remember I still want, as soon as John is well enough, to be free."

John shouted from the room that she must "speak louder". He had not been able to hear what she had said... she did not reply but went downstairs to the dining-room; she heard the heavy door close behind her as she rang the bell in the dining-room, and on Nelly Tanner's suspiciously quick appearance (surely she had not had time to come up the basement stairs), gave her Richard's orders.

"In ten minutes' time... they're talking together on business.... I shall go up too, then, and you must follow me." May smiled, almost humorously, at Tanner's peering face. "Why, Nelly," she added, "you look very anxious. You seem always to be gazing and muttering like those women in Virginia whom we used to call descendants of the witches—as if you were casting spells. Pray, Nelly, don't cast any over me; I've enough trouble as it is...."

The lean housemaid replied angrily with a grim tightening of her mouth, "I'm sorry if I've been uncivil, ma'am, I'm sorry if you are in trouble; nobody would think so in looking at you, if you will excuse me, madam...."

"Seeing the fine house you've got and the fine clothes and easy life," added May, with increasing good humour, using that gentle familiarity with the servants that her husband so resented. "Yes, I've been told that I make that impression, but you mustn't envy me, Nelly. I was badly brought up, I suppose—certainly not brought up for this kind of life—and so I make a good many mistakes, but believe me I pay for them...."

Nelly Tanner was baffled, as she always was by her mistress's manner. This candour, that had nothing in it of condescension, this easiness that had nothing in it of self-betrayal or coarse familiarity, she found quite impossible to deal with. It had never been used towards her before for Nelly, unlike Mrs. Pilch, had not ever been in the service of well-bred women.

The dining-room looked on the north and was already cold. "June," said May, "and one could do with a fire! Now I think we may go upstairs,—I suppose it's ten minutes...." She looked at the clock with the ugly bronze figure of Time as a naked dotard with a scythe leaning over an hourglass; ornate, over-elaborated, in May's opinion, detestable, as was every thing at Stone Pynes. One could not even learn the hour of the day without being offended by some hideous ornament, some ostentatious design, a tradesmen's conception of art as something to be bought, as cheaply as possible, and "stuck about".

She sighed regretfully, considered the only pleasant object in the room—herself; her flounced lace gown, her pretty clasped fingers—on the forefinger of the left hand was a fine emerald that her mother had given her on her wedding day and that had belonged to her grandmother. She kept it there for the dazzle of the green fire—it was exquisitely cut and flashed long beams and glitters of light in any illumination, sun, moon, candle or gas.... Yes, when she looked at it she could forget the wedding-ring on the third finger of the same hand....

Nelly Tanner remained in hostile silence, very much alert, quite ready to take any part in any scene. The muttered suspicions and speculations of the servants that Mrs. Pilch's good-humoured expostulations and loyalty had not in the least subdued, had recently risen to a confusion of excitement and malice that entirely absorbed the three women who, with the cook, formed the domestic staff of Stone Pynes.

Nelly Tanner was therefore very glad to follow her mistress up the heavily carpeted stairs with the brass stair-rods and the massive varnished banisters to the parlour where the two gentlemen presumably had finished their conference; so May entered with the servant behind her carrying a tray of liqueur bottles and glasses. John, although he detested his wife and regarded her as an active enemy, and though he had chosen the servant himself and kept her by bribery in his interest, muttered in furious resentment at May's action in holding the door for the maid; Richard put in some genial comment to cover this up and in an amiable voice asked Nelly Tanner to bring the coffee as soon as possible.

As the door closed upon her John broke out again furiously. He wanted to know, and with the emphasis of coarse and powerful adjectives, why Richard should think so much of drinks and coffee… they had more serious matters to attend to.…

"I hope," said May quickly as Richard picked up the liqueur bottle and held it with a reflective air towards the light, "that you have come to some conclusion—that Richard has been able to tell you behind my back what he could not before my face—something perhaps in my favour, that you would not think so hardly of me—"

"In your favour…" John seemed incapable of finishing the sentence, and May glanced at him in concern. She thought him about to have a seizure or some stroke; his usually pallid face was disagreeably flushed, his eyes suffused, he shuddered and shook where he stood, thrusting his hands in and out of his pockets and stamping with his right foot, as if he wished to relieve numbness, on the heavy crimson rug in front of the fireplace that now was curtained for the summer with chenille and wool lace.

May was checked in what she was about to say by the man's obvious fury; she looked at Richard; what could Richard have told him? He answered her glance with a cleverness she had not expected.

"I said nothing to John to put him in this state. It's bad for his health as I've told him, but he won't listen to me nor to reason. Don't go near him, May, I don't trust his mood."

"He's ill, indeed we should send for Dr. Harman. John, you mustn't agitate yourself so. Did Richard tell you why I went to London?"

"Richard said something that I don't want to believe...."

"I *suggested*," amended Richard, "that possibly, May, you, as an inexperienced young woman, had gone to London with some ill-advised design of getting advice about that divorce you were so recklessly proposing."

"Is it true?" asked John, and took a clumsy step towards her as she backed against the wall with the over-patterned paper. "Is it true that behind my back you were daring—"

"What if I were to say it is true? I've a right, I suppose—"

She felt Richard's hand on her arm. He drew her away from the other man towards the door, he delayed action and conversation with more skill than he himself knew he possessed; his timing proved perfect... a word here, a word there... non-committal and exasperating... a withdrawal of May, small as a doll in the light grasp of his heavy hand, brought the climax exactly where he wished it. He heard the servant's footstep on the stair and opened the door for her entry as John, inflamed beyond endurance by May's courteous yet contemptuous defiance, approached her, as Richard had furtively swung her forward, and struck her across the face that he had once so admired and for so long detested.

Nelly Tanner ran swiftly upstairs to the nursery. She did not need to go as far as the door, for Lizzie Burt was leaning over the banisters that in the upper part of Stone Pynes were of a meaner character, being of pitch pine painted an ugly light yellow.

"What's going on?" she asked rapidly.

Nelly Tanner could hardly gasp out her momentous news quickly enough.

"He's given her a black eye, that he has! There was a quarrel on there… I heard some of it, not all…. Mr. Richard trying to make the peace as usual—but she's a proper high flyer, she is!"

"Did you see him black her eye?" asked Lizzie Burt, her face working with excitement.

"That I did—and so did Mr. Richard."

"There's her two witnesses if she wants evidence for a divorce."

"I don't know as I should give it," answered Nelly Tanner. "I could say what I liked, couldn't I? The police couldn't get anything out of me I didn't want to say. I'll be bound she deserved it, too."

"What's she going to do?"

The two women spoke simultaneously and crept in a furtive manner down the ill-lit upper stairs and peered over the banisters on to the landing below where May's bedroom was situate.

"She's lit the gas there and is moving about," reported Lizzie Burt without any thought of her charges; it was the other woman who whispered, "Hadn't you better look after the children—you don't want them to start hollering?"

"They're asleep and they know better than to whimper if they do wake up in the dark. We'd best go down and see what's happened."

But Nelly Tanner, with the lifelong habit of servitude upon her, was so unused to direct action and so used to underhand and secretive methods that she hesitated.

Lizzie Burt was more suave. "The poor lady'll need a little comfort," she smirked. "Women oughter stand by women. If someone behaved like a brute, I'm not going to stand by and take his part."

The other servant glanced suspiciously at one whom she had hitherto regarded as a fellow conspirator, then deciding that Lizzie Burt was deep but could be relied on, she followed her to their mistress's room.

The door was ajar and May was standing by the open wardrobe, pulling down clothes as it seemed at random and throwing them lightly into a small open trunk. She turned, and her composure abashed them both, for one side of her face was stained an angry red from her husband's blow.

"I'm glad you've come, both of you," she said. "I have asked Dolly to get me a cab—there should be one on the rank now."

"Oh, ma'am," exclaimed Nelly Tanner with a glibness that rather surprised the nurse who had hitherto despised the housemaid as being clumsy, stupid and greatly her own inferior. "What's happened? I couldn't help seeing that there was trouble—"

May Tyler interrupted, "You couldn't help seeing, Nelly, that my husband struck me and for no reason at all; now you can't help seeing that I am leaving this house at once and going away till I know what to do."

This encouraged the nurse to sidle up to her mistress and say in an insinuating tone, "We're shocked, madam, both of us. Nelly came running up to me saying terrible things were happening. I can assure you we're your friends, both of us, although Mrs. Pilch don't believe it and has stood in our way—"

"I don't want to talk about that now, Lizzie, I'm not even stopping to change my dress—this lace gown will do very well under a cape.... Will you please fetch it out—a long velvet cloak...?"

Nelly Tanner did so almost mechanically and May slipped her arms into the handsome garment the colour of parma violets and lined with a pale rose hue that gave, over the guipure lace gown, an incongruous air of festival to her delicate figure.

Lizzie Burt rapidly asked practical questions. "Are you leaving the master, madam? And if you are, where are you going… Madame Dumont being abroad…? And have you got enough money?"

"I don't know, Lizzie—I've not looked to see what's in my purse—enough for the cabman and the train fare somewhere, I suppose; and then I have some jewellery of my own that I brought from Virginia that I can sell until I can get in touch with my mother and my bankers…."

"But if you leave the house, madam," whispered Nelly Tanner, genuinely impressed and even awestruck by the long expected but nevertheless overwhelming drama that had at last shaken the daily routine of Stone Pynes with its undercurrent of suspicion and crude intrigue, "if you leave the master you'll never be able to come back—"

"Do you suppose that I wish to return?"

May smiled. She gave a glance into the long cheval mirror, then turned to the overloaded toilet table and opening a jar of cut-glass took out a peach-coloured powder puff and dabbed it over the mark on her face.

"It's no use, it's no use," she kept whispering to herself, as if she did not realize the presence of the other two women who were gaping at her with scarcely restrained excitement and curiosity. "It will always show, it will always show…. Fasten up my case, Nelly, if you please, but before you do put in it— Oh, I don't know—some soap, some perfume… what shall I need? I hardly know what there is…"

"But it's worse, madam," said Lizzie Burt, "not to know where you're going… you can't leave the house like this…."

"But I do… this is how I leave Stone Pynes and for ever. You will look after the children, Lizzie, as your master bids you. They couldn't be separated from me more than they are now. Pray don't endeavour to restrain me…."

"I'll come with you if you like," suggested Lizzie eagerly, "so that you're not quite alone, madam…."

Mrs. Tyler's faint and generous smile seemed to show that she understood the spy's meaning in this offer.

"I don't require either you or Nelly or Dolly; if I wanted anyone I would take Mrs. Pilch, but I don't want anyone...."

"But where are you going?" insisted both the women at once.

"I couldn't say until I get to the station, until I see how much money I've got; you must not trouble yourself about me. There are a number of ornaments here—bracelets and ear-rings, clasps and buckles—you may each take one. I will write to my husband—to Mr. Tyler..." the last title seemed to wipe the first, and for ever, from her lips, "to tell him I wish this—and there must be one for Dolly too... but Mrs. Pilch I am taking something myself—"

"You're going downstairs to see Mrs. Pilch?" the women repeated together.

Mrs. Tyler had passed them without answering, save in so far as the words "She has been so kind to me" that floated up the stairs as she went down them might be taken as an answer. She passed the door of the parlour; it was ajar—no doubt John and Richard were behind it, waiting to see what she would do. John did not come out to express his horror at his action; well as she knew him, that cowardice seemed to her to have a peculiar shame; it was surely strange, too, that Richard did not come to champion her, even to the extent of escorting her to the cab; but perhaps (she was always ready to accept a magnanimous interpretation of other people's conduct) he was doing his best to restrain or comfort—her mind fell on that word—John.

She went down to the kitchen where Mrs. Pilch was seated at the table beating eggs with a wooden spoon in a blue jug; the enormous range, blazing with a coal fire that had been let down to the last rung, heated the basement and partially underground kitchen insufferably. Nothing was quite clean and there was too much of everything—but there was a certain homeliness about the clutter, about the large moonlike face of the clock painted with representations of the sun and moon… something cheerful in Mrs. Pilch's common face, worn by the stresses of life into harsh lines, but expressing a placid goodwill nevertheless… something that reminded May of the black servants in her Virginian home in Mrs. Pilch's large white starched apron and large white starched cap.

Dolly Hoey stood the other side of the table with a piece of green baize in front of her on which was laid the silver that would be used for dinner. Piece by piece she was, with an idling air, running this through a rouge cloth; some of the red dye was on her coarse fingers.

The cook rose with a concerned exclamation; Dolly stared, an avid spectator, as May went up to the elder woman, put her arms round her neck and kissed her.

"I'm going away, Mrs. Pilch—here is something for you—those greenish stones you said once you liked when I wore them to a dinner—do you remember?"

"Going away, madam?" Mrs. Pilch had flushed directly with emotion when her mistress embraced her. "And giving me this—but it is valuable, and for a lady's wear—"

"Therefore it is for you. Please keep it. It is really mine to do what I wish with—I've no money to give you, and I wouldn't offer it if I had, for we've been friends, haven't we? Dolly, you will find something upstairs; you may take what you please—but tell your master first. I shall write to him about it…. I am leaving Stone Pynes." She listened. "That's the cab… you found one, did you, Dolly?"

"No, madam," breathed Dolly heavily, "there wasn't one on the rank when I was there, but I left a message with the old cab washer who hangs about."

All these commonplace and unnecessary words served to tide the three women over a moment so terrible to one, so heartrending to another, and full of such sensational interest for the third.

"Don't try to keep me, Mrs. Pilch—don't try to run after me—but I don't think you would. I think you understand too well."

"Yes, madam, I do, and I wouldn't try to stop you, and if you want me or I can help you, let me know."

"I will, Mrs. Pilch. I don't know where I shall be, but I shall write to you."

This candid arrangement at once impressed even Dolly as ridiculous, for if Mrs. Tyler was leaving her husband in this sudden and dramatic fashion, concealing her whereabouts from him, why, it was absurd to think that she could send her address to the cook.... But Mrs. Pilch remained standing rigid by the table, staring down at the bowl in which were the frothy eggs, the yellow bubbles beginning to subside; Dolly, in the presence of her superior servant and the cook, remained at her place, though longing to run upstairs to see what "the gentlemen were doing".

May ran up the kitchen stairs and pushed open the baize door; they were all in the hall—John, Richard, the nurse, the parlourmaid.

"You can't go like this," began John.

For the first time since she had known him, she saw him humble himself. He was alarmed, perhaps frightened.... Richard standing behind him said nothing, but smiled at her as if approving her action, Nelly Tanner with voluble and ignorant exclamations was protesting against the action of her mistress.

"I am going," said Mrs. Tyler. "Good-bye to all of you. You'll hear about me from someone, I suppose...." She looked at her husband without giving him his name.

Richard came forward to open the front door for her; she thanked him and went down the steps. On the pretentious gravel sweep known as the double drive stood the four-wheeler, the man on the box, to whom the family was well known, peering at his fare and the group that he had seen for a second in the lit hall when she had opened the door.

The summons, the scene, the appearance of his passenger was sufficient even to arouse masculine curiosity to a suspicion of domestic strife.

"You'll drive to the station, if you please," said Mrs. Tyler, adding, "I think I have enough money to pay you and to buy my ticket too. If I haven't you will please ask my husband for the fare."

The man, who had returned to the rank to find the excited servant running out again for a cab, agreed quickly and civilly. The Tylers, who had not got a carriage, gave him frequent employment. He had, too, a sudden sense of compassion for, and indignation on behalf of, the pretty young woman who looked at him so candidly and with such courage, and whose face was marked, he could see, by that livid stain that precedes a bruise. No one liked or respected John Tyler, and his family affairs had been more keenly discussed in his neighbourhood than any of his household was aware of; the cabman warmly assured May Tyler, as she opened the door, that he would drive her where she liked and that she mustn't think of the money.... But the handle stuck, and May's strength was very slight and the cabman could not quickly get down from the box as his legs were wrapped in a rug and the horse was fidgety.

In this slight delay Lizzie Burt was through the door of Stone Pynes and down the steps and by the side of Mrs. Tyler.

"Won't you say good-bye to your children?" she cried in a weeping voice. "Never mind the master and the wrongs he's done you... think of those innocent little ones.... You wouldn't forsake them, would you? You ought to stay with them—I've done my best, but I'm not their mother...."

May stared at the woman whom she had always disliked and resented as much as it was in her power to dislike and resent anyone. Had she misjudged Lizzie Burt? Was there a true friend here after all?

"Will you please bring my case? I was waiting for that," she stammered.

The nurse was sharp to notice her faltering tone. "You can't go like this, madam, indeed you can't. If you don't care for the scandal and your own reputation, you've got to think of the children. This is going to ruin the master and even if you don't concern yourself about that, and say he brought it on himself as he may have done," hurried on the nurse with increasing glibness, "and mind you, I don't say he hasn't done—still you've got those little angels upstairs to think about. Come up at least and say good-bye to them."

May hesitated, in agony.

"You'd better get in, madam," urged the coachman, cutting in from his box; "the train you're wanting to catch is due in another ten minutes—I can just make it if you're quick—"

May did not understand this chivalrous attempt to aid her in her escape. She stared at the man hardly hearing what he said, for the nurse's insinuating words were ringing in her ears. For the first time since she had come to Manchester, for the first time indeed in her life (but it was not until her marriage that she had been put to proof), did her courage, her resolution sink.

She suffered the older, the stronger woman to turn her aside from her purpose, to lead her up the steps, the stairs.

"I'm only going to say good-bye," she protested. She called out in a faint voice to the cabman, "Wait for me."

The pretentious front door closed upon her.

The man waited, staring in front of him at his well-kept horse, at the prim beds of geraniums that never to May had looked real, that showed in the light of his carriage lamps a hard scarlet against the dingy, mottled leaves of the suburban laurels. In the semi-circular flower bed cut off from the street by the outer stone wall grew some foreign shrubs that had not flourished in the Manchester air—stunted and soot laden they raised wilting branches and dingy leaves. Beyond were the two always open gates, each of which was emphasized by a pillar of ugly thickness on the top of which, in imitation of a more elegant and reasonable century, was a large pine conventionally shaped. These pompous ornaments were like everything else about the tasteless residence that John Tyler termed a mansion, shams, for they were not stone, but made, like their supports, of Portland cement....

The coachman, a knowledgeable fellow, observant and of quiet manners, had always instinctively disliked the house and all the occupants, save the mistress. There was nothing genuine about any of it—fakes, humbugs and shams—vulgar common people apeing gentry. Cement (and no doubt Mr. Tyler had shares in the company) apeing stone... potted flowers grown in greenhouses apeing the blooms seen in real gardens... half-blighted shrubs and trees imitating the woodlands and plantations of exotics found in gentlemen's residences....

The coachman glanced up at the house with contempt. As far as he could see it in the thickening shadows, it was odious; the gables, the eaves, the ornaments, the crockets, the drain pipes all clumsily made and inconveniently placed.... Blinds were drawn at all the windows; there was neither light nor sun for Stone Pynes.

Without hope the man patiently waited, then what he had expected happened. Nelly Tanner came tripping out, a small lantern in her hand, the door kept open by the shoe scraper that the housemaid, with ostentatious deliberation, had put in place.

"The master says," she remarked shrewishly, "that you're not to wait any longer. The mistress has changed her mind about going out to-night—if there's any charge, will you please send the bill in to the master...."

"There's no charge," replied the cabman, and without more comment touched up his horse and drove slowly away from Stone Pynes, the crunching of his wheels and the sound of his horses' hooves on the gravel that was always kept so clean and well raked, being the only sound in the chill summer evening.

*

Richard was plausible and ingratiating. He supplied at least in some measure that comfort and protection for which May was, beneath her well-bred composure, desperately seeking.

"You must overlook it, my dear girl. You must consider that he wasn't himself.... It was an outrageous thing to do... it was not what one would have expected from a man in John's position...."

She answered as if she were talking to herself. "It was exactly what one would have expected from John, from a man in John's position. It seems to me as if he had often done it before, but with an invisible hand that left no trace. This does, you see—I'm marked...."

"It will pass... there is stuff you can put on that. It won't be a bruise...."

"You did nothing," accused May, staring at him with a candour that to him had an almost terrifying blankness. "You did nothing, Richard."

"There was nothing I could do. You didn't want a scene, did you? You did the best thing in leaving the room, though of course you lost your head when you tried to leave the house."

"I think I lost it when I returned," replied May softly. "Those servants pulling at me to go upstairs to the nursery.... I wonder if Lizzie is really fond of the children, and Nelly really fond of me. I have never guessed it."

"You're not very good at reading people's characters, are you?" Richard laughed softly to himself, so softly she hardly noticed it and attached no importance either to the man or his manner.

She was intent on her own problem. "They seemed kind and troubled last night," continued May, "but what were they to me—those sleeping children? As soon as I got upstairs I was told not to disturb them.... They've been taken from me ever since they were born. A better way for me to have recovered them would have been to leave John, to have divorced him, then perhaps he would have had to give them up to me. It is terrible that I had to leave London before I had the advice of your lawyers, Richard. Do you not know yourself, your own law?"

"It's very intricate," he assured her soothingly. "I know that you've pretty good cause now—a blow struck in front of two witnesses—"

"My brother-in-law and a servant."

"Well, you mustn't mind that."

A slight uneasiness that he disdained troubled his speech. He kept his will fixed on his purpose and continued, "Try and forget all about it. A divorce isn't a pretty business for a lady, but if you want your freedom why not put up a fight for it?"

"I can fight," said May, at which he laughed aloud; but she took no heed of this gross affront to her courage and her sincerity. "Indeed I can fight," she repeated as if stating a mere matter of fact, "but so far there has been nothing worth fighting for...."

"Not even the children?" asked Richard, sincerely shocked, for he had an ideal deeply ingrained in his nature of the plaster saint type of maternity being inherent in all good women.

"Not even the children," replied May, who knew so little that she did not realize the deep-seated conventionality of the sex to which Richard belonged. "How could I? They were taken away from me... they were made, I think, to dislike me by John and the servants he put over them—"

"Tut tut, you mustn't speak like that. John would never do anything of the kind—it was merely that you were incompetent, untrained.... But we mustn't go over that old ground. Come, you've been crying, I think. Your pretty eyes are quite red...."

"I've not been crying, I never cry—I am disfigured by the thoughts I have of John. Will you not take me to town at once so that I can see your lawyers openly? Will you not lend me a little money so that I can get away from Stone Pynes? Why not?"

"I'm John's brother," replied Richard awkwardly, somewhat outmanœuvred by a suggestion to do frankly what he intended to do in an underhand way.

He found May as difficult as she was fascinating.

What a strange creature she was, wanting to fly in the face of God and the Devil—of all the decencies, of all the respectabilities when if she'd only have a little sense she could get her ends and preserve appearances at the same time; appearances, that is, for himself and his brother, nothing of course would be left of *her* reputation (under this word Richard included everything that made life in England tolerable for a woman) when she had once "gone through" the divorce court. Probably only her priests would remember her then... and yet, perhaps in the eyes of her priests she was not married at all....

He considered her keenly. She was an enigma, as different from him as the splendid peacock struggling in net had been from John; as different as the guarded peaches on the sunny wall had been from John's and his daily food in their childhood and youth.

"What am I to do?" she asked, looking at him. "I can't remain here.... I wish I had not come back from London; John was not so ill. I think Dr. Harman asked me to return merely because he thought I should never have gone away. I shall write to my mother, she's in Rouen now and it will be a long time before I get a reply—"

"You mustn't send a telegram," said Richard quickly. "If once anything like that goes through the Manchester post office, the scandal will be all over the place."

"Is no one to be trusted then?"

"I am. You may trust me—remember to-morrow is the carnival at the Pomona."

"But I cannot go, of course," interjected the young woman with a spasm of dreadful horror on her disfigured face.

"But, of course you can. You must go—just to put a face on it… not for John's sake, I do not ask that now… but for your own, to show that you have nothing to be ashamed of, to show that John's brother supports you, that everything is as it should be at Stone Pynes."

"But nothing is as it should be at Stone Pynes, Richard, and why should I pretend? That seems to me dishonourable and foolish."

"You must pretend for a little while at least,—that's not hypocrisy. You don't want the servants to know everything—"

"But the servants do know everything. Nelly came into the room and saw it all, saw me treated as my father and my grandfather would not have treated a slave they had bought in the market-place. They were courteous men and respectful even to the negroes…."

"You mustn't think of such things. Come with me to the Pomona to-morrow, put on your smartest gown and then we can talk in a way we can't here in John's house—and I don't like to ask you to my rooms, they're untidy. I keep my housekeeper because she's old and getting blind, but she's not much use. Wouldn't you like to hear a little music… see a little dancing, to get away from all this?" He moved his large white hand that was to May so unpleasantly like John's, in a slow gesture round the room that was to him handsome and comfortable enough, but which he knew May detested. "Once you were free of him and got your money affairs straightened out, you could take a nice little place outside London—in St. John's Wood or on the river perhaps…. I could find it for you. You could get your own friends about you… you've got some striking talents I'm sure… you play the pianoforte, don't you, and paint in water-colours?"

"I used to," said May, with a faint smile that he could not interpret.

He hurried on. "You know how to dress, too—anyone can see that. What makes a scandal in Manchester would make a success in London…. I shouldn't be surprised if you went on the stage. Ladies are beginning to, you know, and to do pretty well too."

"I've no talents," said May.

She looked at him with a surprise that seemed touched by compassion, compassion at some blunder of well-meaning ignorance.

"We'll see, we'll see!" Richard's eyes sparkled. "Your mother would help, of course," he added hastily. "She'd come over—she's got introductions...."

"She knows very few people in England. Why should she? And why are we talking of this? It is the immediate future I have to think of—"

"The immediate future," put in Richard with authority, "is to-morrow and the carnival at the Pomona. Have you seen John?" he added abruptly.

"No. It is curious to think he's sleeping next to me with only the curtain in the alcove between us, and there's no other room that either of us can go to without upsetting this household. Have you ever thought, Richard, how strange a place Stone Pynes is? I'm a poor housekeeper—extravagant, wasteful, and everything goes in a free and easy manner. Amelia Chorley calls it Liberty Hall, yet in truth there is no privacy, no freedom... one cannot even change a room or the time of a meal.... All goes by a kind of crazy clockwork. I wish you had let me leave the other evening, you and Lizzie Burt.... What brought me back, I wonder? Custom. Didn't some poet say that—'Custom, cold as frost and deep as life itself'?"

"I don't know any poets," replied Richard with amiable condescension. "I expect it's Tennyson—you're always reading him. You spoke of the verses on the bells in the town hall...."

"Perhaps... perhaps..." May rose and put her handkerchief that was soaked in *eau-de-Cologne* to her bruised cheek. "I must talk to you! I must talk to someone.... It's a question of getting some money, too... there are all those debts and John hasn't paid them yet, and I have to go on running bills at the shops. Think of it, Richard, at a moment like this one is pulled up by—"

"Pence—shillings and pence," interrupted Richard with grim cheerfulness. "I know. You must leave that to me. It's not a woman's affair. I'll manage your bankers and I'll manage John.... I'll see your debts are paid and you get some money. You won't want to dance to-morrow evening, I suppose. Keep close to me and we'll find a table somewhere, a private room, where we can talk. You'll wear a domino and a mask, I suppose?"

"I've got no mask," replied May. "I'll see if I can buy one in Manchester.... But is it necessary?"

Unimaginative as he was, he was impressed by the symbolism of her words. May Tyler had never found a mask necessary. He couldn't answer her question as to whether it was or not. He was not sure whether it mattered if she went disguised to the Pomona. He thought perhaps it would be better if she were there openly, and said so.

"But my face.... Am I to explain to everyone that I have met with an accident? I could do that, of course."

"There'll be no need," replied Richard. "It's a faint mark—nearly gone.... A good thing he wasn't wearing his ring, it might have cut you.... Now I won't stay any longer; I've got some business about that cotton substitute ramie grass to do, and you must rest and keep quiet; and don't put yourself in John's way, leave him alone.... Who's looking after him?"

"Mrs. Crimpton—she's not trained but she's used to sick rooms. I don't think John's really ill, he's only sulking. He's seen the Chorleys this morning, I don't think he said anything to them as they were quite friendly to me; I met them as I was coming down."

'How impossible,' Richard Tyler thought with exasperation, 'to engage this young woman in any kind of conspiracy,' yet in a way this quality was her main, her dazzling attraction, and in a way, too, it made his manœuvres easier.

"I'll go upstairs and see John. I'll say all I can that is soothing and kind. I hope Lizzie Burt is respectful to you?"

"Oh yes, I've hardly spoken to her since yesterday. I don't wish, of course, for the condolences of the servants. I have no confidence to give them; they are, as you say, respectful and Mrs. Pilch is always my friend."

"She's not been worrying you about yesterday?" demanded Richard, thinking that this might be an excuse to get rid of the over-officious cook.

"I said she was my friend," repeated May.

"Oh. I see what you mean…" He was clumsy, out of his depth. "Yes, of course—delicacy and all that kind of thing.… Well, you must trust me and nobody else. I've spoken to Dr. Harman. He's given me a sleeping draught for you if you need it."

"I never take such things, I don't know that I wish to sleep; it's better to lie awake and think one's problems out. If one slept one might dream. I think that's been said before—was it in a play I saw once when I was at school? You know, Richard, I've seen so little, been to such few places.…"

"But when you were a child—a girl…" he was still fascinated by the presence of this woman though he wanted to be away and manage matters with John, "you went all over the continent—you must have been about a deal.…"

"But I took everything for granted then. I must have lived in a world entirely my own. It's very difficult, you know, to become disenchanted."

He grinned, not knowing in the least what she meant, and left her with further words of complacent comfort to go upstairs and soothe, as best he could, the restless and peevish invalid who, at once irritable from nervous tension and drowsy from George Harman's medicines, was alternately coaxing and cursing Mrs. Crimpton who moved heavily about the room performing the routine of "attending the sick", familiar to her, and one that she followed with a scarcely disguised gusto.

Downstairs, May looked at her face in the long mirror on which was a faint film of dust; pictures and mirrors were seldom polished at Stone Pynes. The mark was on her face; it would be worse presently, a bruise deepening to blue and purple. At present it might be disguised.

She remembered the face-wash that she had made in the Parisian convent and the recipe Rose Bernier had given her. She had tried once or twice to obtain Fowler's solution at the Manchester chemist's, but in vain. It had seemed as if it were unknown in England. Useless, then, to bother the man again, and she did not wish his professional eye glancing at her face. Was it not from flypapers that they had obtained the ingredient that took the place of the Fowler's solution? Yes, she was sure of that... but had it been Fowler's solution? She had almost forgotten, even when she had asked in the chemist's she had not been quite sure.... If only she could find the recipe... but how hopeless after all these years, she had lost it at once, she remembered. She might easily, however, obtain the other ingredients—the chlorate of potash, the rose water, the rectified alcohol, and then half a dozen soaked flypapers—the grocer had them. She detested them when used for their original purpose; nothing could be more horrible than to see the helpless insects stuck on the gluey substance. There had been no flypapers in Stone Pynes since she had been the mistress there, but now she resolved to buy some, and to make the face-wash that she had used as a girl, in order to disguise the bruise that John had made, before she went to the carnival at the Pomona.

"Do you know what I saw in her room?" whispered Lizzie Burt.

The lowered voice was merely because of her sense of the dramatic value of what she was about to say, for she and Nelly Tanner were alone in the ugly nursery where the housemaid, with a careless, slightly disgusted air, was dragging a dirty rag over the glazed linoleum.

"Nothing would surprise me I'm sure," replied the other servant.

"Well, I think *this* would—she had flypapers soaking in her basin—six of them, just enough water to cover them and then a clean folded towel on the top."

The nurse's vicious face showed disappointment at the other woman's blank stare.

"Well, what if she did? What's in that?"

"Oh, you don't understand me," said the nurse peevishly. "Do you mean to say you've forgotten that horrible murder case in Liverpool? Those baby farmers who murdered the poor innocents, with arsenic got out of flypapers?"

"Heaven help us!" exclaimed Nelly Tanner, shocked. Her malice had always been as vague and circumscribed as dull. "Murder!" she repeated feebly.

"Oh, I don't say anything about it being murder here," replied the nurse, throwing back her head impatiently and stabbing the long needle spitefully into the little sock she held on the egg of polished wood. "I just said, what's she doing with them—and I think it's strange, coming on top of all these goings on, all her bad behaviour and trying to run away and making herself talked of with Mr. Thorne—"

"*Did* she make herself talked of?" asked the other servant keenly. "Did it get as far as that? It seemed to me she was really too open for there to be anything in it."

"Don't you believe it!" replied the other woman with authority. "Those that seem the most open are usually the worst of all; brazen I call it, not open...."

"What do you think she might be doing with the flypapers? I never knew you could do anything with them—I'd forgotten about the baby farmers, I don't read horrors...."

"Well I do," replied the nurse. "What else is there to read I should like to know? I was in Liverpool at the time and everyone was talking about it. The poor little creatures were all murdered by those two hags—Smart and Cunningham—those were their names and well I remember them.... Hanged they were and a mob howling outside the jail in righteous indignation...."

"I should think so indeed," replied Tanner with an elegant shudder, standing with her back to the damp and glistening wallpaper, the wet, dirty rag squeezed in her hand and dripping on the floor. "But you don't say the mistress—"she paused.

"Oh, I don't say anything," replied Lizzie Burt, "except keep your eyes open."

"I never knew there was arsenic in flypapers—I knew it was poison, of course, by the way the flies die...."

"Well it *is* arsenic," pronounced the nurse tersely. "All that came out at the trial."

"I wonder they're allowed to sell 'em!" exclaimed the parlourmaid, still partly fascinated, partly appalled, by Lizzie Burt's grim talk. "There wouldn't be enough on 'em perhaps to do harm to any but a fly," she added; but the nurse would have none of this,

"Didn't I tell you that those dear little babies was poisoned from flypapers—dozens of them as I remember. Well I don't go so far as to say the mistress is trying anything of that sort," she added with vicious reluctance. "Perhaps she's just got enough to make the master go to sleep when it's convenient, when she could get off and be about her goings-on without him knowing...."

"But there's Mrs. Crimpton in and out," protested Nelly Tanner. "She'd have an eye to that."

"She cannot have an eye to everything, and with all the medicines he takes, those he gives himself from his medicine chest, those that come in parcels from London—you know what I mean, those parcels from Joshua and Blunt—and what with what the doctor gives him, something fresh every time, who'd notice an extra drop of something or other? And then there's all those patent foods that Mrs. Pilch messes up that he takes to the office, poor gentleman, when he's well enough to go. I'm sure she doesn't wash that brown jug properly—I had a look at it yesterday and there was still stuff sticking in the crannies."

Nelly Tanner's slower brain did not at once grasp the implication of this, so the nurse explained impatiently.

"There'd be a way of finding out, don't you see? The doctors would know how to find out if there's any of that nasty stuff left in the basins—I remember that in the other case, it was what was left sticking in the pap boats that gave them away." The housemaid was still floundering and the nurse thought it prudent to leave the subject with this warning. "Don't say I've been putting thoughts in your head, because I haven't. I just said the whole thing's queer, and we've a right—indeed it's our duty as good Christians, to keep our eyes open."

"Well, I'd leave the place," replied the other servant, "if I thought there was any goings-on like that. I don't want to be mixed up in anything of that kind."

"You oughter stay," replied the nurse quickly, rolling the sock, rising and with a swift motion of her lean hands brushing down her starched apron. "Now I've got to go and take the children out, little treasures. It makes your heart bleed, doesn't it, to think of what may be in store for them?"

Nelly Tanner was on safer ground here; she agreed, adding—"It makes your heart bleed thinking they've got a mother who neglects them, such sweet children as they are, too. Never a bit of bother or making a bit of noise, thanks to your care, Mrs. Burt...."

The nurse accepted the compliment with a condescending smile and went into the night nursery where, under heavy blankets in a darkened, overheated room, (the afternoon sun was beating on the holland blinds) the two weakly children were taking their afternoon nap. The nurse looked in a detached manner first at the boy's sleeping face; he was an unattractive child, with a yellowish complexion, sleek dark hair and eyes and, even in his slumbers, a sly expression. He, as the nurse put it, "favoured" his father. She tucked him up mechanically, drawing the blankets closer round his neck regardless of his forehead beaded by sweat. Then she went to look at the little girl who did not in any way "favour" her mother. She, too, had a likeness to her father, but she was paler in colour, less determinate in feature; a petulant expression was on her face, her eyes were not closed—dark and intent they gazed at the nurse.

"Can't I get up now? I'm so hot and tired of lying here. Can't we go out? Can't we have something new for tea? Haven't you finished that red dress of mine, I hate the blue one."

"A proper nuisance, Miss May, that's what you are! Can't you lie still?" the nurse mocked her charge. "Say your prayers and try to go to sleep."

"I've said my prayers and I can't go to sleep," retorted little May. "I want something exciting to happen."

"Well, you'll get it," replied Lizzie Burt tartly. "Don't you worry, my pet, you'll have something exciting quite soon, though I don't know if you'll understand much about it."

May prepared the face lotion, indolently regretting the while the lost recipe. What was the name of the ingredient that took the place of the wash she was obtaining from the flypapers? She was not at all sure now that it had been Fowler's solution; she could be quite sure, however, that the substitute had come from flypapers. One did not forget anything like that.... The white room in the convent, the tresses of lilac the colour of sugared almonds... (*dragées*—she remembered the French name as more familiar than the English one) yes, lilac, the colour of sugared almonds, two shades of mauve, light and dark... multitudes of florets forming the lovely truss of blossom, and she standing there with a basin on which was painted in gold, sprigs of laurel and soaking, with faint distaste, the flypapers... They were so ugly, both in themselves and in their association, but the solution had been a success. She could remember that... and all the girls had exclaimed that every blemish had been removed from their complexions, even freckles covered up, and that they had become as diaphanous—yes, that was the word—as the lilies in the dusk that the nuns tended so carefully in the convent garden in order that there might always be during the summer months these flowers, emblems of purity, to gather for their chapel altar, beside which, in a shrine of faded gold, stood the image of Our Lady in a silk frock heavily embroidered, that May had helped to make.

The memory of that scene effaced her present surroundings. There was that power of memory in the hideous papers floating in the hand basin. May proceeded cautiously; she detested the heavy marble topped wash-hand-stand and all the paraphernalia... she knew how easy it was to break the cumbersome articles with this combination of china, glass, and marble, all slippery, and hands slippery, too, from soap.... The servants were continually chipping or cracking basin, ewer, slop-pail or the various stands and bowls that comprised the set and were intended for soap carriers, soap drainers, tooth brush and nail brush stands. May had been told by Lizzie Burt that ladies who really took an interest in their homes had mats underneath these easily broken articles, and May remembered once setting out mats of linen with borders of crochet, but these had soon become soaked and stained and looked even more distasteful than the white marble with the blue veins.

Now she posed the large basin with difficulty in her small hands, breathing quickly, and forgetting everything in the physical strain. The water was finally poured off into the bottom of the soap dish that she had previously washed, but there were some drops on the Axminster mat and on the polished mahogany legs of the wash-hand-stand. May mopped these up with a face-towel. She always lived under a slight inner uneasiness as to her own servants disapproval of her extravagance or carelessness. The papers from which all the substance had now been soaked she put on top of the slop-pail, a heavy white china contraption with a handle of cane bound over metal. May then proceeded, too intent upon her task even to think over her miseries, daintily to prepare the face-wash. The articles from the chemist she mixed, according to the proportions she could remember, with the water from the flypapers in the bottom of the soap dish, then turned the whole resultant lotion into a large cut-glass scent bottle with a heavy silver top that she took from her overloaded dressing-table.

She wished that Rose Bernier or her mother were there to advise her just how long this wash should stand; she smelt it, trying to recall the precise odour, that seemed to be the faint perfume of rose leaves as she remembered. She hoped, almost with passion, that it would prove successful in removing the bruise from her face, or at least in concealing it... her natural gaiety, not to be subdued by any misfortunes, stirred in her a wistful, subdued desire to be away from Stone Pynes, to be among the lights and the dancers in the large Pomona Hall. She had not for some time been to any entertainment that suited her taste; perhaps to-night at the Carnival people would be masked, disguised.... She might forget they were cotton merchants and their wives, she might try to imagine that she was in some elegant house in Paris, Rouen, Vienna or Venice. The purple gown she had bought in London would do very well, and her long cloak of sapphire blue velvet would pass as a domino... she could not wear the other that she had flung over her shoulders in her futile attempt at escape....

She was glad that John seemed "better"; she had been in alarm lest Mrs. Crimpton should say "He's not so well to-night, madam, you'll have to stay at home." She could be of no use, if she did stay, to the morose and sullen man who seemed to resent her presence in his room; but there was always convention heavy over all of them. She was his wife. She must attend him, she must respect and love him—a Christian woman, a Christian marriage.... She must, she knew, too, redeem herself in the eyes of the household from at least the charge of flightiness. They knew perfectly well that she had tried to escape, every one of them; all the tradespeople, too, by now. She had, indeed, made no disguise of it, and however meek they might be, they were watchful; and however outwardly respectful, they were covertly insolent.

May knew so much as this, though she did not know or even suspect that they were in any way spies, she had even forgotten the episode of Mrs. Bingham's letter, and, at the time had really believed her husband had taken it from her desk that was still unprotected, as it had nothing to conceal.

Mrs. Pilch gave her looks of sympathy when she had been in the kitchen that morning, but she could not, save by a return glance, accept her servant's championship against her husband. Mrs. Pilch had, without saying anything, returned the piece of jewellery to the jewel-box, but the other women had kept what May had meant to be parting gifts.

'Why do I trouble myself about small, absurd details that do not matter in the least? I still have to think what I am going to do.... I hope Richard will really be able to help me to-night, I must insist on it that he does.... Perhaps he will come back with me early and we can talk to John; perhaps I should write to Dr. Harman again, or Dr. Fitch. I feel so alone, so uncertain, and I despise myself for this weakness....' So ran her disturbed thoughts, though she did not put them into exact words. What the sum of her misery amounted to was that she was an alien. These people, friendly or hostile, were all foreigners, in every way different from her; except perhaps Jerome Thorne who reminded her of the chivalrous gentlemen of Virginia, so many of whom had died gallantly in the Civil War, among them the man whom she ought to have married.... This thought, too poignant to be whimsical, struck her like a dart as she stood with her hand cautiously holding back the unwieldy drapery of the alcove that separated her husband's room from her own.

He was asleep, or feigning to be asleep, tidily arranged in his bed. On the pedestal table beside him numerous glass bottles, glasses, boxes, spoons and tins and packages of patent foods. Mrs. Crimpton, who sat there in her cap and gown and shawl, with the decorous yet slightly menacing air of a priestess attending a ritual, gave this array now and then more interested and concerned inspection than she did the patient. She was in fact, as professional nurses usually are, more interested in the remedies than either the disease or the victim of the disease. A pleasant, placid woman and inured to all forms of sickness and accident, she contemplated with a gentle satisfaction the array of medicines.

"He's sleeping peacefully, madam," she remarked, rising respectfully.

John Tyler opened his swollen eyes and retorted peevishly, "No, I'm not, I've had a fever all day and been in pain too; those fools of doctors don't know their business—I always said so."

"Will you have other advice?" asked May with that sincere concern that was her immediate response to pain and suffering.

"No—more expense for nothing," grumbled her husband. "It's only my own medicines that do me any good."

"Well, I'm not sure, Mr. Tyler, that I ought to allow you to have them," put in Mrs. Crimpton, "especially without telling the doctor. You're always having sips of private medicine behind his back, you know, and I don't think it does you any good."

"I'm the best judge of what does me good, aren't I?" replied John Tyler.

May, still not entering the room but watching from the alcove, anxiously considered him; he was moving freely in the bed, his face was not unnaturally pale or flushed, his eyes seemed as clear as usual; she could not consider him desperately sick.

"I'm going with Richard to the Pomona masquerade, as you wished me. You don't wish me to stay at home and attend you, John?"

He did not reply; unable to bring anything agreeable across his lips he had to restrain himself in front of Mrs. Crimpton, who smoothed over the moment with soothing conventionalities.

Of course Mr. Tyler would like to think that his wife and brother were having a little bit of change and enjoyment, and of course she would look after him until they came back… it wasn't likely that they would be late, was it? And if Mr. Tyler was took bad, or wanted them (she changed the first expression quickly on a malignant look from the patient, who did not wish to be reminded that his illness might be serious, although he exacted all the attention due to one gravely ill)—why, she concluded, somewhat agitated, she could always send a messenger to the Pomona. It wasn't far off, was it, and the cab rank was just round the corner and she was sure that Nelly Tanner or the other girl—Dolly, wasn't her name?—or Mrs. Pilch would go, even if the gardener was not to be found….

"He wouldn't be—he's always at the 'Red Lion'," sneered John. "Well, run away, May, and enjoy yourself. Is that the dress you bought in London? I don't like it at all—it's not suitable for Manchester…."

"No," replied May, without any offence, but indeed sweetly, "but it is suitable to me just as I am not suitable to Manchester. Good night, John… and I shouldn't take too much of your own medicines." Her gentle face was almost pleading. "Please don't. And if, Mrs. Crimpton, you think there's the least occasion, pray send for Dr. Harman immediately, and Dr. Fitch, too… it would be better if they came together…. Marsden, that's our gardener and odd-job man, Mrs. Crimpton, you remember him, will not be at the 'Red Lion' I am sure. I have asked him to stay in to-night and be at your service."

She stared through narrowed eyes at the bedroom scene. The ugliness had undoubted fascination; it was so strange too, and so strange that it should be strange.... She had been eight years in Manchester, eight years married to that man lying there on the narrow bed piled with blankets and linen sheets pulled away, with the medicine bottles and boxes of pills and tins of invalid food like a satanic battalion on the bedside table, with reinforcements on the top of the washstand, all shown in the raw light of the gas that was falling from the bracket on the wall.... Why was it so ugly? She ought to have been familiar with it by now—and her own room was very little better, nor indeed was any room at Stone Pynes where she had never been allowed to have her way in any matter of taste or management....

She dropped the curtain and returned to her crowded chamber. 'I must get away, I must get away. It's that strychnine he's taking. I'm sure. I'll speak to Richard about that to-night.' She took up the heavy cut-glass bottle and peered at the solution she had made; it had changed to a pale yellow colour; that was correct, surely.

As she was turning it into the basin in order to bathe her face, she heard her husband's voice calling her peevishly in a low, insistent tone.

Again she was at the alcove, again drawing the curtain. Hurriedly John Tyler, raised on his elbow in the bed, begged a favour of her.... Mrs. Crimpton had gone out of the room; "slipped down to the kitchen," in her own terms, to fetch up some posset.

"I want my own special medicine. You know—that white stuff I take. My legs were so numbed to-day I couldn't get out of bed when that old hag wasn't in the room...."

"Perhaps you shouldn't have it?" May no longer remembered her distaste for the room and its occupant as she crossed the threshold. "Where is it—and yet perhaps I shouldn't give it you...."

He pleaded with her, and his persistent, agonized appeals were unendurable, besides, commonsense told her that if he had been taking it so long he might go on taking it... She followed his directions, opened the tall-boy and then the pigskin hat-box, took out the packet of white powder on which was written "For cats" and brought it, pityingly, hesitant to the bedside.

To her surprise he put in an eager finger and thumb and, abstracting a pinch of the powder, put it into his mouth as if it had been food, grinning up coarsely at her astonishment.

"That's the way to do it. That's what the doctors don't know anything about—eat the stuff and it gives you new life.... Put a little into that meat juice, too... I'll know when to ask for it at the proper interval of time and that'll mean two doses to-night.... And put that powder where I can get at it without Mrs. Crimpton seeing, down among the medicines."

"I don't see how I can. How much do you want put in this meat juice?"

"That little spoon...."

He watched her with eager eyes, only relaxing when she had fulfilled his directions.

"But I cannot leave the powder here unless you don't mind it being seen. I think it would be so much wiser, John, if you would tell the doctor..."

John cursed the doctor and rousing himself still higher in the bed searched impatiently with his eyes for a place where the powder could be concealed.

"Is it so necessary to have it hidden?" asked May. "I feel like a conspirator..."—'and not on this account only,' her sensitive conscience reminded her.

"If it is found," said John furiously, "it will be taken away, don't you understand? and then I shall die. These fools—scoundrels, too, I think they are—they don't know what is keeping me alive."

With the quick ears of one who guards a precious secret he had heard a sound on the stairs, a creak of a step. "That infernal old hag or someone is back again already. Put the stuff in the hat-box, May, and come in another time when I am alone."

She obeyed him swiftly and had just closed the door of the press when Mrs. Crimpton entered.

May Tyler would never have been, even under happy circumstances, gay in the Pomona Rooms. They were everything she disliked—garish, ostentatious, painted in bright colours that jarred, hung with ugly incongruous decorations in harsh tinted tinsels. The gas lights hung in iron circles, twelve lights to a circle, each acrid flame enclosed in a globe of clear glass. This overhead illumination cast unbecoming shadows on faces, draperies and objects, making everyone and everything bright and flat at the top, dark at the bottom. There were boxes round the floor in which were tables, set with what the programme termed "refreshments".

The revellers were, as May had known they must be, far too provincial, flat-footed and dull for this kind of amusement, that she had seen done so well by the people who had invented it in Italy or France. Even when the various dominoes, who wore awkward masks and ill-fitting cloaks, had grossly indulged in cheap brandy, sherry and champagne, they became riotous and noisy, or fell asleep on the heavy gilt and plush chairs instead of making the evening witty and gay with delicate and fantastic adventure. May had pulled her hood slightly over her face as she had not been able to find a mask in her untidy belongings and it had been too late to try to buy one.

Richard was in a dark grey domino that lent, in her judgment, absurdity to his tall, stout figure, that was ill-cut, and showed the edges of his grey trousers; he was so out of tune, even with an attempt at this mannered merriment, that she felt vicariously embarrassed; she regretted that Richard could not have found some other place, some other opportunity in which to speak to her privately.

Early in the almost intolerable evening, speaking under the noise of the stamping of the dancers in ragged quadrilles and fast waltzes, she begged him to find time for their private interview.

"I mustn't be here too long with John so ill.... I don't know how we can talk in this noise. What made you think of it, Richard? Is there any place we can go?"

"We can go into one of the alcoves or boxes."

He had not left her the whole evening, his hand under her arm, he had assumed an air of protection for which she was grateful.

"Who's the fellow in the white domino who keeps so close to us? That's an odd set-out—a queer colour for a man to wear," he added with a sneer.

May had not noticed that any white domino was following them; she did notice that he had used the word "colour". Richard's minute mistakes always fretted her taste, always on edge, easily fretted now.

"There are several white dominoes here."

"Yes, but this fellow always keeps close to us, he has a silly pointed mask of paper, badly glued. Is it anyone whom you've been encouraging, May?"

This remark seemed to her so odd and incongruous that she peered at him from under the shadow of her hood without replying, and he, seeing her ingenuous look, laughed and drew her away to the end of the large hall. Here wide steps set out with artificial palms, led to an upper gallery where a desolate and sinister contraption was making doleful sounds. This was an orchestra played by invisible means; drums, cymbals, bells and triangles were suspended from the ceiling, a dome painted pea-green, and they moved to a mechanical rhythm of uncouth melody. This Magic Orchestra, as it was termed, was one of the great attractions of the Pomona Hall and had now been set in motion to please a section of the dancers who wished to indulge their curiosity about this novelty. Their stout figures in their badly made dominos and ill-fitting masks were jumping and turning about on the balcony to the strains of the mechanical music that could with difficulty be picked out from the lush swell of the waltz being pounded out by the tired human orchestra below on the dais of dirty crimson.

May, who was little given to reflect on anything, did vaguely reflect on humanity's pleasure in a mask, even these traders of Manchester felt that Puritans and hypocrites required yet another disguise as well as that they usually wore. May had found all of them so enclosed in tradition, superstition, so inarticulate, so enmeshed in routine and catchwords, that they seemed like pasteboard marionettes, jerking to the puppet master's strings, and yet these creatures had still something they wanted to hide, something that could live only behind a mask, something that must be moved from everyday by a domino, a hood, a false identity, something that must be encouraged by blinding lights, the rhythm of sensuous music, the swinging together of heavy bodies, clasped tightly, so that the buckram, the cotton backed velvet, the dyed tow hair were dark and damp with sweat. What was it that thrived in the foul smell of dust beaten up from dirty carpets, from long filthy curtains that shook as the revellers knocked into them, from the dingy clothes beneath the cheap finery? That battened in the crude gaslight, the reek of scents that came from bottles with pictured lilies, violets and roses pasted on their flat sides, but which smelt of no earthly perfume; it was little matter that the Midlands had created an atmosphere so polluted that no flower would grow in it, the industrious chemists could supply the deficiency... alcohol, from the persons of the women, alcohol from the wines and spirits served at the bar, nicotine from segars and cigarettes... what need such incense?

"Pretty smell," said Richard. "You never get any of this kind of thing. Perfume? Do you, poor May." May remembered the attar of roses her stepfather had sent her, that she had used to make the wash with in the convent—was that which she had made from memory any use to hide her bruise? How foolish of her to lose the recipe, if she had had that no need to have bought those hideous flypapers; she saw them now, sodden, falling into thick morsels, on the ugly slop-pail.

May put her hands to her ears and willingly followed Richard to a small room, that appeared to be a disused bar at the side of the gallery. There she paused, slightly panting, shaken by the harsh noise, her throat dry from the dust the dancers stamped out from the floor, the crude hues of the ugly garments worn by the company. Everything about her was uncongenial, both to her nature and her mood, even after eight years of Manchester she felt sharply alien.

"Richard, tell me quickly what it is you have to say. I must go home—get away from this place. I go out so little, I did not know that it was like this."

She looked at herself apprehensively in the long mirror behind the shelf beyond the bar, where stood vivid hued bottles, bottles of liqueur brandies, she wanted to see if the home-brewed lotion had effaced the bruise from her cheek; not being sure of this, for her face was troubled with many shadows and the hard rays of the gas overhead, she pulled out her handkerchief and dabbed her cheek.

"Tell me what you want," asked Richard hoarsely, as if choked by the dust, leaning on the brass-rimmed bar. "That is what I want to know. Are you determined to go through with the divorce, you have evidence now, you know...? I don't mind telling you I had a hand in staging that."

"Please don't say so," she answered hurriedly, almost at random. "I don't want to believe it, and yet I suppose I don't care very much. It all seems to me so distasteful—and that's a weak word, isn't it?—that it cannot be discussed. Yes, I do want a divorce, I'll go through anything to get one. I must leave this place.... I must leave John. If only he hadn't been ill—that makes it all the more difficult."

"It's a pity your stay in London was so unfortunate," muttered Richard thickly. He had not removed his mask and she could see his eyes, dense and bright, through the holes in the painted cardboard, his thick, dry lips moving under the clumsily fitting nose of the vizor. "There's likely to be trouble there, I think."

"Oh, Richard!" she beseeched him. "Do please not think of the past, but the future. What am I to do? Can you get me some money? I'll write to my mother, I'll entreat her to come to Manchester."

"She will be of no use to you, you want someone to look after you. I'd do that, you know, but you're such a queer sort of girl, one is never sure of you."

He talked thickly, incoherently, and May did not understand what he was saying. Her senses were beginning to sway under the impact of the atmosphere poisoned by human breath, the whirling shapes that had been for the last hour bouncing round her with giggles and guffaws, the rhythm of the waltz played loudly by the orchestra in the crimson velvet uniforms, by the strident clanking of the instruments fixed to the pea-green ceiling that beat out a melody unknown to her with metallic precision, accompanied by the thump of the feet of the dancers in the gallery without, who, loutish and slightly drunk, were clutching one another with coarse cries and hooting bursts of laughter; one couple was bound together by a chain of paper roses, clumsily clipped into shape.

It was past May's powers even to ask Richard to explain himself. She was now, without her own volition, at a point at which her desire was to escape from Richard as well as from everything else in Manchester; and then, staring away from the empty bar with its stained and polished counter, its pulleys and siphons, to the doorway that led to the balcony she saw the white domino Richard had mentioned; there for a second and gone again. She knew herself utterly unfitted to deal with the world; first she had gone to London, then wished herself away, then she had come here and wished herself away.

Now Richard had come close to her, lolling along the bar; what he muttered was incomprehensible and incredible; she averted her face from the reek of drink, tobacco and hair oil; it was forced on her consciousness that he was what he would have called himself "making love to her", assuring her that "if you got a divorce from John I'd look after you...." There needn't be any scandal, she'd get her own money and he knew places where she could live without the gossips getting their claws into her... why not? It was done every day. A fine woman like her was a fool to stick it—"don't be shocked—if you knew how the upper-classes behave..."

May was fascinated by this discourse that held her rigid; it was so utterly unexpected, so entirely grotesque that she could not rally herself to answer, and he mistook this motionless attitude for one of interest, of consent; of course she would be interested, there had never been anyone but John and she had been a grass widow four years and more; she was human, for all her proud airs. He had been drinking more than his wont to get up his courage and had now gone beyond his commonsense, that cold judgment of a tradesman, that was usually, with very narrow limits, correct. He had not meant to force the situation to-night, only to feel his way, but the music, the drink, the whirligig of the dances, the lewd atmosphere of sly licence and secret lust, had driven him beyond his usual discretion; he wanted to maul her as John had wanted to maul the peacock and the peaches.

"You married the wrong man, May—what's he done for you? Well *you* know best..." he was edging her gradually towards the end of the bar, for as he sidled nearer, she fell back. "Come now, you ought to know a good friend when you see one—didn't you ever guess that I was sweet on you?"

"I thought," she stammered, like someone speaking through waters fatally enclosing, "you would have married me...." She heard him laughing behind the strip of pasteboard and muslin that was becoming sticky from his sweat. "You did, did you; then why did you jump at him, you little fool?"

She was that all right, she confessed as much; always understanding so little, the victim of good breeding that taught that women must be impervious to any assaults on their passions, must always smile and be well behaved, always be ignorant of evil—always ignore ugliness, must live by a rigid, but irrational code that was never explained, a little fool, never at one with the people into whose midst she had married, never able to understand even her own fortitude, even her own attempt to escape, even why she had married John Tyler.

"*Why* do you want to get away?" Richard urged, "because you remembered you *could* have married me?"

"No," she was trying to be honest, trying not to be frightened; even if she was not quite aware of it herself, she was, by nature, tradition and upbringing, so aloof, so much more what is meant by "respectable" than the Manchester women who thought her "fast", that she had endured eight years of Stone Pynes rather than affront a conventionality that to her was concrete as manacles, as sacrosanct as the laws of God. Even now she could not believe that Richard, so neutral a figure, until now, in her lazy imagination, was looking at her as hitherto John alone had looked at her, her mind was not touched, he had roused her instincts as John had roused them before she knew what instincts were. Now there were none of the pretty disguises she had thrown over her feeling for her husband, but the feeling itself, roused suddenly, stripped like one of the maskers unexpectedly and dancing naked in brutal triumph. She leaned towards him, as the nymph crouching amid the reeds might have leaned towards the centaur. Richard, pressing closely, snarled and whimpered, and pulled at her shoulders, too clumsily, too quickly, making a butting movement that threw back his hood and mask; his distorted and congested face was to the woman like a reflection of her own. Between them they had evoked some primitive lust that was all the more terrible to her, that she felt it to be partly due to her acceptance of it; she was bare of pretences in her own eyes; to this lust had been due her marriage, so stupid and so horrible. She had more than acquiesced in John's brief need of her; with all his shams, his vulgarities, his coarseness, she had been drawn to him, wanted him; if not for long, at least long enough to ruin her—not the fault in him, who never pretended to any virtue of any kind, but the fault in her, whose exquisite chastity had masked her so perfectly, even to her own eyes, had brought them both to ruin… now she had allowed it to happen again. Her face was so drawn into an expression of blasted simplicity, the disillusionment of the delicate minded who find suddenly their own animal passions so awful, that Richard recoiled. He had only one interpretation of the monstrous disgust with which she forced herself away from him, that he had startled her by being too quick; he was sobered by her agony of alarm, he had made a gross, perhaps a dangerous error, yet triumph flared amidst his fear. May *was* a good, pure woman; in that moment he would have devoted his life to keeping her so, rescued from John, safe in an embowered cottage, with singing birds and a flower garden, guileless over a piece of needlework, welcoming his tender visits with a gratitude untinged by any hint of sex. As this all darted into his mind he tried to stammer something that would cover his blunder. But May had seen too much, she too had lost her head and all the ladylike arts that would have helped her to pretend she had not seen her breeding was in the dust with her caution. May ran away, as much in a panic as a schoolgirl kissed against her will at a Sunday school treat. She stumbled in her long cloak from the deserted bar, tripped in this, and fell against the white domino waiting outside the door, so that he had to half lift her to her feet, talking loudly and merrily to cover the episode.

Richard Tyler, not quick enough to turn this incident to his advantage, and indeed dumbfounded, remained clumsily where he stood, ignominiously in the wrong, ready to do penance if he could get her alone; the white domino took May Tyler's arm through the cloak and led her through the maze of the stamping dancers.

"I've been watching you all the evening; I thought he was up to no good."

May had no language for such a moment as this; she was struggling not to cry, she shut her eyes in the bitter endeavour to regain her self-respect.

"You must trust me."

"I don't know who you are...." She could contrive that between sobs but no more; he supported her down the gilt stairs and again through the spinning figures into one of the alcoves off the large gas-lit ballroom.

The waltz had been encored; the kaleidoscope of colour shifted; everyone shifting out of step round the large room where the light was like acid on the shoddy mantles of sham silk and velvet.

"I'm sorry you don't know my voice. I hoped you hadn't forgotten me." He had taken off his white pointed mask as his name came into her mind—Jerome Thorne, the knight errant, but the mask had turned him into the likeness of a large rat. "You must," he insisted, "let me know how I can help you. You know, of course, that I would do anything for you. I've made it my business to find out how matters stand...."

He continued talking suavely, saying nothing to alarm or annoy, and she did not hear more than the tone of his voice which did not please.

"No one else, no one else," she whispered to herself.

He caught the words. "You must trust me—not Richard, or the doctors, or anybody whom they put about you. Send for me and I'll do what I can. Someday there may be some happiness for both of us." His voice became keener as he added, "You haven't let your husband know we were together in that London hotel?"

"No," she forced herself to speak, coughing and stammering. "There was no harm in it, but since I have understood that it was foolish of me to stay there with you. You must think me very inexperienced and unworldly...."

"Why so you are," replied Mr. Thorne pleasantly. "That's understood, isn't it? But I really came here to-night (not knowing how your gallant escort was going to behave, though I had my own ideas on that subject) just to warn you, my dear, not to tell your husband about that episode in London.... I don't like to come to Stone Pynes, eh?—and I thought you might come here—with Richard, since John is ill. Don't bother him while he is ill."

"No, I won't," she promised immediately.

"It was a great wrong, you know," insisted Mr. Thorne with a slight air of reproach.

"I suppose it was wrong, a great wrong to try to get a divorce. The scandal will ruin his business, I suppose, but I can think of nothing now but getting away from Richard...."

"John, you mean; you often use one name for another. So you came up to see what you could do about a divorce! Well, there's a sly boots! I thought you so 'unspotted from the world', my dear. Who was helping you?"

She lied mechanically; after to-night she would be likely to lie when Richard was mentioned in connection with her affairs.

"No one. I just wanted to see my bankers, to advise me where to find a lawyer, then there was a telegram from the doctor, and I had to go home."

"But you went to Blackheath first? Why? If no one was advising you."

"I met Mrs. Bingham by chance; she had had the telegram—she told me I was being very indiscreet and that I had better stay with her—even for a night."

"So she would, funny meeting her!" Thorne was suspicious. Was she really a fool or "a deep one"? Funny about the lawyers. "I wondered," he gave her the full sleepy glow of his fine eyes, his voice took on the deep tones of the professional philanderer unsure of his ground. "Yes, do you know, I *wondered* why you were going alone to London."

She was still trembling from the encounter with Richard that had been an encounter with herself; she answered at random:

"Why did you think I was?"

"I thought it just might have been..." he saw the first surge of some frantic disgust in her face, and shrewder, more sober and more cold-blooded than Richard, added tenderly, "My *dear* girl, *don't* think I suspected you of going to meet some man—you simply mustn't think like that about me. I *do* respect you."

This was true, but he hoped that some day it would not be; she was a fool, then, after all; odd, but no need to allow that brute, the younger Tyler, to have the advantage of this folly; that scene in the bar-room was surely unmistakable; he continued, with the complacency of a man from whom no woman had rushed away in a panic.

"I want to help you, indeed I do." Chivalry was the role that he found easiest; he knew he had the appearance that suited with the kind of feminine romanticism that delighted in knight errantry, and though this pose made his love affairs very long drawn out, it also made them cheap; delay suited a temperament essentially sluggish, and vanity more than passion being the motive of his intrigue, the slow drama on Arthurian lines, that could end in a semi-mystical climax of material renunciation and spiritual negation of worldly passion, suited his pocket as it suited the vanity of the women. If Jerome Thorne had never had to pay for more than sweets and flowers on the excuse that "love was without price" for any of the women he had attracted, at least they could skip out of the adventure feeling there had been nothing "sordid" about it; thus his straight features, flung back yellow hair, noble air and the manner that Manchester considered "chivalrous" had ensured Jerome Thorne that he need never run into debt for his amours, and this he found convenient, for his income was far from sufficient for the vices that had to be paid cash down.

"Why do you think," he asked with great tenderness, "I followed you to London, if not to watch over you in your loneliness? To protect you?" he added, for he was never so sure of himself that he did not underline his effects.

"Follow me? I thought we met by chance? At the station?"

So she *was* a fool; there was not a hint of coquetry in her wide eyes, flushed by tears, staring at him blankly; he took his cue, emphasized his pose of knight errant and had the satisfaction of seeing she took him at his face value; she did not even ask how he had come to follow her to the station, no need then to account for this, which could only be accounted for by the truth, that Lizzie Burt, for a fee small to him, large to her, kept him informed of the movements of her mistress, "for her protection, she ought never to be unguarded."

To May this was salve, after Richard, after herself and Richard, after herself and John; she was reassured as to the monster she seemed both to have housed and created; she looked at him most anxiously; he was passive enough to give her complete faith in him; he would never rouse some instinct in her that shamed and bewildered, he would never remind her that she had once wanted to marry John. She retreated further behind the barriers Richard had so roughly trampled down, that Jerome Thorne had helped her to raise again; with him she would always be safe, he would always behave as she wished; she was as wrong with Jerome Thorne as she had been with Richard Tyler, and this time did not even glimpse, for a second, the truth about herself, which was that Thorne had really no essential attraction for her at all, and was quite incapable of disturbing her as did the Tylers; she would always be safe from herself with Thorne, and it was this unconscious knowledge that gave her confidence in him. So, gradually losing her alarm, she listened to his specious, soothing talk, not realizing his words; she became concerned only in getting away from this dance hall which now to her had an infernal aspect, with the rasping waltz tune, the splitting, greasy masks, the clumsy shapes, embracing one another in their flowing crude-coloured dominoes like tops in draperies set spinning for ever.

"The porter will get me a cab"; she suddenly rose. "There's no need for you to come to the door...." She was conscious of a relief, even of a pleasure in having found, in her unexpected misery and degradation, this help and championship. "No, of course I shall say nothing to my husband, and of course I'll let you know if you can help me; but it seems I've done wrong more than I meant, or thought of. I'm confused—you must forgive me.... Good night."

He was quickly after her and quickly found the porter, paid the man and saw that she was escorted into a prepaid cab with the dexterity of one used at least to homespun gallantries.

He returned leisurely through groups who stared, for they were both well known, to find Richard Tyler. That humiliated and discomfited man, his laborious schemes of many months completely ruined, was, as Mr. Thorne had supposed he would be, at one of the bars—the third at which the enemy so unknown to him had looked to find him.

Thorne knew very well how he and May Tyler were "talked about"; he had helped on the flattering gossip himself. He had been vexed that neither John nor Richard Tyler seemed to know or care about this; he suspected, truly, that they completely trusted the reckless little woman... yet Richard, the sly, clumsy devil, was after her himself, and she'd turned him down flat, been scared too, that showed she really was "straight". He was flattered, pleased, a little excited, with his usual tricks of knight errantry he'd get her in the end; meanwhile he would like to put the elder man who had been so often rude to him in his place. He didn't intend to let anyone think she'd made him ridiculous with that baulked London meeting—but no doubt Richard didn't know he, Thorne, had been at the Mentone; if he had he'd have rounded on May, not secretly championed her, egged her on, lost his head and tried to snatch at her in a public place. No, Thorne was sure that May, who was the only person who held this secret, had not mentioned his, Thorne's, presence at the Mentone; yet he must; it might come out she'd given him the slip, one never knew who was watching. Also, he had compromised himself to-night, not legally, of course, nothing John could get him for, but sufficiently to permit him to go a step further, and flaunt a conquest he had not made. He had done this before, with little dexterity but much success, for he had traded on the stupidity of roused passion, and the readiness of the world, quite justifiably, "to believe in evil".

He drank a glass of brandy with an easiness too jaunty to be well-bred; the younger domino approached the elder and greeted him by his name. He pushed his mask aside from his smooth face that had not lost the calm, almost majestic expression that May thought spiritual, tender and manly.

"I've done you a good turn," he whispered, tapping Richard Tyler on the arm. "She's gone home safely. I told her not to say anything about anything... you understand me...?"

Richard, whose mask was hanging by the elastic round his neck as he had torn it off and it had caught on the fastening of his domino, stared at the speaker with eyes suffused with blood; he looked more than middle-aged, bloated, stupid and sad.

"The white domino," he muttered, eyeing the young man's expensive cloak. "I suspected that it was you following us all the evening."

"Lucky for you, don't you think? She might have—well, kicked up a fuss if it hadn't been for me," he continued in a pleasant and patronizing tone, leaning on the bar with an air of impertinent freedom, exaggerating his part, in "soothing" May Tyler, as he termed it, and in "getting her quietly from the building". Had she been left alone she would have gone as rapidly and as quietly, but Richard was not quite sure about this, nor did he care; one point only absorbed his furious attention.

He could have endured her rebuff, he could almost have found a morbid pleasure in it, a regretful relish in the knowledge that she was utterly unobtainable, not even to be clutched at, pulled down and destroyed as John had pulled down and destroyed the guarded peaches on the wall… but what was this man saying, what was the purport of his mincing sentences, his smirks and winks? One sentence penetrated Richard's wits, bemused with rage, whispered fiercely into his ear.

"You'd better be careful about the hotel episode… that would quite go against her in a divorce…."

"How do you know that I took her to a hotel?" answered Richard slowly, so as not to stammer. "Besides, she went away so soon I had no chance of seeing her for more than half an hour or so…."

"I know," replied Jerome, with a slow smile of complete triumph, "but she went there to meet me, my good fellow, as you'll find out if you refer to the hotel books. If you're cooking up any divorce evidence, you'd better be careful about that."

Richard Tyler remained enclosed within the dreary battle-ground of his own gloom, fury and disappointment. Outside events had, compared to his own emotional disturbances, very little interest for him—not even the events that might be taking place at Stone Pynes. He had none of the qualities that would have helped him to keep his situation in hand. He could not for a while even say what it was he desired, such was his confusion, and when he knew, his wish was one that he could not admit, for it was revenge.

He had no distinct purpose in his mind when, that rainy afternoon in June, he went over to Stone Pynes to learn something of the fortunes of the people who interested him more than anything in the world. There had been one or two peevish notes from John, complaining of his state of health since the carnival ball, but as some of these were written from the office, thus showing that John was able to go about,

Richard had taken little heed of them. Now, by an effort of his memory and a consultation of the calendar, he could recall the lapse of time that had become smudged in his mind… some ten days after the mask at the Pomona Rooms Richard Tyler went to Stone Pynes.

It was Nelly Tanner who opened the door to him; she seemed to have been crying and her greeting was hysterical.

"Oh, thank God you've come, sir! There's queer things going on here…. Master's very ill and the mistress—" She glanced furtively behind her up the stairs, then grew so close to Richard in the dark vestibule, that he could smell the rice powder on her face, "Mistress… well, I don't like to say it, sir, but she's giving him all sorts of things…."

"Haven't you had the doctor?" asked Richard mechanically.

Nelly Tanner answered still in a whisper. "Oh yes, Dr. Fitch and Dr. Harman and another… specialist I think they call 'em… but they don't seem to know what's the matter with master, though they've ordered him a parcel of medicines, I can tell you, and patent foods, too… the kitchen's full of them and Cook doesn't know where to turn for all the tins and bottles and cooking up this and that…."

"Anybody upstairs with your master?"

"Only the mistress, sir."

Nelly Tanner contrived to give a very sinister intonation to these very simple words.

"Mr. and Mrs. Chorley's been more than once, but they weren't allowed in. Mistress said the master wasn't to be disturbed…. Dr. Harman seemed to think she ought to have a professional nurse—you know, sir from the Institute—but she said she could manage all right by herself. Mrs. Crimpton was sent away by the master. *She* gives him all his drink and food and everything…."

"I'd better come downstairs to the kitchen and talk to you before I go up. I ought to know the lie of the land."

The maidservant's face tightened with pleasure. "I'm sure we shall be glad to tell you all we can, sir, the same as we told Mrs. Chorley and her husband... they thought it wasn't right and that you ought to be sent for, but the master said no, he'd rather get well by himself. He wants the mistress with him day and night waiting on him—but then he doesn't *know*, poor gentleman...."

By now they had opened and shut the baize door that enclosed the basement and were downstairs in the little sitting-room at the back of the kitchen that John liked to call the servants' hall. Dolly Hoey was there, aimlessly turning over the leaves of a book. She started as her master's brother came in, and rose quickly, putting the volume *Fortune Telling Made Easy* under her apron.

"Now what's all this nonsense?" demanded Richard with a clumsy disguising of his intense interest. "I can't have this going on, you know—gossiping and whispering in my brother's house, and he ill. I wonder the doctors didn't let me know before and I'd have come round and taken a hold of things."

"I wish you had, sir, but the master didn't wish it, and what could we do?" It was Nelly Tanner who spoke. She was by far the most fluent of them all, but she had not said more than this when Mrs. Pilch entered from the kitchen, drying her floury hands on a large soiled tea-cloth.

"Now don't you go putting ideas into Master Richard's head like you've been trying to do with me," she objected stolidly. "Don't you take any notice of them, sir, they're just fools making something out of nothing."

"I've no doubt you are all fools, a pack of gossips, but I want to know what this 'something' is that you are making out of 'nothing'."

"I'm not going to be silenced by Mrs. Pilch," snapped Nelly Tanner viciously. "Why should I be? It's my duty as a Christian to speak out... there's *funny goings on* in this house and if I hadn't thought I should do a bit of good by remaining, I should have cleared out long ago."

"Tell me what's happened," demanded the heavy man, settling himself at the table which was covered by a cloth with a blurred pattern of scarlet and dark blue.

They all began talking at once; he silenced them, and gave the word to the first housemaid, who, pleased by this distinction, flowed on glibly; in his mind, as he listened the business man made a summary of her talk which ran thus... his brother had been ill on and off since the night of the ball, now worse now better... twice able to go down to the office and take with him patent food cooked by Mrs. Pilch in the brown jug with which Richard was so familiar, from seeing it on his brother's untidy desk.... Dr. Harman had been in constant attendance talking vainly about a chill and prescribing this medicine and that; another parcel of medicine had arrived from London from Messrs. Joshua and Blunt, of course no one but the master knew what was in it... his wife "had nursed him day and night," as the saying went; that is, she had sat up in her room ready to wait on him at any time should he require medicine, drink or food.

Mrs. Pilch put in more than once, "And very kind and good she's been, doing for him as much as any lady could, with no thought for herself...."

"But she stood out against having the nurses," insisted Nelly Tanner, "not on any account would she have them, though the doctors spoke of it...." And then the woman's eyes gleamed with venom. "She gave me a letter to post one morning when things seemed very bad and we didn't think the master was going to live.... Oh, you were going to be sent for, sir, but as he recovered it wasn't done."

"What about the letter... what do you know of it?"

The woman who had hitherto been silent, the nurse, now spoke; she was seated in the back of the room, knitting in the shadows.

"You wonder perhaps," she remarked, "why I am here, sir. The little darlings are both safe asleep in their cots and I came down to get their supper, special dishes you understand that I don't let anyone but myself touch." She glided off this into a cool and deadly accusation that fell on Richard Tyler's ears with an extraordinary pleasure. "*She* gave me a letter to post when I was going out with the children. I came to the road and I was going to send Master John across with it—I do, you know, I let them go across the road with the letters when there isn't much traffic about—and he fell down and the letter got covered with mud, and so I took it out of the envelope to put it in another. Then I saw that it was a very wicked letter, sir, and I've got it here now, and you can have it if you like...."

Richard's glance tried to convey to the woman that she only fooled him because it suited him.

"To whom was the letter addressed?"

"Why, to Mr. Jerome Thorne, sir, the gentleman who used to come here after her and stay alone with her in the parlour, if you ever heard of such goings on—and I can tell you that the one time the master did go out there was trouble about him, too."

"How trouble?" demanded Richard. "And how do you know of it?"

His massive cold fingers were on the scrap of paper that bore on the top the coronet and initial D that headed all Madame Dumont's notepaper. He thought swiftly, "Yes, once again, a fool, writing on her mother's paper, and in a hand that's not disguised." Often enough he had seen it on the friendly notes she had sent him.... The servants crowding greedily about him, he read May Tyler's letter to Jerome Thorne.

I feel I ought to tell you that he knows nothing of the London visit. You seemed so disturbed about this that it has concerned me very much. I am with him day and night. The doctors are constantly here. Sometimes he doesn't know me; sometimes he speaks to me reproachfully. I fear I have committed a fearful sin. What is one to do? What am I to do? Would it be possible to see you? I cannot leave the house, he is sick unto death.

Yours thankfully, May.

Richard Tyler's blood seemed to him to turn sour in his veins as he read. His monstrous fancies were, then, justified; they were no progeny of disordered passion or of a seething brain, the whelp Thorne had not lied, here was plain fact. He folded up the letter and put it in his pocket. He contrived to speak quietly to the nurse who was gazing at him with grim intensity.

"You did quite right to keep this and to give it to me. I shall have to take charge here now. It's not fit that she should be left with him."

"Indeed it isn't," broke in Lizzie Burt, "not with them flypapers and all—"

"Flypapers?" he exclaimed. "What do you mean by that?"

The three of them broke out at once. "Those what she bought just before the master was took bad and had soaking in her basin."

"There's nothing in it," said the cook quickly. "Ladies often do that; it makes a face-wash—"

"I have been in service for a good many years," protested Nelly Tanner contemptuously, "and *I've* never seen it done. Flypapers for face-wash, indeed! I've never known a mistress use flypapers... and wasn't it flypapers those awful two women used in Liverpool to murder those two poor innocents with? Everybody knows there's *arsenic* in flypapers—"

"Perhaps the mistress didn't know," interrupted Mrs. Pilch, whose lined face was of a pallor that showed her freckles unpleasantly. "You've no right to judge, Tanner; you've been saying awful things...."

"Perhaps," said Richard, heavily, "she's a right to say what you call 'awful things'. I don't like the look of it at all. Has anyone been here beside the doctors?"

"No, she sent for a nurse this morning, at last... we'd been asking for one for ever so long—"

"Mr. and Mrs. Chorley came," put in the cook, "but Tanner wouldn't let them upstairs."

"It was the mistress that wouldn't see them. Mrs. Chorley tried her best to get into the poor gentleman's room, but the mistress kept on saying he must have rest and quiet. Mrs. Chorley said she didn't like the look of it at all."

"What could have made one lady say that about another?" demanded the cook sternly, "if it wasn't wicked, idle gossip hadn't put it into her head? And whose wicked idle gossip could it have been but yours...?"

"Has she had all her letters?" demanded Richard.

The servants admitted with some reluctance that this must be the case since Mrs. Tyler seemed to go down early to the letter-box herself, and could not therefore give Richard Tyler the information he required as to whether or no there had been a letter from Jerome Thorne. Certainly that gentleman himself had not been to Stone Pynes.

"I'll go upstairs and see my brother." He peered round at the four women, his secret allies. "You've done very well. I ought to have come before, but I've been very busy, and I had a little note from my brother to my office deceiving me into thinking he is better than he really is,"

"I'll come up with you, sir, if you like," said the nurse eagerly. "The woman they've sent—Nurse Goff from the Institute—is up there. She's doing what she can for him; he's always in pain, poor gentleman, and such a power of medicines as the doctors give him... why, the place is nothing but medicine bottles and tins and jars of patient food—"

"Getting more than is good for him, I should think," protested the cook. "What with this mess and that mess—why, he couldn't go down to the office but I had to give him something to take up in the brown jug, and then he complained I'd put sherry in it and spoiled it for him.

He won't stand anything that's sweetened. Then again, sir, if you will allow me to say so, why does he keep taking his own medicines when he's got two doctors in charge of him?"

Richard brushed this aside as irrelevant, as to his purpose it was, and went upstairs to the small bedroom where his brother lay.

His first glance was not for the restless invalid, but for the woman who sat beside him. The mark of the bruise, now fading, was still discernible upon her cheek. She wore a dressing-gown of a pale blue colour, with flounces of lace, and over that an apron of a French design tied carelessly round her waist; her fair hair was untidily gathered at the top of her head. She was pallid and her face had the slack, disinterested expression of one exhausted almost to the point of insensibility.

But she started when she saw Richard and whispered, "I thought you'd have"—she glanced at her husband—"the kindness to keep away."

"I'm sorry," he replied sarcastically, "that I offend you. I regret that I stayed away so long.... I hear that my brother is very ill...."

By now Tanner, who had come behind Mr. Tyler, was in the doorway, but the heavy man motioned her away. "Wait outside on the landing till I give you leave to enter," he said with authority.

"Do you give orders in my house?" asked May, rising. "Why have you come? John is very ill but he did not wish me to send for you."

"Where is the nurse?" demanded Richard.

"She's in the bathroom or the closet—I don't know—mixing medicines. They give him so much medicine there is no end to it, and every day he's worse."

"You were writing to Jerome Thorne," whispered Richard, taking May by the arm and leading her to the window.

"How do you know that?"

"Never mind, I've got some sort of a watch on you."

"Why shouldn't I write? He seemed to me a friend and I have none—really none."

"Amelia Chorley," replied her brother-in-law, "came here, did she not? Why should you not have made a friend of her?"

"Because she dislikes me," replied May simply; "she only came here to spy and make mischief."

"Women who act as you do must expect to be spied on," answered Richard harshly. "I do not like the look of things at all. Have you been tampering with his food and drink?"

May, not seeing the purpose of this question, answered at once, "I've given him some of the powders he begged for that the doctors don't like him to have, and once I shook up a bottle and added something to it, but it was the same medicine. I only wanted to pour it together into one large bottle."

He made a gesture as if he brushed this aside as incoherent nonsense.

"What is the matter with you, Richard? Why do you look at me like that? *This defeats all my plans*—I have to be with him always. No divorce now. He will not allow me out of his sight."

"For good reasons as I suppose," replied Richard morosely, eyeing her with dull fury, "and yet I suppose the poor fool suspects nothing."

"You mean," she answered, "of my design to get the divorce… yes, I see now that that was sin, a really fearful sin… the scandal would have ruined him and it is against my faith. That is what it means being so far away from a priest or a church. I wish I could find one now."

"You may well try to cover things up by talking like that. Priests, and the *sin* of divorce and all the rest of the nonsense! You know that it is something else you are referring to—another *sin*."

The voices had now roused the sick man who heaved up in the narrow bed and stared with unseeing eyes at the couple in the window-place.

"You must go," said May, with more authority than she had ever used to her brother-in-law. "This is John's house and after that mine."

"Oh! so you've thought that out, have you? I suppose you know the terms of his will."

"Who is talking about a will?" interrupted John drowsily. "Everything I've got goes to May, of course… why shouldn't it?"

Richard looked at the young woman and then at the sick man, a lightning glance that endeavoured to penetrate their minds; then he went to his brother's bed and murmured conventional sympathy with his sufferings.

John complained eagerly and sourly of all his symptoms, of the inhumanity and stupidity of the doctors who did not know how to treat him… muttered lamentations of a chill, whispered of pains in his throat, of a sensation like a hair in his gullet… protested against the doctor's order that allowed him to gargle with but not to drink lemonade…. Richard listened to none of this but looked with as much confidence as if he had been learned instead of ignorant at the half-opened packages of patent foods, at the uncorked and unscrewed bottles and tins of beef tea and calves foot jelly, the array of bottles of all sorts and sizes, at the soiled glasses, handkerchiefs and plates that littered the large table beside the bed that Nurse Goff had brought in place of the usual commode.

"You will have to speak to the doctors," interrupted May, "if you want to know what they are giving him. I have no idea at all, I carry out their instructions. I think," she added, speaking rapidly, for she heard a footstep, "that it is in bad taste for you to come now…. I think you should stay away."

John mistook the meaning of her words. "Oh, Richard won't mind our little matrimonial differences; he knows that you were trying to get a divorce…. I never thought you really would carry it so far, but there it is, and we're good friends now, aren't we, May?"

She did not reply directly but said, "I'll nurse you while I can, John. I shall not think of leaving you while you're sick."

Nurse Goff entered the room, a small, dry, impassive personality, outwardly most scrupulous, inwardly a callous cheat.

"This is my brother-in-law," faltered May, looking the more disordered, lovely, rich and warm when beside this precise personality. "Mr. Richard Tyler."

"What do you think of the invalid?" grinned Richard. "Eh, nurse?"

John had now fallen back in the bed with a groan, at once demanding the presence of, and abusing the skill of, the doctors.

"I don't like the look of him at all," announced the nurse with an authoritative air, "indeed I don't, and I wish Mrs. Tyler would leave the nursing to me."

How often this had been said: "I don't like the look of him...."

John roused himself to argue against this but the nurse, with a practised hand, tucked the clothes round him and told him to lie quiet and compose himself for he should have nothing till the doctor came and that would not be long.

May turned and went into her own bedroom, dropping the heavy dusty draperies over the alcove. Richard at once sidled up to the nurse and whispered, "What do you make of it, nurse? Anything odd?"

"Why should there be anything odd?" snarled John who had been listening keenly. "I caught a chill... I've not been well since I had the malaria... the doctors' medicines are no good...."

"Perhaps what you've taken yourself, Mr. Tyler, have been no good. I'm sure I wish I knew where you hide all those parcels you get from London." The nurse spoke as if rebuking a small child.

"Oh they're nothing—stuff I have been taking for years...."

"I'll wait and see the doctor," said Richard. "I didn't know you were so bad or I'd have been round here before. Now lie quiet and trust in me. We'll get you better, if I have all the specialists in London down to see you."

John groaned but acquiesced; his senses were confused. He held out his hand but could not focus where his brother was, grunted, groped, gave up the attempt and adjusted himself clumsily on his tumbled pillows.

The nurse went ostentatiously out of the room and Richard followed at once, exchanging words on the landing.

"What's all this talk I hear in the kitchen?"

"Oh, domestic trouble I suppose," replied the nurse tartly. "The usual thing... they've been quarrelling and let the servants know, as I daresay you're well aware, Mr. Tyler."

"But the trouble's worse than that, isn't it?"

"Worse than that? I don't know... I hear she tried to leave the house and was brought back by force... and then she has been buying fly-papers, and heaven knows how many of them... and people still think of that Liverpool case.... I keep a strict watch over his food, but I have no authority to keep her out of his room."

"Do you think she ought to be kept out?" asked Richard eagerly.

The nurse looked at him straightly. "The doctors don't suspect anything, but then they don't know the case like the servants do. I think Lizzie Burt is a very honest sort, and the others faithful to their master. I hear *she's* getting everything from the will and that your brother's a very wealthy man.... One has heard of such things before," she added evasively, primly.

Richard turned and went with the directness of purpose given by a sudden tremendous idea to the library, took a sheet of paper from the writing-case, a quill and the bottle of ink and carried them to his brother's room. Nurse Goff was sitting by the bed of the sick man who was unconscious but grumbling monotonously.

"Where's Mrs. Tyler?" whispered Richard.

"Oh, in her own room I suppose, I haven't seen her. She's always in and out, and he's always calling for her. He's asleep now... I've given him a draught to keep him quiet...."

"When will he wake up?"

"Oh, in about an hour, I should think."

"Well, you can go and take a walk or have a rest, or do whatever you want to—I think you ought to get another nurse to take the night duty so that my sister-in-law need not come in here at all."

The nurse rose and Richard Tyler sank in her chair beside the bed, picked up the novel that she had dropped on the floor, rested his sheet of paper on it and began to write, saying as his pen scratched along, "I'll wait till he wakes. I want him only to sign his name to this, and I'll ring for you and Tanner to witness his signature...."

Amelia Chorley thrust herself into Stone Pynes with the excited violence of someone who intrudes upon the unusual. She had the air of expecting circumstances so odd that any oddity in herself might be excused. Disdaining the disguise of the social conventions that she usually aped, she asked Nelly Tanner, who opened the door, "how matters were going," adding: "I've heard the *strangest* things."

"From whom, madam?" asked the servant with relish tempered by discretion.

"Oh, I met Lizzie Burt and she told me about the letter. Of course we've all noticed it for a long time. What a dreadful state of affairs—I'm glad Mr. Richard's in charge. I hope he is?" she added briskly, placing her parasol and gloves on the imitation Tudor chest in the hall.

"Oh yes, he's in charge." Nelly Tanner whispered with eager ferocity. "He won't let mistress into master's room, she's not to touch *any* of the things he eats or drinks... the nurses are to watch over him day and night."

"What's the doctor think of all this?" asked Mrs. Chorley brusquely. She had gone into the parlour and was patting her bright, stiffly crimped hair into place beneath her round tulle hat with the seagull's wings and velvet bows on the temples.

"I don't rightly know, ma'am," gabbled the housemaid. "There's so many doctors coming and going, and so many orders being sent down to the kitchen, and every time I can get into master's room he doesn't seem in his right mind, and mistress seems pretty well shut up, no one sees her."

"So you can't make head or tail of it, I suppose?" Mrs. Chorley smiled with the contempt of the expert for the amateur. "Well, I'll go upstairs and find out what *is* happening."

This she proceeded to do and went with a cool, alert manner into May Tyler's bedroom, lightly tapping on the door and then immediately opening it with feline swiftness.

May was seated on a low chair covered in soiled satin at the foot of the over-adorned bed. The room, as Mrs. Chorley at once noticed, was in considerable confusion; the curtain of the alcove that led to John Tyler's room was partially pulled aside; on the mantelshelf and on the dressing-table bottles of medicine stood among the brilliant and frivolous ornaments that May had brought from Paris and London.

"My dear, you look worn out." Amelia Chorley's eyes glittered on her prey; she had always, for reasons she had never concerned herself to analyse, disliked May Tyler. "Whatever is happening here? Oughtn't you to be with John?"

"There are two nurses," replied May, rising, and holding out her hand. "I don't quite know what to do, I'm not mistress here any longer."

"Whatever *do* you mean?" exclaimed the other woman with zest. "But you'd better be discreet, hadn't you, my dear?"

She pulled the drapery over the alcove after a quick glance into the other chamber that showed her the invalid asleep and the nurse watching beside him.

"I mean," Amelia Chorley added, turning quickly, "of course you can count on me as a friend and speak *quite* frankly. I heard something from my husband that *he'd* heard from Richard... oh, just men's talk at the clubs, you know... but really I was *quite* disturbed about you. What *is* John's illness, *does* anybody know?"

"No one knows," replied May, "not even the doctors. I am blamed for it, you know."

"*You* are blamed for it?" Amelia Chorley darted on this to her, incredible admission. "Why? How?"

"Because I didn't get a trained nurse in sooner, and another doctor—that's why it has all been taken out of my hands. I have no money and am not allowed even to telegraph to my mother."

Amelia Chorley was disappointed. This was not the high drama she had been hoping for from her husband's hints and glances, from Richard's black looks and sombre words. She had tried to get into Stone Pynes on several occasions, but this was the first time she had succeeded and she meant to make the utmost of her success.

With the duplicity and shrewdness some women have as natural gifts she questioned May directly and obliquely as to John's illness and the domestic situation; the exhausted woman gazed at her with a candour that weariness was beginning to eclipse as the twilight once eclipsed the lilies growing in the garden of the Parisian convent.

"I'm so fatigued, Amelia, I hardly know what I'm saying or doing. I've been up several nights, never knowing when I might be called. There is nothing to conceal from anyone that I know of, except..." She paused, thinking of the white powder that she had, on more than one occasion, given John at his passionate solicitation.

"Except what?" pressed Amelia Chorley, stroking her hand.

"I don't know what I was going to say."

This was near the truth, for she had been doubtful, everything about the white powder was doubtful, it might be doing her husband good for all she knew, she had no idea of its name, after all, neither Richard nor the doctor had taken any notice of her fears, and she promised John not to speak of this private medicine.

Mrs. Chorley was not to be thus put off; she settled herself down in a red velvet buttoned chair by the dressing-table with the torn lace flounces tied up with bows of frayed blue ribbon.

"My dear, what a confusion you've got this room into—with two nurses and Mrs. Crimpton as well! Are you sure they've been doing their duties... and then Tanner and that other maid.... Forgive me, dear, but it looks as if the whole household had got out of hand."

"Richard's the master," repeated May, in a tired, flat voice. "He thinks I'm quite incompetent, perhaps he's right. He's been very offended because I tried, or thought of trying, to get a divorce.... I suppose you've heard of that?" she asked with an innocent directness that disconcerted the other woman, and made her dislike May more because of her own flush of shame.

"Well, I've heard something about it, but I don't know... it's all a lot of nonsense, I suppose?"

"Oh no, I was quite sincere, but now I feel sorry, of course, while he's ill.... The doctor spoke to me and said that he was fretting over it and that I should have what they called a reconciliation, though that didn't seem to me the right word... but I could see that it was a fearful sin...."

"*What* was a fearful sin?" interrupted Mrs. Chorley, with more eagerness than was clever to show; she pushed her chair closer to the other woman.

"Why, trying to get a divorce," replied May faintly. "First, it is against my Faith that I have forsaken, yet my Faith would not accept this marriage, you know, so perhaps a divorce would mean nothing now—since I am not married— But among *his* friends—and the children—it would have ruined him—caused a scandal, brought the business down.... I was selfish, thinking of myself only. Yet, I was right too.... I haven't got it at all clear yet, Amelia; I'm very much alone, there's no one to whom I can turn."

"You can confide everything to me."

May smiled. "I don't think I could. I expect that's my fault."

"We've known each other a long time," pleaded Amelia Chorley, and her hopeful desire to be put in possession of a fascinating secret lent a warmth to her voice that might well have been genuine friendship.

"Yes, but that makes no difference. This business is so much my own, I cannot even tell it to my mother...."

"But you want help and how are you to get help?" retorted the other woman with some stiffness, "if you don't confide in someone? Dr. Harman now—*he* knows the whole story, I suppose?"

"The doctors think of nothing but how to get John well and I must think of nothing but that, too. I'm shut out," she repeated again, "he does nothing but call for me. I can hear him through the curtains... the nurses have orders to shut me out, Amelia, I'm not mistress here at all; Mrs. Pilch has some kindness for me, but none of the others."

Mrs. Chorley tried to penetrate into May's confidence by persistent and what appeared to be affectionate offers of service, but May shook her head.

"There's nothing you can do for me, Amelia, and you're more John's friend than mine."

"Well, that ought to make no difference."

"But it does." May's smile, as if she gracefully but emphatically ruled the other out of her confidence, suddenly infuriated Amelia Chorley.

"Well then," said that lady with a sudden sneer, "why don't you write to Jerome Thorne? *He* might help you."

"Do you think so?" replied May quietly. "Is that your advice?"

Amelia Chorley's plump hand went to her veil, pulling it about in an effort to control herself. Was she dealing with an incredible effrontery or an incredible innocence?

"Why, of course it would be a good idea. He's well known to be very chivalrous and he's paid you a great deal of attention, hasn't he...? Of course in the most gentlemanly and proper sort of way."

May seemed oblivious to the double meaning of these homely words.

"He doesn't wish to be involved in my concerns," she answered. "I have made a mistake—several mistakes with regard to him, but I still believe that what you say is true; he will help me—why not?"

"Write to him now then, at once." Mrs. Chorley was busily looking round the room for writing materials; these she soon found; coroneted paper of Madame Dumont's was thrown down in a heap behind some scent bottles and a silver tarnished inkstand with pencils and pens standing among a number of boxes that contained pills and pastilles.

May, who had been walking slowly up and down, sank again on the edge of the bed and wrote on the pad and with the pencil that Mrs. Chorley, controlling her eagerness, brought to her.

> *I am writing to you to help me in my present fearful trouble. I am in custody without any of my family with me and without money. The truth is known about my visit to London. Appearances may be against me, but before God I swear I am innocent.*
>
> *May Tyler.*

May handed the letter, addressed to Jerome Thorne, to the woman who stood over her and who could scarcely restrain herself from snatching this precious piece of evidence.

"Now, you ought to try and get a little rest, dear May. Shall I send Tanner in to you? Have you had any refreshments lately?"

"I can't rest and I can't eat, everything seems grotesque… I'll wait and hear what Mr. Thorne says. If he can suggest anything… give me a little help… I'm so very much alone."

"So you keep saying, but of course you're surrounded by friends. There's Richard, and Dr. Harman, and myself, and my husband and dear Nurse Bart…"

"Do you think she's a friend? I always felt that she disliked me. She's left the house, you know, with the children; Richard sent them away this morning—I don't know where."

"Richard's taking a good deal on himself," observed Mrs. Chorley with satisfaction. "He must have *some good* reason."

"He thinks I'm careless—no use—either as a housekeeper or a nurse," smiled May faintly. "Also he can never forgive me for having spoken of a divorce."

"But you too had *some good* reason, hadn't you?" Mrs. Chorley could not leave her prey yet, although she held the compromising letter firmly in her smooth fingers. "I mean, you found out something about the woman at Salford, didn't you? And then you quarrelled, and Richard saw him raise his hand to you..."

"Nothing of that kind happened," replied May steadily. "If it had, I wouldn't remember it—Richard shouldn't remember it... I don't know anything of anyone in Salford. If it were true, one shouldn't think of it now. Will you ask someone to send my letter at once, please, Amelia? It is a service you can do me. I haven't the money for the stamp. Richard has locked up the cash box."

"I'll lend you that. My husband does not let me take much about with me, but I can manage a stamp. Now I must go in and see John. I'll be sure your letter goes."

May thanked Amelia for this service, then stood still by the end of the bed. Her soiled water-lily-green dressing-gown with the heavy flounces of lace, trailed about her on the thick carpet, the thick pile thick with biscuit crumbs and dust; her fair hair had come down from the pins and lay loosely on her shoulders. She looked at once forlorn and indomitable. Mrs. Chorley, embarrassed, stooped and kissed her, because there was nothing else to do.

*

"There are some queer things knocking about this house," complained John Tyler. "All these comings and goings, all these bottles of medicine, and gargles, and plasters, and—nothing doing me any good."

"None of that is queer," replied Richard, staring harshly down at the sick man's changed features. "That's ordinary enough."

But John continued to grumble, to lament, to protest and complain. He'd heard whisperings… he'd seen figures.… He wanted May to come and give him some of his private medicine.… At these words Richard glanced knowingly across at Nurse Goff.

"He means the *nux vomica* that Joshua and Blunt sent him from London."

"Yes, sir." The nurse was glib. "But I don't like him to have anything except what the doctors prescribe.…"

"And *that's* enough, I should think," remarked Richard, "why, they change the medicines every day."

"Why can't May come in?" persisted John. "I know she's behaved herself very badly with all that talk of a divorce, but I want to see her—I want to see her alone."

Richard resisted this request without quite knowing his own reason for so doing. His hatred of May as someone who had cheated, deluded and failed him was at present a blind unreasoning power. He knew that he meant to destroy her in the most hideous way possible, but he was not quite sure as to the means he would employ. As he was putting his brother off with cool and clumsy subterfuges, Mrs. Chorley tiptoed into the room from the alcove.

John received her with discourteous gloom, making the most of all his pains and blaming everyone for the state in which he found himself, and repeating again that there "were queer things knocking about the house."

Mrs. Chorley smiled at the invalid, with conventional expressions of sympathy, spoke cheerfully of John's certain recovery and his re-appearance in his usual haunts at club and race-course, in that inane tone used by many when speaking to the sick.

Whilst she was speaking, she was signalling with her fine eyes at Richard, glances that he well understood to mean that she had something important to reveal; he therefore soon made an end of her fussing over the sick man and drew her away. John was left in the charge of Nurse Goff who, with professional callousness, continued reading the novel she had slipped under her chair; John Tyler groaned and complained on his large down pillows.

As soon as they were on the landing, Amelia Chorley thrust May's letter to Jerome Thorne into Richard's unsteady grasp. "She's just written to him again, I couldn't have believed it! She asked me to post it for her. Think of *that!*"

"To that fellow?" Richard sighed; Mrs. Chorley began mechanically to vaunt her own cleverness in having obtained this incriminating missive.

"What will you do? Keep it or send it to him? He might," she suggested in an even lower whisper, "compromise himself further by his answer."

"He won't," replied Richard sullenly. "We have got one of his letters and *he* doesn't give himself away. Does *she* in this?"

"Well, of course," bridled Mrs. Chorley as they slowly descended the dusty pile of the stair-carpet together, "she gives herself away by the fact that she has written to him, doesn't she? Naturally she writes guardedly, but you and I know, don't we Richard, what they do mean? Why, even Lizzie Burt rushed up to me when I tried to get in yesterday, and said 'Thank God you've come, madam, the mistress is trying to poison the master'."

"I've sent her off with the children."

They had reached the parlour and he went to the window and opened the letter as he spoke.

"Burt'll be back again though. She knows a great deal, and I may need her." He glanced over the letter, showed it to Mrs. Chorley and then put it in his pocket as soon as she returned it.

"She *is* a fool, isn't she?" muttered Amelia, almost confounded by the ease with which May had been trapped.

"A fool," repeated Richard. "I don't know who's being a fool... all of us I should think, by being so taken in by *her*. It's a good thing two of the servants saw those arsenic papers."

"Flypapers you mean?" whispered Amelia.

"Well, it's the same thing; they're covered with arsenic, of course. She must have got a pretty strong solution. I hope they'll save him... I'll see to it she is kept out of the room."

"What a wicked, wicked woman!" exclaimed Mrs. Chorley, yet cautiously under her breath. "One can hardly believe it!"

"When a wife goes wrong like that, one can believe anything. I went to the shop to-day and found she *did* buy those papers the day I took her to the Pomona Rooms—funny, isn't it? The very day—"

Mrs. Chorley did not know to what he alluded; she continued to press for details about the flypapers... they had come into the house, open, rolled, tied with a string... they had been left on the hall table... John had picked them up and looked at them, two of the servants, if not three, had seen them soaking in the basin in May's room with a towel over them... all of them, of course, had begun talking about the baby-farming case in Liverpool only a few years ago.... Where had the solution gone? Were not John's symptoms exactly those of arsenic poisoning? Why it was all as clear as need be.... So she extracted and commented on her information.

"What are you going to do?" she asked as Richard sank at last into silence; she felt a genuine excitement, not untouched with dismay, at this sudden revelation of the drama being played in Stone Pynes. She had only half believed, hardly believed at all, in any of it, the lover, the poisoning; and now, suddenly, the house was full of horror as if dark winds bearing the seeds of plague had blown through the pretentious windows. She dare not put into plain terms her present emotion, half relish, half fear; she was a woman always frightened of clear thinking and accurate speech; neither did Richard yet know what his plan of action would be....

"We shall have to see if John recovers or not," he whispered vaguely and knew that he would prefer, from many points of view, that John should not recover.

The two left the room together, he, heavy, dark, reeking of tobacco, castille soap scented with that manly odour, orange flower water made at Cologne, she reeking of *Violettes de Parme*; their artificial scents were not powerful enough to dissipate the smell of boiling cabbage that escaped even through the baize doors that shut off the basement.

Half an hour later John was dying; the exhausted doctors said and wondered why the London specialist for whom Richard had telegraphed was so late, too late—a missed train no doubt, well, too late.

"Take her out of the room," added Dr. Harman, glancing at May, who sat huddled by the wash-hand-stand, on a low, hard chair. "He would have her in, but he won't ask for her again now—she seems half unconscious too, anyone dosed her with anything?"

"The sedative you gave me sir, only," replied Nurse Goff.

"That all? She seems very drowsy."

"She was hysterical, I made it strong—there's enough to do with the patient, sir."

"Yes. Take her to her own room, will you, Mr. Tyler?"

Richard who had been watching his brother's agonies with coarse curiosity, started.

"I? I am to—take her? To her bedroom? How?"

"Pick her up, can't you?" asked Dr. Fitch impatiently. "Get her out of the way—she's as light as a child...."

Richard stared; Nurse Goff pulled back the curtains of the alcove; in May's room a night-light was burning, the litter of the sick-room had spread from John's chamber to that of his wife; bottles crowded everywhere, but the bed was trim.

"My brother is dying?"

"Yes, Mr. Tyler." Dr. Harman was dry. "And I've asked you to take your sister-in-law away."

He approached her; bent over her; the others, blotted into one thick shadow excluded his last air from the dying man whose convulsions shook the bed; rattling teeth, rattling iron. Richard heard neither, he whispered tenderly: "May, May."

She drooped sideways; it was easy for him to raise her; a light weight, yes, there was some essence in her hair that, fine as a child's, hung over her eyes, something very different from the stuff the others used; he twisted her long pale-green flounced gown over her body and carried her through the alcove; he had longed to do this since he had first met her in Paris, many years ago, when John had snatched her; now John was dying and he had May in his arms.

He laid her on the curtained bed; she was hardly conscious but the doctor's stuff was not strong enough; he knew where they kept the opium pills that had blotted out even John's agonies, he knew everything that happened, that was, at Stone Pynes; he was at her dressing-table, there was the box where Nurse Goff had thrust it, grumbling there wasn't room to place as much as a pin more in the patient's room, it was so overcrowded; he removed one pill delicately, silently approached May and forced it between her yielding lips, forced down water out of the dirty glass, the dirty decanter, laid her tenderly on the pillow smoothing her hair.

He would willingly have murdered all those drab people in the next room, piled their bodies on the corpse and drawn the curtains of the alcove without a pang, for the rest of the night alone with May, but the beast was drab, too, and prudent and well-hidden in the dark thicket. Already they were calling him, the London doctor had arrived. Well, she was powerless at least, he had had her in his arms, and now he kissed her, not with passion, but tenderly, on the brow.

In the ugly parlour of Stone Pynes where the gas lights in the metal circle dependent from the ceiling had been burning for several hours and the heavy crimson curtains shut out the early summer air, Richard Tyler faced the three doctors, talking first to one and then to another in a jerky, yet controlled manner. The three medical men sat at a round table with the dark purple chenille cloth that slid about at a touch. Their faces were weary and impassive; a flicker of half humorous resentment now and then passed over Dr. Harman's lean features; Dr. Fitch appeared uneasy, slightly disgusted, while the third medical man, Dr. Harris, who was "a London specialist", held himself a little apart from his colleagues, and looked severe, with the aloof, suspicious air of a man baffled by what he despises; in the trained mind, in the smooth features of this detached onlooker of the affairs of the Tylers was a well-contained astonishment as to circumstances that seemed horrible, grotesque, yet completely commonplace. What could have been more ordinary than this dreary household? But Richard's face... it might have been looking from behind bars.... Dr. Harris had seen such an expression on the features of a condemned murderer; yet the man was very quiet. The story seemed to the man of experience, so insignificant; a cotton merchant of no importance whatever, dissipated and vulgar, an invalidish sort of man fond of dosing himself, had indulged coarse appetites, eating heavy meals of indigestible and gross foods, had drunk quantities of inferior wine and brandy, had taken a chill through being out in the cold and wet, and had after an illness of fourteen days of random dosing, died as Dr. Harris would have expected him to die—of gastro-enteritis. Dr. Harris had been called in too late to do anything save examine the corpse and now found himself in the midst of an extraordinary condition of affairs; this brutish-looking brother of the dead man was accusing his sister-in-law of murder.

He waited, with a sense of responsibility and of disdain, to learn something from what these three people had to say; he liked none of them. Richard Tyler he thought an objectionable type of successful and uneducated business man, to the London doctor his only interesting point was that he seemed driven by some energetic passion; what that was Dr. Harris could not at present even guess. The two provincial medical men he thought slightly incompetent and extremely self-assured; he knew that physicians in the wealthy Midlands, flattered by a large and ignorant following, were apt to assume too much authority and to rate their own powers too high.

Dr. Harris held in his well-kept hand a paper on which was a list of all the medicines that had been administered during his fortnight's illness to the man lying dead upstairs. The London physician now and then glanced at it, while thoughtfully inclining his head at some professional remark made by one of his colleagues.

Ordinary liver medicine. Inferior sherry. Farinaceous food, warmed in a saucepan. Inferior brandy and soda. A dose of physic. Orso's meat juice. Arrowroot. Bread and milk. Helier's food, with vanilla. Lemonade—as a gargle. Oxtail soup (tinned). Pompadour food. A parcel of pills, bottles of medicine sent from Messrs. Joshua & Blunt, London. Strong tea. Diluted prussic acid. Nux vomica. Strychnine. Mustard and water. Bromide of potassium. Tincture of henbane. Revalenta Food. Coffee. Mordant's papaine and indin. Legs rubbed with turpentine. A Turkish bath. Morphine. Ipecacuanha wine. Fowler's solution (white arsenic, carbonate of potash and lavender water, I per cent arsenic). A blister to the stomach. Jalorandi and antipyrine. Mouth-wash of chlorine water. Bismuth. Sulphonal Cocaine. Nitro-glycerine. Phosphoric acid. Bromides. Fellows syrup (quinine, iron, arsenic and hypophosphates). Podophyllin pills. Hop bitters. A pill of rhubarb, aloes and camomile. Sulphur. Spirits of nitre. Sulphuret of antimony. Sips from 28 bottles of private medicine. Tincture of potassium. Mercury.

Dr. Harris suddenly asked of the dark-haired, stout man in front of him, "What first made you have any suspicions as to your sister-in-law? The accusation could not be a more serious one, you know, Mr. Tyler."

"There was talk," the thick answer was ready at once. "Old friends of mine—Amelia Chorley and her husband… and the nurse, Lizzie Burt.… I have sent her away with the children now, they are staying with friends, but Burt will soon return; and then there were the intercepted letters…"—he pulled at the cloth and stammered, "to her *lover*—her lover."

"You'd better, perhaps," suggested Dr. Harman, "let me finish the story of how your suspicions began, Mr. Tyler. I think, perhaps, I can put it more briefly—it is exceedingly painful for you, of course. It was the letters, Dr. Harris, that Mrs. Tyler sent to a young man who is undoubtedly her lover, she stayed with him at an hotel in London—that is proved—it was these unhappy letters that aroused suspicion. She was trying to get a divorce from her husband—that is also *proved*; there had been several unpleasant scenes between them… Mrs. Tyler suspected her husband of infidelity. We intercepted these letters.…"

"You had your suspicions, then," asked Dr. Harris gazing on the list, "before you read them? What were these based on?"

"Her behaviour generally," put in Richard Tyler thickly, "there had been trouble between them for a long while. She bought flypapers… I hardly remember all the details of what happened. It was the nurse told me about the letter-writing to Mr. Thorne.… It was read to me at the house.… I met my sister-in-law in my brother's bedroom.… I found Nurse Goff there... I was shocked at his condition. I can hardly remember what I said; I believe I told my sister-in-law I had very strong suspicions about the case... she asked me what I meant and I replied that she ought to have called in professional nurses, and also another doctor earlier.... I was not satisfied with the case; I sent for you Dr. Fitch and took charge of the house, giving all the orders.... I told the nurses I should hold them responsible for all foods and medicines given to him, and that no one was to attend him at all except the nurses... but I did not mention any names.... Thorne is a scoundrel. This isn't the first time. Yes, they were to exclude everyone."

"But there was no one else to exclude?" asked Dr. Harris.

"There might have been a servant for all I knew...."

"But at all events, it was your sister-in-law you had in your mind...?"

"Yes."

Dr. Harris remarked, "It seems a very extraordinary state of affairs. Where is the poor lady now?"

"She's shut in her room. She fainted before my brother died."

"Nothing can be done," put in Dr. Harman. "Nothing really should be done, or even said, until we have had a post mortem...."

The other two physicians agreed but Dr. Harman added that he thought the evidence was, to say the least, "very uncomfortable. Everyone who's in the house with Mrs. Tyler has suspicions of her. One cannot forget the Liverpool case... arsenic in solution might have procured this gentleman's death. Then we have the lover, the letters, the access of the wife to the husband...."

Richard Tyler, rising suddenly and standing well out of the harsh light shed by the gas in the brass brackets overhead, pulled out his handkerchief and dabbed at his brow. Seeing his great excitement, Dr. Harris asked, "I suppose, sir, you are struggling under a conflicting sense of what is due to your brother and possible injustice to your brother's wife?"

"God forbid that I should unjustly suspect anyone… but do you not think I have serious grounds for fearing that all may not be right, and that it was my duty to do what I did?"

"I agree." Dr. Harman supported a friend in distress. "I know enough of the case," he bowed slightly towards the London man, "the trouble there was between husband and wife—the differences of their temperament, the flypaper episode, the intercepted letters—well, we need not go over it again, but I think that Mr. Tyler is certainly acting rightly in taking complete control of this house and of seeing that his sister-in-law is kept under lock and key."

"To whom," asked the London physician rising, "does the house now belong? Possibly the lady is in a position to ask us all to depart?" he added with a slight smile.

"Stone Pynes and all its contents belong to me as trustee for the two children," replied Richard, and his ill-controlled agitation increased. "To me—I've taken steps—for a sale—of *everything*."

Dr. Harman remarked swiftly. "Oh, the will has been altered? You know when I made that reconciliation, everything was to be left to your sister-in-law; she was to be trustee for the children…."

"That has been altered now. When I first had my suspicions, I advised John to leave everything in my hands. He did so. You remember, Mr. Fitch, on the day that you told me—last Thursday—that he was in his right mind. I can show you the last will. It was witnessed by Nurse Goff and the housemaid, Nelly Tanner, neither of whom are beneficiaries."

The London man was beginning to be impressed by this accumulated evidence; he sensed some miserable story of spite, jealousy and vulgar passion underneath these suspicions of murder that seemed to have risen so easily, and to have been held so tenaciously; he had heard, with tedium, the evidence of the servants whom Richard Tyler had taken upon himself to bring up into the parlour; Dr. Harris had soon cut them short, but he had heard enough to enable him to gauge their attitude.

The cook was friendly disposed towards her mistress and had cried, refusing to believe she was a bad woman; and Dolly Hoey seemed frightened and doubtful, but the others—including the gardener and his wife—were grimly satisfied that May Tyler had poisoned her husband, and so were the two nurses. There were a hundred confused scraps of evidence among which stood out the constant disputes between husband and wife, the ill terms upon which they had been living together for so long… the interview that had ended in a blow, the mistress's flight to London, the intercepted letters, the obvious attentions of Jerome Thorne who had what Nelly Tanner declared, "the worst of names for a lady's man." Dr. Harris had heard also the evidence of Mrs. Chorley, discreetly cloaked by tears and regrets, but deadly as far as May Tyler was concerned; well, he thanked his stars he was not a lawyer.

"What do you propose to do?" he asked of the heavy-eyed cotton merchant. "I suppose you'll wait for the post mortem?"

"No," replied Richard firmly, "I've sent for the police, the police…. The inspector should be here any moment."

"I think that's rather putting the cart before the horse," protested Dr. Harris, but the other two pronounced almost in a breath that they "refused a death certificate".

"You really have then your suspicions, gentlemen?" asked the London physician, turning towards them, "of—murder?"

"Sir, if we had not," replied Dr. Fitch with an air of offence, "we should not have gone so far in the matter…."

Richard came forward to the table that stood a pool of light in the hot shaded room where knick-knacks showed fantastic reflections on the thickly patterned wallpaper.

"Excuse me, gentlemen," he said hoarsely, and they noticed his twitching brows and convulsed mouth, his tradesman's manner, the loss of his sham gentility, "you'll have professional matters to talk over, I've no doubt. I want to go up and look at my poor brother again; I'd like to have a little respite, you understand?"

"Time for a prayer or two?" suggested Dr. Harris with a suavity that could hardly be termed satirical.

Richard Tyler went out of the parlour and directly into the dining-room where were seated the two professional nurses, Goff and Newton who looked tired, irritable and excited, and Amelia Chorley talking rapidly to an audience of Dolly Hoey, the gardener and his wife who had previously been a servant in the house.

"I'm going upstairs," whispered Richard hoarsely. *"She's* all right, I suppose?"

Nurse Goff, blinking in the gaslight, answered that Mrs. Tyler was "in a deathlike swoon" and looked as if she would remain so for several hours… no need to trouble… nothing could be done.

"Then we must go up and see to things before the police come," smiled Mr. Tyler. "You know the police are coming?"

He went up the stairs with the thick red carpet and told the nurses who had followed to wait outside on the landing as he wished "to have a few moments alone with his dead brother."

It was not, however, towards the neatly arranged deathbed with the curtains hung in precise folds that Richard turned. He paused, and stared round the room; a low jet of gas illuminated the neat order; the nurses had done their work efficiently, there was not a crumb on the carpet, a stain on the furniture; dingy, draped and well polished and brushed, chairs and tables were in rigid array. Everywhere stood medicine bottles; they crowded on the marble top of the wash-hand-stand, on the table that still stood by the bed, on the mantelpiece, and behind the brass fender on the marble hearth, like menacing battalions of demoniacal symbols they seemed to press forward slowly round the dead man and the living man.

Richard examined these bottles carefully, one by one put them down and began searching the room. His brother meant so little to him that he had forgotten that a corpse was lying on the bed beneath the well-folded linen sheet, concealed by the straight curtain. He went carefully through his brother's clothes and drawers, and in the hat-box of pigskin leather found what he was searching for; three packets, one of white powder mingled with soot, one of white powder mingled with indigo, one of pure white powder. This last was marked "For cats"; all had been depleted of their contents, the paper that was labelled contained only a small amount of the white powder.

"So," said Richard, speaking his lie aloud through the concentrated emphasis of his desire to believe it, "she tried to play this on us when she put *them* back in here." He took the packages up, lifting the curtains between the two rooms almost in a gesture, and stood in his sister-in-law's bedroom.

The nurse had lit a small night-light and stood it behind the fender. These wavering rays alone disturbed the hot shadows.

May, in her twisted, stained gown of water-lily-green, with the flounces of untidy lace, was lying like a wax doll carelessly dropped down on the large bed. The nurse had pulled the curtains straightly either side of her, but the incongruous and ostentatious finery of the room and of May's clothes scattered here and there on different chairs, gave the apartment a tawdry appearance like that of a second-rate actress who apes a great courtesan.

Richard opened the cupboard and stared at the dresses that like so many ghosts of May herself hung before him; the dress he had seen her wear when he had followed her to the dressmaker's in London, the dress she had worn when he had taken her to Salford, the dress she had worn to the carnival, the dress she had worn when his brother had struck her across the face.... He put his hand down the length of them, and then reminded himself that women did not wear pockets.

In the bottom of the cupboard, among a medley of shoes, high heeled, with brilliant buckles, was a large chocolate-box with crumpled yellow ribbons, the lid half-pushed aside, a few chocolates in tinsel papers lay in one corner; there was a seal with a bird with a branch in its mouth (as he ascertained by peering at it closely) thrown carelessly among the sweetmeats and a small bottle with a gilt design on it, standing upright and stoppered. He opened this and smelt it eagerly; there escaped a faint, sickly floral perfume. He put it back and tossed down into the chocolate-box the three packages he had brought from his brother's room. He then began to look through his sister-in-law's drawers, turning over handkerchiefs, packets of face powder, oddments of cosmetics.... There was nothing there that he considered of any use to his design; but he did not put it so in his own mind. Indeed, he insisted to himself that he was an avenger, seeking justice on the dead. He pulled out some of her handkerchiefs and threw them into the chocolate-box, some more handkerchiefs and sprinkled them with some of the liquid in the gold-flecked bottle. All this was done quickly. He could move more swiftly, more lightly than he knew, yet he had taken up and thrown down more of her possessions than he needed to; many years she had lived here, shut away, out of reach, his brother's wife, and he had respected her, thought her a good woman, never intrigued for her, never tempted her, and all the while she had fooled him; he raged as if he, not John, had been made a wittol. Escaping his watchful admiration she had taken a lover, a shoddy young scoundrel, on the edge of bankruptcy, who could not even pay for his vices, a boaster, a liar... yet Richard had believed him. What had Thorne to give her? No doubt *she* had paid the bill at the Mentone; he, Richard, would have paid highly had he known she was for sale. But she had gone, for nothing, to a cheap fool because he was young, with a face like a sick girl's.

Richard stood in the alcove, between husband and wife, he, neat for his coffin, in the half-light of the gas jet, lowered to a blue spurt of flame, half-hidden by the long dull curtains, she, tossed down as Richard had flung her, lying awkwardly, all her draggled finery aheap about her, her head so sunk in the pillow that he could see nothing but the tufts of pale hair, the untidy, tasteless extravagance showing in the flickering rays of the night-light; he looked from one silent room to the other. He triumphed in that John was dead, John who had seized her, in Paris, and that she was very low, and should be lower, for all her dainty ways and aloof airs.

He dared not approach her bed; there were those other women outside, the hateful accomplices; she was lost to him, well, by the time he had done with her, no one else would want her... pretty little doll, with the innocent eyes and the harlot's heart, who had lain in young Thorne's arms in a house of ill-fame; he might have guessed from the way she had looked at him across that empty bar, she had leaned near at first, not drawn instantly back.

They were tapping discreetly on the door of the death chamber, he damned them all, with silent emphasis, then went and opened to them; Amelia Chorley was there now, behind the two nurses, beside Lizzie Burt, who wore her travelling-cloak and black straw bonnet; it was Mrs. Chorley who rapidly explained her arrival and that "the poor little darlings were safe at Blackheath with the Binghams. *I* think she ought to have stayed, but she says *you* told her to return here."

"So I did, her evidence will be wanted—come in, all of you—five, yes, with me that makes five witnesses—I've touched nothing, of course, but a few business letters—no need to let the police know business. That doesn't concern the case."

They followed him into John Tyler's room; the two nurses noted at once that nothing *had* been touched since their arrangements; Lizzie Burt giggled hysterically, "I never saw so many bottles!"

"Some of the cupboards were locked, in both rooms," said Nurse Goff.

"I have the keys of everything," Richard answered. "I haven't been to the cupboards," he took the keys from the pocket where he had just returned them, and gave them to Amelia Chorley who was keeping away from the bed.

"You ought to go and look through everything at once, Amelia, so we know what to tell the police when they get here. Look through all her clothes… there are all kinds of bottles in her room, too, you'd better leave those for the police…."

"I won't do it without a witness," protested Mrs. Chorley taking the key, but the servants and the two nurses were eager enough "to help". Richard Tyler sat down by the side of his dead brother while the three women went through the alcove and, after cautiously turning up the gas, and even more cautiously peering at the unconscious woman on the bed, began to search May Tyler's room.

"Won't she wake up?" whispered Mrs. Chorley.

Nurse Goff replied, "No, she had a sleeping-pill—she was hysterical, *as* you might suppose. Dr. Harman ordered it—*she's* safe enough."

"How untidy she always was," sneered Amelia Chorley. "Just *look* at this room!"

"Always the trouble, ma'am," put in Lizzie Burt, "waste, idleness." She opened the cupboard door. "All these fine clothes! She bought them in London, *hundreds* of pounds they must have cost!"

"Perhaps she didn't pay for them," suggested Nurse Newton. "I shouldn't have come had I known the sort *she* was."

The four women turned over the dresses, searched the drawers, and every receptacle in the room.

"It doesn't matter how untidy you leave it," said Mrs. Chorley, "the police won't know what it looked like before—but don't leave things *scattered.*"

None of them knew what they were trying to do, or why; May Tyler had always offended all of them, both Amelia Chorley and Lizzie Burt who knew her well and the nurses who knew her so slightly. Amelia Chorley had once had the amorous interest of John Tyler, and he had spent a good deal on her before he married May and Amelia became too stout and showed in her complexion that she shared at least one of her husband's vices, drinking. Amelia Chorley had tried to ogle young Thorne, and he had preferred May.... Lizzie Burt hated her mistress on principle, class-hatred, and the hatred of the underdog, mingled with feminine vindictiveness; the nurses mechanically took the "worst side", as they termed it, of humanity for granted, and liked drama; as single women wishful of marriage they regarded an adultress as a cheat for whom no punishment could be too hard, since she had contrived to cajole one man into matrimony and another into sin.

"Goodness, look at all these cosmetics! Rouge, skin food, complexion cream—hair lotion—"

Amelia Chorley was interrupted by Lizzie Burt.

"There's something funny in the chocolate-box, ma'am."

Richard Tyler had not long to wait; Amelia Chorley came through the alcove as he rose from his short vigil by his brother's body.

"There were three packages in the chocolate-box, Richard, and a handkerchief and a bottle of—stuff—I expect *that's* what she got from the flypapers.... There are all manner of bottles and packages there, too, and one of the Orso's meat-juice tins. There's a spoon stuck in it. Oh, and cosmetics—you'd never guess—"

With a raised hand, Richard Tyler silenced the woman's chatter.

"Bring the packages here to me." He turned to the professional nurses. "*You* ought to witness what is being done, *you* see these things are being brought out of my sister-in-law's room."

"From a chocolate-box!" giggled Lizzie Burt. "And Tanner told me where *that* came from—the master indeed!"

The nurses gave her an indignant look; whatever they were doing, it must be done decorously; Nurse Goff was deft, used to controlling the disorder of the sick and to arranging the order of the dead; she now took the leadership.

Soon, on a little tray, she had the three packages, the silk handkerchief, the bottle with the gold ornamentation, the apron, the handkerchiefs and a dressing-gown with several lavender-coloured stains on it that she had found hanging over the chair at the foot of May Tyler's bed.

"Take them downstairs," whispered Richard, eyeing them, "you will not show them to the doctors. Lock them in the cellar." He was giving these orders to Nelly Tanner. "There's witnesses to all you do—and bring the keys back to me. I'll go down and wait for the police."

"The police?" Nurse Newton's voice was frightened; she began to lose nerve, and shivered and wept, here between the murdered man and the woman who had murdered him.

Mrs. Chorley put a large arm round her and said she "must go down to the kitchen and get a warm drink."

"But Mrs. Pilch won't have anything to do with us… she says she's leaving the house."

"She can't do that," said Richard sharply, "she'll have to wait till the police come. The cook is a witness, too. There ought to be a lawyer to advise us."

"A lawyer, I don't know," Mrs. Chorley looked uneasy; "perhaps all that stuff is just bicarbonate of soda or rice powder—but why was there 'For cats' on it?"

"The mistress was always fond of cats," said Lizzie Burt, and Amelia Chorley and Nurse Newton began to laugh, unable to control themselves, suddenly conscious of the insensible woman behind the curtain alcove and the dead man on the bed.

Richard asserted himself, drove them out of the room. The gas was flaming in May's room; no one wanted to return to lower it.

They crept downstairs, not seeing one another very distinctly, the women hardly remembering what they had done or how they had done it, aware of nothing save that quantities of suspicious powder had been found in May Tyler's wardrobe and in a chocolate-box, of all places.... They recalled nothing of the definite scene... how shocking it all was.

"Yes, you ought to send for a lawyer," said Mrs. Chorley, clutching at Richard. He had preceded them and now came up from the cellar where he had locked away what had been taken from his sister-in-law's room; the keys, large and small, dangled on his hand.

"I've done it," replied the heavy man sombrely. "What do you suppose? I've sent for the lawyers and the police—I don't know who will be here first."

"Somebody ought to stay with *her*, I suppose," whimpered Mrs. Chorley doubtfully, "but I'm sure I couldn't."

"It had better be one of the nurses," said Richard, speaking in a mumbling voice, and yet with directness as if he had had all his plans long since prepared; he seemed, as Lizzie Burt noted with admiration, "to have thought of everything."

He asked Mrs. Chorley if she would stay the night in the house, and she agreed, as long as she could sleep on the sofa downstairs. Nurse Goff would stay up with Mrs. Tyler; Nurse Newton might return to the Institute; everything could be arranged quite comfortably and respectably.

*

The physicians were still closeted in the parlour; Mrs. Pilch had with some reluctance taken up some refreshment. Everyone in Stone Pynes was yawning and seemed to have a headache... it was such a hot summer and it occurred to no one to turn down the gas or to draw the curtains in order to let in a little air. Even in the death chamber all remained warm, enclosed, stale. Everyone was absorbed, as if they had been puppets in a box, in their own silences.

At midnight the lawyer, a Mr. Claypole, a personal friend of Richard's, appeared. He at once gave his advice "that the police should be sent for". Richard remarked that he had already done this, but "they seemed to be a very long time. Anyway," he added, "they couldn't arrest her now, because she's still unconscious."

The London physician asked, "I suppose she had a sleeping-draught?"

Dr. Harman and Dr. Fitch declared they had not given Mrs. Tyler anything, save a light sedative earlier in the day, but Richard admitted that he had, on his own authority, given his sister-in-law, who had been in a painful state of hysteria, a heavy sleeping-drug, but one quite harmless that had been prescribed by Dr. Harman himself some time before to be used in a case of emergency.

Soon after the lawyer had joined the gathering in the parlour, a representative of the police arrived in the person of Inspector Bigalow. He was a man of an insignificant appearance who did not seem impressed by the case that he had been called upon to deal with; in a methodical yet stupid manner he began to search the premises, permitting Mrs. Chorley, who controlled her desperate fatigue in order not to miss this new excitement, to accompany him on that lady's statement that she was "a close family friend."

When Inspector Bigalow returned to the hot parlour he showed to Richard Tyler the opened tin of meat extract that Mrs. Chorley had already remarked on, a green bottle with clear liquid and black powder in a broken box, a bottle labelled "Compound Mixture of Bismuth", a bottle with a little sediment at the bottom, a parcel of white crystals and a soiled glass in which was deposited what appeared to be medicine; he also laid on the table several garments stained deeply especially round the pockets, and in a businesslike manner demanded that all the "stuff" should be analysed. He seemed to think this was Dr. Fitch's task.

"I shan't be able to do all this myself immediately," protested that tired man with a sigh. He found the case uninteresting, unwholesome, and in a way that he could not have expressed, unreal. These people all moved before him like painted figures on a cardboard background. They were at least no concern of his, at least he hoped not—surely a criminal charge could not arise from this muddle.

"Take this stuff to the chemist," he said. "He can do it. I suppose we can have a little sleep now?"

But it seemed not; Dr. Harris wanted to know what other medicine there was in the house.

Richard stated that there were upwards of three hundred medicine bottles between the bedroom, the dressing-room, a linen closet on the landing and the bathroom… no one could undertake even to gather together these articles; all save Mr. Harris and the inspector were fatigued to the point of prostration; even Richard was merely galvanized by his strong emotions, like a corpse by a charge of electricity.

"I'll make inquiries and take particulars, gentlemen," said the inspector coolly. "I'll stay upstairs—until the morning; I shall have my eye on things. I'll see that no one comes in or out. I'll send for the superintendent to-morrow."

He left the room, intent on his duty.

Mrs. Chorley could no longer hold herself on her feet; she limped into the back parlour where Nelly Tanner was putting up a bed on the horsehair sofa.

"I hardly like to sleep in the same house with a murdered corpse," she whispered with a fear that was hardly feigned. "You will have to stay in the same room with me, Tanner, sleeping on a chair."

The servant could hardly refuse, but she made a grimace. Her own bed was hard and uncomfortable, but the chair would be even more so; still, there was nothing to be done; even she, who had no imagination and but few feelings, was aware that something fantastical and unconnected with everyday events was occurring.

Mrs. Pilch said that Stone Pynes was "like Hell opened for the Devil's return". What was happening? Three doctors, and now a policeman, and everyone talking of murder? She had kept the fire down, until the kitchen was like an oven; people were always wanting meals, the nurses were eating like fighting-cocks and the servants kept thieving food, whenever her back was turned—in and out of the kitchen and the little room beyond that the master liked to call the servants' hall; now, a huge pile of soiled linen from the sick room on the kitchen floor, pails, jugs, pans of slops standing about unemptied.... Nurse Newton had had a meal before leaving, the doctors had had "trays", Mr. Richard kept sending down for drink; Mrs. Chorley had demanded tea and cake; Lizzie Burt, panting downstairs after her help in the search, had asked for "something hot" after her long journey. "If anyone else asks me for..." she threatened wanly.

Dolly Hoey was crying, huddled on her Windsor chair, weary and frightened, tired and resentful.

"They keep talking of murder," she complained. "A policeman in her room now; Mr. Richard sent for him."

"He always meant to—the lot of you always meant to."

"Why?"

"I don't know if you don't," protested Mrs. Pilch. She sat down heavily, too exhausted to climb up to her attic bedroom, nursing a swollen foot with a scalded hand. "Seems mad—*such* spite—and why? Have they got a warrant out?"

"I don't know. Oh dear, it's terrible! The London doctor he said he didn't see cause, or something like that; I heard him, when I went in for one of them trays, but Dr. Fitch he said that after what Mr. Richard's said he couldn't give a certificate, so Mr. Richard had every right to send for the police."

"Haven't they got no further after all these hours of arguing?" groaned Mrs. Pilch. "I must put my feet… where's the money for the housekeeping coming from? What did the policeman say, Dolly?"

"That he'd make inquiries and take particulars, and that to-morrow the superintendent would come to make inquiries and take particulars…."

"It'll all be proved to be a pack of nonsense. Where's the money coming from? We was always paying cash because of the bills—"

"Oh, Mrs. Pilch!" cried Dolly, "there won't be no housekeeping, will there? There's master dead, and the children sent away, and mistress—"

"Don't say it," interrupted Mrs. Pilch, sternly. "This is a Christian country, I should hope, where the innocent don't get punished." She gloomily eyed the bell-board. "If anyone rings for food—or drinks…"

George Harman drove home in a hired cab, it was too late for his own neat brougham. He recalled his cherished Dante, locked safely in the cabinet at home; he would be glad to get away from this Stone Pynes business to another world.

With a shock that made him clutch at the carriage cord he realized that it was not another world; the spectres had escaped from the printed pages and flocked to Stone Pynes; the Florentine had not set down any more horrible story than this, no fiend he had invented looked more terrible than—than who? The doctor jerked himself into what he supposed was reality. They were just ordinary people in ordinary trouble at Stone Pynes; "but there's nothing else," he argued, struggling with exhaustion; "there wasn't, even in Dante's Inferno. A damned soul in a frock-coat—I don't know what I'm talking about; almost delirious, eh?"

Edmund Fitch lay on an iron bedstead in the children's nursery, in case the nurse called him for May Tyler; he felt uneasy about a good many things, so uneasy that he forgot his offended dignity. Harman should never have driven off and left him to this... of course it would end in smoke; a pity to have called in the police; Richard Tyler was undoubtedly showing vindictiveness. 'I never thought he was so fond of his brother. I suppose it is natural; they were in close association for so long, and she is foreign—and then the lover, disgusting, one must admit.'

But he wished that Richard had not drugged her... and who was it he had seen lately who looked... damned? He could not remember.

Glyn Harris made notes, seated at ease in his expensive hotel bedroom, tore them up and wrote others. Unlike his colleagues he did not suffer from insomnia or fatigue; he had come fresh to the case, and was quite detached from it; interested slightly in one person only. 'Why is that man hounding his sister-in-law? Love of his brother? Motive much too weak.'

The woman he considered a common type, weak, silly, married to a man a generation ahead, with a lover and neglected children, debts, a taste for extravagant finery—'an unpleasant set, vulgarians, with too much money and no wits to spend it—no ideas beyond races, drinks, a shoddy establishment like Stone Pynes—the medical evidence will clear her, no Borgia there, and if, poor wretch, the fellow had been taking arsenic'—the thoughtful physician paused before the centre of the puzzle, 'the motive of the brother-in-law? He has already secured all the money by that last minute will. Why wash all this very dirty linen in public? The police, and the miserable woman drugged—interesting to watch that man's behaviour; fifty or so, unmarried, a coarse heavy type, probably shrewd at his business, could be brutal or servile, cringed to me and bullied the servants to-night, nearly lost his head, but *not quite*. What is he up to?'

Dr. Harris's cool summary was suddenly interrupted by a crackle of red lightning, an acrid blue rush of flame. He put up his hand; only the wind in the pipes, and the gas hissing and glaring; he turned it off and rang the bell, again perfectly self-composed, but in that second of complete surprise he had had a sense that lately he had seen something utterly horrible—in a human face; then it was gone, and he waited patiently in the dark for the chambermaid.

Upstairs at Stone Pynes Nurse Goff and Inspector Bigalow after a cool and professional scrutiny of the corpse, proceeded to the widow's room and sat in stiff attitudes on the frivolous quilted and satin chairs either side of the bed on which May Tyler lay in her tumbled pale-green silk and lace; they left the gas turned high, and the untidiness of the room was ugly in the ugly light.

"A good thing for her," remarked the nurse, staring at her patient, "if she never woke up again."

"If all they say is proved, I agree with you," remarked the Inspector. "I never saw so many bottles—I'll have to send a deal of stuff to Parkinson for analysis—the doctors won't do it."

He then asked if there was any beer in the house, and the nurse replied that she would ring for Mrs. Pilch to send up beer and sandwiches a little later on—"about three o'clock, as you might say, Inspector."

"That's very thoughtful, very thoughtful indeed, ma'am."

IV

PRISONER'S POSY
FLOWERS OF RHETORIC

MAY TYLER RETURNED TO A WORLD OF A STARTLING UNREALITY; then the tumbled bed and the tawdry curtains were faintly familiar. She remembered, 'I meant to get Tanner to mend those rents.' She stared up at the lace flounces on the curtains and these remained solid, but everything else slid into confusion, faint, repellent, out of focus.

Two policemen were seated by her bed; Nurse Goff with quick nervous movements was tatting a long string of yellow-coloured twine between them. The door was ajar and there was another policeman in the corridor.

"What has happened?" she asked, smiling foolishly, like a child, sitting up, wondering why her mouth was stiff and dry, touching her tumbled hair with vague fingers.

The nurse glanced at her with a cruel interest.

"You're in custody, Mrs. Tyler, on suspicion of causing the death of your husband. Didn't you hear the superintendent?"

The young woman in the tousled water-lily-green dressing-gown laughed feebly.

"How did I cause his death?"

"By arsenic in the Orso's meat juice for one thing," replied the nurse. "The doctors have found it there—and in your husband's body too. There was a *post-mortem*—"

"Arsenic...? No, that was the powder he always asked me to give him."

The policeman at the door looked in. The Inspector commanded Mrs. Tyler to be silent—"for your own sake."

"Yes, that's what you've got to do, hold your tongue!" said the nurse. "Lie quiet and I'll get you a cup of milk."

"Lie quiet…? Where is my husband?"

"He's being buried to-day," replied the nurse. "Not that that'll concern you much. You've got yourself to think of."

"John is being buried to-day?"

"She's not as stupid as she seems," remarked Nurse Goff to Inspector Bigalow. "I found her quick and clever when she was nursing the poor gentleman. You've been unconscious a long time," she added sharply, glancing sideways at her patient.

The room was in darkness save for the glimmer of the gas overhead.

"I've been in a stupor," murmured Mrs. Tyler, holding her head. "I've heard things though; doors banging, people coming and going whispering, and once Richard standing over me gripping my arms and shaking me. 'I want your keys,' he said. 'Where are your keys, do you hear?' But I lost that again, then someone reading something."

"I don't suppose the first is true," said the nurse flatly, "and the second was the superintendent charging you; he wasn't reading."

"Why am I lying in my clothes?" demanded May. "Neglected and uncared for? Can I see my children?" She repeated the demand.

In a cold, deliberate voice Nurse Goff said, "No. Mr. Richard Tyler is master in this house now and he sent the children away to the Binghams with Nurse Burt, but she's back again to help him."

"Who's looking after the children?" asked May vaguely.

"Oh, they're with friends—I shouldn't worry about *that* if I were you," replied the nurse sarcastically.

May fell back on the pillow and tried to turn again into the phantasmagoria of her drugged sleep. Dr. Fitch entered and felt her pulse and, without a word, left the room. May listened to the echoes of her dream; she heard footsteps outside… many feet stopping at her door; she saw a crowd of men approaching her bed; she smiled vaguely; the grotesque distortion of the scene resembled a play enacted by clowns; mounted on hybrid animals big men clothed in blue galloped round the room; Richard, with a long white false nose, leered above the cymbals he was crashing together; gigantic medicine bottles rose and sank, turned and twisted, as if dancing. Someone in a white domino whispered, "Mrs. Tyler, I am Superintendent of Police, and I'm about to say something to you. You must be careful how you reply because whatever you say may be used as evidence against you. Mrs. Tyler, you are in custody on suspicion of causing the death of your late husband, John Tyler."

May frowned in an effort to distinguish one figure from another; they were all pressed so close, like a solid block of puppets in the thick half-light; she began to laugh, and the crowd passed out of the room, saluting her mockingly.

"What shall I do?" she asked thoughtfully.

Someone replied brusquely, "Well, ma'am, you can get in touch with your lawyers. You can send a telegram to any relatives.…"

"My mother, I should like my mother to come."

"May she send a letter to her mother?" demanded a stiff feminine voice.

May was dragged up in bed and told to write; she did not know what to say, she kept laughing; the nurse had already secured her mother's address in Rouen, and put this down on a scrap of paper, adding: "I am in extreme danger. Please come at once."

The nurse asked the crumpled figure on the bed for the money.

"I've no money; you must look among my things, there might be a few shillings somewhere."

"The *things* have all been searched," replied the nurse, "and no *money* was found."

"Will you ask the doctor for some money? What is it for? Please send for my mother. There are so many people in the room. Richard has the keys of my cash box."

"Ask Dr. Fitch to lend her five shillings," the Inspector said, and May laughed again. "I split my new gloves—when I went to Salford. John got a chill at the races."

She asked, "Is there no one who can help me… no one?"

"You ought to know that," replied Dr. Fitch. "No friends have been near you so far. We found enough arsenic in your husband's body to justify further search; we found arsenic in solution in a bottle in your chocolate-box and traces of arsenic on your handkerchiefs and apron."

"I don't know anything about your law," replied May with a half-imbecile look. "I don't know the names of any lawyers in Manchester. I should have known some in London…." She paused.

"Take care what you say," advised the doctor with mechanical friendliness. "There is a policeman in the room and another at the door; they've got to do their duty, you know. You're not fit to be moved and the formal proceedings will have to take place here in your room. You're fully conscious now, I suppose?"

"What's all this noise in the house?" she smiled.

"It's your *husband's* funeral," said the nurse; "but for you he would have been buried three days ago."

"A funeral so late!" exclaimed May. "Why, the gas is lit—it must be well on in the evening."

"You're very cool, I must say," remarked Dr. Fitch in some distaste, "for a young woman in your position. There has been an autopsy; we found enough poison to justify further research, do you understand? Here in the house. I shouldn't concern yourself about the funeral."

May, however, had stumbled from the bed, helped by Nurse Goff. "Can I no longer do anything here? Am I not mistress?"

"Certainly not. Your husband left everything in the charge of Richard Tyler, and apart from that, my dear young lady, must I remind you of the horrible situation you are in—in custody—on such a charge."

May grasped the nurse's arm.

"I sent your cable to Rouen. I have asked Messrs. Endicott & Martin to come; so far the police don't allow entry. I'm afraid," he added with the annoyance of a man who has reached the limits of his patience with an exasperating set of circumstances, "there's very little that they or anyone can do for you."

As soon as he had left the room, the nurse remarked, "If you want to see the last of the husband you've poisoned you'd better come at once. I suppose she can?" she added, looking at Inspector Bigalow. "There's a plain clothes man at the gate—besides, she's too weak to walk."

"How am I being treated as—a prisoner? I've been a prisoner too long," whispered May faintly.

She laughed again; the mutterings had begun again and the clowns' faces were pushed close to hers; where was she going and what was she doing? The slow stumbling down the ugly stairs seemed like a descent into perpetual darkness; there were meaningless noises and crossing lights that seemed random and could not be distinguished one from the other; the nurse was guiding her into the parlour… everything seemed to be as she had left it, untidy, ostentatious, hateful; the nurse had her at the window and had drawn the holland blinds; the large gas light above the Portland stone porch had been lit… there was the handsome hearse clear in that gloomy illumination, black, picked out with gold, the russet colour of the horses' haunches showing between the well-polished harness. Behind the bevelled plate glass was a coffin covered with white flowers, unwholesome and sickly as the flowers of the convent garden in Paris that had once been so fresh now appeared in her memory.

"Who is in that coffin?"

"You do well to look at it. Take care, you'll fall over."

She sagged on her feet and clutched at the window-sill, then pulled herself upright, seated herself at the chair by the desk from which Lizzie Burt had taken Mrs. Bingham's letter.

"Please, nurse, help me to get this straightly. Am I in a delirium? I can remember so little... if only I had a friend here."

"It looks bad for you that you haven't got a friend."

"There is one—I supposed he never answered—Jerome Thorne?"

"I think," replied the nurse, a soft drop in her voice, "a letter from him was found among your belongings. You'd better write to him again—if you think it will be of any use to you?"

May stood still; the nurse put a piece of paper under her hand, a pencil between her fingers; May knew she had done this before, yes, exactly the same action, only it had been Amelia Chorley standing over her....

She began to scrawl:

> *Will you, please, help me in my desperate trouble? Why didn't you answer my other letters? I have no money, no friends. Everything is known, but none of it can harm you. It was my sin and I asked his forgiveness—I don't know if he heard me....*

"I never did," interrupted the nurse, who was reading over her shoulder.

May made a movement as if to tear the paper up, but the nurse drew it quickly from under her lax fingers.

"Don't send it, nurse, better not, as he did not answer before—what letter was it they found...?"

"Mr. Richard had it...."

"Oh, but I must have help," whispered May.

"I'll write to Dr. Fitch, too," she added vaguely, but the nurse smiled contemptuously.

"The doctor's in and out of the house… you can speak to him when you like."

She could hardly resist glancing at the letter, yet kept her eyes discreetly on her patient. "You'd better come upstairs to bed again. The inquest wasn't favourable to you. And if you could see the papers—"

"About what?"

"Oh, you know, my pretty!" said the nurse. "Don't play any of those games with me!"

May returned to the window, staring down. There was a woman down there in the murk, trying to escape; she had a bruised face. "If you want to catch that train…" "But I do, I *must* catch that train. I've been in prison so long." "You can't, the drive is covered with broken medicine bottles, and those geraniums grow so well because they put white powder in the soil." "They have pulled her in, shut the door…." "Poor thing," whispered May, "can't someone help her?"

She stared down and saw a group of men in weather coats; the thick sooty rain was falling as the woman in the smart, soiled dress tried to escape; she was in the London train now, and in a strange hotel; the clowns began dancing and mocking again. "A deadly sin, you know. First you leave your Church, and then you want to break this tie, and there are your dear little children, so sweet and loving, and you are a respectable married woman, the woman at Salford? Oh, nothing in that, but *you must behave yourself.*"

The hearse took shape again; the horses shook their heads, rattling their harness.

"Chains," said May. The nurse lowered the holland blind, she had satisfied her own curiosity; the hearse, followed by the sleek carriages, dripping water, had moved slowly along the drive, between the Stone Pynes made of cement.

How quick it had all been! The police, Superintendent Browning taking Mrs. Tyler into custody, the post mortems, the inquest at the

Crown Hotel, the coroner's statement, the adjournment for a fortnight, the journalist's reports; Nurse Goff had a paper tightly folded in her bag that contained a column headed "The Tyler Mystery".

As May still stared at the holland blind as if she could see through it, the nurse glanced over the letter she had just scrawled, then hastily returned it to her pocket, and taking May by the arms led her from the room.

"She got away in the hearse," whispered May. "*That* time. No other way, but in a hearse, eh? Would the nuns take her back?"

"Your nonsense don't take me in, you wicked woman."

"Please, nurse, if you would stop the mechanical music. I *ought* to have looked in the blue Bible; I never did, not once."

Up the stairs again, gaslight, dust, people whispering, tip-toeing about, rancid smells, sour smells of cooking-fat, of hair oil, of scent, the convent garden lilies decaying, the elder-flower rotting, the face-lotion flyblown... yes... that was it, flypapers, mayflies....

"Who was the god of flies, nurse?" May asked suddenly, clinging to the banisters. The nurse was startled, half-pushed away the woman she was supporting.

"*You* ought to know."

May was in the tousled bed again. The procession of grotesque figures had returned; there was a clown giving her a cup of milk, there was a clown holding her hand again, there was John—or Richard—staring down at her through a cheap mask. Then there was a pause, a sense of everyone slipping... her own voice asking for the door to be shut, and the voice of the policeman standing there declaring that it could not be shut... and then her own voice again whispering, "But I couldn't escape, whatever you did, I couldn't escape." Then it was Amelia Chorley or another woman... her sight was failing... she could not be sure, but some woman was there whispering to the nurse.... And then it was the doctors, and then it was a crowd of clowns pressing into the room and one of them leaning over her and saying he was her lawyer, a member of the firm of Messrs. Endicott & Martin… it was Mr. Endicott himself speaking, the clown said, he was complaining that he had had difficulty in getting into the house, and May repeated the word "Difficulty… difficulty…" thickly, several times. He had pen and ink and a paper in his hand… that seemed a recurrent pattern—papers, pens and ink. She was to sign her name as a guarantee, the clown was explaining… of course she had no money and they needed payment… she was giving them some charge on her estate.… She smiled courteously and with help from the nurse contrived to place her signature at the bottom of the document. The clowns began to whisper and to dance to the mechanical orchestra. "She can't escape, she can't escape," the little man who was standing at the foot of the bed was speaking. She asked for a handkerchief, for something to drink; but her voice was so low no one heard her; the clown with the long white nose coughed and said, "This person is Mrs. Tyler charged with causing John Tyler's death by administering poison to him. I understand that her consent is given to a remand, therefore I need not introduce nor give evidence."

Another carnival figure squeaked from the group of dancers. "You ask for a remand for eight days?" And the small, spruce figure floating at the end of the bed, a drab puppet at the end of a string, replied, "Very well, I consent to remand. That is all."

They dissolved. "Are they gone?" asked May. "Is the room empty?"

"The room's quite empty," replied the nurse sarcastically. "Don't try and pretend with me. I know that you're not so bad as you would like to make out. You'll have to appear in court to-morrow so make the best of this last night in your own home. If I were you, I wouldn't worry much; it's just as well to be in jail as in one's own home with a policeman in one's room."

It was Dr. Harman... she tried to understand what he was saying. He was reproaching her, "You should never have written those letters—the last one has been handed to the police. What do you suppose? You make it difficult for anyone to help you."

"Who is trying to help me?" asked May. "What letters? The letters were to ask for help."

Madame Dumont who had travelled without pause from Rouen since she had received her daughter's telegram, arrived at Stone Pynes supported by that strength of will that women can show when in the extreme of physical and nervous exhaustion. Followed by Rose Bernier and staring with an unseeing glance, that was worse than contempt, at everyone—nurses, police, servants whom she met—she went upstairs to her daughter's room. The policeman at the door tried to prevent her entering, but she took no notice of him and passed straight into her daughter's bedroom; policemen again—one by the foot of the bed, one at the side of it—and the nurse, with her foot up on a chair reading a newspaper; May, wearing a disordered, soiled, pale green dressing-gown was lying stretched out on the pillow, smiling at the flies circling above the bed.

"I'm her mother," said Madame Dumont. The company who were waiting for this foreigner to make a dramatic scene were disappointed, for the lady went quietly to the bed, grasped her daughter's hand and added, "This is some absurd mistake. I shall soon put it right, of course.... Who is looking after you?"

"She's being very well looked after," replied the nurse sourly and without rising, "and I must ask you not to come here and make a disturbance. The policemen are in charge as you can see. She's been arrested for poisoning her husband; I expect they'll take her away to-night."

"Everyone seems against me, Mother," smiled May from the pillow, "but I didn't do it."

"I'm sorry," whispered Madame Dumont with steady lips, "that you should say that, May. You know that it is unnecessary."

Then, in French, she began to ask her daughter how this incredible disaster had overtaken her, but the policeman interrupted, saying that she must speak in English, as Richard Tyler came into the room.

"What does this farcical situation mean?" demanded Madame Dumont, now standing by the bed.

"The police will tell you everything," he replied sullenly. "I'm sorry you came just to distress yourself. The police will tell you everything—it's a case of murder and there's a man in it—"

"I can understand nothing. You seem much agitated. What does it all mean? Why did you not send for me before?"

He answered with a sulky downward look, "May did not ask for it and no one knew your address."

"Everyone knew it; *Rouen* would have found me. Tell me, what has happened? Why are the police in the house?"

"I suppose you know that it is said that John was poisoned?"

"Poisoned by whom?" demanded Madame Dumont.

Richard Tyler answered in a broken but persistent manner, "Why, the doctor—Dr. Harman—and I thought John was not properly nursed; Dr. Fitch came and we had a specialist from London… the nurse said May put something in the meat juice and I gave it to Dr. Harman… he refused a certificate of death, and then the police came in…."

"Why not have sent for me? How could you have sent for the police in this way, and not a friend by her? Who has been here?"

"I couldn't tell you," replied Richard heavily. "There's been comings and goings in this house. What do you think it has meant to me, with the death, the autopsy, the funeral, the inquest?… I had Amelia Chorley here, but she wouldn't stay. I had no idea matters would result in this way. I would rather cut my hand off than have it so—"

"But the children?" broke in Madame Dumont. "How can you ruin their future? Your suspicions are horrible... and for a girl like May, unprotected.... You are doing her to death among you, and *for what motive?*"

As Madame Dumont asked this question in a manner the more emphatic because it was so controlled, everyone in the room was still as if waiting for a climax to a long drawn out drama.

Richard Tyler moved about the room clumsily, picking up first this object and then the other. May watched him out of half-closed eyes; she had no idea of what was happening; they were talking about her... there was some confusion that seemed to envelop her like the tangles of a neglected vine that she remembered once in the old Virginian days, stepping lightly through a disused pleasure ground she had suddenly become involved with the vine. She moved her hands now to push its tendrils off to see clowns grinning at her in malice.

Richard stood steadfast, making up those lies smeared with truth that have so much vitality.

"I have been very fond of May. I would never have believed anything wrong of her. I would have stood by her and did until the letter to a man was found—"

"Letter to a man?" exclaimed Madame Dumont. "Do, Richard, tell me a straight story."

"Why, to the man Thorne... she wrote him a letter and it was found, I tell you."

"Who found it? And who is Thorne? When did she know him? She never mentioned him to me."

"She met him this winter," muttered Richard, "and she was always so quiet and domestic before, and would never look at anyone. I would never have believed it of May. She became changed and went out to dances... she went up to London and stayed with him.... I wish I could meet Thorne...."

"Yes, that is about the best thing you could have done. In my country and among the men I have known they *would* have met this man instead of calling in the police.... But about this letter—who found it?"

"Nurse—Lizzie Burt." Richard grinned ferociously. "There were three in all, three letters."

"And if she found it, why did she not give it back to her mistress? What have you to do with it?"

"Lizzie Burt found it on the floor," said Richard slowly. "It fell from *her* dress when she fainted and I carried her into the bedroom."

"From May's dress? How did you know it was to Thorne?" demanded Madame Dumont.

"That was easy; it was directed to him, it was written in pencil and fell on the floor."

"Your disconnected story fills me with disgust and dismay." Madame Dumont glanced round the room. "Who are these people? What are they doing here? My daughter looks very ill. May I not even kiss her...? Why am I held away from the bed like this?"

The Inspector roused himself from a dense staring at the scene. "I warn you, madam, I shall write down what you say."

She glanced at him coolly and replied, "You may write as much as you like, my friend. I've nothing wrong to say, but it strikes me as very strange to see you in this room...."

The young woman on the bed murmured, "Dear mammie, don't excite yourself, the Inspector is only doing his duty...."

But Madame Dumont demanded, "What is the nurse for, and who are the people outside? I consider it infamous! What on earth does it mean?"

"They think I have poisoned John."

"Poisoned John," replied Madame Dumont with disdain. "Why, if he is poisoned, he poisoned himself. He made a perfect apothecaries' shop of himself, as we all know."

May Tyler struggled up on the pillow and entreated, "Mammie, go into the town and see my solicitor. He will explain everything—please don't say anything here. The doctors, and Richard and Mrs. Chorley believe me guilty, but, mammie, I am innocent."

Madame Dumont was staring at Richard Tyler; she asked him to leave the room with her, adding:

"Is there anywhere we can speak in this house—where there are no spies?"

"There are no spies," he returned slowly, going with her into the passage beyond earshot of the policemen. "You don't know the story or what we have been through here. Remember, there's another man… we've discovered an intrigue… we had to get the children away, we thought that if we could send her back to you that would be the best thing. We told Dr. Harman that she was incompetent to nurse him; the doctors went further than we thought, they searched the place and found arsenic—"

"I can make nothing of this," interrupted Madame Dumont. "I am concerned only with my daughter; dying, she looks to me, so white and wretched. Why may I not nurse her instead of that strange hostile woman? Why may not the policemen leave the room? Not a friend in the house… even the children gone, and every minute," she added with exasperation, "since I've been here that woman Tanner has been bringing up a tray of food for some of these wretched creatures."

"We cannot do anything," said Richard with a sly look. "She's going to be taken to jail to-night—there's a remand for eight days, but she'll have to go to jail to-day."

"I cannot make anything out of you, Richard, I don't understand you or this case. May has always been miserable with your brother; she wished to get a divorce, I know, and I would have helped her; but we are not the sort of women who can intrigue, so I left her alone. She would never say anything to me.…" She broke off. "What are those fearful cries coming from her room?"

"You may go up and see, I suppose," conceded Richard.

Madame Dumont hurried into the bedroom, the exhaustion of that hurried and anxious journey making her lightheaded.

In the ostentatious and disordered bedroom May Tyler was weeping and struggling on the bed; the two policemen restraining her attempts to rise, the nurse watching them.

"Please!" cried Madame Dumont. "Let me soothe her. She will be quiet—I know how to help her; these men have no right in a lady's room."

The nurse turned and flung out insolently, "I can put you out if you don't take care. I'm in charge and can act as I think best."

Madame Dumont stared at the scene; she saw, with the clarity of one physically at the end of her resources and mentally shocked almost beyond endurance, what May's marriage had ended in—two policemen, grasping her bare legs and arms, were holding her down in the tawdry bed that the taste of the cotton merchant had provided, where she had slept alone for more than four years now.

She muttered, not remembering that she was overheard, "Death would be better than this!"

One policeman left the shrieking woman to put the mother out of the room and turned to remark to the other constable,

"You hear what she says? Now the young woman's found out her mother's going to give her a dose of something to help her over the worst of it. See they don't get together."

"I'll see to that," promised Nurse Goff viciously. "And there's everyone in the house will help me. Now she's quiet. Leave her alone. No wonder she has had dreams."

"The clowns," sobbed May, then lay still.

Madame Dumont crept downstairs; in the hall she saw Richard; it seemed to her that he must be a phantom. She had not been conscious of his having followed her, of his leaving her at her daughter's bedroom;

he was everywhere, he seemed to be whispering now, as if making excuses, pleading for forgiveness.

"May swooned in the room where John was dying and I took her up, unconscious, and placed her where she is; she didn't come to her senses till yesterday, she never moved or spoke. I'm afraid," he added dismally, "they all lost their heads. She never knew what was happening. She keeps talking about clowns."

Madame Dumont stared, uncomprehending, and stumbled down into the kitchen. The cook was seated at the table cutting thick slices of bread-and-butter. A woman, who was no stranger to Madame Dumont, was sitting near her, her arms folded on the table, her lips moving quickly. Everything was in disorder; the place was littered with trays of half-eaten food, dirty beer mugs, trays full of tobacco ash.

"I know you, Mrs. Pilch," said Madame Dumont, holding on to the door. "But you are the nurse?"

"I'm the children's nurse," replied Lizzie Burt insolently.

The cook rose. "I'm glad to see you, Mrs.—I mean Baroness—I wish I could help."

"I wish you could, but I myself understand nothing. There is no way of having any conversation in the house—the policemen and nurses are always listening; they all have paper and pencils and always taking down notes of Heaven knows what, and whispering together."

"All the downstairs rooms," answered Mrs. Pilch, "are locked except the morning room; not a place open except Mrs. Tyler's room and the attics where we sleep...."

"It's all along of the flypapers," remarked Lizzie Burt, with a disagreeable laugh. "She shouldn't have been such a fool about them, not after that case in Liverpool...."

Ignoring her, Madame Dumont looked at the other servant who was mechanically piling slices of bread-and-butter on to a coarse blue plate.

"What were the flypapers for?"

"Why, for cosmetics, madam."

"Tell me, Mrs. Pilch, has anything terrible really happened in this house?"

"I wouldn't like to say that," replied the cook guardedly, with a steadfast glance at Lizzie Burt. "There's been a lot of little things, like tale telling and tale bearing, that are terrible enough to my way of thinking—but the mistress is innocent, she's never done anything wrong to her husband."

Madame Dumont stood motionless, checked and at a loss, though she did not reveal her own despair.

"Who are my daughter's solicitors?" she asked.

"It's Mr. Martin who comes here, madam."

"I must go down to them, but I don't know my way about Manchester."

"I'll show you," replied Mrs. Pilch quickly.

"It's after office hours," sneered Lizzie Burt, "and you won't find anyone there."

"We can go to his private house," countered the cook. "Remember, mistress is going away to-day...."

"Yes, to the jail," said the nurse. "That's where she ought to have been long ago."

"Don't take any heed of her." The cook had taken down her straw bonnet and Paisley shawl from a peg. "If you don't mind being seen with me, madam...."

"I'm very grateful to you." Madame Dumont put her hand on the cook's shoulder. "You can help me to get a hired carriage, if you will.... I'm very tired, I understand so little of this."

"You're not going out leaving that bread-and-butter there, are you?" demanded Lizzie Burt. "Mr. Richard said the nurse would want something more at five o'clock."

"You can take it up yourself," replied Mrs. Pilch. "If you don't mind coming up the area steps, madam...."

"Anywhere with a friend," said Madame Dumont faintly. "I hope I shall keep my wits, my senses; I cannot believe it, you see. No, I won't take any food. I can't eat—no, not even brandy, in this house."

She was up the area steps and on the grey pavement, the air was oppressive, the sky veiled, a slight fog abroad; the heat had come early and harshly.

"Mr. Martin'll be gone," whispered Mrs. Pilch. "We'd better go to his private house."

Madame Dumont moved with heavy steps to the entrance gates on which stood the stone pines and looked back at the outline of the house with loathing and dread.

"How hot... and dark." She leant heavily on Mrs. Pilch's arm. "Not a star to be seen! I hope we shall find a cab."

The Medical Officer of Rockingham Jail decided that Mrs. Tyler was not fit to attend the inquest. The coroner proceeded with the case, remarking, "Mrs. Tyler is not here to-day, sooner or later she will have to be present in order that she may be identified by a witness."

The inquest was adjourned for a week.

To Richard Tyler the coroner's words tolled like discordant bells; he confounded them with the clanging of the mechanical orchestra in the Pomona Rooms, with the ticking of the house clock in May's bedroom when he had carried her in her water-lily-green dressing-gown to her bed; in the course of a week they had said she would be able to attend the inquest—to be identified by a witness, meanwhile she was in prison. How easy it had been; out of that welter of lies and gossip he had contrived already, though nothing was proved against her, to bring her pretty low; fine lady, well-bred gentlewoman as she might be, she was in that jail that he had mentioned to her as one of the sights of Manchester when he had been taking her to Salford—in the hands of justice, and how would justice proceed?

Richard had already given his evidence; a story that he had already told many times to many people... he had it well by heart.

He returned to his dingy rooms; interviewed the auctioneer's clerk who had brought a proof of the bills advertising the sale of Stone Pynes; Richard himself had helped make the inventory; everything should be sold; Madame Dumont had begged hopelessly for some of her daughter's possessions, Richard had allowed her a blue Bible, a Popish Bible, he was sure, and a purple evening dress that May had worn too often for his liking.

This business done he sat down and considered his position; so many lies had been told that his could never be discovered among them; when he had handed over the three packets, the bottle of solution to the police, not even *her* lawyer had questioned his assertion that he had found them in a chocolate-box in *her* room. He would be out of pocket; there was a nasty list of debts, neither Stone Pynes nor the contents would fetch much, John's insurance would not go far in bringing up his brats and Dora would have to be kept quiet with at least enough money to emigrate; he ought to get her out of the way before May's lawyers found her; May wouldn't speak yet... perhaps never.

He unfolded the papers that he had had so little time to read that day; he had heard the bare-foot newsboys crying out their headlines: *Astounding Evidence, Sensational Disclosures, Mrs. Tyler's purchase of fly-papers, Arsenic the cause of death, The Poisoned beef tea the cause of death, Further compromising letters.* The journalists were trying the case, far ahead of the Assizes; well, there had been a good many people to chatter to the reporters who had hung about Stone Pynes, the servants, the nurses, Amelia Chorley, the doctors, the police, the tradespeople...

he, himself, with his steady tale, quite watertight by now; no one disbelieved him for a second, unless it was that London doctor, with his sneer at "the undoubted purity of your motives, Mr. Tyler" and Dr. Harris could do nothing, he was a stranger.

Richard Tyler returned to his accounts; what could he afford to pay? He would drive a hard bargain, but it would be worth anything up to a thousand pounds.

Richard was precise for his appointment at Stone Pynes; he had his brother's keys and entered the house, leaving the front door ajar; the shutters were closed in the dining-room, it was safe to light the gas; as the coarse blue flame spurted up he looked about; the auctioneer's numbered slips were already on the furniture; *Lot 197* was pasted on the table where John's corpse had lain to be dismembered, where he, and Richard and May had so often sat; she, exactly where John's head had been, when the doctors were at work, May, in her peacock dress, her purple dress, her lace guipure dress; he had asked the police "how *she* was?" and had been told "very quiet and docile."

There was a feeble knock on the door; John went into the passage and said, "Come in."

The visitor advanced, closed the door behind him, came into the dining-room and stood rigid.

Richard looked him up and down; Jerome Thorne tried to pull off his muffler, could not, fumbled for a seat, sliding on to the red plush sofa.

"You didn't go for that Mediterranean cruise? Why?"

"I was advised to stay," whispered the young man, "face it out, you know. I have to appear at the inquest to be identified—what gave it all away?"

"Her letters, of course. She sent openly."

"Why did you want to see me—secretly, like this?"

"To find out what you are going to say," said Richard. "You'll both be confronted with the waiter at the Mentone. Why look so yellow? *You* won't be arrested, not a shred of evidence."

Thorne was too frightened to be reassured by this; he had feared many things during his life, never that he might be "mixed up" in a murder case; he cowered into a corner of the sofa, and asked for a drink that Richard refused—"All locked up."

The hatred that encompassed him disturbed him horribly… and this house… but he had not dared to refuse Richard's demand of an interview at Stone Pynes.

"I wish I'd never seen her," his weak lamentations overflowed his control; he had not yet decided what to do; it never occurred to him to champion, or even to support passively the woman who might be a murderess; he thought of May with disgust, with anger, because she had entangled him in such a horrible affair; all Manchester knew by now who her lover was; he might tell the truth; it would sound a queer story, but if she went for trial, her counsel ought to be able to prove it, that would be a long way to save her; but what would *he* look like? A man boasting of the success of tricks to get hold of a woman that had really failed.

"You didn't lie to me?" suggested Richard, "when you told me you'd been with her at the Mentone?"

Thorne was silent, harassed, ill from insomnia, reckless drinking.

"If I thought you had lied…" added Richard quietly, "I'd kill you, butcher you, and put your body down the cesspool."

"Of course I didn't lie, why should I? It's true—there'll be the waiter's evidence…."

"*Her* counsel—if it gets as far—might shake that—"

"Why, in Heaven's name, do you speak so violently? *You* had better be careful, too, Tyler. *I* saw something at the Pomona Rooms…."

"It would seem a stupid lie, if *you* told *that* story."

"I don't know—people must see you hate her—are hounding her...."

"I loved my dear brother, like a good Christian." Richard's thick white hand passed down the length of the table where John's corpse had lain. "*There's* the motive."

Thorne's fright mounted to panic. "What do you *want* me to say?"

"You'll soon know, and you'll never leave this place until you've said and signed it...." Richard looked up. "*She* mustn't escape. An adulteress, a murderess. *If* it was true..."

'I'm cornered,' thought Thorne. 'I'll never be believed if I do tell the truth—this brute will show me up—there's the waiter, too, damn them all.'

"A question of money," continued Richard. "I'll pay you to stay in Manchester—to put in an affidavit, if necessary."

"I don't understand— Money?"

"Money. That's plain enough? You're in difficulties, I know. Too many chocolate-boxes. You get the women cheaply enough, but there's racing, where you've *got* to pay—had her for a few chocolates, eh? And now you can make money out of her, too—up to a thousand pounds."

Thorne laughed hysterically; how he'd wanted her, the old goat, with his greasy poll and heavy figure! Well, no one would listen to that story, indeed, the Tylers were popular in Manchester, there were so many like them... better to stick to a good likely lie than a most unnatural sounding truth... better make a little money if one could... she was a murderess for all he knew.

"If I've to loiter round Manchester I'll need more than a thousand," he said insolently.

"An affidavit, before a lawyer, or your evidence on oath, if you're called, that she stayed with you at the Mentone. One thousand, five hundred pounds the last offer."

"Very well, it will only be telling the truth." Richard brought paper, ink in a case, a quill from his pocket.

"Come to the table, sit at your usual place, where you used to ogle her—write what I dictate."

He slowly repeated the words he had so often rehearsed; Thorne wrote them down and signed the paper; Richard put a roll of bank-notes on the table. "The sale of Stone Pynes will cover it—now, get out, quick...."

"Can't I have a drink? I'm in a wretched state."

"No. Get out. You've been paid. If you force me to throw you out, I shan't stop until I've murdered you."

Thorne pocketed the money, and went feebly away; Richard stood motionless until he heard the front door softly close, then went upstairs, striking matches to light his way.

Her bedroom was in more than usual disorder; so many searchers, the servants suddenly dismissed, sluttish women, thievish women, for all his care much had been stolen; he lit the gas and stared at the empty bed, the match burnt till the flame touched his fingers, the stump fell and sizzled on the dusty carpet.

"Quiet and docile, was she?" If it did not come to a trial he had wasted his money on that scoundrel Thorne.

Wasted.

The word suddenly wreathed the room; the heavy, stout man in his striped trousers and frock-coat, shook in despair, in rage, with a sense of utter loss he began to weep, difficult tears reddened his eyes, as with a howl he hurled himself on the bed where she had lain until the sheets and pillows reeked from the essence of lilac in her hair, and took down the flounced curtains and ripped them into shreds.

There they were again in the coroner's court—all the familiar figures one by one reeling out their tales. Lizzie Burt, the children's nurse, with her story of having observed Mrs. Tyler soaking some flypapers in a sponge-basin, with her story of having intercepted a pencilled letter to Jerome Thorne which Mrs. Tyler had sent her to put in the post office, and her account of quarrels between Mr. and Mrs. Tyler. Nelly Tanner, the housemaid, with her story of the quarrel and the blow, and her story about seeing the flypapers soaking in the bedroom; the family chemist with his evidence that Mrs. Tyler had bought some flypapers from him—another chemist with his account that a smart young lady, fair haired and elegant, had bought flypapers from him; the cook, with her story, reluctantly drawn from her, of the quarrels between husband and wife and about preparing Mr. John Tyler's patent food that was to be taken down to the office. Dolly Hoey, the parlourmaid, with the story that Mrs. Tyler had tied up the brown jug with some mess for the office with paper and string she had brought her, Nurse Goff with her story about Mrs. Tyler taking a bottle of Orso's meat juice into the dressing-room and replacing it in the bedroom, adding that "she took care that the patient should have none of it." Nurse Newton with her story that "she kept her eye on the bottle of Orso's meat juice" and wouldn't let the patient touch it; the tittle-tattle that the dying man had whispered to his wife, "How could you do it! I didn't think it of you."

Richard Tyler gave his evidence, then took his place in court again, watching a little door on the right where, he had been told, *she* would appear. Thorne was already present, looking ill and jaunty, the waiter at the Mentone had identified him easily enough; he knew him well, a regular client, the police had schooled him; he was frightened, confused, his foreign accent was emphasized, he stumbled in his evidence, there had been another gentleman who had visited a lady on that date, no, he could not remember him at all.

Richard shaded his face with his hand. Was the fool lying, or was he part of a "got up" case? 'But he might not know me, I've never been there before, that's why I sent her there—so Thorne goes often? I wish I'd known.'

It was all a welter of lies; the little door opened and she appeared for a moment, like a mechanical figure in a clock; in widow's black, between two wardresses; the waiter identified her; then Thorne.

"That's the lady, that's the gentleman, they shared the same room."

She was gone.

No one in Manchester could avoid the subject, the Tyler brothers were well known, but May had always been an alien, no one, not even the Chorleys, had known what was happening at Stone Pynes, so quiet she had been until, of course, "the talk" about Thorne....

"Where does this 'talk' come from?" asked Madame Dumont in anguish, appealing to Mr. Martin. "Who begins it? Who listens? Who spies? Who are in these conclaves of whispering gossips?"

Mr. Martin did not attempt to answer these questions; he had been hampered in getting up his case, the police were ahead of him on all counts; he was not very able and he did not believe in the innocence of his client.

Every day "things looked worse" for her, he assured the frantic mother; there had been an exhumation, more arsenic had been found in John Tyler's body; the press clamoured against her; penny prints were hawked in the streets. She had not a friend in Manchester; so far, the evidence at the inquest, the identifications of the waiter.... "You ought to have stayed—it is different with me. I could do no good by attending. I *know* everyone is lying, you ought to be able to *prove* it." Mr. Martin repeated that his partner was present in the coroner's court, and that Madame Dumont was in no fit state to be left alone... one of his clerks came in softly, discreetly, whispered, "Wilful murder."

"How she was dragged into that cab—half dressed, when I returned with you," lamented Madame Dumont, "the police, the nurses—*thirteen men* in the house, I hardly understood—no time even to pack her toilet articles—*no* money, but a few shillings from Dr. Harman, they pushed me away—I ran upstairs to look from the window, to try to see her face—she was being *hustled*...."

"Madam," interrupted Mr. Martin. "Madam, I fear again you hardly understand—my clerk brings me a message from Mr. Endicott—the coroner's jury's verdict is *wilful murder*."

Wilful murder; the words in huge black letters were printed on all the headlines of all the papers; in a week or so she would be charged before the magistrates. Richard Tyler had time to go to Salford and get Dora Lestrange out of the way, she thought of nothing but her children, money for the future, and flying from any possible connection with the case; her passion for John Tyler had proved as feeble as Thorne's for May Tyler.

As the prisoner had been committed on the coroner's warrant there was little need of another charge; she was, however, brought before the magistrates a fortnight later, the Superintendent having got up the case against her, after consulting the doctors.

Richard did not notice the informal ugliness of the scene, ugliness was the background of his life; he had heard that the prisoner who had recovered her health, even her composure, was to be present, and, for the first time, would hear the evidence.

She came in after everyone was seated and Richard forgot all in staring at her through his fingers, a habit he had formed when as a boy he had been forced to go to church, and to kneel decorously on the hard hassock and to assume the attitude of prayer. Here was May Tyler brought as low as the floundering peacock that had once been grasped in his brother's coarse white hands, as the peaches that had been snatched off the warm brick wall....

A female warder was behind her and she wore a dress of black bombazine that hung too large on her slight figure, a widow's bonnet and a crape veil below which her fair hair showed in a fringe....

Richard was infuriated to observe her composure. She bowed, as if unconscious of her shameful position, to all the gentlemen and took her seat at the end of the table, and though a look of care and anxiety contrasted with her youthful and rounded outlines, she was tranquil and held a small notebook and pencil, steadily.

All the evidence was formal; there were no new points of importance.

Richard Tyler looked at the police with dull hatred; they were usurping his revenge, serving it yet usurping it; he himself would have wished to cast on the fair and pallid young woman in her mockery of black, all the incriminating evidence these strangers had got together. The magistrates committed her for trial and Mr. Martin reserved the defence. She disappeared through the pitch-pine door in the white-washed wall, again bowing, as if in her own drawing-room, to the company.

It seemed however that she had had a request to make; a heavy-footed official brought it to Richard. Could she see him a few minutes in the antechamber?

The tall, heavy man in his correct mourning which, with his black hair, made him appear so sombre, followed the usher without a word.

May was standing in the dark, gloomy room termed "reception", a bench ran along each side, a bare wooden table stood in the middle, a weighing machine by the door with a foot measure was beside this; the light was high placed and northern. The wardress was standing at attention.

"I'm sorry to put you to any concern on my account, Richard," whispered May. "But there's no one else."

"There's your lawyers. Wouldn't it be more suitable for you to ask them?"

Was she such a fool that she had forgotten the scene in the Pomona Rooms or so wicked that she meant to turn it to account?

She spoke as if their relationship was most ordinary. "I've not been allowed to have my handbag and my toilet articles. I have not been allowed to have the Bible my mother gave me, I have not been allowed to see my children. Could you contrive these things for me?"

He replied brutally, "I thought that you had asked Mr. Thorne to come to your rescue… and your mother is here."

"Mr. Thorne did not answer my letters. Perhaps I was wrong to involve him… that was Amelia Chorley's advice; my mother is a foreigner and can do very little. What of the requests I have made to you?"

Richard Tyler would gladly have prolonged the moment; he glanced malevolently at the wardress. "How do they treat you?" he asked softly.

"Like all the others, I suppose. I never knew before how women in prison were treated. I think I have sleeping-draughts. I tried to see my mother when they took me away, in a hired carriage, from Stone Pynes, but I couldn't for there were blinds at all the windows. I seemed to be asleep until I woke up in a bare cell. There was a chair beside me with a cup of milk on it, a plate of bread—nothing else. The window was dirty and barred. I didn't mind that so much as the dreadful stillness. My main thought was…" she paused and Richard looked at the wardress as if wondering if this was permitted, but the woman seemed disposed to allow the prisoner to talk.

"What was your main thought, May?"

"Who had contrived and directed suspicion against me," replied the young woman. "Oh, I have been more comfortable since Mr. Martin visited me and was kind. I have a room now such as prisoners awaiting trial, who can afford to pay five shillings weekly, may enjoy; I have a chair, a table, a washstand...."

"Her food is sent in from an hotel outside, she goes to chapel in the morning and has an hour's exercise in the prison yard," put in the wardress briskly.

"And all the rest of the time I am locked in the cell."

"It is all out of my hands, I can do nothing for you. Do you not see the governor, the doctor and the chaplain?"

"I see them, but they have nothing to say but formalities. They are strangers to me—my mother is not allowed to visit me, it is feared that she would procure me poison...."

"She threatened to do as much," put in the wardress.

"Oh no!" interrupted May gently. "She said 'better death than this', meaning what I was enduring, that is all, she explained to me. Richard, will you get me some of those things I asked of you?"

"You know that the children have been sent to Blackheath?"

"With Lizzie Burt?"

"No, I found Lizzie some work in Manchester. As a matter of fact she is acting as housekeeper to me."

May's candid eyes had no reproach. "Are the children well—are they happy? I was not allowed to see them before I was taken away. I always thought it would be better for them in the country than in Manchester; with John and me.... So everything is left to you, Richard.... I have nothing at all?"

"Oh, you have a small income, but I dare say you won't need it. Your mother's able to get money. I'm going to sell up by auction everything in the house in a day or two's time. John did not leave much. I have to sell every stick."

"That's no regret to me, I always thought that house a joyless place."

"A nice thing for a woman to say of her home where she has lived many years," remarked the wardress in a tone of contempt.

"I gave your mother the Bible and a few things out of your room. Ask her for them," said Richard, biting his forefinger. "What Bible is it? I never saw you with a Bible—save once...."

"I should have liked the blue Bible that is in the wardrobe in my room. I want the recipe for a face-wash that I had made up in Paris before I was married... it is somewhere in Stone Pynes, but of course it won't be found now."

"I shall find it if it is there," replied Richard. "I shall search very well, of course. It will be found, *if it exists*."

He had to forego these moments of poignant pleasure. Was she ready to turn to him now in her anguish, in her terrible plight? He used these words in his mind of her but he could not see that she was in any agony; she smiled at him with the courtesy she had always shown as he left the room.

Dr. Harman discussed the tragedy with Richard Tyler.

"Before she came before the magistrates, Mr. Tyler, she passed the night here in a cell with a plank board for a bed. I believe one of the policemen gave her a blanket to lie on... damp, dark, dirty, with drunken men raving next door... with no light, with no one to speak to.... It's odd, isn't it," added the doctor in a juridical manner, "that no one comes forward to take her part?"

"You're wrong," whispered Richard, leaning along the table. "There's a greengrocer's wife where she used to deal—she sends her in some fruit with a sympathetic note."

"A greengrocer's wife!" The doctor smiled sadly.

He recalled the dreary scene; the crowded court, lawyers, reporters, witnesses, spectators; the prisoner the most insignificant figure there.

"She was already judged and condemned," remarked Dr. Harman. "A needless anguish."

"There wasn't a man on the Bench and hardly one in court," smiled Richard, "who hasn't dined at Stone Pynes."

Dr. Harman spoke again, deeply troubled. "I took little notice of the proceedings, formal, dry and confused, were they not? How composed she was, as if those people were her guests and she their hostess! I admired, perhaps with an exasperated respect, a breeding that stood so severe a test."

Richard remembered how the appearance of the prisoner had caused an uneasy and shuffling silence in the overheated and over-crowded court, where gross bluebottles buzzed on the dirty window-pane. May Tyler had taken notes. The formalities proceeded dully.

"Have you agreed upon your verdict, gentlemen?"

"We have."

"Do you find that death resulted from the administration of an irritant poison?"

"Unanimously."

"Do you say by whom that poison was administered?"

"We have decided that the poison was administered by Mrs. Tyler."

"Do you find that the poison was administered with the intention of taking life?"

"We have come to that conclusion."

There was a second's pause, then the Chairman of the Magistrates, deliberately turning his head away from the prisoner had remarked, "That means a verdict of murder and commitment to the Assizes."

The scene flickered before Richard's eyes, the words hummed in his ears. May alone before these hostile men, all of whom she had entertained, who had liked her or had flirted with her a little, or had begged her to sing this song and that; who had praised her table and her wine, who had crowded round her at the race-course, who had pressed her hand a little longer than politeness allowed; who had been pleased and flattered to be seen with the fair Virginian with her blonde hair, her wide candid eyes, her smile at once that of a child and of a great lady, and her smart uncommon clothes.

Something in Richard's heart, conscience, soul—he knew not what—was outraged.

Guilty of murder!... the Assizes commenced soon, she would not have long to wait.

"There is nothing I can do. You will have seen in the papers, Dr. Harman, that I am reluctant—very reluctant for the trial."

He gazed round the room that Lizzie Burt had exerted herself to make tidy and comfortable; she entered with a pile of newspapers, the ink still wet on them, and laid them on the table; they were like fellow conspirators. He was paying her too much and she knew it; their luck seemed to them of that uncommon quality of which one has to be wary lest it be fiendish.

Richard felt slightly giddy. "It's a hot day, Dr. Harman," he remarked. "There's thunder and a good many flies about. This won't be the last edition of the papers."

"I waited here a long time, Mr. Tyler," said Dr. Harman coolly. "Mrs. Burt told me you were expected earlier."

"I went into the club," replied Richard. "You're right, I didn't come straight.... I had a few drinks, I talked the thing over...."

"Can you help her, Mr. Tyler? I know the newspapers give you *and* the police a generous air—loth to prosecute—and so on, but *who* began the suspicions? *Who* sent for the police?"

"You'll have it all threshed out in court."

"I'm shocked to know as much. But you haven't answered."

"Why should *I* answer? Her letters to Thorne were enough."

"By no means. And you noted, of course, that they are in pencil, and could have all been forged? Oh, the malice of servants, ignorant—spiteful—I don't like it, Mr. Tyler, everyone lied, I don't trust that rat of a waiter, the police had got hold of him...."

"It will all be threshed out at the trial," replied Richard sullenly, obstinately. "*I* couldn't stop it now, if I wished, could I?"

"Money? Has she any?" asked Dr. Harman uneasily. "I hear she signed away her entire estate to Martin and Endicott."

"Her mother has the money—she is looking after the defence." Richard sullenly roused himself into anger. "What has all this to do with me?"

"Dr. Harris, before he returned to London, spoke to me very earnestly about Mrs. Tyler. He thought she had been harshly dealt with—for instance, those packets of arsenic, why didn't you leave them in her room?"

"Dangerous stuff to have about...."

"How did you *know* they were arsenic? You seemed to have assumed a good deal, Mr. Tyler."

"There was so much talk—you and Dr. Fitch didn't like the look of things, did you? And the *post mortem* proved you were right."

"We didn't find a fatal dose, remember that—after two tests—the medical evidence will be in favour of the defence—talk, yes there was too much talk. Did you know your brother ate arsenic?"

"No—I knew he dosed himself—some harmless pick-me-up—nothing in it...."

"But Mrs. Tyler told you of this—white powder, he took? She told me. I thought it unimportant, as your brother took so many medicines..."

"So did I—she is such a foolish woman."

"If she—did this—she must be—mingled cunning, stupidity and ferocity—perhaps one could find her insane..." Dr. Harman looked troubled, stared at the heap of papers. "A pity the press got hold of all this 'sensational' stuff as they call it—I wonder you are so against her, Mr. Tyler."

"I was fond of my brother. I'm not in the witness-box—yet. I've nothing but a straight story to tell, I wonder you can doubt it—an unfaithful wife—trying for a divorce, poison to her hand, in and out of the sick-room..."

"The police can't find any evidence anywhere that she bought arsenic...."

"Well, it was there, in her room, in the chocolate-box."

"Why," wondered Dr. Harman, "should she buy flypapers—with all that arsenic in her possession?"

"A foolish woman," grinned Richard.

"She swears it was for a face-wash, a recipe that she used as a schoolgirl...."

"Well, where is it?" Richard recalled that she had said, "Of course it won't be found now"—but this was not on his conscience, with all his searchings, he had not found the recipe.

"Young Thorne is behaving like a scoundrel," Dr. Harman frowned. "Going about the place, as if he was a hero—in the saloon bars if not in the drawing-rooms. I would not give much for that waiter's evidence—her counsel ought to be able to shake that—those letters were faked—not love-letters—of course Thorne lets it go by default, rather proud of the publicity—and she won't speak...."

"You mean—they never stayed at the hotel together?" Richard's tone was so urgent that the doctor felt relieved, hoping that the brother of the dead man might be softened in his attitude towards his sister-in-law, if doubt could be thrown on the amorous intrigue.

"I dare say they met there, he may even have suggested the place to her, certainly odd she didn't go to her usual hotel—her head was full of this divorce plan—but the adultery—I doubt it. Very much."

"But she admits it...."

"By default, as he does. When she says 'my sin'—she means the divorce, even the marriage; she is not, as you say, at all clever. She has been stunned, too, half out of her mind, with horror—and drugged—too much. Bred a Catholic, the marriage was null to her—it meant she left the Church, but she put 'Catholic' on the prison register...."

Richard turned aside, being unable to control his features—had he made some fiendish mistake? Why, after all, had he believed Thorne? But Richard's mind was too coarse, downright and dull for him ever to be able to disbelieve what the commonplace consider the obvious. He laughed grossly. "Get a jury to believe she's a respectable woman, *I* don't."

The tradesman showed in the choice of the word—"respectable". Dr. Harman rose, useless to argue with such a man; and it was true that the case was full of confusion, mystery, error, lies, contradictions; not the least remarkable feature was the reserve of the prisoner, neither to her mother, her lawyers, nor her physicians would she in any way explain herself, beyond the childish—"I didn't do it."

Dr. Harman took his leave.

Richard picked up the papers, one after another, with the banner headlines, paused at one that flourished, "The Flypaper Theory—a Reminiscence"; here was mention of the flypaper poisoning case in Liverpool for which two baby-farmers had been hanged.

"Hanged!" whispered Richard; then he read stories of May Tyler, many of which he knew to be untrue; supposing he had loosed a pack of hell hounds on her track and she would be torn to pieces?"

"Mr. and Mrs. Chorley came round and wanted to speak to you," said Mrs. Burt opening the door and putting her head round it, while speaking in an insinuating tone, "and a number of other people whom I don't know. They left their cards," she put down a salver of Sheffield plate heaped with squares of pasteboard, that slipped over on to the newspapers.

"I won't see anyone, no matter when they come or what I'm doing. Do you understand? You can tell them what you like."

He held up the news-sheet, lounging. How many lies about May Tyler? There was an account of her husband's life insurances—all incorrect, of the vast sums she would inherit, of the enormous wealth of Madame Dumont. The heading of another paragraph was "Mrs. Tyler's Financial Difficulties", and there was a description of her keen interest in racing and cards, a statement that her life consisted of going from one race-meeting to another, one card party or dance hall to another.

Richard Tyler was amazed. The journalists had far outstripped anything that he might have imagined or tried to put about in his clumsy way.

Flinging down the papers he remarked to Mrs. Burt who, with meticulous care was arranging his supper, "Where do these fellows get all this nonsense? My sister-in-law never gambled or went to race-meetings—she wasn't in debt for anything except household expenses—"

But the woman was not as candid as the man. "One never knows," she hinted primly. "She was out of the house a good deal, wasn't she?"

"I never heard that, I thought she lay on a sofa and read light novels and strummed on the piano."

"I wouldn't care to say that!" Mrs. Burt was very knowing. "What about the times when Mr. Thorne was there? He's a racing gentleman, isn't he? And she was gone from the house often enough.... And all those fine clothes she bought in London, I suppose they weren't purchased just to do the shopping in."

Richard sat silent, then took his head in his hands. He was trying, and it was difficult for a man of his type who had never been honest in any way about anything, to be candid with himself. It was, of course, easy to pretend he believed all these slanders against May. But did he? The way she had looked at him, that pale hair under the widow's bonnet—widowed—yes, she really was free of John now.

Why could not he, Richard, have married her? They were not blood relations? But the law forbade. What was she doing? He had her pretty well spied upon… a bribe here and there…. The prison doctors attended her with scrupulous regard for the rules, her mother, far more passionate and practical than her daughter, came and went as often as allowed, which was seldom, and so did the lawyer, Mr. Martin, and Dr. Harman. She wrote letters to her mother; he knew that; but there was nothing in them except expressions of dismay and bewilderment, the prison authorities read them before they were sent out.

By what means could he discover her mind; who held the key to that? So far she was in his power. He had her stripped; her mother had the dress, the Bible, for the rest, he had taken everything. He would need every penny for John's brats… and how long would she be in prison? He began to calculate that, regardless of Mrs. Burt's sharp "You'll be late for your supper, sir." Until the Assizes, another few days…. The trial, how long would that take? And then she would be condemned to death…. No, the medical evidence was conflicting, but in her favour, even the experts were doubtful; the defence had some good points. Madame Dumont, who was high-spirited and vigilant, even though she had everyone against her, had secured Sir Jonathan Docwra, Q.C., for the defence, a man like that would pick holes in the evidence of the waiter, perhaps save her reputation, as well as her life; Lord Barnfield was the judge on circuit… Richard knew nothing about him, but the merchant had an exaggerated respect for the law; the judge would see everything, perhaps even the truth… at least enough of the truth for May to be released… as Dr. Harman seemed to see it. Richard would have liked to have asked him about the judge and the lawyers but could not find the courage to do so.

"Your supper's getting cold, sir," repeated Lizzie Burt.

"I'm trying to straighten the tangle." Richard looked up and seemed so like his elder brother that Lizzie Burt moved away. Not until one of the men was dead, had she remarked how they resembled one another.

"Living in the house with a ghost," she muttered, "that's what it is."

She eyed the newspapers enviously; she wanted to read "all these lies" that she had helped to breed.

Richard moved heavily to the table; he had had his revenge; when May was released she would not be such a highstepper, he would probably be able then to do what he liked with her... the devil of it was there would not be anything he would want to do; she had deceived him, she belonged to Jerome Thorne, that boasting fool... what could women see in him? He had nothing to recommend him but a face that was like those wax blocks one saw in barbers' shops.... What would May have thought of him had she seen him pocketing the roll of notes.

"Just hard, sir, how they're calling the papers again in the street! It doesn't seem as if they could have enough of the story. No one can talk of anything else...."

"They're not on to the truth yet...."

"They're on to a few things worse than the truth it seems to me, sir," said Lizzie Burt, staring out of the window.

She allowed herself much familiarity with her new master, knowing herself indispensable to him, at least for the present; any anecdote that she could tell of Stone Pynes was received with such avidity by Richard Tyler that she employed her considerable leisure in inventing more crude slander of May Tyler.

"I wonder if Thorne's left the city," mused Richard, turning over the well-cooked cutlet on his plate. "I wonder if he'll be called...."

"Supposing, sir, he was to go into the box and say nothing ever happened?"

"He won't do that." Richard thought of the letter he kept so carefully locked up.

He was surprised that he had no appetite. It was the weather, that's what it was… too much thunder in the air.…

"Mr. Thorne must feel a bit awkward, mustn't he, sir?" goaded Lizzie Burt. "He's been pretty well hinted at in the papers; nobody could be far off a good guess as to who the gentleman in the case *was*."

"He's no reputation to lose. He was always a wastrel, throwing away the money his father earned."

He was surprised that he did not now feel that livid hatred towards the man that he did towards the woman, yet he had no goodwill towards Jerome Thorne either.

"I wonder…" he paused on those words, and Lizzie Burt shot him a glance of contempt. She knew what he was about and thought him laggard in the performance of it. Had she been in his place there was a good deal she could have done to see that the noose was firmly thrown round the neck of this wicked woman; but he, the big heavy man with money, position and independence, seemed, to Lizzie, to lag and hesitate.

"I don't want to pry into your affairs, sir," she ventured. "Everybody knows about Mrs. Lestrange—it would be a pity if that came out, wouldn't it?"

"It won't come out," grinned Richard, looking up from his plate. "Dora Lestrange, as she calls herself, and her children have been sent away. She won't speak—I've promised her an annuity as long as she doesn't."

"But if Mrs. Tyler tells her lawyers?" objected Lizzie.

Richard made a contemptuous movement with his fat white hand. "Her lawyers are no good, they don't believe in her themselves. She's got a big man coming down I believe—Docwra—but he's been on that government case… *The Times* libel action… you wouldn't know of it." Richard slurred it over, not knowing much of it himself. "He'll be disgusted once he finds out about Thorne; everyone will be disgusted—an unfaithful wife and one with such a large allowance, too."

Lizzie Burt giggled. "It does interest me to read of that in the papers, sir—just what she used to spend even on the biscuits and fruit and wine...."

"I suppose you didn't supply any of those details?" asked Richard and Mrs. Burt answered bitterly, "Oh no, they wouldn't come to *me*. I was only the children's nurse. I told them what I know about the way she always kept out of the nursery and showed no interest in the little blessings; but of course it was Tanner and Hoey as to the other things, as if I couldn't have told them just as well. But I had *my* story about the flypapers...."

"The London man, Harris," mused Richard, "says there wasn't enough arsenic in the flypapers to have killed a kitten... at least, if that was the solution in the bottle with the gold ornamentation."

"Ah!" countered Lizzie, "not in *those* papers perhaps—but who knows how many more she had that we weren't aware of? Nothing was to prevent her buying them up by the dozen all over the place and soaking them secretly. It was just a mistake on her part that time that she let us see them, don't you think so, sir?"

"I suppose so."

"And now you've finished your chop I'll bring you up a nice rice pudding," said Lizzie Burt with an ingratiating smile. "I'm sure you need to keep your strength up."

The case seemed confused but ordinary. Messrs. Endicott & Martin had prepared it with all the industry of provincial lawyers concerned for the first time in an important trial. Sir Jonathan Docwra smiled with professional understanding, not untouched by compassion as he looked at the large pile of documents from which he was to prepare his brief. His own motives as to undertaking the case he hardly knew. He was a tired man who had given for months all his concentrated energies to a political case in London. He had been successful but he was exhausted and he rather regretted this new case as he looked out of the window at the dreary façade of the pompous houses opposite him. The best hotel in Manchester could only offer sombre accommodation.

May Tyer was a Catholic though sadly lax in her religious duties, and her mother, who had waited on Sir Jonathan in London, was certainly a well-bred woman, rather a surprising type Sir Jonathan thought to have come from America, a country he associated with the new and the crude; but then Virginia—good English families had gone there.

Now there was very little time in which to prepare his brief—the Assizes opened in a few days and the Tyler case was the first to be heard. Sir Jonathan leant back in the green velvet chair beside the large mahogany desk on which were piled all the solicitors' documents. His assistant, Mr. Cornford, had already been through them, arranging them, dating them, yet obliged to leave them full of gaps and queries; Sir Jonathan had himself read them but had not come to any definite conclusions, she was probably innocent of the murder; she would be acquitted on the medical evidence; such a small quantity of arsenic had been found in the body that there was hardly, some must argue, a case to go to the jury; besides, the experts disagreed. The victim might have rejected the arsenic, during the last few days of his illness; the local physicians had been careless there. In fact the carelessness in the case was amazing. That search before the police were called in—the arrest while she was hardly conscious. The strong feeling against her in Manchester—the case should have been heard elsewhere, the journalists had made hay with the story, how discover the truth behind their lies?

Sir Jonathan, a handsome man, who owed much of his success to his noble presence and splendid voice, lay back in the long chair covered with rich velvet, and tried to put the case together; at the inquest, in the magistrate's court, everyone had lied, everyone would lie again at the trial. Already there had been contradictions, confusions, Endicott and Martin had got up the case badly, they had been handicapped, of course, still, they might have done better.

The man was an arsenic eater, a trump card there, an unfaithful husband, a man of whom little good could be said, even in Manchester, except that he was popular because of his vices and his easy way with money—when abroad. Nagging his wife about the housekeeping expenses and throwing money away on gambling, drinks to friends, racing and a second establishment; but the defence was to be conducted on the most generous lines, and John Tyler's faults, by his widow's request were to be lightly passed over, not mentioned at all, if possible.

Sir Jonathan suspected the manner in which the local police had got up their case, but it might be difficult to shake that now.

The adultery was the main obstacle against an acquittal; she would really be tried for that, not for the murder—if she had been a constant wife, good, fine, long suffering, it would not have been difficult to dispose even of the three packages of arsenic found in the chocolate-box, they might have been her husband's store, displaced by the hand of malice—or carelessness, in a household like that!

As a Catholic, Sir Jonathan considered his client debased by the Anglican marriage, to him a mockery; as a fastidious man, he considered her degraded by her infidelity to this union; as a lawyer, he knew he would be addressing a British jury, with Puritan instincts, to whom she would be "a fallen woman."

Still, he hoped there would not be much difficulty in securing the lady's acquittal—but he wondered as he idly turned over the pile of journals that had been collected for him; all the papers published in the Midlands since her arrest, each with a sensational and violent account of May Tyler's tragedy, what use that same acquittal would be to May Tyler. Sir Jonathan was surprised at the warmth with which the journalists had been allowed to express themselves; it was against, at least, an unwritten law, to have this trial by newspaper before there was a trial by jury. It was hardly his business, though his sense of abstract justice and his humanity, for he was an upright, kindly man, were shocked as he saw, reading the headlines only, May Tyler described as a murderess, a woman who had recklessly spent her husband's money on race-courses and gambling-tables, who had run his house with the most careless extravagance, who had plunged him into unnecessary debts while carrying on a sordid intrigue with one of the best known local Lotharios.

None of this interested Sir Jonathan, except the curious dissimilarity of the personalities of the prisoner and her mother with these reports; they were refined, elegant, even in their extremity, exceedingly well-bred. The younger woman's self-control was remarkable; even though he had been able with a good conscience to assure her that he had good hopes of an acquittal, still her position was horrible and would after the trial be worse. She would have no reputation, no position. Her children…? This man Richard, the brother, the self-righteous cotton merchant—he had sent them away to friends. No one would blame him. She would not have a friend, an acquaintance.… His legal mind paused at this… she did not seem to have a friend or an acquaintance, as it was. Everyone was against her; even her own servants, except the cook, whom, no doubt, she had in her easy way bribed by overlooking faked accounts. Her close intimate, the Chorley woman, seemed eager for her punishment; her brother-in-law who should, Sir Jonathan considered, by the ordinary rules of humanity, have been her champion, was her enemy. Many years in Manchester and no friends! And this falling away from her own Church, too… in her extremity she had turned to the family doctor, not to a priest, and she could easily have found one to accept her penitence. "An empty-headed frivolous little fool, I suppose."

He recalled the prisoner in her black bombazine, with her wide eyes, her fair hair carelessly dressed, her courteous manner, her answers that had seemed so frank and yet were so evasive. Purposely evasive? He did not know. It might not be difficult to get her off, but morally she was blasted for ever.

There was the usual waiter's evidence, the chambermaid's too? No, that had not been put in. Probably neither she nor the man Thorne would deny the charge; perhaps he was not the first.... Sir Jonathan could get nothing from her, save her protestation of her innocence, and his ears were jaded with assertions of innocence. But it was his business now to endeavour to understand May Tyler.

Sir Jonathan, a man of agreeable manners and mild tastes who enjoyed a happy domestic life, had occasionally made fictitious excursions into the realm of the horrible and the, to him, incomprehensible. He had never forgotten reading *Madame Bovary* and the criticisms upon the novelist's daring unmasking of human nature. Was this the case here? The woman was bored with her provincial life perhaps and had found no alleviation of tedium save in sordid intrigues?

The lawyer was honest enough to question his mental use of the word sordid; perhaps that slight young woman whom he had interviewed in jail with a wardress always present had not found these adventures gross or squalid. To her they might have had a fairy-tale quality and she was, he admitted with the candour of a man beyond temptation, fascinating. Yes, that was the word for her—fascinating; and he wondered, allowing his mind to wander from the strictly legal aspect of the case, why she had ever married a brute like John Tyler, for a brute he must have been if he in any way resembled his brother, the worst type of uneducated, prosperous Midlander.

Everyone concerned in the case was repellent, almost disgusting, to the aristocratic Catholic lawyer; here was revealed provincialism and Puritanism at their worst, ostentatious, without principles or background, without tradition or elegance. The way, for instance, they allowed their press to turn over this story before the Assizes—a gutter press indeed... who had supplied all these details of the victim's private life? She must have had spies and traitors at her elbow all the time—some of the servants, of course, and of course they had all been lying. The journalists had needed very little on which to base their tales for the bar-room and the kitchen. He had heard that the prisoner, on being taken from the jail to the coroner's court, had been hissed by the crowd. That was the obvious reaction of the public to the campaign in the newspapers; he was even surprised that there was not one of them that had not, for the sake of novelty, championed the forlorn woman, so pretty and engaging.

He wished he knew more about her... there must be something behind those wide set eyes, those small features, that look of appealing yet reserved innocence....

The case presented few technical difficulties; the misconduct would be admitted, the usual quotation from the New Testament could be brought in to the opening speech, no one could object to an appeal for Christian charity though Sir Jonathan in his long experience had never known anyone act upon it... the medical evidence would dispose of the charge of murder. He could not (and he had examined keenly all the evidence) see that there was anything even to direct suspicion against May Tyler. The intercepted letters between herself and Jerome Thorne were so cold and dry that they might not have been letters of lovers at all, in pencil, too, and might have been tampered with, while the traces of arsenic found on her dressing-gown, apron, handkerchiefs from spilled medicine given to her husband, of course—as for the arsenic found in the chocolate-box... three packets of it and a bottle of weak arsenic in solution. The packets were easily accounted for. The man had been an arsenic eater. This subject had been a new one to Sir Jonathan. He had had to do some research in order to find out the facts; he had them now in a notebook by his side. The arsenic in solution she had said she had procured from some flypapers without even knowing what it was—for a cosmetic wash. Sir Jonathan had never heard of women using arsenic as a cosmetic. Here again was a subject to which he had given little attention. He was rather sorry that she had bought flypapers… there had been far too much in the press about the baby-farming case at Liverpool.… Still, commonsense must override rumour. And there was a beauty specialist to testify how arsenic was used in cosmetics—a pity she could not find that recipe.

He returned to the medical evidence. She was a frivolous and unfaithful wife, a negligent mother, a woman who was, in his opinion, scarcely worth the pains that must be taken to get her out of the horrible position into which her own folly had brought her; but was she a murderess? Certainly the strong point was the medical evidence; the Crown could not prove death from arsenic administered by the wife when the husband was an arsenic addict. The Crown would have almost to throw in the sponge; Sir Jonathan rather regretted that the passionate entreaties of Madame Dumont had persuaded his good nature to undertake something so distasteful, he had no wish to see a delicate-looking gentlewoman in the dock on any charge, and something so horrible.… As soon as May Tyler was free he intended to forget he had ever seen her; but now there were points in the case that continually obtruded upon his keen and well-trained mind, weary as he was.

The enmity of everyone about May Tyler, in particular the enmity of the brother, the will altered by the sick man at the last moment. "I suppose he had heard of that visit to London… yet… odd!" The selling up of everything at Stone Pynes by Richard Tyler a fortnight after his brother's death, the disappearance of the recipe for the face-wash that May Tyler had declared was somewhere in the house; the impossibility of sorting out confused and conflicting evidence as to the drugs the sick man had been taking. Even the doctors were contradictory and, in Sir Jonathan's opinion, baffling on this most important matter. What had the wretched man taken, and when had he taken it? No one seemed to know. The lawyer drew from the heap of papers the list of medicines administered during the last fortnight of John Tyler's illness and glanced at them half in contempt and half in despair. Surely the amount of arsenic found in the body might have been accounted for by all these various drugs?

It was merciful, especially considering his own fatigue, that the case was so simple that he would not be called upon to go into all these details accurately. Why, it would be impossible to do so!

The police had been careless—that Inspector Bigalow, for instance, why, he had taken no trouble at all to find out what was and was not in the house. So many people coming and going… that search when May Tyler had been unconscious, unconscious for a long time surely, a drug would not have been permissible in the circumstances…? He sighed, depressed despite his surroundings, neatly put together his papers and began to prepare the speech for the defence.

For a while he could not concentrate. A stupid and inappropriate sentence danced before his closed eyes, as if written in lightning fire. Two hundred and fifty bottles of medicine, three packets of arsenic found in the house… arsenic on the clothes, arsenic in the drinking vessels, arsenic in the slops—arsenic everywhere… Stone Pynes contaminated with arsenic, in the sinks, the closets, in the brown jug the dead man had taken to the office. How did either John Tyler or his wife procure so much poison?

Mr. Mark Steele, Q.C., advocate for the Crown, was considering the same evidence as that which Sir Jonathan Docwra found so unsatisfactory. He was not a lawyer of the same standing, nor a man of the same quality of character; but he was alert, able and intensely interested in his career. He did not resent the sensational publicity that the case had been surrounded with because this was, in every sense of the word, favourable to the Crown, and though he had no animus against the young woman on trial for her life, he felt a professional zeal in securing a conviction. It would not be easy because of the medical evidence; the doctors disagreed there and of course Sir Jonathan, a formidable opponent, would make the most of that and of the small quantity of arsenic found at the autopsy; such a small amount that it might easily have been the residue of one of the very many medicines the dead man had taken. Madeleine Smith's supposed victim's body had been found to contain seventy grains and here was less than half a grain, and Madeleine Smith had got off on a verdict of *non proven*.

Still, something might be done for the Crown. An atmosphere of hostility had been created against the prisoner, the story ran on those familiar lines so acceptable to the public—a betrayed husband, a frivolous, extravagant, faithless wife who further shocked morality by neglecting two young children, a woman who was a foreigner, who had kept herself apart and seemed to despise her neighbours and yet who had been cunning enough to carry on an intrigue with the most likely young scoundrel in the place; who had been crafty enough to arrange the visit to London, to the disreputable hotel. The police had done that part of the business very well. There was the waiter's evidence, the servants' evidence, the intercepted letters—even what she had said herself, talking and writing to Dr. Harman of her sin, her crime—expressions almost as useful as a confession, but not quite for she had maintained with an almost remote dignity that she knew nothing whatever as to the death of her husband, save that she had put at his request some white powder into some meat extract and given him some in a spoon. She believed this white powder to be strychnine and had often protested against his use of it and had allowed him to have it in compassion only. That was a stupid story for her to put up; a complete denial would have been better.

It was rather awkward for the Crown that the man seemed to have been an arsenic eater, but that could be got over Mr. Steele thought because it was an obscure subject of which even the doctors seemed to know little, and there was enough arsenic in the house to account both for Mr. Tyler's secret indulgence and for his wife's criminal intentions.

"She is probably as clever as the devil," he thought, looking with an unconscious disgust at the gloomy hotel room. "She knew he took the stuff and thought it would be an easy thing to give him a little more in her own way. But why was she such a fool as to let those servants see the flypapers soaking in the basin? And that intrigue—well, cleverly managed to a point, yet she made some bad slips there. I suppose like most of these criminals she's astute in the main but makes some clumsy mistakes."

He got the notes for his brief together with energy and concentrated zeal for his subject; the case seemed to him as it had seemed to Sir Jonathan Docwra, commonplace and sordid; he despised Manchester, the cotton brokers and merchants that formed the bulk of its wealthier citizens. In such an atmosphere it was difficult to imagine any agreeable existence or even any pleasant vices flourishing. He felt contempt for the press that had been so useful to him. It was grossly unjust that everyone should discuss the case before it had been tried—yet no one, not even the Recorder himself had appeared to be disturbed; even those in the city whom one would have supposed to have had a little public conscience had merely lifted their brows when Mr. Steele had pointed out how the case against May Tyler was being prejudiced before it was heard. Well, so much the better for him. If he could secure her conviction it would only rid the world of an extremely dangerous criminal.

Mr. Steele, even more definitely than Sir Jonathan, had a genuine horror of the type of woman May Tyler appeared to him to be. She outraged all his masculine conventions; married to a man with money and position who was by all accounts kind and indulgent to her until provoked beyond endurance (after all what was one blow in the face during a married life of many years?) and she had not only been unfaithful to him with the first rascal who had come along, but remained in his house playing a sinister part.

As to what this sinister part was, Mr. Steele did not know. Like his colleague, Sir Jonathan, he was baffled. The medical evidence would probably get her off... the man had been an arsenic eater. Somehow that would have to be put in the background, made light of... Mr. Steele did not know what witnesses the defence had on that subject. Had she done it? It was not his business to find out. He did not as a man, believe she had; as a lawyer he could make out a very specious case—the immorality first of all, then the debts, the looseness and extravagance of her life, her neglect of her children, the fact that she had no friends, that all the servants except the cook (whom no doubt she had bribed by passing her faked accounts), were against her, even the professional nurses disliking her, suspecting her, the brother-in-law, her natural protector, hating her bitterly.

Well, that was the intangible part of the evidence. As to the tangible there was practically none. The traces of arsenic found on her garments might have been accounted for by the fact that she had handled medicines for her husband that contained arsenic. And what could one do with a man who was continually dosing himself? Mr. Steele glanced once more at the list—so many "doses of private medicine".... Messrs. Joshua and Blunt had given a very garbled and, Mr. Steele thought, untruthful account of the drugs they had made up for Mr. Tyler. Then the arsenic in the packets—one mixed with soot, one with indigo, one pure arsenic labelled "cats" and found in a chocolate-box in her room....

Inspector Bigalow was a gift from heaven to Mr. Steele; he had only searched Stone Pynes himself several hours after Mr. Tyler's death and had accepted without protest the articles that Richard Tyler said he had found in his sister-in-law's room, accepted without demur the account of the brother-in-law, the friends, the servants as to the whole affair. Whereas, as Mr. Steele clearly saw, any one of those people might have been accused of the murder of John Tyler, especially the brother who had had the will altered so shortly before the death, who had sold up everything in the place before the trial so that further searches were impossible, who had undoubtedly given his sister-in-law a sleeping-draught that had kept her insensible for twenty-four hours and then searched her private drawers and boxes.... 'I wonder what Sir Jonathan will make of that?' thought Mr. Steele. It seemed to him a difficult piece of business for him to tackle, but perhaps he would not have to do so; perhaps Sir Jonathan, who, as he knew, was not very eager to undertake the case, who was worn out with the big London libel trial, who would be quite sure that May Tyler would get off on the medical evidence, would not take much trouble to build up the defence.

'There's the moral guilt,' Mr. Steele reminded himself. 'That will go a long way to making it easy for me. The newspapers have damned her in every issue, it reads already like a French serial....'

Then he allowed his mind to turn from the legal aspect of the affair (the only one that really concerned him) to the humanities behind it. What sort of people were these... the vulgarians, the cotton merchants and brokers, the American woman and her mother....? How had they all come to such a pass? And that house, now empty and locked up, Stone Pynes, in the suburb that these provincials had called "genteel" but that was now fast being overgrown by streets of offices and slums.

Arsenic everywhere... packets of arsenic in a chocolate-box... arsenic in solution in a scent bottle... traces of arsenic on aprons, handkerchiefs and dressing-gowns... servants gossiping, lying, contradicting one another... a young, pretty and, as it seemed, impassive woman, moving carelessly through an extravagant household... the brothers alike as he had been told—brutal common men with money and no idea how to spend it; the nurses who had come in more like vultures to watch over carrion than as "ministering angels".... The tag from the trite quotation made him laugh.

Well, he did not suppose that he would secure a conviction. The case was hardly worth considering in detail. He was glad that he did not have to do so. What a confusion… two hundred and fifty bottles of medicine at least the police had listed and that was not all.…

The prisoner could understand very little of what was happening about her; she had really never understood the world in which she lived, nor her own acceptance of the society into which she was born. To be in prison was not so much more grotesque than it had been to be at Stone Pynes. Everything here, as there, was to her out of focus. The life that had closed round her when she had married John Tyler had been as unexpected and as strange as the routine of the jail. She could not, though she repeated her plight over to herself, realize that this present pain and jeopardy was worse than her former pain and jeopardy.

She slept very little and the prison doctor, who was kind and sympathetic, gave her sleeping-draughts which further increased her apathy. She would be found innocent, of course, and she supposed that when she was acquitted she would be free. She and her mother would return to France or to Virginia—but she had been told that Richard was the trustee for the children, that he had sold everything at Stone Pynes, that the house was now as locked up and desolate as the ostentatious marble covered vault where her husband lay beside his father and mother. That part of her life had gone for ever and in the future lay some measure of freedom, but it had no zest or flavour. There was no large and stimulating passion to keep her animated.

She lay or sat exhausted on the narrow bed or the straight chair remembering nothing but the rules of good breeding—one must have control, one must not distress or torment other people by giving way, nor must one's dignity be affronted by the exposure of one's feelings to public scrutiny. This, out of all she had been taught, was all she remembered.

Her solicitor and her counsel often came to speak to her; she believed she had given the impression of being very stupid; there was so little she could really remember of what they had asked her; everything they wanted to know the truth about seemed entangled among the myriads of small falsehoods. The fact that she was innocent seemed to her sufficient. Mr. Martin thought so too, or pretended, out of kindness. Sir Jonathan put it more evasively, stressed everything on the medical evidence. In the bottle of solution that she had identified as containing the cosmetic she had made from the flypaper was one-hundredth part of a grain of arsenic, and the experts had remarked that it was scarcely sufficient to have produced a really good flypaper. There remained the packets of arsenic found in the chocolate-box, but the defence had gathered evidence that Mr. Tyler had been an arsenic eater.... May had been a little startled, even through her apathy—the white powders that she had thought strychnine... yes, that fitted in very well. Perhaps it was arsenic then that she had given him in the meat juice, but that need not lie on her mind as he had not taken it. It had been found in the extract. As for the spoonful—yes, that had come out of the package in his room—who had put it in hers?

She had been given a list of two hundred and fifty bottles of medicine, all opened and partially used, discovered in Stone Pynes; she read it through without it having much meaning to her; Mr. Martin blamed her listlessness, her mother, who was taking the affair with a tempestuous fury of anguish and courage, tried to rouse her, telling her she must rouse herself, fight—asking her who she thought were her enemies, for enemies there must undoubtedly be, Madame Dumont maintained.

May did not know—"Perhaps it's merely bad luck," she said. She could not answer her mother's probing questions about Jerome Thorne; she did not know why she had written to him, except that she had believed he would be kind; she would not talk of him, nor of the London visit.

Madame Dumont was not satisfied. She considered such reserve foolish, and yet she admitted herself quite at a loss with the behaviour of these Manchester cotton brokers of whom she spoke with the most anguished contempt. Why was Richard behaving so? On this subject May had nothing to say. This secret was safe because it was shared between herself and one other person who would always be silent.... Richard Tyler would never speak of the scene in the Pomona Rooms and neither would she; not even because she thought it would not be believed and Richard would overwhelm her with lies, but because of fastidiousness. She could now hardly credit what had happened in the empty bar; it seemed part of the ugly fantasy induced by the vulgar carnival, the orchestra played by invisible hands, the paltry and noisy festival.... Jerome Thorne also she put out of her mind; she could not get him clearly enough to understand anything about him. She moved bewildered and beset among mysteries and strangers, knowing only that she must keep her fortitude and not cry out.

She said little to her mother about her project for divorce; beyond telling Madame Dumont that she had gone to London to find some lawyer—"But why that hotel?" "I don't know, it was the first I saw." She said little to the priest who, on hearing of her faith, came to visit her in her cell. She admitted guilt in a large sense, the guilt of the Anglican marriage, of having disobeyed her husband, of having planned to divorce him, of having been rash and foolish in her behaviour towards Jerome Thorne. She was not allowed to see the children, and after a while ceased asking after them.

Lying in prison week after week, she heard of the proceedings of her case, brought to her by the solicitors, Sir Jonathan or her mother; she had no other friends—she was cut off and abandoned, and she wondered why. Everyone had deserted her... in what sort of society had she been moving, what kind of people were these among whom, for several years, she had mingled? The wonder of that oppressed her even more than the wonder of how she came to be in her present plight. The lost recipe for the face lotion bothered her; everyone seemed to attach so much importance to it; now it could never be found. She asked for the *Blue* Bible—"I should read it now"—but the prison authorities found the plain Bibles they provided more suitable.

How much longer before the trial? They had told her, of course, but she had forgotten. She knew nothing of English law; what her solicitors said to her she did not understand, thereby causing even her mother's anguished impatience. She roused herself to utter commonplaces that were spoken with an almost childish candour. To her mother, who was so seldom allowed to see her, she wrote, "I am feeling better on the whole, but my faith in human nature is at an end."

She found it difficult to attach any importance to what people said, the law, the Assizes, the judge. She was concentrating on gathering control, on being patient, on putting through this last phase of a martyrdom, of fixing her mind on the future when she would be free. What future? She saw it as a mirror of the past, in the shape of pictures of Paris in the spring-time with the tresses of laburnum and wisteria, the smooth green grass outside the lake and palace of Bagatelle and herself or her children, young, lightly clad, with parasols, moving gaily through the sunshine with friends on every hand.

She was still allowed her own clothes, but this hot, clumsy and ugly mourning seemed to her to belong to a stranger. She often stared down at her small hands lying on the dull bombazine, wondering to whom they belonged; it seemed hypocritical to wear the wedding ring; she showed some animation when she told Sir Jonathan that she would not have anything "brought up against John".

"How much do you know, Mrs. Tyler? His was a peculiar history."

"I don't want to know now. It would be useless, would it not? I know of the woman at Salford. He ought to have married her. There were others—then, his health—and the powders. Please, nothing of that."

"I shall keep out as much as I can; I fear you are being too generous."

"What *did* John die of?" she asked sadly.

"Gastro-enteritis. The problem is—what caused it?"

She looked at him vaguely; he reminded her more of the men whom she had met in Virginia than anyone whom she had met in Manchester; he used a courtesy that restored her bruised self-respect; but he was remote, aloof, almost unreal.

"The judge—what is the judge like? How strange to have a judge. If there could be a judge who knew everything."

Sir Jonathan thought of Lord Barnfield, the upright, austere, puritanical man, ambitious, cold, wholly absorbed in his profession and in intellectual pursuits, severe to harshness in his opinion of human frailty, with a horror amounting to morbidity of unchaste women; May Tyler's counsel again regretted that she was not a good and faithful wife, or at least that another judge was not taking the case, he was sorry for his own sake, too, the old tag tormented him—"Lilies that fester, smell worse than weeds."

"Please, Mrs. Tyler, if you would be frank about that hotel visit...."

"I wanted to find some lawyers—about a divorce."

"I know. But who was helping you? How did you come to such a place as the Hotel Mentone? Who was the other man, not Thorne, the waiter saw you with, but can't identify?"

"There was no one, the waiter is mistaken." May lied like a child, obstinately, unconvincingly. "I wanted a divorce—I came up to London—walking about I saw that hotel—Mr. Thorne was there by chance. I wrote to him because I had no friends, no money. Amelia Chorley advised me to do so...."

Sir Jonathan sighed; he knew that had she looked even more childish than she did that story would never have been believed—in Manchester.

"Mrs. Tyler, what—I ask again—exactly do you mean by your sin—your crime?"

"The marriage was the first—the second, the trying to get a divorce—it would have ruined John, and the children. I ought to have gone on enduring it."

"No doubt it was your duty to do so, Mrs. Tyler, according to the laws of this country you were married to this man, but what makes *you* say—'I ought to have gone on enduring it'?"

"Because I wanted to marry him once, I was part of it—the whole mistake. I ought to pay, too." She closed her eyes, recalling Richard at the Pomona Rooms; at first she had leaned towards him, as if swept by a dark wind. "I deserve my punishment," she added, with a smile so incongruous that Sir Jonathan wondered—'unstable in her mind?'

He made an unconscious gesture, as if washing his hands; the rest of his conversation was official; Lord Barnfield had arrived in Manchester—Mr. Martin would explain to the prisoner, so little versed in English law, the use of a Grand Jury.

"The Grand Jury," said Mr. Martin, "have been summoned to consider whether the magistrates were justified, Mrs. Tyler, in committing you, Case No. 24, on the charge set forth in that calendar, the charge of murder. The judge will have the depositions of the witnesses of the prosecution as given at the magisterial inquiry, and as the defence was reserved the question, and the only question for the Grand Jury, will be whether the evidence of those witnesses for the Crown showed sufficient grounds for justifying the Crown in exposing you to the trouble and risk of a trial by jury upon the specific charge of murder upon which you are indicted."

Mr. Martin was at pains to explain to his apathetic client that the functions of a Grand Jury, one of the great bulwarks of British law, were such as make it necessary that their judgment should be left absolutely unfettered by any constraint whatsoever. "The Grand Jury must consist of not less than twelve and not more than twenty-three men, and is selected out of persons of sufficiently high rank in the county to make them as free as possible from any chance of being influenced by any local feelings on the one hand or any restraint by the Crown on the other."

"I shall then be free immediately," remarked May without either animation or excitement.

Mr. Martin was also inclined to think the Grand Jury would not return a true bill. May asked if her mother might be allowed to see her and that they might make together arrangements for instantly leaving the country; she could not think of anything but that escape, from the prison, from England, and when Mr. Martin called her attention to a long written list of all the bottles of medicine and patent food found in Stone Pynes and begged she would study it, she took no heed, but left it lying on the small table where the wardress every night, out of consideration for her prisoner's health, left a small cup of cold milk that was always there in the morning, untouched and sour.

The Grand Jury assembled in the Manchester Assize Hall. Everything was orderly and had the dignity of long established routine; the journalists were present, but subdued and silent, the formal and dignified proceedings had the air of a symbolic drama, but little concerned with real life. No one expected that the Tyler drama would yield much further excitement or sensation. Nothing was likely to come out in open court that had not already been debated violently in the newspapers, drawing-rooms, bar parlours, clubs and streets of Manchester. Everyone thought they knew all it was possible to know about the domestic life of John Tyler who had undoubtedly poisoned himself by over-indulgence in drug taking, and the foolish, frivolous and, at the same time, aloof and proud young woman who had been stupid enough to buy flypapers and make cosmetics from them at the same time as she was involved in an intrigue with Jerome Thorne. That young man was not in court, but as he was a man who was frequently concerned in illicit sex affairs, and as there was not the least suspicion that he had been concerned in any plot to murder John Tyler, his absence was the less regretted.

The public of Manchester, on the day that the Assizes opened were in the state of the tyrant who has tortured his victim to the limit and must now give up this pleasure as the victim is to be snatched from him. The trial, indeed, would be somewhat of an anti-climax since it would, even shrewd experts like the Recorder of the city had said, certainly be short, certainly produce no different witnesses and probably much less dramatic evidence than had been already produced, and certainly would end by the curtain falling forever on the story of Stone Pynes.

May Tyler had her own lawyers in New York; her stepfather was known to be coming to England; she had far away but powerful relatives and friends; once she had been acquitted it would be impossible even to discuss her case for fear of libel actions. So the gossips regretfully licked their lips over the scandal that was almost at an end.

The citizens of Manchester until now had not given any thought to the personality of the judge, Lord Barnfield. As soon as he arrived in Manchester he was discussed; he had a reputation for the highest sagacity and integrity, was considered a cold man of a scientific bent, regarded as one of the most lucid and penetrating intellects on the bench; so far no case in which he had ever been concerned had provided much drama for the spectators. He had written several books, half rationalist, half philosophical, that had pleased a small number of highly educated and intensively trained men of his own type. He was unmarried and had lived a life so secluded from all save formalities that even those friends who considered themselves his intimates knew very little about him. He was greatly respected, but certainly not liked and, in an unaccountable way, not much esteemed. No one had any reason for believing anything but what was extremely favourable about him; there had never been the slightest reproach on either his private or public conduct, and yet even those who were obliged to pay tribute to his obvious virtues did so in a fashion slightly resentful. It had been felt in Manchester that the fact that Lord Barnfield would take the Assizes would rob them of much of the excitement they might have had from another type of judge. This man seemed to chill the very atmosphere in which he moved and to reduce everyone about him to a depressed and timid condition. The vulgar and flaming melodrama that gutter journalism had been able to make of May Tyler's story would disappear, even those most delighted by it were sure, in the grim, juridical atmosphere that the precise, learned and unemotional judge would give to the case. Indeed, among those who whispered at the back of the Assize Court were many who pessimistically declared that they were certain Lord Barnfield would charge the jury not to bring in a true bill, and then all the palatable tragedy that had absorbed the great city for nearly three months would disappear.

Some of the journalists had already written their copy about the young and beautiful woman who should now receive all the homage due to her virtue and sufferings; speculations were being made as to whom she would marry—not Thorne, of course… after this she would be able to do far better, and as for the scandal, no one supposed for a moment that a Q.C. like Sir Jonathan would not be able to tear up the usual evidence of the usual waiter, and rapidly to dispose of such a common type of vulgar Don Juan as every other male in Manchester knew Thorne to be.

The Judge addressed the Grand Jury, and his words were such as everyone had expected. His voice was dry and increased the dullness of his demeanour, he was so scrupulous that of course he would do all he could to allay the suspicions that had been directed, for very little reason when people of commonsense looked into the matter, against May Tyler. As his speech would be reported in the papers, and as these papers would be read by the jurymen who would act as May

Tyler's judges, he would, of course, be extremely careful. He would show that his own mind was absolutely open and that he had formed no opinion of his own. Therefore his opening words were heard with but little interest.

Turning first to the Grand Jury composed of well-to-do citizens of Manchester, among whom was the mayor and some opulent merchants who had occasionally condescended to have the Tylers at their tables, Mr. Justice Barnfield began his monotonous discourse.

"I refer to the case of May Tyler who is charged with the wilful murder of her husband, John Tyler."

He made one or two other formal remarks that caused his audience to shrink into themselves with the foreboding sense that a long period of boredom was before them, then as the hard voice crept on and on, seeming to wind round and round the room, the reporters, the men on the Grand Jury, those in the body of the hall glanced at one another as men will when trying to see if what they have noticed themselves has been noticed by others.

"I believe this case," said Lord Barnfield, "is one that has excited very great attention in this country and certainly if the prisoner is guilty of the crime alleged to her in the charge, it is the most cruel and horrible murder that could be committed. The case is one which will, no doubt, occupy a very considerable time and as I have said, it has attracted a good deal of attention. I will speak very shortly on the nature of the circumstances and the nature of the case, because to anyone who has been accustomed to the transaction of criminal business it is perfectly obvious that the case is one in which every part of the allegations will be vigorously contradicted and in which the circumstances will be questioned. I know not, of course, what the evidence may be which may be set up for Mrs. Tyler, but it is quite possible that evidence may be given on her behalf which may be of very great importance. You have nothing to do with that, however, and all I have to say is to point out to you, very briefly, the facts apparently proved by the prosecution as far as they bear on the case."

All present who had read numerous versions of this drama and found them contradictory, listened with keen attention as to what the brilliant legal mind of the judge had made of the tangled story.

"Gentlemen, I think you know Mrs. Tyler's husband was a cotton merchant in the city, and although these matters are hardly contested, let me say he *appears* to have been unhappy enough to have had an unfaithful wife. Whatever may be thought of the rest of the case, letters are produced which make it very difficult not to believe, in fact I should think it almost necessary to admit, that she was carrying on an adulterous intrigue. There were many violent quarrels between Mrs. Tyler and her husband. Some time after one of these quarrels, suspicious circumstances were noted. For one thing, she put into water a certain quantity of flypapers which contained arsenic. These papers, which nobody can have proper occasion to use, except it be to kill flies, were found soaking in water. This water would have become impregnated with arsenic and might have been used for poisoning. A good many incidents occurred, then there were bodily symptoms in Mr. Tyler, the nature of which can be explained to you by the medical men. Soon after he was taken very ill a very striking and remarkable incident happened, to which your attention will be directed. Mrs. Tyler gave one of her servants—a nurse—a letter addressed to her friend, Mr. Thorne, which she wished to be posted. The servant went out with a child, whom she called the baby, and she gave it the letter to hold. The child carried it for some distance and dropped it into a puddle. The nurse picked it up and then it was dirty. She then went to the post office with the intention, as she said, of getting a new envelope and re-directing it. However, when she got to the post office she opened the letter and in doing so she noticed some expressions which attracted her attention—which, indeed, would have attracted anyone's attention.

The nurse did not post the letter but gave it to Mr. Tyler's brother; there can hardly be any doubt that the letter implied in its terms an adulterous connection between Mrs. Tyler and Mr. Thorne, then in addition to that, there are in that letter expressions which there may be many ways of reading. It contained these expressions very nearly in the first lines. 'He is sick unto death…' the reference apparently being to Mr. Tyler. This, of course, means that Mr. Tyler was sick unto death when at the time it did not appear that anyone had told her that he was in danger—a circumstance of the greatest possible suspicion. It shows, too, the terms on which she was with Mr. Thorne. There is evidence to show that she had been to London and met a gentleman. There are some strange peculiarities about that part of the story which I will leave out. She had been to London and there met Mr. Thorne with whom she had stayed on two occasions during her absence from home. Of course, if that is proved, there can be no doubt as to what her relations with him were, but certainly if she stood in those relations to him—I hardly know how to put it otherwise than this—that if a woman does carry on an adulterous intrigue with another man it may supply every sort of motive for murder—that of saving her own reputation, that of breaking through the connection which under such circumstances one would think would be dreadfully painful. It certainly may quite well supply—I won't go further—a very strong motive why she should wish to get rid of her husband. Gentlemen, these matters will be brought before you, and you will have to consider them.

"After this, Mr. Tyler appears to have got worse. He had but a short time to live. There will be a good deal of evidence as to the different things of which he partook. I will pass over very lightly indeed what was found immediately after his death, a variety of things were found which rendered it natural to suppose he had been poisoned. There was what I have already mentioned, the flypapers; but I will also mention that there were several things which the medical men say were found to contain arsenic. There was the bottle of meat juice that contained arsenic. There was a bottle of brandy and other things, all of which were said to have arsenic in them. In the course of the *post mortem* examination it appeared that they found arsenic in a number of the parts of the body, but I am speaking entirely from memory. That, of course, is a matter of the utmost suspicion. It appears the wife administered the medicine to him until they called in a nurse. There were several professional nurses, but I don't think they were called in until a day or two before his death. It was by then that the medicine and other things were found.

"After the death, after the examination of the man himself, I may tell you that they made a search through the house and they found a variety of things, some of them contained arsenic. There were some things kept in a chocolate-box which contained arsenic, and there was in addition (I hardly know what to call it) some kind of stuff which apparently contained arsenic because there was the word 'Poison' on it, and afterwards, like a sort of postscript written in ink, the words 'for cats' so as to make it read 'Poison for cats'.

"That is a very bare outline of the case, and I have made it a very bare outline because you have to consider, not whether she is guilty or not guilty, but whether there is sufficient evidence to put her on her trial for poisoning her husband. I may sum it all up in a very few words which, however, may be sufficient to guide you in your inquiries. It seems that a state of things existed between her and her husband and Mr. Thorne which might operate as a strong motive to her to get rid of him. It appears she had nursed him very nearly the whole of his illness, nursed and administered to him the food and medicine which he took. It appears, I say again it is in evidence, though you have not evidence on the other side and do not know what may be put in—but certainly there is evidence that poison was found in various parts of his body and the symptoms of disease from which he suffered were symptoms of arsenic poisoning. If after that you think it desirable that the matter should have further investigation, you will find a true bill against the prisoner."

The judge's charge to the Grand Jury was like the ringing-up of a curtain on a new act of the melodrama that had seemed exhausted by its own stupid violence. There had been a medley of obscure and uninteresting figures turning over with mutual contradiction the details of the infidelity of the little American married to a petty cotton merchant who had dosed himself once too often with a secret drug. Intelligent people had thus understood the affair from the first, and even those by no means intelligent had begun to realize that there was nothing but conjecture and gossip in the whole case. The journalists might do their best and had done very well indeed in turning over every possible aspect of May Tyler's life. As a woman in prison, as a suspect murderess of her husband, as a woman who had dared to take a lover, she was an object of intense interest, and there was after all very little to feed this interest.

The journalists could write about the flypapers and packets of arsenic, and what the nurse had said, and what the parlourmaid had said, and what the brother had said, and the visit to London and the matrimonial quarrels, but after all there was very little in it and by the time that Lord Barnfield made his charge to the Grand Jury everyone was conscious of raking over ashes. The woman was almost certainly not a murderess. Many people in Manchester knew, as a matter of fact, that she was neither loose living nor extravagant. She had, on the contrary, kept herself apart and even romantic episodes with Jerome Thorne seemed scarcely proved and were not at all in character with the cool and courteous gentlewoman who had offended most of them by her indifference to their attentions or their society. Men and women disliked her for being solitary, for being superior, for being reserved;

and there had been a good deal of malicious pleasure in seeing her so suddenly and so violently pulled down—but nearly three months scavenging into the affairs of May Tyler had yielded little result and everyone, those who understood a little and pitied a little, those who disdained the whole affair, and those who wanted to believe the most outrageous and gruesome incidents the Midland journalists could invent, were alike convinced that there was soon going to be an end of the story of May Tyler, and a flat end, too. But now a figure of whom no one had thought, save in his symbolic aspect of routine justice, had come upon the stage and suddenly everyone was alert, whispering, excited. From the moment that the judge's speech was read in the evening papers, everyone concerned in the case sprang into a brisker life, while the fatigue and apathy of those principally engaged (for by now every detail had been so constantly conned over that exhaustion had taken the place of the zeal of either vindictiveness or honest detailing) was galvanized by a charge to the Grand Jury that was in essence a speech for the Crown.

Mr. Steele read it with amazement and ran over it with a lawyer's eye. It was inaccurate, prejudiced, poorly expressed and showed that the judge had not read much of the evidence and that he was almost passionately biased against the prisoner. Why? Mr. Steele wondered. The old man had a fine, lucid brain, harsh, yes, but he had never been known to be ferocious or careless… "Old man?" Mr. Steele caught himself up; the judge was still in what was kindly termed "the prime of life"—fifty-eight years of age.

'There must be something more in the case than I found out,' he mused with chagrin, stung by his sense of his own ineptitude. He did not want the case handed him on a platter as it would be before a judge who spoke like this. 'He's made up his mind already,' reflected Mr. Steele, and again asked himself why? These little provincial people, what can they be to him? How he stresses the infidelity, a rigid man of puritanical life… but his animus seems almost personal. He's not seen her… perhaps if he does he will be less virulent. Mr. Steele was not at all inclined himself to face the prospect of May Tyler being hanged. He believed, on the evidence, that he had taken no great trouble to analyse, that she might be innocent, and though he regarded her with dislike because she had broken that unwritten law that men most value, he did not wish to see one so slight, foolish and in a way harmless, brought to the gallows.… 'But she won't be,' he said to himself, comfortably looking over his papers again with an eye to discover on what the judge had founded his rancour. 'She won't be—there's the medical evidence, hardly any arsenic at all in the bottle of her cosmetic, hardly any arsenic in the body, and the man a confirmed arsenic eater.'

Sir Jonathan had heard with equal amazement Lord Barnfield's speech. With him it caused a deeper uneasiness than it had with Mr. Steele. He was a conscientious man who felt his responsibilities keenly. He had not got up the case as carefully as he might have done had he not been so sure of an acquittal. He turned over in an acute but fatigued mind what could be the possible meaning of the ferocity—he used that word deliberately—of the judge who came from such another world, who would soon return to it, to whom the Tylers and all their friends, acquaintances and servants could not be anything but insignificant provincials. 'And he has,' Sir Jonathan pondered as Mr. Steele pondered, 'not even seen her.'

Sir Jonathan wished there was time for him to go into the evidence more carefully. It was all confused and obviously most of these people had been lying; the pompous lies of the police, anxious to exaggerate their own authority, the spiteful lies of the servants who wished to whip up a melodrama, the vindictive lies of the so-called friends. Sir Jonathan pulled himself up. Why was everybody lying about this seemingly harmless woman? She had lived many years in Manchester and there was nothing against her, nothing whatever; he had been at pains to discover that. He had been impressed both by the good breeding and the devout sincerity of Madame Dumont. He had understood, being himself of that class, how these frivolous, aristocratic and thoughtless women had been trapped by their own negligent gaiety into this marriage with a vulgarian—a detestable man, Sir Jonathan thought, a man for whom he had not the least sympathy. Yet he was what his fellow citizens termed a good fellow, and seemed to have been much liked and had had many partisans... well, they were all the same class, gross, low minded, spiteful.

Yes, they had been spiteful towards May Tyler and her mother and they had seized hold of her foolishness in buying flypapers and the coincidence of the wretched man's furtive vice to fasten on her a charge of murder. He had found the story, since Madame Dumont had first come to him with the case, ludicrous. Now he found it appalling.

All these people talking, lying; all these bottles of medicine, all this dosing, plastering and blistering, all these jugs and bottles and pans of invalid food...

He visited his client, he noticed that she had still lying beside the few papers on her deal table, the list of the bottles of medicine found in Stone Pynes. She asked for the "Blue Bible".

"You mustn't concern yourself with that," he said kindly, "but tell me if you can of more important matters."

But May Tyler knew of no more important matters.

He asked her what she was thinking of? She replied that she felt utterly forsaken, as if everybody had turned their hand against her.... The reading of the judge's speech in the papers had completed her sense of fearful solitude... nothing remained but the hope of maintaining some fortitude.

Sir Jonathan again spoke to her about Thorne.

"That is not properly understood," she replied in great agitation.

Sir Jonathan tried, with melancholy firmness, to keep her to the point. "It is admitted there is evidence, we cannot deny it, it will make a very bad impression. You must remember that the jury are ignorant tradesmen and workmen. They are extremely respectable. They will consider your conduct so disgraceful that you will be greatly prejudiced in their eyes...." And then the lawyer in him overcoming the Catholic and the gentleman, he demanded, "Why did you admit it? Why did you send those letters, writing to him even when the police were in the house?"

She looked at him, frowning like a child trying to understand an adult's speech. "I thought Amelia Chorley was—not my friend, but well-disposed towards me. She advised me to write to Mr. Thorne. I have told you so often."

"Could you not discern the sarcasm of this vile woman?" demanded Sir Jonathan.

"No," replied May and smiled, as if asking pardon for her fault.

He kept both his patience and his compassion well in hand. Once more he went over the old ground, the judge's hostility had altered everything. "This visit to London, could it not have been contrived with more discretion? Where is this miserable man who has been your undoing?"

May Tyler shook her head. "I know nothing. He didn't answer my last letters. I thought he would have been a true friend to me in the little I asked of him. I needed only some advice, a small sum of money.... I wanted to cable to my New York lawyers and to my mother. I was quite forsaken in that house...." She suddenly smiled again. "This is no more a prison to me than Stone Pynes was for years."

This manner of talk made Sir Jonathan uneasy, both as a Christian and a lawyer. "I wish to bring out in evidence," he warned her, "the fact that your husband was keeping a woman who named herself Dora Lestrange and four children that he had had by her. That, at least, will balance your misconduct in the eyes of the jury. Once more, I ask your permission. The judge's attitude is serious."

"That is one thing I can do," she said, "to make amends for my sins. I will not have John's affairs and those of that poor woman brought up in court. You must manage your defence, sir, without that…" and she asked with an interest that irritated Sir Jonathan if Mrs. Lestrange was being looked after, if her husband had left her and her children any provision.

The lawyer was confounded by so difficult a client. He felt, sensitive as he was to human character and behaviour, that she was concealing something from him. He asked her outright why she had written to the doctor about her "sin", why, as she had not been discovered, she had so readily betrayed herself. He could not as a Christian urge that she should have been sly as well as unfaithful, but as a man of the world and as her barrister he was bound to point out the almost infantile folly of her conduct. But May's answers were hesitant and evasive. She appeared either not to understand what he meant or to be determined not to answer clearly. Her insistence that her sin was her attempt to get a divorce in face of her wifely duties and her hereditary faith was to the lawyer exasperating in face of the judge's hostility. He pointed to the evening papers.

"You must understand Lord Barnfield's attitude…."

"But he is a judge—a stranger—what reason could he have to be—against me?"

Richard Tyler had been in the Assize Court and listened to Lord Barnfield's charge to the Grand Jury; he had watched the universal surprise and excitement and gone home quickly to the dingy tidy chambers that Lizzie Burt kept for him and sat down to think over this change in the situation. He saw himself faced by a need for sudden decision. With the judge in this mood there was just a chance that she would be—he could not finish the sentence in his mind—found guilty. He wrote "Guilty" on a piece of paper on the desk ready to his hand, then tore it up. But no, the charge was too flimsy.... He inwardly marvelled that even with the aid of the journalists the matter had gone so far. In common with the great majority he had expected the Grand Jury to refuse a true bill. He had expected a dull ending to this violent episode in his life, that he would be left with John's small fortune, with John's two families, with John's debts, with he did not care to surmise what tormented thoughts; and May, having been pulled down and despoiled of all her dignity, modesty and pride, would go abroad with her rich mother, casting off the scoundrel Thorne, of course, and making no doubt a splendid marriage on the strength of her mother's fortune and position, and her own notoriety. But now things looked different, and what was he to do? To continue his course of putting on her the guilt of murder and letting judge, jury and lawyers decide among themselves how far he lied, or should he withdraw, contradict himself, at least soften his evidence and give his sister-in-law the best chance he could? Whatever happened, she would undergo a severe punishment before the staring, jostling crowds of Manchester; she would have to stand on trial for her life. Was not that enough to satisfy Richard Tyler for the evening at the Pomona Rooms and the knowledge that this candid-eyed creature had made a fool of him with a cheap rascal?

Richard soon decided that it was not enough. His cruelty had increased with indulgence. He was more determined than before to have the last ounce of revenge out of this extraordinary affair where events had turned so oddly in favour of his design. He had hardly planned it, everything seemed to have fallen into place so easily; she was a foreigner and a stranger, she had no friends.... Thorne was a scoundrel, she had long been disliked by the servants. By some extraordinary coincidence she had bought flypapers, excusing herself by talk of a cosmetic wash. Richard believed that this was true, he also was certain that she would never be able to find the recipe for the cosmetic. He knew her so well—and here again when he had come to this conclusion he was confounded—knew her so well yet she had been able to intrigue with Thorne under his very nose, under his watchful gloating eyes, with spies set about her by her husband. Of course he did not know her well, and why was he so certain that she was not a murderess? At least he would—and his soul that could not long remain unbared, took refuge in a platitude—"he would let justice take its course".

It would be a satisfaction to stand in the witness-box and tell as many damaging lies as he could about May Tyler. He was a capable business man and a realist, and he did not neglect the practical side of the matter. He was well aware of the dangers of going too far, but he had a strong suspicion that the case had been already so confounded and debated and become so complicated through carelessly taken evidence, lost evidence, false evidence and the helpless position of the prisoner, that the truth, or even any particle of the truth, it would be almost impossible for anyone to find.

The judge, now, they called him a man with a remarkable legal mind, but Richard knew that his brief account of the case had been totally inaccurate, and what did all these details matter—who moved bottles of medicine from this room to that, what the dying man's symptoms were, how many times the nurses gave him meat, jelly or chicken broth.... The main points were, as Richard could clearly see, the unfaithful wife quarrelling bitterly with an outraged husband, a house full of arsenic, a man suddenly ill, a wife nursing him and then arsenic in the body. That would be enough—the quarrel, the lover, the arsenic....

Richard was not sure whether or not he wished May Tyler to be hanged. He had not sufficient imagination to gauge what his feelings might be in the event of her being condemned to death. He might go as far as he would, he might enjoy his sport punishing her, torturing her, bring her down as low as a woman could be brought, and yet have no guilt or even remorse on his mind. 'For she will be,' he mused, leaning back in his chair with a sigh, 'acquitted on the medical evidence...' but the trial might be a long torment.

He had heard in common with many of his fellow business men that there was a strong dislike between the judge and the counsel for the defence. There was high political feeling all over the country on the question of Irish Home Rule; Sir Jonathan, as a Catholic and a man of partial Irish birth, had brilliantly undertaken the defence of some of the Home Rule leaders before the Commission set up to investigate an alleged forged letter to *The Times*. Not only had Sir Jonathan been exhausted by the strain of this long investigation, but the judge, Lord Barnfield, had been on the other side and had shown himself passionately partisan; not while the inquiry was taking place, then he had maintained his usual cool decorum, but in his club and among his friends he had expressed himself with pointed sarcasm against the Home Rulers, so openly that it was now common talk even among the people with whom Richard Tyler mingled in Manchester. All this would go against her, or so Richard Tyler thought, judging these great men to be no better than himself, unless (and here he wondered) she, the woman in the dock, roused any compassion. For himself, obsessed by his hatred, this seemed impossible. Nobody could feel any compassion for such a woman surely... but he admitted reluctantly that there was a possibility that these other men might feel for her as he had felt when he had seen her first in Paris, many years ago, as he had felt at the Pomona carnival.

This reflection salved his conscience a little; these legal men would no doubt be secretly her champions, they would see that she was not hanged and he could indulge his lust for vengeance, without taking on himself the risk of sending a woman to the gallows.

"She'll get off," he said partly in relief, partly in disgust, "on the medical evidence."

"The medical evidence" was the catchword of the case; everyone was using it; Richard felt his head reel, his hands cold, he curtly dismissed Lizzie Burt, so eager to comment on the reports in the evening papers, and sat alone with his bewilderment.

Who had been on the bench to-day?

He saw himself there enlarged, bloated beyond recognition, robed in scarlet and ermine, wearing a wig with stiff powdered curls, denouncing May Tyler, not the great lawyer, the judge who inspired awe and respect, but himself, Richard Tyler, swollen with fury, with lust, with desire for revenge, denouncing the woman who had cheated him; he, a small, mean devil, had watched with fear and horror, a large, grand devil whom he had evoked. There he was, the incarnate form of all his own secret hatreds, set up on high, all bowing and trembling before him—the judge.

Lord Barnfield also sat quiet in an easy chair, and sagged wearily, allowing his thoughts to race aimlessly while the books his secretary had unpacked lay untouched on the table; he made a movement, as if pulling something to pieces, then sank back again. No books to-night, no cool reasoning, no Puritanical moralists, no legal treatises; an enemy (and he had many) had once dared to say to him, "How much you've missed, Barnfield."

An ascetic, one who had successfully suppressed half of his nature, the gross vile half, what had he missed? Passion, lust, pleasure, he had conquered them, despised them always—now, he was nearly sixty years of age, no fear of temptation. No hope of temptation, all lost, gone, vanished… no secret meeting in the Hotel Mentone for him, no woman running secretly to his arms, no woman to write to him, to lie and poison for him… an adulteress… perhaps a murderess… to be destroyed… to be hanged… to have the breath choked out of her, while he, the judge, drank his wine, and read his tomes.

He had not more than glanced at the case against her; adultery, that doomed her… what was she like? Fair, they said, and small… foolish, too… Sir Jonathan would have some difficulty with her… a Catholic, the Judge despised Catholics for their bigotry and arrogance.

How did Sir Jonathan like defending a Catholic woman on a charge of murder?

Lord Barnfield turned to his books, dashed them aside like Faust… too late… and no devil's bargain possible now… his mind dwelt on the small, disreputable hotel, the furtive meetings, the hushed meal, the locked bedroom and the young man (ah, *young*!) taking to his arms the adulteress—fair, did they not say, small, twenty-five years old? "What I would have given…."

He smiled with contempt at his own plight; the long struggle to get where he was had left him dry, grey, barren of all the warmer humanities; but the thick lips, the fleshy nose of the sensualist were not wholly disguised, he held his enemy down, but he had not conquered—not yet, you old, righteous man, you judge who loathes criminal women? How dare they disturb him? *She* would not; he would see to that, he would observe her coldly, with detached justice… 'What I would have given….' 'Why did not you take it?—When you could have done, so easily? A mistress, a wife, little, bought women in hidden places….' 'Because I was too proud, too ambitious, too much the Puritan, because I thought of nothing but being—the Judge.'

Since she had read his speech in the papers the prisoner had thought of little but the Judge. The word itself was one of terror; early childhood memories of the day of judgment and of doom were revived; she brooded over this unknown and dreadful personage who, as it appeared to her, had her fate entirely in his hands. She took little heed of those who came and went in her cell. Her demeanour was so abstracted that some thought her callous and others half imbecile.

Her lawyers came and went, the doctors came and went, there were the wardresses, and now and then her mother, although her only tears were for her mother's anguish no one concerned her much. They understood, she knew, nothing of her story, nothing of the emotions that had made her the wife of John Tyler and that now had made her accused of his murder. This was a fantasy with which none but herself could deal. She had but few resources with which to struggle against the confused figments of her own dulled imagination; neither training, nor philosophy, nor religion, nor any great love.

She discovered now, with an aloof curiosity, that she had never loved or been loved save by her mother; interested, peering, prying faces came up from the past and mocked her with sneers... to the most harmless of them she had been nothing but an object of compassion—to her own servant, Mrs. Pilch, to the pariah woman in Salford, perhaps to Rose Bernier her mother's servant—a creature to be pitied? What had she been to Jerome Thorne? Everything about that was misunderstood. She could not speak of it, nor of Richard, such things were not for daylight. Jerome Thorne had disappeared into the confusion which was now one to her with the night of carnival at the Pomona Rooms. Everyone she had ever known appeared intermingled in a masked dance, where parti-coloured garments flapped in bewildering fashion round dancing figures who now and then pulled aside their masks to leer, or pry at her, and out of all this confusion whirled and rose with satanic power the figure of the Judge.... "At last, I am to be *judged?*"

He was much as she had expected him. She heard the trumpets as if they sounded on the day of judgment. She saw, amid a dazzle, the man in scarlet and ermine enthroned high above the crowd, disguised as the maskers had been by the garments of another age, the strange stiff curls of the floured and pomaded wig falling either side of his withered face.

He was staring at her with the same intensity that she was staring at him. To him also there was but one person in the packed court, and that was the young woman who stood in the dock.

May was as regardless as the judge of the panting sighs of excitement, of the staring eyes peering through the gold mother-of-pearl and ivory opera glasses, the stir and soft trample of the press of people who had come to see this cruel comedy played out. She had been allowed as a great concession that many objected to, a seat. She had risen as the judge had entered, and both the old man and the young woman stood for a barely perceptible second gazing thus at one another. Strangers until now, only knowing of the existence of one another since a few weeks on his part, a few days on hers, but now all absorbed each in the other.

He saw her too exactly as he had imagined her. Fair, delicate, lovely with a fragility that could only be compared to the most delicate things he had ever seen—early spring lilies or breaking foam on a summer sea—clad in heavy and unbecoming black for the man whom she was charged with murdering. Their common curiosity was so intense that it raised them above the moment and apart from the issue at stake.

When the judge sat down he was so obviously moved that the lawyers looked at him with a sharp scrutiny, not untinged with apprehension. They were jealous for an abstraction—the dignity of the law. His charge to the Grand Jury had been odd. There must be some reason surely for a man so eminent, so distinguished, so notable for his dignified detachment and reserve, thus exposing himself? And the legal men glanced sharply at the prisoner, wondering a little at the woman and the case even while they laid out their papers and whispered to one another.

The prisoner was charged. She wore a veil edged with crape; as the wardress touched her elbow she put this aside and answered "Not guilty." The names of the jury were read over. They were small tradespeople of Manchester. All peered with inquisitive eagerness at the young woman described as "May Tyler, aged twenty-six, of no occupation, well educated, committed by the Grand Jury and the coroner for having feloniously, wilfully and of malice aforethought killed and murdered one John Tyler."

Mr. Steele rose to make the opening statement for the prosecution. The witnesses were requested to leave the court but Richard Tyler was allowed to remain. May saw him in the well of the court as she saw the women who had sat at her table and chattered with her over her tea cups in their bright summer dresses with their luncheon baskets gently poised on their knees, looking at her, staring, whispering together, peering, criticizing. Richard meant no more to her than did any of these. The only person who mattered was the judge. She looked at him again as the rabbit may look at the rattlesnake; a heavy jowled man with small eyes, some nobility of the brow and a gross mouth, the face expressionless, trained to complete secrecy, but looking at her steadily with eyes that seemed to peer from a mask as Richard's eyes had seemed to peer from a mask on the night of the Pomona carnival.

Mr. Steele's voice rose and fell like a monotonous sound in the background; she heard it without understanding. He was talking of herself, of her husband, of her children, of their life... none of it seemed to coincide with what she remembered of that life. There was the visit to London, there was the quarrel, there was mention of a Manchester gentleman, a cotton broker, "whose name cannot possibly be kept out of the case—a gentleman named Thorne." She heard Mr. Steele say they lived there together as man and wife in a London hotel, went out together and left together, he paying the bill....

She made a little movement at that, but she had been schooled by Sir Jonathan to keep silent, as he would speak for her—of course, the truth would come out....

Mr. Steele went on. She heard the description of how she had tried to leave the house and been brought back, how she had been struck in the face and how the doctor had tried to make peace between her husband and herself; now they were talking about the illness and the wearisome horror of that fortnight was described again. Now he was talking about the flypapers and who had seen them and what she had done with them, and she took little heed for she could not understand... it was all a dancing confusion.... She looked as the wardress drew her attention to a paper she had in her hand. It had been put there when she had gone up the narrow stairs to the dock. It was the list of two hundred and fifty bottles of medicine found in the house after her husband's death. Sir Jonathan had made marks on certain items that he wished to draw her attention to... she looked at them now, and the figures and the letters moved about into twisting patterns.

Tumblers... arsenic mixed with charcoal... handkerchief, black-stained with charcoal... outside marked arsenic... bottle labelled solution of morphia... bottle no label... box of crystals... bedding from bedroom in which deceased died... flannel shirts worn two or three days before death... sealed package.... seal with bird with branch in its mouth... arsenic poison for cats... handkerchief... mixture... Messrs. Joshua and Blunt gargle... Messrs. Joshua and Blunt scent bottle no label... small bottle containing pills labelled poison... small bottle of dark brown pills... bottles found locked up in Mr. Tyler's private desk in office... old liqueur brandy... medicine bottles no label... from spare bedroom a case containing pills, small bottle in blue paper....

For the first time she heard the judge's voice; it caused her to glance up startled from the paper; the enthroned man in his scarlet and ermine had said, "Did they say what he had for lunch?"

Mr. Steele was answering with great respect, "My Lord, I think it was beef tea, but I may be wrong...."

Then he continued with the talk that was meaningless to May. She heard him reading the letter Jerome Thorne had written to her, and she heard him reading the letters she had written to Jerome Thorne, altered, yes, she had never written those endearments. She heard talk of herself coming and going with bottles—always bottles—and more accounts of the brown jug at the office, and of what had been found in the hat boxes and the chocolate-box. She heard him reading the last letter she had sent to Jerome Thorne, that she had given to Amelia Chorley, Amelia had given it to Richard.... Her attention returned to the list in her hand... blue bottle... glycerine... small packet like chocolate... large bottle labelled poison... wash containing few drops of arsenic... round bottle of oil and mustard... blue bottle liquorice powder.... She took up the pencil with which she had been provided and wrote on the side of one section "My room." She had been told by the doctor that it would be better for her to concentrate on something, something trivial.... "This was what they found in my room. They were all medicines that had been used for my husband, I had better go over the list..." One bottle of cod-liver oil... black bottle containing small quantity carbolic acid... bottle of liquid for cleaning cloth... empty hair-wash bottle... lavender water bottle... empty spirit bottle... blue bottle containing carbolic acid.... "My room," she wrote on the side. "My room...." But the room in Stone Pynes had never been hers, and now it no longer existed any more than her life in Manchester existed.

Mr. Steele had come to the end of his address and the witnesses were called. Why were they showing plans of Stone Pynes? That seemed little more lunatic than anything else that was happening, but she noted it... the drawings handed about.

Now there was Richard in the box and he, without, as it seemed, emotion or even interest, again went over the case. His brother's age, his marriage, the children....

May tried to think of the children. She saw them as prim pasty-faced marionettes standing obediently when she entered the nursery, saying "yes" and "no" with sullen looks while her husband's servant treated her with ill-concealed insolence. Their figures were interwoven with the list that she tried to concentrate on... "tin box containing insect powder, small bottle of white powder...." Some of the things she knew, some to her were strange. What mattered was, surely, the three packets of arsenic, poison found in the chocolate-box.... Who had put them there...? "Poison for cats..." she would never have poisoned a cat or any animal... no one in Stone Pynes wished to destroy cats. This triviality was before her like a huge stumbling block—"Poison for cats..." Three packets of arsenic in her chocolate-box.... If John, as they said, had been taking arsenic, if this white powder that had always alarmed her had really been arsenic, why these packages must represent some of his supplies. But who had put them in the chocolate-box given her by Jerome Thorne? Who hated her so much...? But the absurdity would come out, surely.

Richard was speaking now. He was telling the story in such a way that she could not recognize it and she heard him say, "After having a segar, I went back into the bedroom and found my sister-in-law changing the medicine. I said, 'May, how dare you tamper with the medicine!' She explained that she was putting it into a larger bottle so that it might be more easily shaken up. He continued about his brother's illness. The prisoner thought, 'Did it look like that to him? How differently to me.' He mentioned his brother's death—the hour and the manner of it—and that reminded her that she had known nothing of his deathbed. She had fallen headlong, as it seemed to her, into blackness. She could recall nothing until she was roused to find the police sitting by her bed."

The judge spoke again; his voice brought her round, like an automatic figure obeying its machinery, to turn slightly and stare at him. The judge said: "In the parcel labelled 'Arsenic, Poison for Cats', arsenic was underlined."

Sir Jonathan Docwra was on his feet cross-examining the witness. She could make nothing of his questions; there were the same words repeated again and again... the patent foods, the medicines, the meat juice, the servants' evidence, the contents of the chocolate-box, arsenic found here and there... two hundred and fifty bottles of medicine found at Stone Pynes.

Richard and Sir Jonathan were exchanging what seemed to May brisk and hostile comments on two people who must be, she supposed, herself and Jerome Thorne. She heard the words "guilty meeting", "adultery", "infidelity".... But Richard knew the truth of that London visit. The truth... did anyone know it, much less herself?

The long summer day had ended. The darkness encroached upon the court though someone had opened the windows, and flies buzzed here and there in the dusty corners; the air was close from the packed audience.

May looked about vaguely, holding her list of two hundred and fifty medicine bottles in her hand. She had taken off her thin black kid gloves and then put them on again. They were sticking to her palm with the moisture from her hand.

"I wish," she thought, "I had some *eau-de-Cologne*," and it seemed as if she would only have to turn about and pass into her over-furnished untidy bedroom and take up a bottle.... She stopped herself on this word. What were they doing? She tried to peer at Richard, but surely there were thick shadows between him and her? He was in every way a stranger, a being of whom she knew nothing; cut off and divided from her for ever, a heavy man with a plain face, in a correct morning-suit, speaking slowly and precisely as was his habit in order to disguise his Midland accent.

She looked again at the judge. The court was rising. Mr. Steele remarked that all the exhibits should be placed somewhere altogether, and again the judge spoke. Everything he said was trivial, but it had a tremendous power over May. He remarked, "The proper custodian of these things is the custodian of the court." He then turned to the jury and made a little speech in terms of cold courtesy.

"This case is likely to last some time. You may not receive letters and telegrams or send them off. You must not allow any influence from outside to bear upon this case. If anyone attempts to communicate with you, I give you warning that such person will be guilty of gross contempt of court and will be treated accordingly. It is the practice that juries be locked up, but I shall not order that in this case but trust to your honour and discretion. If you want an airing, you will go in a closed carriage."

To the prisoner no one seemed of importance save the judge, and to the judge no one seemed of importance save the prisoner. Round them surged the city, eager to turn over these details, now publicly avowed, of the life and habits of a dead man and the woman accused of his murder. In every billiard-room, in every hotel, in every tap-room of every public house the case was discussed. The jurymen went to and fro having taken no notice of the words of the judge. They played their games, smoked their pipes and made their observations with anyone who cared to hear. The talk flowed in an increasing confusion; words and phrases clashing against one another until they broke like the spume of the waves of foul water against the prison where the woman sat alone in her cell, against the hotel parlour where a judge sat alone with his books.

She thought of him as a symbol of power above humanity, enthroned in brilliant and costly garments, implacable, immaculate, the arbiter of her fate. No one else mattered at all, neither the wardress nor the nurses who came and went, nor the doctor, nor her lawyers, nor even Sir Jonathan who was kind and, she thought vaguely, a little troubled. Only the judge.... She had ceased to wonder about anything. Now and then she made a spasmodic effort to explain herself, but somebody always soothed her as they might have soothed a fretful child, hushing her with compassion into silence.

The judge thought of the prisoner and turned over his notes of the case, but did not read them and could not concentrate on the close writing, on the paragraphs of dry legal reporting, full of blunders, errors and contradictions. His gaze seemed to see through the walls of the ugly, heavy building as the gaze of the woman saw through the walls of her prison, and they stood face to face; she disguised in her mourning black, he disguised in his scarlet and ermine, one peering at the other, curious, afraid. He menacing and hostile, she beseeching and at a loss.

He had heard of such women, but never, he believed in his austere, ascetic life, seen one, save for a brief glance in a street or a public place. A Jezebel, a Delilah, a murderess and yet one who had the softness of a dove, a shy and beseeching loveliness.

Only the three of them mattered, the woman being judged, the man who set her in the dock, the man who judged her, the others were earning their fees, or feeding their curiosity that had been so long starved by humbug and hypocrisy; the avid gaping, the strained listening of these expensively dressed women, and their pompous escorts showed how thin was the smear of civilization over Manchester, their sham careful gentility fell from them, and as they gloated over this banquet of murder, adultery, drugs, kept-women, secret vices, their long suppressed grossness showed in their eager faces. But the three were set apart; they knew one another by a dark instinct; Richard sat rigid, eyeing in this exalted, fearful man, of a class and rank so much above his own, the fell vengeance he had evoked against the untouchable woman whom he had respected, who had broken the moral law, but not for him, who had dared to set herself so high above all of them, while wantoning with the least of them.

He had, perhaps, not quite known what he was doing, as he had piled up the evidence against her, he had wanted her degraded, exposed as Thorne's mistress, hardly had he wanted her hanged… she would not be, everyone said… "the medical evidence." But the question of her punishment was out of his hands now, he overlooked the jury, those ignorant, bewildered tradesmen, he thought only of the judge.

Richard knew that the judge hated May and for the same reason that he hated her; she disturbed him and she was unattainable; Richard almost pitied him, the worn, ageing man, with the sensual mouth, lonely, a recluse, a man who had cared for nothing but the intellect, and who lately had been so virulent against unchaste women, who had fulminated so sharply against immorality; the little devil crouched among the sweating crowd and stared up at the great devil he had evoked.

The prisoner thought only of the judge, she was on her guard for his glance, for the sound of his voice. He looked at her, the old, bedizened man, as John had looked at her in Paris, as Richard had looked at her in the Pomona Rooms; the drowsiness of the nightly sedative clouded her mind, the court receded in a blur of vapour; she was in a jungle, the undergrowth was very thick, dark and tangled, and the flabby satyrs with grey whiskers slowly closed in on her, moving clumsily, on hands and knees. The judge was speaking, one of the medical experts was in the witness-box.

"Have you ever heard of a case of arsenic-eating?"

"Never, my lord."

"Why is it taken?"

"I understand, as an aphrodisiac, my lord."

Few of the inhabitants of Manchester had heard that word before, though most of them had jeered about "pick-me-ups"....

"The learned witness means a love potion," the judge explained; his grey face was impassive; Richard had a glitter of triumph, not all the drugs in the world would relieve the judge's torment, his desires were for his own dead youth at whom the beauty of the woman in the dock mocked; John had been a fool, going headlong to destruction... the subject was hurried over; it had been the edge of the pit for respectability and humbug... the dead man had taken arsenic to ward off attacks of malaria... everything shrivelled into the commonplace horror of a trial at the Assizes.

On the morrow they were confronted again and the evidence continued. The prisoner and the judge looked away from one another, and again she tried to concentrate on the paper in her hand. One after another the witnesses came and went, her servants, Amelia Chorley whom she had once thought her friend, the doctors... there was the examination and the cross examination, the details of the illness, of the two hundred and fifty bottles, of the three packets of arsenic in the chocolate-box, of the unhappy household, of the unfaithful wife. Now and then the judge spoke; commonplace words, questions that seemed to have no purpose, interrupting the evidence, and every time his voice was heard the prisoner turned and looked at him and then glanced back again at the list in her hand.

It was proved that her husband had eaten arsenic. She gathered that Sir Jonathan had forced several witnesses to admit as much. Arsenic had been found in a bottle of Orso's meat juice, arsenic had been found in the stains on her dressing-gown, on her apron and handkerchiefs.... She saw Stone Pynes as soaked in arsenic from floor to ceiling, solution of arsenic dripping over the clothes in her cupboard, the gay and unsuitable gowns that she had bought in London, the shoes in which she had danced at the Pomona Rooms, the ostrich feather fan that she had waved in moments of idleness, the blue velvet Bible her mother had given her; arsenic in powder sprinkled among her toilet-set and trinkets, among her feathered hats and combs and the folds of the lace curtain of her bed; arsenic in the pockets of Richard when he had gripped her arms through the thin sleeves of her domino while the orchestra, played by invisible machinery, jangled overhead.

The wardress touched her arm. The second day was over.

It was the third day and they were talking about the flypapers. This sent her mind back to the prescription. She tried to understand what they were saying. If she could have found the prescription that would have helped she knew. She had not even known that there was arsenic in Fowler's solution, nor arsenic in flypapers... murderesses had used flypapers it seemed two years ago. She had known nothing of that; it was all as remote and curious as a puppet show at a fair.

The charwoman was speaking.... Medicine bottles in the office... saucepans, basins and spoons... used to eat the patent food that was taken down to the office in a brown jug... she had never been able to get the food out of the crannies.... The doctors were there again and the chemists, their assistants. Now the nurse once again... the story of how May Tyler had tried to escape, the story of the letter—the letter that had been dropped in the mud and Sir Jonathan proving that the servant had lied and opened the letter to betray her mistress.

Then the end of the next day the close of the prosecution for the case for the Crown was concluded. May Tyler had been told by those automatic figures, as they seemed to her, who came and went in her cell, that to-day, the third day, was to be decisive. Sir Jonathan was to speak in her defence. He was to bring forward the evidence that would clear her, but she could not attach any importance to this. When she was not in court everything was the same. She thought of it like one of those mechanical games she had once seen at a pier-head, when she had gone with the children for a dull holiday. A north-east wind had been blowing and the sea was the colour of ashes and vinegar and she had stood there with Lizzie Burt, the women holding on their bonnets and protecting the children from the wind with their cloaks while they put pence into a slot and saw a drama enacted. A castle door opened, two knights came out, tilted at one another until one was vanquished, then the victor returned into the castle and the doors were closed....

So every time a coin was placed in the slot this scene would be enacted, and so to May Tyler seemed the days of her trial; every day the same thing, the same people talking about the same story, the same details, all of them becoming more and more confused, more and more untruthful and further away from the core of reality, as when she had gazed at the little scene on the pier, the tiny marionette show that had become, every time she gazed, more and more grotesque and foolish and yet with a deepening power of hypnosis so that between the wind blowing and the waves breaking and the children putting in their pence, and the figures performing their antics and disappearing she had become numbed and foolish, as she was numbed and foolish now—only conscious of one thing, the figure of the man in the scarlet and the ermine, with the heavy false grey curls either side of his massive face who now and then looked at her, and now and then made notes on the paper in front of him.

She could not hear what Sir Jonathan was saying. His voice flowed on and on. Now and then there was a sentence that, incongruous and even ridiculous, flashed into her mind and out again like summer lightning, without point. He spoke of "a cloud of doubt and mystery," he spoke of "the verdict, which must snap the thread of this poor woman's life...." He spoke of "this lady when she was forsaken and alone"... he spoke at great, wearisome length of John Tyler's habit of eating arsenic—arsenic... that was the white powder over which she had been so concerned, of which she had tried to warn the doctors and Richard; and no one had told her....

Now Sir Jonathan was speaking of her. He looked at her with an intensity that caused her to give him some attention. He was asking the judge to allow her to make a statement, the judge was saying that she might do so. He would allow it, "but," he added, "it would be a statement made without the possibility of cross examination and without the sanction and weight attached to the oath." What did that mean? Probably someone had told her and she had forgotten....

May Tyler wondered at the weight attached to an oath. All the witnesses had been on oath and all of them had lied or made mistakes, but she, without an oath, would tell the truth....

Her lawyer was pleading for her, preparing the judge and the jury for the failure she would make—she could understand that he was trying to excuse her, talking of her distress, her untrained mind, the fact that she was a woman and foolish. He did not use that word but he implied it... he was talking now of the visit to the hotel, referring to it with an air of repugnance as "the dark cloud that passed over her life and must for all time rest on her character as a woman and a wife." He glanced at her and she at him, the paper shaking in her hands; he had spoken of her as "the woman taken in adultery," but she thought he had understood. Why did he not bring Jerome Thorne forward? Would he, too, lie? Richard had lied and lied and never looked at her....

He added, "But I would earnestly entreat you not to allow any repugnance that you might find in your minds against a sin so abhorrent as that, to lead you to the conclusion, unless the evidence drives you irresistibly there, that because a woman has forgotten her duty to her husband, she is to be regarded as one who will deliberately and wickedly seek to destroy his life."

The witnesses for her defence. First a man who gave evidence that John Tyler had taken arsenic, the evidence of the chemist who had sold him the arsenic, then the evidence of the great experts.

"How many *post mortems* have you assisted at?"

"It is difficult to say, something short of a thousand."

The judge was interested in the experts. He asked them simple questions with an air of keen attention.

May saw the wardress give her a weak smile and make a slight indication towards the body of the court. It took the prisoner a moment or so to understand that the woman was trying to convey to her that the evidence was favourable, that the people who had hissed her when she had first appeared in the dock were beginning to turn to her side. Here was a hairdresser and perfumer, he spoke of arsenic being used for face-washes; "There's an impression among ladies that it is good for the complexion."

There was a beauty specialist; she swore that thousands of her clients used arsenic as "a lotion for the complexion." Nothing could be more common, but "gentlemen were usually ignorant of these secrets of the toilet."

Richard was recalled. What could that mean? She could understand nothing of what he was saying... it was about pills again, medicine, arsenic. He had not known what his brother was taking.... Sir Jonathan cast some suspicion on the quick sale of the furniture and all the effects at Stone Pynes before there had been a thorough examination by the police, but the judge seemed impatient and the lawyer, seeing that, let the witness go down from the box.

Now they were speaking of her, the wardress touched her arm again. She must leave the dock and go into the witness-box and make her statement without oath, without cross examination. She noted with a smile of courteous sympathy the frown of anxiety, almost of despair on the face of her counsel, the blank complacency on the countenance of Mr. Steele; sharp and painful curiosity on the faces of the packed audience. Yes, it was an audience and she must play a part, forgetting what she really knew, what she really felt, what had really happened and standing up and saying as best she could what she was determined to say.

Sir Jonathan was speaking to her and she could not hear what he said. It was the first time she had spoken save in a small room among a few people. Pressing her hand with a nervous intensity, he told her to raise her voice. She clutched the rail in front of her. She must speak clearly. She crossed the court, from the dock to the witness-box. 'I am playing a part—like the charades at the convent, I must be very quiet.'

There was a hush and yet a murmuring about her, her clumsy mourning was like a disguise. She spoke, staring past the judge.

"My lord, I wish to make a statement, as well as I can to you, a few facts in connection with the dreadful, crushing charge that has been made against me. I wish to refer to the use of the flypapers and to the bottle of meat essence. The flypapers were bought with the intention of using as a cosmetic. I have been in the habit of using a face-wash prescribed for me and my mother, I used it at school.... This was lost or mislaid. I had an eruption on my face," she put her hand to the cheek that her husband had struck, "and I thought of this face-wash. I had to go to a ball with my brother-in-law, I remembered when I had been at school in Paris, in a convent, that we had used flypapers. I did not know that there was arsenic either in Fowler's solution or in the flypapers. My mother knows that this is true. I wish to refer to the bottle of meat essence. I knew my husband took some white powders and when he was very sick and very depressed he implored me to give him one of these powders. I was overwrought, terribly anxious, miserably unhappy and his evident distress utterly unnerved me. He told me the powder would not harm him and I could put it in his food. I found it where he told me—it was in a package in a hat box. I put it into the meat juice. I had not one true or honest friend in the house, I had no one to consult and no one to advise me. I was deposed from my position as mistress in my own house. I did what I thought was right, to soothe one who was in such distress. I put the powder into the meat extract...." She paused and the court seemed locked in silence so unnatural that the possibility of anyone breaking it appeared remote indeed. But the prisoner began again in her faint and feeble voice. "Until some days after my husband's death when this terrible charge was made against me, no one had informed me of the fact that a death certificate had been refused. It was only when I heard that there was arsenic in the meat juice that I was made aware of the nature of the powder my husband had asked me to give him. I tried to explain but a policeman interrupted me. I would like to add..." she did not see Sir Jonathan trying to convey to her with an agonized concentration of his gaze, that she must stop, for she had already said too much and harmed herself; nothing was in her mind but gathering together the strength to say what she had resolved to say. "I know I did my husband a fearful wrong. I made full atonement. I have no more to say."

She came down from the witness-box and returned to the dock, a small figure in her heavy black and everyone looking with that expression of reserved wonder that people use when confronted with what is almost incredible.

There was complete silence. Sir Jonathan, with the movement of one who is undergoing a great strain, was on his feet. He wished to call witnesses to corroborate the prisoner's statement, but the judge refused. "I cannot go beyond what the law allows."

Sir Jonathan was making his closing speech for the defence, the prisoner heard him call it "an anxious, wearisome case," heard him speak of "the mysteries and conflict of evidence," heard him go over again the story. It was her story, but by now had become to her without interest. She was "this lady" in Sir Jonathan's speech, the lady "who fell, who forgot her self-respect, who forgot her duty to her husband." It was the visit to London... she heard him talk of the Thorne scene, the touching and painful incident of the wife desiring to leave her husband....

He was speaking for her and yet he uttered lies. He mentioned about her being brought back to the house to see her babies, "a woman so yielding is not wholly bad...." And then it was talk again—the visit to London, the letters, the poison, the arsenic in the box, the bottles, the medical evidence, the evidence of the nurses, of the servants, of the experts... her own conduct... the quantity of arsenic found in the body... his insistence that poison by arsenic was not proved, that there was no direct evidence against the accused.

Now he was speaking of her again and her handkerchief, of Mr. Tyler's use of arsenic and as he spoke he showed increasing signs of uneasiness, of fatigue to the point of exhaustion.

There was a large clock in the court, but May had never noticed it before, for time had not existed since the day of her husband's death; suddenly she heard the ticking.

The wardress touched her arm and almost imperceptibly whispered as the weary lawyer sat down, "He's been speaking for nearly three hours, and for no purpose as it seems to me."

Mr. Steele's speech, continuing the case for the prosecution had a routine air, an acquittal was still considered as certain by everyone. The jury, who had mingled so freely with their fellow citizens in the city and who had even discussed the Tyler scandal with journalists, were known to have made up their minds that "the medical evidence" was not sufficient for them to return a verdict of guilty. These words were repeated even by those who scarcely knew their meaning; sullen, narrow-eyed Richard Tyler sat huddled in his place; he wished that he had not spent that money on Jerome Thorne, for neither side had called him as a witness, the Crown because his appearance was likely to create sympathy for the prisoner, the defence because they could not trust the scoundrel not to say something damaging to May Tyler, and Sir Jonathan having admitted the adultery there was little object in calling the lover; when Richard had given that bribe he had thought that May's counsel would deny what was, in court, ponderously called "the moral lapse."

Richard was surprised at the manner in which Sir Jonathan had thrown his client's "virtue," as he termed it, to the dogs, could not the evidence of that foreign waiter, terrified by the police, confused by his memory of so many "ladies and gentlemen" coming and going at the Mentone, have been easy to shake? Where was the chambermaid? Why had not Sir Jonathan put Thorne in the box, and exposed him as the base cur he was? Thereby gaining sympathy for May as the victim of a designing libertine?

Had May "confessed" in prison? How eager they all were to pounce on her and her sin, while John's ugly life was hushed up, glossed over.... Nothing seemed to interest any of them save the woman's guilt... no excuse for her, none, not four years of a mock marriage to a vulgar, brutal—well, Richard knew what these London gentry thought of the Midlands... odd how they all hunted her, odd he should find it odd for this was what he had done himself... he believed that Thorne had spoken the truth that night in Stone Pynes, yet he was amazed that anyone besides himself should credit it... didn't she seem proud, untouchable—yet the evidence of that miserable little waiter, the few pencil letters so easily tampered with... he looked up at the judge and shrivelled into himself... it was only the judge that mattered now.... Richard's exhausted mind centred on the man in scarlet and ermine who was staring down at his notes, cold, harsh, impassive, only, now and then, making a small convulsive movement, that he was at pains to hide by a quick adjustment of his sleeves or notes. May was impassive, too, stupidly she stared down at the sheet of paper that contained the list of medicines found at Stone Pynes. Even gross horror had its formula, it slipped into long established usage, there was decorum even in this ugly hall, on this fearful occasion; Mr. Steele had a smooth personality, he conducted his case with the utmost decency; the ladies with their luncheon baskets and opera glasses found him dull, the men thought him fair, the lawyer thought him restrained as became a counsel certain of losing the verdict, the twelve working men in the jury box listened dully; there was a great deal in the trial that they had not understood, they had tacitly agreed on "not guilty" because of the medical evidence.

Mr. Steele said his task was disagreeable; Sir Jonathan had been able to enthuse an air of chivalry into his appeal for a "morally guilty" woman falsely accused by spite and jealousy of a monstrous crime. Mr. Steele had the unsympathetic role of putting the worst side of the case against May Tyler forward as impressively as possible. "One's natural feeling is enlisted in favour of a woman who is attractive by her cleverness, her appearance and even by her social position which is similar to our own. To have to urge before twelve men that she has been guilty of a deliberate and cruel murder is not by any means a pleasant or agreeable task. I must say, as far as I can judge for anyone concerned, all in the case have been labouring more or less under the same feeling."

Mr. Steele then touched on what had become a much debated feature of the Tyler tragedy, the free comments in the press before the jury had come to their decision. Sir Jonathan had made some stinging allusions to this disgraceful behaviour on the part of the local journalists. Now Mr. Steele, countered with, "As far as I can judge, having read the papers, although they did try to gratify the natural curiosity of the public and the right of the public to know what was going on, they did so most carefully and guardedly, and in a way which does them credit. Nothing which seemed to prejudice the case appeared."

This was in such glaring contrast to the truth that a murmur, half-protest, half-laughter went through the packed court, some of the journalists themselves guffawing.

Mr. Steele continued unmoved with his line of attack and once again went over the life of the Tylers that had been already, as he himself admitted, put before the court with minuteness and care.

May did not understand what was being said. Her mind was far away. Again the scene to her was like the little set piece of mechanical figures that she had watched that stormy summer day, on one of those dismal holidays she had taken with the children when they had stood at the end of the pier and pushed their pennies into the slot. She saw Mr. Steele's lips move, his hand go up and down on his pile of papers, juniors leaning towards one another and whispering now and then; but none of them meant anything. She tried to concentrate on the list in her hand as the doctor had ordered... two hundred and fifty bottles of medicine... poisoned in Stone Pynes... arsenic in closets, in cupboards, in pots, in bottles....

There was a stir, a hum, a leaning forward, a pressing together among the crowd when Mr. Steele touched on the three packets of arsenic found in the chocolate-box, he quickly followed up his mention of this dramatic fact by reminding the jury of the London visit, using words that were never heard in the drawing-rooms of Manchester but that had been very often employed in this trial. "Adulterous intercourse," he said, and then he admitted that Sir Jonathan had been correct in his comment that a woman who was unfaithful to her husband was not necessarily a murderess, and even added some moralizing on his own, "there is a wide chasm between the moral guilt of unfaithfulness and the cruelty that would cause the death of a husband. Notwithstanding many men, even very guilty ones, are ready to throw stones at an adulteress, certainly we know that as regards a woman,

Every fault a tear may claim
Except an erring sister's shame,

but, unfortunately, this is not a case in which discovery of an adulterous intercourse has been put before you as the motive for the act of administering poison. Unfortunately this woman, at that very time, by her own handwriting and her actual deeds, had so interwoven her adultery with her conduct that it was impossible to treat it as an ordinary case of adultery, and not treat it as in actual connection with the alleged crime."

Once more there was the account of the London visit, of the letters, of the flypapers, of the quarrel and the blow, of the illness, of the *post mortem* evidence, of the medical evidence, of what was found in Mrs. Tyler's room—bottles of arsenic in various degrees of solution, meat extract with arsenic in it, arsenic on handkerchiefs, aprons and dressing-gowns, three packets of arsenic in a chocolate-box.

May raised her eyes from the paper and stared at the judge, massive-jowled, pale and bent over his papers, he sat above them all… soon it would be over; the jury would go out, she had been told, to consider their verdict… they would come back and say "Not guilty" and she would go away with her mother "to forget" Madame Dumont had said… but May knew better… she would never escape from Stone Pynes, from her marriage to John Tyler.

The court adjourned with an air of fatigue and flatness over everyone. There would be to-morrow an end of the show; no one would be able any longer even to discuss it. It had been already ascertained by the journalists that neither Mrs. Tyler nor her mother would entertain any suggestion from the press of interviews on any subject whatsoever. They would leave the country immediately, disappearing from Manchester for ever. People gossiped about the children—Richard had the custody by that last-minute will, *she* would have to leave her children behind.

Would Jerome Thorne come forward from wherever he had been skulking and marry her? Not likely, nor that she would accept him now.... So people made their crude and baffled guesses, so the speculations went to and fro in the hotel bars, in the tap-rooms of the public houses, in the clubs, in the parlours, on the slum doorsteps that thunderous, summer night. Public feeling had turned, there were no longer hisses when the police van drew up at the Court House.

Richard Tyler was uneasy, for no reason that he could define. He had brought himself to a state of fierce resignation to the loss of May; she would escape him and for ever. He could think of no possible device whereby he could either follow up his revenge or bring her to look kindly on him. It was not that prospect of immense loss that made him restless, nervous and shaken, but the fear of some intangible justice overtaking him while she had stood her trial for the crime that he knew she had not committed, for a crime that had never been committed at all. He had felt, sitting biting his forefinger, or standing at the back of the court with his hands in his pockets, as if he had been on trial though the heavy-faced judge had never looked at him nor even when he had been in the witness-box seemed to take any heed of his personality. Now Richard feared something from the verdict of to-morrow, as if some mysterious and unforeseen judgment would fall on him for what he had done. He cast over in his shrewd mind for what this could possibly be. She had no champion—none—a foreigner, a stranger; that scoundrel Thorne would keep well out of the way, and there was no one else. Besides, his part in her torment was secret. No one knew positively what he had done the night of his brother's death at Stone Pynes. If Amelia Chorley and the servants and the nurses guessed, they could not, for their own sakes, speak.

The trial would go against him in many ways; the scandal would do the business no good. The forced sale of Stone Pynes and its contents had meant a loss, he had taken far less than the place and furniture were worth. John's insurance money would not pay for the liabilities that he, Richard, had undertaken in educating and bringing up the two brats. He would probably have to leave Manchester; but it was something more than these accumulated annoyances that threatened him.

In an attempt to distract himself he took out of his pocket a note that Mr. Martin had given him earlier in the day. It was to the effect that a young man named Tarrant had written to state that not long ago he had given John Tyler three packets of arsenic—one pure white, one stained with indigo, one with soot in exchange for putting on the market a substitute for cotton. He had understood that Mr. Tyler was an arsenic eater and therefore had not felt any scruples in leaving such a quantity of poison with him since he believed the man was well able to take care of himself. Now, having read the reports of the trial in the papers, he believed these three packets might have been those found in the chocolate-box. The illness and death of his own wife had absorbed him during the earlier part of the trial, but he was willing to give evidence now if it was not too late.

Mr. Martin had written across the end of the note, "I think we can't do anything about this now. It will be no use to Sir Jonathan who has already done his best with the subject of your brother's habit of eating arsenic."

Richard tore up the note and cast it into the blackleaded grate where Lizzie Burt had arranged goffered pink and yellow paper. If that young man had been put into the witness-box, it might have made a difference, the three packets might have been identified as those that he had given to John Tyler. But what did it matter? No one had been able to prove that May had bought arsenic in packets; no one had been able to prove that she had bought more than the few flypapers that did not contain enough poison to dispose of more than a few miserable insects. She would be acquitted and there was no need to clear up what would remain in the mind of the public a mystery, discreditable to her—the packets of arsenic in the chocolate-box....

The night was of an oppressive heat. The smoke over Manchester hung lower than usual, almost suffocating and stifling those who walked abroad in the attempt to get a little clean air. Richard, with his hands in his pockets, slouched over the narrow bridges that spanned the twisting waters, black from the dye factories, where he had taken May when they had gone on their visit to Dora Lestrange. His own action was not clear to him. He had destroyed something with venom, with skill, with secret violence, and he did not know if he was pleased or not, that he could, for this night at least, dwell on the certain anguish of the woman in her cell waiting for the morrow when she would once more, even if for the last time, have to stand before the curious, contemptuous and spiteful glances of the strangers who had never liked her and whom she had always, by her very kindness and aloof gentleness, disdained. Not guilty of murder, no doubt… guilty of adultery? Yes. Never for the whole of her life would she escape from the sentence that would be imposed for that crime. Yes, she had danced before him, out of his reach, like those insects that bore her name, mayflies, and he had destroyed her, as she had destroyed him, for the rest of life showed grey ahead.

It was the sixth day of the trial and the judge spoke high above the heads of his audience, from behind his pile of notes to which he frequently referred with many pauses, stammerings and retractions. There was an uneasy undercurrent to the outward dullness in the court. Now that the ugly show had come to an end, the men at least were slightly doubtful as to the parts they had played, both in the enjoyment and the stirring up of prejudice, excitement, rumour and malice. The women were mostly confirmed in their curious and pitiless attitude. Such women as had compassion for May Tyler, or did not enjoy the spectacle of this young creature enduring for a week such public torment, had never come to court; those who were there, though yawning occasionally from the enclosed air, the heat of the day, and the sense of anti-climax that had come with the conviction that everyone held that the verdict would be "not guilty," nevertheless hung on the looks of the prisoner when the address of the judge was too tedious to penetrate their own stupidity and absorption in the personal side of the case. All they wanted to know about was the life that had been going on at Stone Pynes, the quarrels between husband and wife, the misbehaviour of this reserved little foreigner with one of their own men. Every detail of that existence interested them; of the greater drama that was taking place in the mind of the judge and in the mind of the prisoner, and somewhere between them as they now and then looked at one another as a delicate silk might be cast from a shuttle to a shuttle, that full fed and low-minded audience were oblivious.

The judge had only spoken hitherto in short and trivial sentences. The prisoner had not heard his address to the Grand Jury. She listened intently to his deep and expressionless voice as with a fine show of judicial calmness he made his formal preamble. The paper with the list of two hundred and fifty bottles was under her hand, neatly gloved in black suede. She had been allowed a chair at Sir Jonathan's earnest request but now preferred to stand, the wardress sitting beside her. She had been told very earnestly, both by her solicitor and her barrister, that she must not take any heed of what the judge said because she was safe—safe "on the medical evidence." There was only one or—if the old man was long-winded—two more days to endure and then she would be free; but though May believed these words they brought but little reassurance to her. She did not expect ever to know what freedom meant, nor happiness, nor content and the fascination of the grotesque and sinister scene in which the judge was the central figure, blurred all her thoughts of past and present; there existed only herself standing erect in her bombazine and crape, in her heavy mourning for a husband whom she had loathed and the stranger who was her judge, and whose leaden eyes accused her of some unnamable sin, not the murder, not the adultery about which everyone had been so explicit but the sin of tormenting, with her beauty, her story, the long-suppressed passions of an intellectual Puritan.

At first Lord Barnfield, speaking slowly and with many contradictions, spread nothing but tedium in the court. Lawyers even ventured to put their elbows on the table and their hands behind their ears, pushing forward their wigs with movements of considerable irritation and boredom. The judge had apologized for having once more to go through the story and the evidence, and proceeded to do this in a halting, stumbling but impassive fashion. His errors were continual. Mr. Martin checked them off on his notes; Sir Jonathan was not in court and his assistant, having been bitterly rebuked by Lord Barnfield for venturing to point out mistakes in the course of the case, was now silent when the judge confused a date, a name, a place. The legal men present were at once aware of these errors, glanced at their neighbours with raised or frowning brows, and scratched down a note on any odd piece of paper they had near them. The Recorder, who was present merely through curiosity, could hardly preserve his patience at the manner in which the judge was summing up, and the dissatisfaction felt by this trained observer spread, not as dissatisfaction but as amazement, slowly through the court.

First the lawyers, then the clerks, then the more intelligent of the men, then all the men, then the women gradually felt a quickening of intense agitation, like an expectancy of something monstrous and unforeseen. Was it possible that after all the speculation, the gossip, the to-ing and fro-ing of debates and discourse, that the melodrama of May Tyler would not end with the Manchester Assizes?

The judge, it had become apparent, and this was the cause of the emotion that with every moment increased in the court, was summing up in contradiction to all the evidence and with deadly animus towards the prisoner. His voice took on more colour, he moved in his chair, shuffling the papers; when he had come to the episode of the flypapers, he made such an obvious mistake in the date of purchase that Sir Jonathan's assistant rose to put him right. The judge stared over the head of the lawyer and replied, "There is no use in disputing what word I use," and then returned to his recital of the case.

There were the incidents with which everyone present was already familiar, retold yet again, and told in a manner and with an accent that they had not heard nor expected to hear. Point by point—though in a confused tangle for he kept no sequence in his speech but went backwards and forwards over the complicated course of petty events—the judge put forward everything that was against the prisoner.

Suddenly, after speaking of the details of John Tyler's illness, he mentioned the brother and Richard, who had been standing leaning against a pillar, his arms folded, and the sweat beading unnoticed on his low and heavy brow, started, as if he had been touched on the shoulder. The judge spoke gently about Mr. Richard Tyler, even distinguishing him by a glance across the court. "Mrs. Tyler pathetically complained of the manner in which she was treated; her lawyer pointed out that in his view it was somewhat harsh. Now, gentlemen, I think it fair to say that any charge of harshness or unkindness that might be brought against Mr. Richard Tyler could also be brought against the nurses, the servants, the friends. They behaved as well as it occurred to them to behave at the time, and I think it is due to them, and to all persons who are placed in so dreadful a position as that of seeing a treacherous domestic murder..." the judge stopped as if jerked into silence and turned to stare at the prisoner, who stared at him without moving, "... of seeing a treacherous domestic murder," he repeated, "it is due to this man, to these people, to remember the unhappy position in which they were placed. If you think of it for a moment you can hardly imagine a more dreadful necessity than that of supposing that your brother's wife, who might be the person to whom you are most attached, is carrying on a plot for secret murder. Conceive how exquisitely painful is this situation. How should a man, placed as Mr. Richard Tyler was, behave if he is unhappy enough to conceive a suspicion? How could he so behave himself as to conduct himself quite properly and prevent himself from being reproached afterwards, either for wicked suspiciousness or for criminal indulgence—namely, reluctance to face a dreadful fact. How could he behave in such a way as to escape those reproaches is a difficulty which will present itself to you more and more vividly, the more you consider the subject. I feel these people were placed in a very difficult position. I can really say nothing beyond this—that it is all part of one dreadful whole.

"Remember the letter written by the prisoner to Thorne. I pass it over at present, contenting myself with this thought: taken by itself, it establishes the unfaithfulness of Mrs. Tyler to her husband. Consider what a shock this letter must have been to the brother, and her friends—even to her servants. It certainly justified amongst them a painful and miserable state of things. This letter is certainly a ground upon which suspicion, strong or weak, might be raised.

"There has been a suggestion put forward that her brother-in-law owed her a spite ever since her marriage. I do not think, however, that you ought to believe that for various reasons. Remember that this was a case of strong suspicion. Remember the letters this woman was writing to her lover...."

It was by now clear, even to the most trivial-minded of the spectators, that the judge was enlarging in an emphatic and precise manner every possible suspicion that could be held of the prisoner. He had gathered from the evidence all the incidents that could do her harm. He referred to the medicines given to the dead man by his wife, he referred to Richard Tyler's remark, "May, how dare you tamper with the medicine!" and he added, "Surely this was a strange, dreadful unwelcome remark to make to a lady in her own house when she is in attendance on her husband. Surely this proves the state of feeling in Mr. Richard Tyler's mind and shows that he must have had strong cause for the most frightful doubt. And what of this chocolate-box that contained three packets of arsenic found in the prisoner's bedroom…?"

The judge paused again, with an unexpected suddenness. He moved awkwardly in his place, clutched the desk in front of him and a slight spasm passed over his face, a grimace so transient that most of them staring at him (and now he had the attention of all the court) could not credit they had seen it; he said something incoherent, staring at the prisoner.

Now he had taken up the threadbare story of the meat juice, of the quarrels, of the suspicions of the nurses, of the bottle with arsenic in solution, of the wife's debts. He touched but lightly on the main contentions of the defence—that the dead man had been an habitual arsenic eater and that not enough arsenic to kill even a mouse had been found at the *post mortem* investigation. He said that the evidence as to John Tyler being an arsenic eater was very contradictory and that though no doubt he took this drug now and then as a stimulant, the jury must not let these circumstances weigh much with them. As for the small amount of arsenic found in the body, he would point out that arsenic was a poison that was retained only for a very brief time and that therefore the dose that had killed this unfortunate man might have been supposed to have passed from him before his death.

He touched on the quarrel when the prisoner had been struck by her husband and had endeavoured to leave the house, and pointed out with a stern insistence that roused the jury, who were now listening in a nervous tension very different from the indifference with which they had heard him begin his speech, that it was ridiculous to suppose that John Tyler had struck his wife for any light cause; nor was it likely that the reconciliation that the family doctor had prided himself on having brought about between the two was more than superficial. "A slight and superficial thing," he repeated with a snarl, "after a quarrel on the question of *jealousy*.... Was this so-called reconciliation brought about by the good offices of the medical man?" and his whole deportment changed so that his listeners moved forward unconsciously in their places, drawn within the powerful range of his denunciation, for by now it was nothing less, as he added with a bitter sneer, "after a desperate quarrel of this nature there simply comes in the family doctor, and all is harmony. I say that such an interpretation of these events does not accord with my knowledge of human nature."

Then with a sudden quickening of his speech he went over the medical evidence, making blunder after blunder as to the reports by the family doctors and the experts, confusing all the symptoms of the patient that he repeated again and again with a cold relish, and with a dramatic force that caused those present, who had hitherto regarded the whole trial lightly as a mere occasion for gossip and scandal, to realize the horror of this agonizing deathbed. Not one symptom of the fortnight's torment did the judge spare. Whatever else he had forgotten, nothing of this escaped his memory. It was almost with a sigh that he turned the last of his medical notes face downwards, but it was with a mutter to himself like triumph of "The letters... ah! the letters," that he referred again to the prisoner's appeals to Jerome Thorne.

He stressed Amelia Chorley's evidence. Was it not odd that she should have suggested to this forlorn woman that she should write to Jerome Thorne, and suggested it, as she said herself, in sarcasm? He made no reference to the prisoner's illness at the time, nor to her frantic attempt to obtain help; none to the fact that her cash box was in the hands of her brother-in-law and that she was literally penniless. Carefully through his notes of examinations and cross examinations he pursued his quarry. The policeman had been right to intercept the letter, the nurses had been right in refusing to leave the room when

Madame Dumont visited her daughter. Everyone had been right but the prisoner. Had not Madame Dumont said, "Better death than this?" when she had seen her daughter under arrest, and might it not fairly have been supposed by those in charge of Stone Pynes, that this meant a threat of suicide both on the part of Madame Dumont and her daughter... and might it not also be inferred that for the prisoner's mother to have come so rapidly to such a frantic decision proved that she had little hope that her daughter could prove her innocence?

He made nothing of the evidence brought by the defence as to the custom of using arsenic in solution as a cosmetic. He had never heard of it, that was sufficient; and if Mrs. Tyler had been in the habit of making up a cosmetic that required arsenic, where was the recipe? Was it not curious that neither she nor her mother could produce this? Were they expected to believe that this woman of the world, this guilty wife who was capable of arranging a rendezvous with her lover in a London hotel of the worst reputation, should yet be so innocent that she did not know that there was arsenic either in Fowler's solution or in the usual brands of flypapers?

Again he came to a check in his speech and now appeared to have forgotten not only his audience but even the prisoner who had hitherto held his constant attention whether he had looked at her or not. Now he stared at the clock in front of him as if concerned with time alone. His old manner returned, his tone was impartial, judicious.

He went over the prescriptions and the brown jug of patent food that John Tyler had taken to his office. "Arsenic everywhere.... Gentlemen, you must remember that. In this house which had been for some eight years supposedly a scene of domestic content we find strains of arsenic on the mistress's handkerchief, on her apron, on her bedclothes... packets of arsenic in the cupboard that is reserved for her own personal use... arsenic in solution in a perfume bottle... arsenic in the closets and cupboards. Gentlemen, that house which we cannot think of without a terrible shudder and a most painful disgust has now been stripped of all its contents by the brother of the dead man—perhaps you will have to say the murdered man. We cannot wonder at the action of Mr. Richard Tyler in thus scattering abroad, dispersing for ever, the objects that must remind him of an experience so detestable that few of us are called upon to undergo it—but may we not ask of ourselves if the furnishings of Stone Pynes had been left in place longer, the traces of arsenic might have been found in the very nurseries? I repeat, gentlemen, nurseries! For this woman who stands before you, indicted on the charge of a crime so monstrous, this unfaithful wife, is the mother of two young children whom it is not surprising to learn she hardly ever saw, and who were left by the anxious care of her husband, solely in the charge of an honest and faithful servant. In considering, as you must consider, the character of the prisoner, I think it will be necessary for you to recall the unnatural disposition this woman showed towards her children, the youngest of whom is of very tender years, the eldest of whom has not yet left home for his first schooling. I think it will be permissible for you to ask yourself if a woman who shows a hardness and a flippancy in regard to her maternal duties, which all women worthy of our respect regard as pleasures, is not likely to be the woman who, having been tempted into one crime and one that can never be forgiven her sex, may not possess the callous disposition that would enable her to commit murder...."

Mr. Martin made a movement, almost as if he was about to interrupt, sank back again in his chair and whispered over his shoulder to Sir Jonathan's assistant, but the young man shook his head, affected not to hear and stared down at the quill pens he had neatly arranged in the dish in front of him; the solicitor had suggested that Sir Jonathan was sent for... the barrister had kept a steadier head—no one could interrupt while the judge was speaking. If Sir Jonathan were to come into court there would be nothing he could do. No one was restless, even the most lightheaded of the women did not unfurl their fans of Japanese paper printed with brilliant chrysanthemums or snow-topped mountains; all were hushed and afraid and expectant.

Was the judge a sick man? Several times a light and quickly controlled tremor passed over his face; more than once, as he pulled to pieces the medical evidence, pointing out in changing tones of scorn and impatience how contradictory and therefore worthless it was, he held with an unnatural grasp on to the desk as if he felt himself falling into a void… stuttered, retracted, went on again stumbling in his speech.…

He mentioned that poison had been found in the body.… He repeated this three times before the junior barrister for the defence, getting to his feet with almost as much difficulty as if he had been partially paralysed interrupted, "A trace only, my lord, a trace.…"

The judge smiled at him, leaving his upper lip in a rigid grin. "A trace then," he said quietly, "We'll leave it at that… yes, very well, a trace.…"

He glanced down at the jury, watching with a reflective air those twelve intent faces all different in feature and all charged with the same expression—one of awe and horror.

"Gentlemen, our learned friend has reminded us there was only a trace found in the body. On this point you must consider the difficulty of the tests, the number of medical witnesses, their constant disagreements. Gentlemen, you must remember that this unhappy man's illness had every symptom of arsenic poison, that his unfaithful wife was in close attendance on him, that in her cupboard were found three packets of arsenic—a deadly poison. As I think you understand, gentlemen, a deadly poison with which this house, Stone Pynes, was—I don't think the expression too strong—tainted and fouled from attic to basement. You will remember, gentlemen, not to use any foolish arguments, or raise any trivial questions in this quite serious question, this question that is one of life and death.…"

He returned to the charge of the letters, he mentioned the guilty visit to London. "It is not my business to speak as a moralist, but there is one horrible, lamentable result of a connection of that sort, which renders it almost a cruel necessity. It furnishes the strongest possible provocation, the strongest possible inducement for entering upon a system of the most disgraceful intriguing and for telling a large number of lies." He took a letter from the papers in front of him. It had been ready to his hand. Staring across the court he said, "It begins, 'My dear May...'"

Mr. Steele remarked, "Yes, my lord."

The judge said, "Do you know Mr. Thorne's handwriting?"

The defence put in, "The handwriting is not proved, that is my recollection."

The judge smiled again, and again appeared to give his entire attention to the jury.

"Well, there is no witness in court who is acquainted with Mr. Thorne's handwriting. Is Mr. Thorne here?"

Mr. Steele replied, "No."

There was a sound like a long-drawn sigh in the court.

The judge continued, "It has been impossible to keep Mr. Thorne's name out of this horrible case and I have nothing to say as to the moral difference, of such a sin as these two were guilty of, in a man and in a woman, but I think that painful and disgraceful as Mr. Thorne's position was, his severing of the guilty connection is to his credit. He said in fact, 'Now, once for all I am not going to be led into telling any more lies or doing any underhand or dangerous missions.' That, gentlemen, is the attitude of the man who had been this woman's lover, when she is in desperate peril and in a position completely forlorn. He is so suspicious of her behaviour, so alarmed and chagrined at all the circumstances in which she finds herself that he says in effect, 'I am in the dark as to what all this mystery is about. I am tired of all this scheming which seems to be endangering your reputation at a most critical time. If I could see I was serving you in any way, I would not write so strongly. I have, besides, my own interests to think of, and although you might think me very selfish, I shall take the utmost care of them. I am thinking of going away, of leaving the country.' If in effect it had been exactly what this misguided young man did, I do not see that you could censure his conduct, but he stayed, and made a frank admission of the adultery. He deliberately dissociates himself from an act of a guilty complexion and from all association with a woman whom he knows has been telling wicked falsehoods, who has been living in a maze of falsehoods, for which she was rightly in very grave and great difficulties. I ask you to consider this other letter, I ask you to remember this phrase in it. 'He is sick unto death…' This is very much like saying, 'Relieve your mind from all fear of discovery now or in the future, my husband is going to die and you need not be afraid that anybody will ever know as to what has passed between us.' I think then, gentlemen, that though we must say this young man was wrong and foolish, as many young men are wrong and foolish when tempted by a wicked woman, we can also say that he behaved as he ought to have done when he abruptly ended all connection with the prisoner…"

Now Lord Barnfield appeared to lose the thread of his discourse. He muttered something to himself and pushed his papers aside with such a nervous hand that some of them fell to the ground and were picked up clumsily by one of the clerks. The rustle of those papers echoed through the court with a sound like that of the hisses that had greeted Mrs. Tyler when she had first appeared in the dock.

"Papers…" exclaimed the judge with an emphatic attempt to regain control, "we were speaking of flypapers.… Mrs. Tyler purchased these," she said, "for the purpose of preparing a cosmetic…" he leant forward and stared at the jury and they gave way before his gaze, each man shuffling a little in his place. "Cosmetics, gentlemen, but she was not a very scrupulous person, as we all ought to be, about telling falsehoods, for she says now that she wished to make a face-wash... but she told the chemist that the flies were beginning to be troublesome in the kitchen. Now I think you will agree with me—I am sure that you will agree with me—that this is not a vindictive, cruel or unfair prosecution. I don't want you to attach too much importance to small things, like the buying of the flypapers, I ask you to be on your guard against such details, and not to attach a degree of weight to them to which they are not entitled. You must not think that because the prisoner told lies and bought the poison, that she is a wicked woman and a poisoner, but I am bound to say, gentlemen, I am bound reluctantly to say that there is strong evidence for the prisoner having had a motive at once strong and disgraceful...." He pulled himself up. "I should have said, if you cannot find a motive, well, you must consider the fact without the light that motive would throw upon it, but I repeat that here there is a motive."

Again he was going over the London visit, the letters, the evidence of the servants, the doctors, the friends and Amelia Chorley, and every few moments he used the words "sick unto death" until they became like a bell tolling, or a refrain chanted at intervals during some gloomy ritual... "sick unto death..." And as the moments passed, the judge piled up, emphasized and drove home to the jury watching him fascinated, dumb and with intent faces, the guilt of the prisoner. There was nothing to be said for her it seems, nothing at all. He repeated the points that told most against her. Why had she not got the prescription for the face-wash? Why was not her mother called to prove that she had been in the habit of using a face-wash with arsenic in it? Why had she admitted in the rambling and unimpressive statement that she had put white powder into the bottle of meat essence? Were they to be impressed by her statement that she was overwrought, terribly anxious, miserably unhappy and utterly unnerved by her husband's distress? Considering what they knew of her character it was not likely they would have been impressed, nor was it likely that they would think very much of the story of her husband being an arsenic eater.

At this point he paused again and looked over his papers. His repetitions, his blunders, the hopeless confusion into which he had got his notes of the evidence, his forgetfulness of many incidents, his distortion of others, caused the lawyers to glance at one another with a bewildered amazement they dare not express by more than glances, caused the audience even themselves baffled and bewildered by the oft repeated details of the case, to move and stir and even to whisper uneasily.... But who was to judge the judge? He must speak as long as he liked and say what he liked, and they must stay and listen to him.

The assistant barrister rose at one point and made a comment again on one of the judge's errors, but he, too, spoke in a style so ineffective that it was almost stuttering and brought in as if in self-protection the name of Sir Jonathan. The judge cut him short with a smiling vanity. "Oh pray, Mr. Martin, dismiss from your head the notion that I in the smallest possible way censure what was done, or that I assume there was any kind of division between Sir Jonathan and the solicitors."

The young man remained for a moment on his feet. The reply had been completely at random; defeated, he sat down and put his head in his hands, glancing through his fingers at the prisoner who was still standing leaning slightly forward on the edge of the dock, her widow's veil neatly folded back from her smooth brow, and the fringe of pale hair.

She appeared to be unconscious of anyone save the judge, she was looking at him with an intensity that to many of those present (even many of those who until now had made callous sport of her tragedy) was almost unendurably painful. Her wide-set clear eyes had lost nothing of their uncommonly candid expression, her lips were slightly parted and the peculiarities of her face—the short nose, the round childish contours—were emphasized by her lack of colour and her lack of expression.

The judge began again with a sudden and unexpected force, for lately his voice had sunk, been almost tremulous, that of an old and troubled man. Now it was loud, forceful and dominating. He had no more to say about the evidence, he appeared to have dismissed that from his mind; the crime and the prisoner alone concerned him—the crime and the prisoner and the words that he could not forget—"sick unto death" that he repeated so often that it seemed to the audience, many of whom were beginning to be at the end of their nervous resources, scrolled in fiery letters round the hall… sick unto death….

"You must not consider the case as a mere medical case in which you decide whether the man died from arsenic, you must decide it as a highly important moral question. You have in the first place to consider all the evidence, you have then to consider that—I had almost better say you ought not to consider for fear you might consider it too much—the horrible nature of the inquiry in which you are engaged. I feel that it is a dreadful thing that you are deliberately considering whether or not you are to convict that poor woman of really as horrible, as dreadful a crime as any poor wretch who stood in the dock was accused of. I could say a good many other things about the awful nature of the charge, but I don't think it necessary to say much more; your own hearts must tell you how horrible was this crime, if crime it was. For a person to go on deliberately administering poison to a poor helpless sick man upon whom she has already inflicted a dreadful injury, an injury fatal to marriage life—a person who can do such a thing as this must indeed be destitute of the least trace of human feeling…. You have to consider the whole story, the question of motives which might act upon this woman's mind, the intrigue which she carried on with her lover and the feelings—they seem impossible to ordinary, innocent people—the feelings, horrible and incredible, that a woman should be plotting the death of her husband in order that she might be left at liberty in order to follow her own degrading vices. There is no doubt that the propensities that lead persons to vices of that kind kill all the more tender, all the more manly, or all the more womanly feelings of the human mind. That is a comment upon which I will not insist. I will spare you what would be exquisitely painful to me, painful to her and painful to you. I will not say anything about it, except that it is easy enough to conceive how a horrible woman in so terrible a position might be assailed by some fearful and terrible temptation. I have read to you the terrible letter which she wrote. Recollect that in two or three unmistakable expressions she has intimated that he is sick unto death, recollect that while her husband lived, and according to her own account while his life was trembling in the balance—even at that awful moment there arose in her heart and flowed from her pen, terms of endearment to the man with whom she had behaved so disgracefully.

"Well, gentlemen, I have done my best and said all I think necessary to say to you upon this most painful subject. I do not wish to spin out the last words to you and I accordingly will ask you to consider your verdict."

He had come to an abrupt end of what had seemed endless. There was a moment's silence, as if the harsh spell of his brutal words was still over them all. Richard Tyler was the first to move; walking slowly, like a man afflicted with the agonies of cramp, he moved round to the back of the court, past the people who were now beginning to whisper, to sigh, to stir, to turn their eyes at last from the judge to the jury who, the bailiffs having been sworn, had risen with a clatter of heavy boots and were standing in an uncertain, shuffling way still staring at the judge as if they did not know what to do. Lord Barnfield made an impatient gesture with his hand as the twelve tradesmen shuffled out.

Richard Tyler moved towards the door of the hall and took his position beside the policeman standing there. The jury, with sudden, jerky movements like a flock of sheep that unexpectedly perceives their savage guardian the watch dog charging at them, stumbled out of the court, none of them appearing in complete command of their limbs, for they clattered and pushed and one helped the other.

When they had gone, the wardress touched May Tyler on the arm and pointed out the seat in the dock; but May shook her head. She folded into four precise portions the list of two hundred and fifty bottles of medicine found at Stone Pynes, she studied her own small, gloved hands, memories of the past, speculations as to the future were alike hidden from her. She was conscious of the present moment only and of one aim only; she must behave herself with dignity and fortitude. There was nothing else—no hope, no help anywhere. She smiled with a faint irony at her own position which appeared to her as ridiculous as tragic, her glances at the judge were full of curiosity. He was completely incomprehensible to her—but almost everything had been since she had come to live at Stone Pynes. Then she looked to where Richard had sat and found he had gone. The people were moving, but in a repressed manner; the eye of the judge was upon them and their murmured comments were of the faintest. Some of them ventured to twist in their seats, to look at the clock, the journalists in particular kept a careful note of the time. To them the judge was now as interesting an object of scandalous comment as the prisoner, but with him they would not be able to have a free hand.

May Tyler unfolded her paper and again studied the list. A pity she had forgotten where she had put the recipe for the face-wash, but it was so long ago… an early summer day in Paris… the day they had bought the Bibles with the blue velvet covers and seen the lilies green as flowers growing under water in the convent garden. Since then everything had been a mistake; but nothing had mattered very much…

there had been only one lesson to learn—how to endure it. That she had learned early and well.

She wished she could compose a coherent whole from the evidence; she had been in the dock for six days and a number of people had been talking about her own life and character; and these people had all been examined and cross-examined by clever lawyers, but now at the end she could make little of any of it. She did not know herself or her life any more clearly. She could not recall that night of the death at Stone Pynes any more definitely, all was still confusion, distasteful, repugnant to all her senses as had been the carnival in the Pomona Rooms when the instruments hanging from the ceiling had played automatically and the heavy dancers in their garish and parti-coloured garments had thumped and whirled on the dusty floor. No use now to try to understand any of it, she was not clever enough, perhaps not interested enough. After this very little could matter....

The jury returned, she heard someone—perhaps the wardress, but the voice seemed to come from nowhere—mutter, "It took them half an hour only."

The Clerk of Arraigns then rose and called over the list of the jury. His voice was repressed, monotonous and he kept his eyelids down as he added quickly:

"Have you agreed upon a verdict, gentlemen?"

The foreman twice tried to speak before his dry throat and lips would allow him to form the words, "We have."

The Clerk of Arraigns, without altering his position, then asked, "And do you find the prisoner guilty of the murder of James Tyler or not guilty?"

The foreman answered now rapidly, "Guilty."

At this there was a general swaying and humming in court; a universal noise, human voices blended with the sound of moving feet, of rustling skirts, of chairs pushed back and the journalists scrambling for the door, of the police pushing them back into their places, of some women sobbing in nervous excitement, of the lawyers folding up and unfolding and bringing down violently on their tables their piles of paper, useless now....

The prisoner felt the wardress touch her again. She was becoming used to that slight pressure on her arm. She understood that she was to face the judge; she observed now that he had placed a triangle of black silk on the pomaded curls of his wig. His voice took on its most strident notes, the tone with which he had repeated with such ferocious zest, "he is sick unto death...."

As he began to pronounce the sentence (he had no longer needed to read it) the Clerk of Arraigns had held up his hand, and the judge had nodded. There was one more formality; the clerk had turned to the prisoner—

"May Tyler, you have been found guilty of wilful murder. Have you anything to say why the court should not pronounce sentence upon you?"

The wardress again touched the prisoner's arm. Her voice, quiet and penetrating, again sounded to the prisoner like the voice of some disembodied entity.

She said, "There's been a confusion in the proceedings... it's all the excitement you see. You have now a chance of saying something for yourself."

But May Tyler knew there was nothing that she could say for herself—only perhaps this one thing.... They were all staring at her again, silent once more, arrested in their various movements of agitation, excitement and amazement.

What the prisoner murmured impressed no one, many could not catch her words. "There has been a great deal said about myself and Mr. Thorne, there have been many mistakes on that point—a great deal not understood and a great deal not true...."

The judge, ignoring this as if she had not spoken, proceeded with the sentence that he had been so eager to pronounce that he had forgotten the routine of the court.

"Prisoner at the bar, I am no longer able to treat you as being innocent of the dreadful crime laid to your charge. You have been convicted by a jury of this city after a lengthy and most painful investigation, followed by a defence which was in every respect worthy of the case. The jury have convicted you and the law leaves to me no discretion and I must pass on you the sentence of the law. This court doth ordain you to be taken from hence to the place from whence you came, and from thence to the place of execution and that you be there hanged by the neck until you are dead, and that your body be afterwards buried within the precincts of the prison within which you shall have been confined after your conviction, and may the Lord have mercy upon your soul."

With this his lordship raised the black cap and the prisoner was led below by two female warders.

V

FLOWERS OF CHARITY

WHAT WAS LEFT IN THE CHOCOLATE-BOX

THE MATRON, MISS SARAH BEE, WAS SHOWING A GROUP OF prison reform enthusiasts over the building where so many condemned women were housed in what was supposed by the enlightened to be very advanced conditions of comfort. The matron found these visits a pleasant break in the routine of her life which she secretly considered as hard as that endured by the convicts. She did not, however, agree with the views held by these grave and earnest men and women; she considered, not without some inward contempt, for what daily passed under her eyes had made her hard and cynical, that these well-meaning philanthropists had no idea whatever of the wrongs they thought they were redressing or the conditions they believed they were altering, but she took, being a woman of some philosophy, what interest and excitement there might be out of the episode and showed off, with the air of the custodian of a museum displaying his treasures, the various exhibits in the female prison where she had passed over a quarter of a century, rising by perseverance from the lowest to the highest rank among the wardresses.

Miss Bee had shown these humane inquirers how a prisoner would arrive, indicating the outer bell that would be rung to summon the gatekeeper to unlock and swing open the great gates. There were two of these and the prisoners would arrive in cab, or omnibus, or prison van that would stop at the side door in the heavy brick building that led directly to the reception-room where the matron would be waiting to hear the name, age and nature of the crime and the length of the sentence which she would then enter in the registry book.

"It is a very simple formality with nothing really shocking or alarming about it," she remarked, using the trite sentences that she had employed so many times before.

As a government servant she had to be careful what she said; as a woman near her pension she had after all no great interest in these matters. She affected a humane smile and deliberately softened that harsh and stern demeanour that she preserved, very necessarily as she believed, before the prisoners.

One of the ladies wished to know exactly what happened when the prisoner's name had been entered in the book.

"Oh, their hair is cut off and you would be surprised the trouble we have about that. Some women make more ado about having their hair shortened than they did when they received a sentence of lifetime imprisonment."

A remark that the matron was accustomed to hear was duly uttered by one of the clergymen in the party. This was to the effect that female vanity was the mainspring of most female crimes.

"They don't get much chance to indulge that here," replied the matron. "As you will see, they have plain brown serge frocks, blue check aprons and muslin caps, with some alteration in the classes, though I must confess they show an extraordinary ingenuity in altering the headgear. It gives us a great deal of trouble."

"Imagine," exclaimed one of the lady visitors, "these unhappy creatures, lost for ever to all decent society, still concerning themselves about their clothes!"

"I assure you they do," said the matron, "and you must not, madam, consider the prisoners as altogether wretched. I can assure you that since the recent reforms, a female prisoner is better off than a woman in a poor-law institute."

"Indeed, I have noticed that myself," another lady remarked. "These miserable women are better cared for, fed better and receive more consideration and kindnesses in prison than those in the poor-law institutions."

There was a murmur among the party and a shaking of heads. Was it right thus to indulge crime? The doubt was increased when the matron remarked, "Some of these lost wretches deliberately follow a steady persistent course of sin because they prefer a prison to the workhouse."

The visitors whispered together in little groups. They were, despite their good intentions, depressed by their surroundings. Not one of them would have admitted that the prison was dreary, unwholesome and indescribably gloomy; all of them had decided already that it was a considerable advance on the old prisons, and that they could really congratulate themselves on the fine work they had done for humanity in obtaining for these unhappy outcasts some measure, not only of decency but of comfort.

As the matron led her party down the long corridors that she termed the wards, she continued her monotonous recital of the prisoners' life. The day began at a quarter to six when the guard went off night duty in the yard, "by six o'clock every prisoner is expected to be dressed and standing in her cell for inspection by the wardresses on duty...."

The steps of the visitors echoed down the straight passage, broken at short intervals with doors, the outer one an iron grating, the inner one with a small high placed window, also grated.

"The wardresses put their arms through the outer to unbolt the inner," explained the matron. "There are bolts secured at nights."

"There must be very little ventilation," remarked one of the women, drawing her dowdy coat closer about her thin shoulders... the place could not of course be damp, but it seemed chilly, though this was an August day.

"Oh, if they are very delicate the surgeon may order the inner door to be left open. When I first came," she added, "the rattle of the bolts down each ward as the doors were opened in the morning had a peculiar effect on me. The noise used to give me a headache. I have long since become used to so much worse than that."

"It seems very quiet," remarked one of the visitors as they proceeded down the ward. "What other noises disturbed you, matron?"

"You'd be surprised to learn," she replied. "Very often we have what is termed a 'breaking out'. I am sorry to have to admit that even now, with all the comfort—almost luxury, that is provided for these criminals—conditions, as we have remarked even better than those given to the industrious poor, there are those so hardened that they will break into furies and tumultuous rebellions which often reach such a proportion that we have to call in male warders to help us."

"What a shocking depth of depravity!" whispered one of the lady visitors earnestly.

"This cell is empty," said the matron suddenly, putting out her arm through an iron grille and opening the inner door.

The visitors noticed the rattle that she had spoken of; though now it was from one door only it echoed for what seemed a considerable time down the long, empty corridor obscured with grey shadows. They all peered into the cell.

Yes, there was no question it was an improvement on the quarters the women had occupied in the old prisons. It was clean and tidy; there was a carefully folded-up bed, there was a polished deal table, there was a rug covering a small portion of the stone floor; though there could be no light since the prisoners were not to be trusted with either gas or lanterns, yet the gas bracket immediately outside each cell threw into it, when the doors were opened, almost as much light as came in the day time from the small, high set and barred window.

"But what do they do when the door is shut? Are they not suffered to have any light at all?"

"It depends upon their conduct," said the matron. "Those who behave themselves may have the inner door permanently open."

"And those," remarked the clergymen, "who do misbehave themselves?"

"They have the door shut," said the matron, "and sit in darkness." She pointed out the tin pint mug hanging on a hook beside that provided for the prisoner's clothes. "The women keep this clean themselves. This cell is a fair sample of the way in which they are looked after. The women, of course, do that work themselves. After their cells are tidy, then begins the work of the day… oakum picking for the probationers, for those who deserve it by their behaviour, bag making, and the sewing of shirts for the male prisoners. Chapel is now at a quarter past nine. The women attend under charge of the wardresses who take them back to their cells. You must understand that not a word are they allowed to exchange with one another, and that each woman sits in her cell working separately."

"I believe water is served in the middle of the morning, is it not?" remarked the clergyman. "We tried to insist on that."

Miss Bee had locked up the empty cell and was proceeding down the passage.

"Yes, indeed, at half past twelve. The dinner bell is rung at a quarter to one. The prisoners have now four ounces of boiled meat, half a pound of potatoes and a six-ounce loaf. When the cans have been collected prisoners return to their work."

"And the exercise—I understand that since the tread-mill was abolished," asked the most officious of the visitors, "a certain amount of exercise is allowed in the yard?"

"Yes, one hour each day. They are not allowed to speak. One ward of women is exercised at a time with a wardress of course in attendance. They go round and round the prison yard in Indian file. I remember," she added thoughtfully, "I used to consider that, when I was a wardress, the most disagreeable part of my duty. It was difficult to withstand the tediousness of that hour, either shivering in winter or exhausted by the heat in summer. After that the women return to their cells and work is resumed till half past five; then the prisoners' mugs are filled with gruel, a few prayers are said by the wardress standing in the centre of each ward so that her voice can be heard by the prisoners as they are then obliged to stand at the doors of their cell. After prayers, each woman answers to her name from the list called out and then the work recommences and continues till a quarter to eight."

"Some recreation is allowed, I suppose?" asked the clergyman.

"Oh yes, from a quarter to eight until half past reading is permitted in the cells. Then the prisoners proceed to make their beds, and at a quarter to nine the gas is turned out by the wardresses and the matron on night duty begins her round of the prisoners, passing once an hour each cell."

The matron had come to the end of her routine information. There were, however, a few more parts of the prison to inspect, among others the cell used for those prisoners who, as a punishment, were condemned to solitary confinement.

"They are known to the women as 'the darks'," she remarked casually and was silent as the little group of men and women inspected for themselves the two small cells secured by heavy doors and thick iron gratings, covered by a sliding pad which one of the party informed his companions was intended to deaden the screams and uproar of the women in solitary confinement.

"This is necessary because the wardresses are sometimes kept awake all night by the incessant shrieking, hammering, kicking and singing of these desperate creatures."

The sole furniture of the dark cell consisted of boards by way of a bedstead with a wooden block for a pillow; the floor was of slate.

"We keep them on bread and water," remarked the matron. "Would you now like to see the kitchens and the laundry?"

"I hope," said the clergyman as they proceeded up the flight of grey stone stairs and along a corridor so similar to that they had just passed that it seemed to all of them as if they were traversing the same passage, "that even the most obstinate of your prisoners, matron, shows a little respect for the Sabbath?"

"Yes, I think I can say they do. They are given a little relaxation—an hour's longer rest—and those whose good behaviour has been conspicuous are allowed a little speech with a companion. There is some difficulty with the Roman Catholics. You know that the government permits no religious intolerance and that there is a priest for the women who are of that faith. This means that they go to an early service in the morning and that leaves the day somewhat barren, so I have known women attend the Protestant service also rather than remain alone in their cells."

The clergyman muttered some protest against this abuse of religion, to which the matron retorted that many women of a brooding or indolent nature were Catholic not merely because of "the Sunday skulk" but because of the absence from chapel in the weekdays. "It is a question," she said, "of disposition."

They passed a wardress and an attendant carrying a pail of cocoa and a large basket of loaves. The humane investigators stopped and examined the food, declaring the quality of it excellent.

"What of the matter of cleanliness?" one lady suggested to the matron in a lowered voice.

"Oh, they have an ounce of soap a week and a hot bath once a week." The lady nodded, satisfied. "But you mustn't think we are too extravagant," the matron added. "In the winter the prisoners get up in the dark and breakfast in the dark to save the expense of gas. You will be surprised how acute their sense of touch becomes owing to their having to do so much without light. You will see," added the matron, "a large number of prisoners in the kitchen. You must not be surprised if they have a sulky demeanour. Some of them are not at all grateful. They even go so far as to say they resent being objects of morbid curiosity as they term it and resent 'the humiliation and degradation'—yes, those were the words I heard one woman use—of people continually coming to see them."

"One must expect such behaviour on the part of members of the criminal class," replied one of the ladies, gazing about her with a curiosity that had not yet been in the least satisfied. She was a new member of the institution and owing to her wealth and zeal had been allowed to join this party. She knew nothing of the prisons before reform and very little of the question at all. She had expected to see something heartrending and even disgusting during this visit and had secretly praised herself for the fortitude with which it had been undertaken.

Now she was merely tired with the tedium of the matron's dry explanations, of the dull monotony of the wards and cells. Miss Bee had begun again, explaining the strict economy with which the prison was run.

"We have no heating in the winter except in the halls where there are two fireplaces and a stove. Of course the heat does not penetrate the cells, but I can assure you that the wardresses are as rigorously treated as the prisoners. The water frequently freezes in my room at night."

She caught herself up, remembering retirement, a pension was near. She must not complain though she would much have liked to tell these people who seemed so concerned with the welfare of the prisoners, something of what the wardresses suffered in their hard, disagreeable, ill-paid task.

They had reached the kitchens which were plain and ill-lit, fitted with clean scrubbed deal tables; on one side were long coal ranges on which various pots and kettles were placed, on the other were shelves for dry goods, and the coarse glass and china used in the prison; the air was hot and reeked of heavy cooking; the prisoners were engaged in preparing the midday meal for the matrons; some joints of mutton were being placed in the oven by some of the women, while others peeled potatoes.

The clergyman made interested inquiries. He was glad to learn that a convict employed in exceptional hard work had an extra allowance of three ounces of bread daily, one ounce of cheese and one ounce of uncooked meat.

"Everything is so nice and homelike," exclaimed the most experienced of the group of philanthropists. "One might almost be in one's own kitchen."

She smiled with a vague sympathy that she felt "suitable", at the group of women by the table peeling the potatoes and piling up the thick plates. She believed in kindness even towards the most degraded of humanity and she had regretted that so far they had not come in contact with any of the prisoners. Now, at sight of them, she brightened and stepping up to a woman under whose quick fingers a long brown curl of potato skin was falling on to the platter in front of her, she said, "How long a time have you to do?"

"Ten years," said the woman looking up. To the busy visitor she was no more than a convict, nothing about her was peculiar. Her small features had the usual unhealthy appearance of those who had undergone a long confinement. There was no lustre, no bloom in her eyes, on her cheeks or lips that were as pallid as her face.

"Well, how long is your sentence?" asked the visitor cheerfully.

The convict replied, "Twenty years."

"Oh, you've done half the time, haven't you? The remaining ten years will soon slip by."

She turned to rejoin her party having done her duty as a gracious lady who gave up much of her time to doing good to others.

When they had left the steaming kitchen, closed the heavy doors behind them and were in the lobby again, the matron remarked, "That was May Tyler to whom you spoke just now."

Everyone was extremely interested. The woman glanced back regretfully at the closed door of the kitchen. If only they had known… but they had been quite unaware, even of the prison in which May Tyler was confined. Those who had not noticed her were with difficulty able to restrain a request to go back and speak to her. The lady who had singled her out smirked with pride, though she too was sorry that she had not made more of her opportunity.

"You must tell us something about her, matron. What an enormous sensation the case made—and does still for that matter. It seems as if people couldn't forget it."

"Oh, they make a great agitation in America," replied the matron. "I suppose she has her sympathizers over here, but not many people come to see her."

"Her mother's been very devoted," remarked the clergyman. He, also, would have liked a few words with May Tyler whose story he had heard discussed so often.

"Yes, Madame Dumont comes whenever visitors are allowed and stays as long as they are permitted to stay. She has taken a room near the prison; I believe she has almost ruined herself. Her husband is dead, you know, and this has become quite an obsession with her. I hear that she thinks and talks of nothing else but her daughter's unjust imprisonment as she terms it…."

"But she's a *murderess*," put in one of the women abruptly. "I wish I had looked at her. I did not distinguish her from the others, she's very ordinary looking, isn't she? I thought she was so fascinating."

"She's frequently ill and in the infirmary," the matron answered, pleased to be able to retail some gossip about a notorious prisoner.

It was always the same, whoever it was she conducted round the prison, their visit was dull and ordinary until they saw May Tyler. The matron was not allowed in any way to attract attention to one prisoner, but she always contrived that whoever visited the convicts should see that notorious one.

They were all willing to go into the little garden where matron and sometimes the wardresses occasionally sat with their books or sewing, a garden never even seen by the prisoners for it was beyond the porter's lodge, and entered by a secret door. They talked in a desultory fashion of prison reform and then they talked of May Tyler, each hoping to obtain from the matron some detail about this, the only interesting woman in the prison, some bit of gossip that might be fresh, though it seemed impossible after ten years of publicity in two continents there could be left anything to be said about May Tyler.

"There is a very powerful party who believes she is innocent," the clergyman remarked, "and who work very hard for her release. I sometimes wonder that it is not granted."

Another man, an eager humanitarian, appeared surprised and even shocked at this. He declared that to grant May Tyler a pardon would be to overset the verdict of a British jury.

"She was found guilty, you know," he repeated this obstinately, "she was found guilty."

"Then she ought to have been hanged," replied the clergyman. "Why was her sentence commuted?"

No one remembered. It was ten years ago and though they had read so much about the case they had never read it carefully. The matron could tell them, she knew the histories of all the prisoners under her charge.

"They hoped she would confess, that would have made everything so much easier. She was, however, ill after the sentence; she was a

Roman Catholic and the last sacraments were taken in to her, but even this did not bring a confession. She must have been a strong-minded woman.... They were putting up the scaffold in the yard outside. She could hear the hammering and they told her what it was. Her sentence was commuted," and the matron had a glance of rebuke for her ignorant audience, "because it was not proved that her husband died of the arsenic she gave him, though it was held proved that she had given him arsenic."

"Yes, I remember," the clergyman sighed, "a legal tangle.... Well, I suppose that's all that they could do. She was a woman of bad moral character, as I remember."

"Yes," agreed the matron, "that is what went against her so."

"And the children?" asked the lady who had spoken to May Tyler.

"Oh, the brother-in-law took charge of them. I think they are abroad with changed names."

"Does she never ask after them?"

"Not now; when she first came we gave her permission to write to Mr. Richard Tyler for their photographs. He refused and enclosed a letter from the little boy in which he said that he did not wish either his photograph or that of his sister to be sent to his mother."

"A child of that age! The letter must have been dictated!" protested the youngest of the visitors. "Besides it seems cruel to have told him."

"Perhaps," replied the matron, "it would have been more cruel to have allowed him to be involved in his mother's existence. She never spoke of them again."

"What kind of prisoner is she?" asked the clergyman.

"I hardly know how to answer. She is extremely quiet and docile, seldom breaks any of the rules; she has been once or twice in solitary confinement, but that was for carelessness, upsetting boiling water on another woman's foot in the kitchen, or tearing her dress on a nail...

we have no nails now," she added quickly, "in the cells. She is not always in the kitchen, sometimes she works in the laundry or even in the library. Lately, however, she has shown a very sullen disposition, almost refusing to speak, resisting even her mother's entreaties to behave with more cheerfulness and respect towards the wardresses. She has become slovenly too, in her dress, and her work in the library was most careless, so she has been returned to the kitchen. Even now she complains—she says the pails of cocoa are too heavy for her to carry and that the continual smell of cooking mutton makes her sick, if you please."

"Still, on the whole a docile prisoner," remarked the clergyman thoughtfully, "and she's been here ten years.... I suppose the young man in the case—well, he wouldn't be so young now—he never came forward in any way?"

"Oh no!" the matron smiled harshly. "He disappeared long ago. I heard that he had gone to Australia."

"She never mentions him of course?" ventured one of the women.

"Oh, she never mentions anything. You would think that her life had been a blank until she arrived here. I have never heard her volunteer a statement, and though she has for some years now been allowed opportunities of conversing with some of the other prisoners, she takes no advantage of it. She has no friends in the prison. Many of the long term convicts become quite attached to one another."

"She's a very small, miserable looking creature, isn't she?" remarked the youngest of the party thoughtfully. "I always supposed she was so pretty. It's a curious case from beginning to end, isn't it?"

"It's a curious thing," said another, "to see a woman of her station in such a plight. I wonder if she did do it? I think I've read most of the arguments for and against—you remember at one time the press was full of it and books were written championing her, but I never could make up my mind."

"I suppose," admitted the clergyman cautiously, "no one will ever be able to make up their minds...." He looked at the matron, "What would you say? You've had charge of her for ten years."

"I should be quite unable to offer an opinion...."

The matron glanced round the group. This moment always came during the afternoons she gave up to what she termed, secretly, 'sight-seers'. They always were interested in May Tyler and she had nothing to tell them; for ten years that prisoner's life had been of a monotony unbroken by anything save her visits to the infirmary, and there she had endured her attacks of illness with the same patience and indifference as she endured her present life.

The visit to the jail was over, and the party of philanthropists settled themselves in the open wagonette they had hired for the afternoon. There were many things they should have been considering, all of them had notebooks and some of them had made notes, but they talked of nothing but May Tyler, not with any eager gossiping air, because there was so little to gossip about, but in a disjointed, puzzled manner, each giving their little surmise, their random suggestion about the mystery that had inflamed, infuriated and baffled Great Britain and America. One of them could remember that she came from Virginia of a good family, another could recall that she had been an excellent horsewoman, a third had recollections of seeing her likeness in some published print—a young woman in a low-cut dress with her fair curls piled on the top of her head. Could that possibly be the same person as the little woman peeling potatoes in the prison kitchens?

They were disappointed at the matron for not being able to tell them more. How strange that anyone in such a plight did not express herself... and this question of religion.... The clergyman was puzzled there. She went to the Roman Catholic services, the matron had said, but the prison priest had admitted that he was not in her confidence.

As the wagonette moved briskly along, the occupants all forgot the prison and each cast his or her mind back into what they could recollect of May Tyler's story, and neither could remember anything coherent or anything that they could put together into a complete whole. There was something lacking, some clue both as to characters and events was surely missing.

"The man ate arsenic, didn't he?" remarked one of the party.

"Yes," the lady who said that she had once been so well informed about the case answered quickly, "but I've heard it said that if she had given him even a mild dose of arsenic in solution she would have killed him, even though he was used to eating the powder dry."

"A medical puzzle," the clergyman declared. "The doctors contradicted one another, and some of them I should say didn't know their job. Well, it's been curious seeing May Tyler; after all one's read and heard about her. She had become to all of us, I think, quite a fabulous creature, and after all she's only a very ordinary little woman peeling potatoes in a prison kitchen."

"One should feel great compassion for her," suggested the experienced lady cautiously, "but then one never knows. Surely if she were innocent, the Home Secretary would release her. Besides," she concluded, comforting the faint stirring of her conscience, "she was in any case an immoral woman."

"What about the judge?" asked the wealthy young woman who knew very little about the case. "Didn't I hear—I seem to remember my mother saying the judge's summing-up was dead against her."

"Oh, the judge," said the clergyman drily. "He became insane, you know. He was hissed on leaving the court—the trial got on his mind—a few months after the verdict he was in an asylum."

EPILOGUE

WAYSIDE POSY

He was a rough sulky little boy and as he slouched along the lane he kicked to pieces the clumps of violets and primroses that grew in the hedge bank, under the budding hawthorn.

The schoolmistress rebuked him, "They're so pretty," she said absently, but she smiled too, because he was good looking and sang so well in the chapel choir.

At the turn of the lane she dismissed him and watched him run ahead to the cottage where he lived. The parish nurse overtook her and the women lingered gossiping over the funeral that had been paid for by the charity of the wealthier members of the chapel congregation.

The woman who had just been buried had been treated with great kindness ever since she came to the village twenty years ago. It was some time now since she had been dependent on this same kindness for her livelihood. The regular and impressive visits from the town lawyer had long ceased and the old woman had confessed to being without means, but the four-roomed cottage she lived in was her own and it had not been much of an effort among the chapel people to provide the few shillings a week that she required for her food.

It was part of the ritual of the funeral to discuss the dead so lately laid in earth, but the two young women standing at the cross-roads were at a loss where to begin; there was so little to discuss. She had been merely one of those eccentric old women found so often in towns and not infrequently in villages, who live alone without relatives or friends, in the midst of others, and yet as solitary as a recluse in the desert; eccentric, harmless and as familiar a sight to all the villagers as the milestone by the church that they passed daily.

"She may have had an interesting life," suggested the nurse rather dubiously. "You never can tell with these poor old things. I wonder what brought her here... it was before my time that she came and I've never heard a reason given."

"I don't suppose there was one," admitted the young schoolmistress, honesty overcoming curiosity and a native love of the marvellous. "She just drifted here like these old creatures do. She told me that she remembered the place because she drove through it once years ago."

"Well, I dare say," agreed the nurse, "it was no more than that. We shall miss her, one gets used to people." She looked over her shoulder thinking of, though she could not see, the small burial ground. "She had become such a familiar figure, hadn't she?"

"Yes, I should think she must have been here twenty years at least."

The two fell silent, each pondering over that other woman's life; however uneventful it might have been, she had been young once and must have had some memories, they felt compassionate, even uneasy.

"Funny she never spoke of herself," remarked the schoolmistress with a vague, a nameless regret, "except to say silly things."

"They never do tell the truth, when they get to that age. I expect she'd forgotten everything, she was always grateful for any kindness—quite childlike in her ways. Never as much as harmed a fly I should say."

"I tried to get her to talk about the past," confided the schoolmistress. "I thought maybe she'd got something on her mind, but she never said a word, only smiled and put me off with nonsense."

"That was to give an air of mystery, dear." The nurse was wise and emphatic. "They do, you know. People to whom nothing has happened never like to confess it. You remember when she was ill—why it must be two years ago—and I went in to look after her? Well, she had a temperature one night and you'd be surprised at the tales she told, quite solemn and serious, she spoke about having children and not having seen them for a long time and, would you believe it, of a trial for murder? I think she was imagining herself the prisoner. She kept on sitting up in bed, for all I could do to keep her warm, and telling me that it would have been all right if she'd been able to find a bit of paper...."

"Something she'd been reading I suppose." The air was warm and balmy, a few clouds of red golden fleece lay about the west.

"No doubt," agreed the nurse. "As for children, I'd swear she's never had any. An old maid, I expect, though she liked you to call her by 'her married name' as she termed it—poor old soul."

"She didn't leave anything behind?"

"Not a thing, not as much as a scrap of paper. Those who were the kindest to her," the nurse spoke with discretion, she was referring to the two elders of the chapel who had kept "the stranger in their midst" as they termed the old woman in the cottage beyond the chapel, "had to pay for her funeral. Absolutely nothing... nowhere they could write to.... Well, they always expected to take the last expenses on themselves and were glad to do it, I'm sure. Many a time she said she'd like to be buried in the chapel ground."

"She didn't come to chapel very often, but there, I suppose she was too old. You know one day she took me in and showed me some old clothes. I felt quite scared, as if I was, you know—talking to a ghost or something like that. You remember how ragged and untidy she'd been for a good bit now...."

"I'm sure I did my best," interrupted the nurse in routine protest.

The schoolmistress nodded in placid agreement and went on with her story in which, after all, there was nothing very much. The old woman had asked the girl to look at some clothes she had hoarded in her broken cupboard. "Everything in the house was broken," said the schoolmistress, "not too clean either, but as good as you could expect at her age and she didn't like people coming in to help. I don't know what she wanted to show me those things for... little better than rags they were though carefully put away in old-fashioned boxes. There was a lace dress and one of a kind of peacock colour—old fashioned! why, they looked to me sixty years old or more... my grandmother wore something more up to date in the photograph that I've got, but the materials were good in those days, they used to last.... There was a funny plaid skirt too, and a jacket. The moth had got into that I should say. She seemed quite proud of them, held them up to the light and of course I had to admire them. I tried to see if there was a name on them anywhere. There had been but it had been cut out. She said they were hers, but her mother had had to buy them back for her—and kept them for her."

"Well, I dare say she had money once, and had to sell her things, but buying them back seems odd. It's an old story—she outlived all her relatives and friends and came to this, drifting down like they do. She was such a quiet old soul, I don't suppose she'd ever felt anything very much but she'd got her bit of vanity too and liked to make up a few tales. They always do, you know—the duller their lives the more romancing they'll go in for."

The conversation came to an end, but the women remained, with the inertia of fatigue, standing at the cross-roads. There was really nothing more to be said; not one sparkle of colour or brilliancy, not one interesting fact, not one exciting rumour could be gathered from the life of the old woman who had just been buried by a decorous charity. Only this—and the nurse who had been reserving it for a final dismissal of the subject remarked, "Poor soul, she was always thankful if you did a thing or two for her. She gave me a Bible—not that plain one she always used, but a fancy book bound in velvet."

"A Bible bound in velvet?"

"Yes, blue velvet, dirty and rubbed, as you may believe. I asked her if she had ever been a Roman Catholic—it looked like that kind of

Bible to me—but she just passed that off and said it had been given to her years and years ago when she was a young girl, and that she had never opened it.... Fancy that, carrying it about with her all those years and never opening it!"

"I don't suppose that story is true," remarked the other young woman shrewdly. "More likely something she'd picked up in a second-hand shop when she used to go for those jaunts in a bus. I've seen her myself wandering up and down the streets in town prying into the shops where they sell that sort of old stuff."

"She's not been in a bus for a good many years now. I don't know... it might have been hers but it might not... looks to me as if it had been opened, and the first page torn out, no name, and I shouldn't think she ever had turned the pages, they were stuck together and all yellowed round the edges."

"Well, there's nothing more to be said about her." The schoolmistress sighed and reluctantly turned upon her way through the spring evening; the old woman in the cottage by the chapel was dead and buried, and quite soon she would be forgotten. "What about her cats? I suppose they'll be destroyed."

"Oh we'll find homes for them," replied the nurse, still lingering, "that was one of her bad dreams, when she was ill—she was so fond of those animals, she kept worrying that someone would come along with a package, labelled 'Poison for cats'...."

They laughed feebly; a pity there wasn't anything at all to be said about the recluse who had dwelt among them for twenty years; both had been trained to disbelieve in romance, to be incredulous of the marvellous, life was very prosaic, that was why people had to lie so much, to brighten it up a little; both were oblivious of the lovely landscape, in muted tones of brown, green and silver, receding into the dusk; there was a faint perfume from the lilies in a cottage garden not far from the sign-post at the cross-roads; it reminded the schoolmistress how beautiful these flowers were after dusk, luminous, yes, like lights that no darkness could put out, but she thought it would be silly to say so... nothing left behind but a few old clothes and a Bible with a dirty blue cover.

"I must get along."

The nurse fell into step beside her. "Just look where that young John has kicked up the bank, tiresome little monkey, never sees anything pretty but he wants to destroy it...."

"Still, he sang nicely at the funeral, and he's such a handsome boy—I wonder what'll happen to her cottage? Needs a bit of cleaning out. Well, nurse, if you couldn't get anything out of her, there was nothing to get, I'll say...."

The nurse was tersely practical.

"No, there never is, poor souls, they have to invent tales because nothing has ever happened to them." She paused, and it was as if she said, "as nothing will ever happen to us," then she went on quickly, "She was very old, she always talked of carriages, never noticed how the world had changed, she said once she heard some people told to get an airing in a closed carriage—and that her life had been like that, trying to get fresh air, but always closed up, in a box."

The schoolmistress lingered; she shivered in the small, chill wind of evening; the nurse spoke again,

"I felt she was like that—you know, her life, I mean, it's difficult to express—you travel in a shut-up bus, you see everything, but you don't get the fresh air—you just pass along understanding nothing, because it's all blurred by being shut in like that."

The schoolmistress did not like this reference to a closed box; not so far away what was left of the old woman was lying in a closed box.

"You couldn't call her a mystery, could you, nurse?"

"No, no mystery there, just a poor harmless old thing whose relatives allowed her a bit of money, and then I suppose they died, or there was an end of whatever was left her. But I tell you one thing," she added as she turned to the routine of an uneventful life. "She'd been quite vain in her time—Why, in that Bible when I was looking through it, I found a piece of paper—fine as tissue paper it was—a chemist's recipe in French, everyone would not have been able to make it out, between the French and the faded ink, but I'm used to spelling out prescriptions."

"What was it?" asked the schoolmistress lingering on her way, languid with unconscious fatigue.

"It was a recipe for a face-wash," whispered the nurse with a sudden smile. "What they used for cosmetics. What a place to keep it in—a Bible..."

"The Bible she'd never opened. What do you make of that? It couldn't be hers...."

"Well, I don't know, maybe it was put there years and years ago, and she'd forgotten all about it—it was almost glued in—pressed so flat."

"Fancy *her* thinking of cosmetics!"

"Oh, she often talked of such things when she was ill, you'd be surprised! No sense in any of it, just a little—you know—weak minded, once she told me her brother-in-law was a judge, and that she remembered going to a dance with him and there were a lot of clowns."

"Poor soul. Well, I don't suppose she'd much feeling left..."

"No, they get past it, you know."

The cross-roads were glimmering out of sight as the fury of colour faded in the sky, and the darkness fell for the first time on the new-made grave of the old recluse.

THE END

ALSO AVAILABLE IN THE BRITISH LIBRARY CRIME CLASSICS SERIES